NO ONE
SLEEPS

JACK ERICKSON

No One Sleeps

This book is a work of fiction. The details of the CIA kidnapping of an Egyptian imam in Milan are based on books and articles from the historical record.

RedBrick Press
www.jackerickson.com
jacklerickson@gmail.com

ISBN: 978-0-941397-11-7

Printed in the United States of America

Cover design by: Jennifer Fitzgerald
Interior design by: 1106 Design

*For Grace, William, Preston, Lukas, Campbell, and Desiree
And of course, for Marilyn*

THE EGYPTIAN IMAM
MILAN

FEBRUARY 17, 2003

Shortly before noon on a bitterly cold February day, a plainclothes *maresciallo* (marshal) of the Carabinieri military police shouted *"Polizia!"* and stopped a Muslim man on Via Guerzoni in Milan.[1]

The Muslim was an imam dressed in a traditional galabia tunic and *taqiyah* skullcap on his way to noon prayers at the Islamic Cultural Institute on Viale Jenner. The policeman flashed his identification and asked for the man's papers. Hasaan Mustafa Osama Nasr, also known as Abu Omar, handed over his passport, residency permit, and identification papers. He said in broken English that he didn't speak Italian.

The policeman took his time examining Omar's papers. Suddenly, a white cargo van that had been parked across the street pulled up, and the panel door swung open. Two husky men pulled Omar into the van and pushed him to the floor. The door slammed shut, and the van sped up Via Guerzoni into Milan's heavy traffic.

Omar was kicked in the head, chest, and stomach. A rag was stuffed in his mouth and a mask pulled over his eyes. Within minutes, the van reached the Milan suburb of Cormano and entered the eastbound A4 *autostrada,* where it was joined by a car and another van as escorts. The vehicles sped north past Bergamo, Brescia, Verona, Vicenza, Padua, and

Venice. The caravan left the A4, turned north on the A28, and four hours later reached a security gate at the joint Italian—U.S. Air Force Aviano Air Base, two hundred miles from Milan.[2]

Omar, a fifty-eight-year-old Egyptian, was a radical imam at Milan's Islamic Cultural Institute (ICI), considered by the American CIA and Italian intelligence as a center for recruiting European Muslims to go to al Qaeda training camps in Afghanistan. Since the 1990s, the ICI, a former garage converted into a mosque, had become a spiritual refuge for thousands of Muslims living in Milan. During Friday services, worshippers spilled onto the streets, kneeling on prayer rugs on sidewalks and around the block, snarling traffic, and forcing retailers to close during prayers.

Italian intelligence knew the ICI was the European headquarters of Gamaa Islamiya, a terrorist Egyptian group responsible for killing hundreds of Egyptians and Westerners in attempts to overthrow the Egyptian government. Tunisian, Libyan, Moroccan, and Algerian radicals also found a spiritual home at the ICI.[3]

Omar's captors flew him on a military plane to Ramstein Air Base in Germany and transferred to a private Learjet contracted by the CIA. The plane flew to Cairo, where Omar was arrested and taken to a prison, where he was stripped, prodded, whipped, and isolated in a small concrete box. He was beaten with clubs, shocked with electrical prods, his hands and feet shackled, and forced to lie on a mat on a hard floor, freezing in cold weather, constantly attacked by mites, fleas, and mosquitoes.

After seven months, Omar was transferred to the notorious Tora prison complex known as Al-Aqrab, "the Scorpion," where he was interrogated twice daily. Both sessions lasted for hours. He was stripped and pushed onto a wet mattress, with guards sitting on wooden chairs over him as electricity surged through the mattress.

After attempts to locate Omar, the Italian police investigated reports that he had been kidnapped. The antiterrorism police, *Divisione Investigazioni Generali e Operazioni Speciali,* or DIGOS, had raided the ICI in 1995 under code name "Sphinx" and had found tools for forging passports and legal documents, radical Islamic publications, and forged papers. On September 4, 2001, DIGOS discovered downloaded photos of the Twin Towers taken at night on a computer at the Via Quaranta mosque in southern Milan, suggesting there was prior knowledge of the 9/11 attack in the Milan Muslim community.[4]

DIGOS studied logs of cell phone SIM cards from cell towers on the Best Western hotel near Via Guerzoni and tracked 10,317 calls made between 11 AM and 1 PM. They narrowed the calls to eleven made to each other in a flurry around 11 AM. The calls trailed off until seven more SIM cards were tracked near Cormano, calling each other from escort vehicles approaching the A4 *autostrada*. DIGOS identified another thirty-four SIM cards, a network of connected callers, leading up to and after the kidnapping. DIGOS traced the owners of the SIM cards with further data collected from hotel registries, car rentals, and frequent flyer numbers. They identified twenty-five Americans, many with post office addresses near the CIA headquarters in McLean, Virginia.[5]

One of the cards belonged to the CIA station chief at the American consulate in Milan. Another SIM card was linked to an American diplomat in Rome known to be a CIA agent. A third SIM card was traced to the American security chief at Aviano Air Base. One caller had photos of Abu Omar on his laptop computer, taken before his kidnapping.

Prosecutor Armando Spataro was assigned to the case to see if charges could be brought against the suspected kidnappers. Spataro was a highly respected jurist who had prosecuted cases in the infamous 1980s *Anni di Piombo* (Years of Lead) involving left- and right-wing terrorists, including the infamous *Brigate Rosse* (Red Brigades), who had murdered hundreds of people in hopes of igniting a violent revolution in Italy. In 1978, the Red Brigades kidnapped and assassinated Aldo Moro, former Prime Minister of Italy in Rome, an incident that was extensively reported by the international press.

In April 2005, Spataro issued indictments and arrest warrants for nineteen Americans traced from SIM cards. The warrants were valid throughout the European Union, making Italy the first country to take such legal actions against American citizens. Prime Minister Silvio Berlusconi summoned the American ambassador to Chigi Palace in Rome for what was described as a stern lecture on Italian sovereignty.[6]

In July 2006, two high-ranking officials of the Italian Military Intelligence and Security Service (SISMI) were also charged with assisting the CIA in the operation.

The kidnapping of foreigners is a violation of American law under the United Nations Convention Against Torture signed by President Clinton in 1994. But after 9/11, President George W. Bush authorized American agencies to kidnap and transport suspected terrorists to foreign prisons to be tortured under the term "extraordinary rendition." Abu Omar was one of hundreds of suspected foreign terrorists American agencies "rendered" after 9/11.[7]

In June 2007, the Tribunal of Milan set a trial for the twenty-three Americans in absentia. Italian law allows trials for defendants who do not show up in court. In November 2009, Judge Oscar Magi convicted twenty-three Americans, all but one were CIA agents. Many were given prison sentences, including the Milan CIA station chief. Two high officials from the Italian Military Intelligence and Security Service (SISMI) were also convicted. In December 2010, the sentences for the convicted Americans were increased to seven to nine years on appeal, and these Americans were ordered to pay damages to Omar.[8]

Italy's Justice Ministry issued a formal request for extradition of the convicted agents. The United States refused the request. Any of the convicted who traveled to the EU faced extradition to Italy.

In April 2016, the Portugal Supreme Court authorized the extradition of one of the convicted CIA agents, a dual citizen of the U.S. and Portugal, to face prison in Italy after she traveled to Portugal in 2015.

Abu Omar spent four years in Egyptian prisons before he was released. In December 2013, he was convicted in absentia by an Italian court of terrorist crimes. He remains living in Egypt.

CHAPTER ONE

The note read simply:

Marco, I'm in trouble. I'm worried about my family. Can we meet Sunday morning for coffee at Caffè Cavour? Gianni

Agent Marco Molinari stared at the note from his brother-in-law. It had been hand-delivered to the duty officer at the La Spezia Polizia di Stato headquarters, where Marco worked. The sealed white envelope had Marco's name scrawled on the front by a pen running out of ink. It looked like Gianni was in a hurry.

Marco was puzzled as to why Gianni had sent a note to the Questura instead of calling if his family was in danger. Strange. The reference to Gianni's family was disturbing; Gianni was married to Marco's sister, Elisabetta. Betta and Gianni had two young children, seven-year-old Anita and three-year-old Davide.

Gianni was a midlevel customs agent at the La Spezia port, between Genoa and Pisa on Italy's northwestern coast along the Ligurian Sea. La Spezia was an important commercial port and arsenal for the Italian Navy. Gianni was assigned to the port's inspection unit, which off-loaded and inspected shipping containers arriving from ports in the Mediterranean, Asia, and the Middle East.

Marco reread the brief note, stuck it in his coat pocket, and headed to the parking lot behind the police station. When Marco reached his car, he took out his cell phone and punched Gianni's cell number. Marco had to find out if this was an emergency that needed immediate attention. As an experienced police officer, he was trained to be suspicious.

Gianni answered after one ring. "Pronto, ciao, Marco."

"Ciao, Gianni. Are you having dinner?"

The background noise of the family dinner table answered Marco's question. Three-year-old Davide was banging his fork on a plate and screaming, "No, no! Don't want, Mamma!"

Marco visualized the chaotic dinner scene that he had experienced on visits to their apartment: Betta struggling to feed Davide while he jerked his head left and right, pushing her hand away, food flying across the table and onto the floor.

Little Davide was a problem child, prone to outbursts. He was aggressive around other children, and he often fell down and screamed when he didn't get his way. He had an emotional condition that doctors hadn't identified yet. Davide's behavior was a strain on anyone who encountered him, especially his family and neighbors.

In the background, a TV was blaring an irksome commercial offering low, low rates for cell phone service. It bothered Marco that Betta's family ate with the TV on in the kitchen, a noisy distraction that added to the chaos.

"Yes," Gianni answered. "I didn't expect you to call so soon."

"I have your note. You should have called if you needed to talk right away. Are you in danger?"

"No, no, not right now. But I have to talk to you."

"Should I come over now?"

"No. It can wait until Sunday. Can we meet Sunday?"

"Of course. Are you sure it can wait? Your note worried me."

Gianni said something, but his words were drowned out by Davide's high-pitched wail in the background and the sound of him banging his fork on his plate. Marco could hear Betta trying to calm Davide down and taking him out of his high chair—he still had to be restrained in one, even at his age. "Davide, Davide . . . shush, shush . . . good boy. . . . Let's go in your bedroom . . . find your pajamas . . . so we can play before bedtime."

The kitchen TV blared another commercial of a weekend sale on summer clothes for children, the announcer bellowing about low prices and clothes that children needed to be popular with their playmates, and promoting Disney Princess and Ninja Turtles schoolbags, Spider-Man's cool diaries, and Winx's pencil cases that children would need for school at the end of the summer.

Gianni said, "Davide's been sick all week. Betta called me this afternoon to come home and help her. He's been fussy, not letting her change his diaper, crying all day, refusing to nap."

"I hope he recovers soon," Marco said, distressed about his sister's family problems, which seemed to only get worse, never better. "It's hard when you have a sick child."

Gianni sighed. "It's been one thing after another. Davide had a cold and the flu in May and fell out of his bed one night and bruised his head. Last week someone pushed him off a swing in the park, and Betta had to rush him to the hospital. Poor Betta; she hasn't had a break in so long. It's so hard on us when Davide is not in kindergarten. Thank God Anita is going to the public summer school."

"Yes, I know Betta is worn out. About your note, Gianni, are you sure you want to wait until Sunday? What about tomorrow? I could come to your apartment."

"No, tomorrow isn't good. I'm taking care of the children while Betta has an appointment with her gyno. She hasn't gone since Davide was born. She's been neglecting her health to take care of the kids. Betta said I can have an hour Sunday morning. I will pick Michele up at noon and bring him to the apartment for the day."

Michele was Gianni's twelve-year-old son from an earlier marriage. Gianni had gotten his girlfriend pregnant in their twenties, both were unemployed and living with their parents. After a nasty divorce, Gianni had been left with monthly child support payments to Michele's mother. It was no secret how stressful it was for Gianni's family when Michele came every other weekend. Michele resented it that his father had another family whose children were too young to play with. To add to the stress, Michele was going through puberty, becoming emotional and moody. There were frequent arguments when he spent the day, with lots of shouting, arguing, and slamming of doors until Gianni took him to a video arcade or the park to kick a soccer ball around.

"I can make it Sunday morning at ten."

"Yes, thank you," Gianni said, his voice anxious.

"I'll see you then," Marco said. "Give my love to Betta and your kids. We'll get everyone together soon."

On his drive home to Costa di Murlo, Marco played back the hurried conversation with Gianni. Marco wasn't surprised about Gianni's note; he had suspected something was going on. His sister had confided to him that Gianni had been acting strangely the last couple weeks, moody and depressed. Some nights after work, he'd go for walks alone or stay in their bedroom with the door closed.

Marco had observed Gianni's withdrawn behavior when the family had come over for Betta's birthday in May. Marco's wife, Serena, had prepared a typical Ligurian menu: trofie pasta with pesto; leek and potato pie; zucchini stuffed with meat, cheese, ham, and grated bread; homemade focaccia; *cima alla Genovese;* lemon and pine nuts cake. She had put a bouquet of fresh flowers on the table and had presents for Betta, as well as gifts for Davide and Anita.

While Betta and Serena had talked in the kitchen, Marco had kept an eye on the kids playing by their pool on the patio. Gianni had spent the afternoon slouched on the sofa, drinking beer and watching a soccer match between AC Spezia Calcio and Carrarese on Tele Liguria Sud. When Marco had tried to engage him in conversation, Gianni had answered in one or two sentences, barely taking his eyes off the TV.

Marco knew Gianni had serious financial problems. Gianni supported two families on a modest customs officer's salary. He had even asked Marco for money when his landlord threatened to evict them if they didn't pay their back rent. It was a sad situation; Marco felt helpless, knowing his sister was struggling with a difficult marriage, a child with emotional problems, and constant money worries.

A once attractive, vivacious young woman, Betta now looked harried and worried, with rings under her eyes and stringy, uncombed hair. She dressed in clothes that should have gone to charity.

If only Betta had not met Gianni . . . had finished university . . . and had found a loving man with a good job and a promising future.

But what did Gianni mean when he said he was worried about his family?

Later that evening, Marco and Serena were on the deck of their hillside apartment overlooking La Spezia's harbor, sipping chilled Sciacchetrà from Cinque Terre after dinner while their children paddled in the little pool next to Serena's herb garden. Marco had given her Gianni's note and told her about the stressful conversation while Davide was throwing a temper tantrum.

Serena studied the note as Marco gazed at the fiery orange sun ball descending across the azure Ligurian Sea.

Sparrows and other songbirds were swirling overhead, settling in the eucalyptus trees and oleander bushes as the evening air cooled and crickets chirped in the garden. It was a peaceful end of a hot, humid summer day.

"That poor family," Serena said, laying down the note. "Every day they have a new crisis. It grieves me. I don't know what to say. They have so many problems . . . poor little Davide; I think he's autistic or has Asperger's syndrome. How are they going to handle that as he grows up? Poor Anita seems lost; all her parents' attention goes to Davide. She needs more affection; she seems needy. Betta is over-whelmed, trying to be a nurse, mother, and wife, with little support from Gianni. Michele's weekend visits all end in disaster, with the children crying, Betta and Gianni arguing, and Michele scowling and angry. He can be so mean. Do you know what Michele called Betta one night when he was leaving? He called her '*brutta puttana.*' The nerve of that dreadful boy! I don't see how Betta can put up with all the chaos."

"What can we do?" Marco said. "I've given them money. We see them once a month . . . what else is there? I feel hopeless. My heart aches for Betta . . . and the children."

Serena changed the subject. "What kind of trouble is Gianni worried about? Is it serious, something legal, or just family problems? Their marriage is in trouble; we know that. Is there something else?"

"It probably is serious," Marco said with a sigh. "But I don't think he wants to talk about their marriage. God, I hope he's not losing his job. What a disaster that would be."

Serena pressed her lips together and then sighed. "Could be. . . . Poor Betta."

Marco was at the Caffè Cavour at ten o'clock on that hot Sunday morning, sipping cappuccino and reading the weekend *Corriere della Sera*. He was seated at an outside table under an umbrella near Piazza Garibaldi, where he could see Gianni approach from any direction.

It was the usual Sunday morning parade on the sun-blazed piazza: young mothers pushing prams with toddlers wearing sun hats, walking in groups of two or three, alternating talking and texting on cell phones; male pensioners following shorthaired terriers and dachshunds on leashes; widowed *nonnas* strolling, arms linked with each other, stooped over with age and from lifetimes of raising children and grandchildren. Some of them were huddled under umbrellas against the intense sunlight.

Marco glanced at his watch. Gianni was late. Typical. At 10:35 AM, Marco ordered another cappuccino. When he returned to his table, he spotted Gianni hurrying into the piazza from behind the *chiesa* where he'd likely parked his car, near the primary school.

Gianni's head shifted nervously left and right as he approached Caffè Cavour. He looked like he'd just gotten out of bed and grabbed clothes off the floor; his wrinkled shirt was untucked, the front drooping over his belt. Gianni's running shoes had tattered laces. His uncombed hair poked from under a cap. He hadn't shaved for a couple of days.

Marco rose and pushed a chair toward Gianni. *"Ciao, Gianni. Come va?"* Gianni refused the chair and motioned to the café. "Let's go inside. It's too hot outside," he said, his voice tense. His left hand was twitching like an electrical current had jabbed his elbow. "The air conditioner in my car isn't working."

Gianni hurried past Marco into the café, went to a corner table, and sat where he could see everyone in the café, on the patio, and on the piazza.

Marco ordered an espresso at the bar and brought the cup and saucer to the table. "Thank you," Gianni said, avoiding Marco's eyes as he sipped the inky-black espresso. Abruptly he said, "Let's go outside. I need a smoke." He tipped his head back, drained the bitter coffee, and set the cup on the tiny saucer.

"I thought you wanted to be inside—" Marco said, but Gianni had already risen and pushed back his chair.

Marco followed Gianni and found an empty table in the shade of one of the café's umbrellas. It was hot and muggy, 38°C already. People were staying in the shade of trees or awnings around the piazza.

Gianni reached into his back pocket and pulled out a Marlboro Rossa tobacco pouch and Rizla cigarette papers. He pinched brown flakes out of the package and dropped them into the paper, with some falling next to his saucer. He rolled the flakes in the paper, creased the ends together, and licked them before popping the rolled stump between his lips. He lit his lumpy cigarette with a plastic lighter, inhaled deeply, and then exhaled smoke over his shoulder.

Marco disliked smoking, believing it was a filthy, dangerous habit and an insult to people forced to breathe nearby. "You look tired, Gianni," Marco said, sipping his cappuccino, wishing Gianni would take off his sunglasses. "Did you sleep last night?"

Gianni took off his sunglasses, revealing bloodshot eyes that made him look older and world-weary. "Not much," he grunted. "Betta was up with Davide most of the night; he was coughing, crying. I got up a couple times to take care of him but then couldn't go back to sleep. I'll need a nap this afternoon."

"Davide's been sick a lot, hasn't he? How's Betta handling the stress? I've left messages for her, but she doesn't seem to have time to call back."

"It's not her fault. She's busy day and night. She needs rest, but I don't know how or when that can happen." He made a fluttering wave with his hand as if brushing away a fly.

Marco watched Gianni, his fingers twitching as he rolled the cigarette around. "What's going on, Gianni? Your note worried me."

Gianni picked a piece of tobacco off his lip and flicked it on the ground, avoiding Marco's eyes. He glanced furtively at people walking by in the shade, then again stood, motioning with his head that it was time to leave.

Gianni walked into the piazza and tossed his cigarette butt into the gravel path, glancing nervously in one direction, then another. Marco followed behind. Gianni meandered around the statue of Garibaldi, the hero of Italy's Risorgimento, mounted on his horse, leading his Redshirts into battle. He glanced up at the statue of the former sea captain who had refused a seat in the Senate to retire to the small island of Caprera and raise cattle. Gianni had told Marco once that Garibaldi was his personal hero; Gianni had even named his daughter after Garibaldi's wife, Anita.

Gianni looked away and strolled around the monument, which was on a stone plinth in a small circular garden with pink and white petunias enclosed by a wooden fence.

Marco followed a half-step behind his brother-in-law, observing his odd behavior, like that of a man seeking to run away and hide from strangers. Marco pointed to a corner of the piazza shaded by trees. "There's an empty bench over there," he said.

Their shoes crunched on the gravel path, kicking up dust and dried leaves. Neither spoke until they were seated in the shade. Gianni took out his Marlboro Rossa packet again to roll another cigarette. "I'm in trouble, Marco," Gianni said. "Big trouble."

"Tell me."

Gianni lit the cigarette, took a long drag, and exhaled to his side. "I made a big mistake," he began, almost blurting out his confession. "A guy—Indian or a Paki, I couldn't tell—came up to me a couple months ago when I got home. He was nicely dressed . . . spoke perfect Italian with a Genovese accent. He knew my name. He asked me if I wanted to make some easy money. Fast. I was suspicious."

"You should have walked away."

Gianni spoke in a staccato fashion, like he wanted to rush through his pathetic tale. "He asked how Betta and the kids were. I was shocked.

How would he know my family? He knew the school where Anita goes. He knew Betta took Davide to the park every morning. How did he know that? I was going to walk away . . . then he asked if I could use some extra money to buy new clothes for Betta and the kids."

"He probably had been spying on you for some time. What was his name?"

"He called himself Mimmo, but I didn't believe him. It's probably just an Italian nickname he uses."

"Foreigners often use phony Italian nicknames."

"But his Italian was good. He talked fast. He was only there about five minutes. He said he wanted to help my family."

"How much did he offer you?"

Gianni narrowed his eyes, avoiding looking at Marco. When he answered, it was with a hushed voice. "Five thousand euros. For an hour's work."

Marco balled his hands into fists. He was furious with Gianni but didn't want him to know. Bribing a customs official was a police matter, not just a family issue. "That's a lot of money, Gianni. He offered you a bribe."

Gianni took another drag, averting his eyes. "I know. Damn it, I should have walked away."

"What did he want you to do?"

Gianni closed his eyes for a moment, sweat glistening on his forehead. When he answered, he spoke in bursts, making Marco believe he hadn't confided in anyone about the incident that had likely caused him sleepless nights while he had suffered in silence.

"A container ship was coming into the harbor in a few days. He knew I was on a team that inspected containers. He wanted me to sign papers for one container without inspecting one of the boxes in it. He knew about the paperwork, who has to sign it. He knew my supervisor's name and even showed me a copy of his signature. I was shocked that he knew so much."

"Where was it going?"

"Milano."

"What did you do?"

Gianni grimaced like he'd bitten into a lime. "I . . . I did as he said. It was easy. My supervisor signed the papers I gave him, and the container was taken to the warehouse and left on the truck a couple days later."

"What was in the shipment?"

"I didn't ask."

Marco was stunned. Gianni had committed a serious crime that could send him to prison. But why had he taken so long to tell him? "You took a bribe, Gianni. You could lose your job and be in trouble with the police."

Gianni sucked his cigarette hard, ash falling on his soiled shoes. "I know . . . but the money . . . you know we don't have much. Betta doesn't work. Two young children take a lot of money. I pay support for Michele. I'm always broke. If it wasn't for the money my father gives me, we'd be living on the street." He blinked away tears, reaching up to wipe his eyes.

"Why did you wait to tell me? We could have arrested this criminal."

Gianni grimaced, looking like he had painful gas in his stomach. "There's more," he continued, speaking rapidly. "Mimmo came back a month later. Same deal. Another envelope with five thousand euros. Another shipment. Just look the other way and sign the documents. He asked if Betta was okay, as he hadn't seen her recently. He was watching our apartment. She was at your mother's in Parma for a couple days. Remember? Serena was there as well."

"I remember." Gianni's story was getting more complicated; he had apparently taken another bribe. Where did this end?

"The shipment came. I signed the paper and gave it to my supervisor, who signed without reading it. The container was put in a warehouse for delivery. It was also going to Milano. I felt guilty, but I'd already spent the money he'd given me before. I was tempted by the money."

"Everyone has a price, Gianni," Marco said, restraining his anger. He had to hear the rest of the story, which he suspected was more incriminating for Gianni. "Some people are corrupted by money. For others it's sex, a new car, a promotion, or a better job. People are tempted by what they don't have."

Gianni nodded, head lowered. He dropped his cigarette onto the gravel and squashed it with his shoe.

"What was in the shipment? You had the manifest."

"The paperwork said bicycle parts and clothes from China. Machine parts from Pakistan."

"There was something else in there."

"I know, but I didn't inspect."

"Does Betta know what you did?"

"No!" he said, raising his head, reacting as if he'd been slapped on the face. "If she did, she'd kill me! She's angry with me . . . we're . . . having problems. Marital problems. I'm sure she's told you."

Marco leaned back and took a moment before he answered. Betta had mentioned that Gianni had been acting strangely the last few weeks, distant and sullen. But he didn't want to let Gianni know Betta was confiding in him. "She did mention that you were worried about something. I called you a month ago, but you didn't return my call."

"I'm know. I'm sorry. I was afraid to tell you. But after . . . this week . . . I knew I had to see you."

Marco blinked. There was more. "What happened?"

Gianni looked away, pinching his forearm with his fingers like he wanted to rip off his skin. He reached for his Marlboro Rossa package but then stopped, stuffing it back into his pocket. "Mimmo was back Tuesday."

"Another bribe?"

Gianni shook his head. "Not a bribe. A threat."

"What did he say?"

"He asked if I thought Anita was safe at her school. He said that the walls around the playground have a breach; someone could reach in and grab a child. He was trying to scare me, Marco. And he did. I was terrified! Someone grabbing Anita? I couldn't sleep for nights after that."

Marco held his breath. He and Serena loved Anita almost like their own child. Serena was Anita's godmother. They had been at the hospital when she was born and had taken care of her so Gianni and Betta could have a weekend vacation before Davide was born. "You should have

called me immediately. I could have had an officer there in minutes.
We could have arrested him."

"It happened so fast. I was angry, and I was afraid for the kids. I
wanted to hit him. He said another shipment was coming next week.
If I didn't let it through, something might happen to Betta or one of
the kids."

A warm breeze from the harbor rustled the towering palm trees in
the park, making a soft scratching sound above their heads. A dried
palm frond drifted to the ground, landing at Marco's feet. Marco was
furious at what he was hearing: his brother-in-law admitting he had
taken bribes, his family threatened. Possibly Marco's own sister's life
was in danger. How could Gianni have been so foolish?

"You're in trouble, Gianni. So is your family."

"Can you help me, Marco, please?" he begged, finally looking at
Marco, tears running down his cheeks into his scruffy, unshaven beard.
"I don't know what to do." He wiped tears away with a knuckle, embarrassed by his confession. He lowered his head into his hands, leaned
over, and started to sob.

Marco took out his cell phone. "I'm going to call the vice questore
immediately. He might want to send an officer to your apartment to see if
this Mimmo comes back. But you have to tell your story to a prosecutor."

Gianni made a sorrowful moan, like he'd been kicked in the belly.
"Oh, no . . . do I really—"

"Yes. And you're coming to the Questura with me tomorrow for
questioning. We'll need a statement about everything you told me."

Gianni uttered another moaning wail, turning away from Marco
so he couldn't see his face.

CHAPTER TWO

"Dottor Paganini, Gianni D'Imporzano is in the interrogation room," Marco said the next morning when he met his boss, Vice Questore Riccardo Paganini, in the hall. Officers from the Questura were making their way to the conference room for the morning briefing.

The gray-haired Paganini was the second-highest-ranking officer and a thirty-year veteran at La Spezia Questura, the Ligurian provincial police headquarters, who handled traffic, fraud, extortion, armed robbery, homicides, Mafia and drug crimes, kidnappings, smuggling, and antiterrorism. Paganini was a highly respected police official who had risen from a street cop to being a detective in narcotics and later homicide. He eventually had been selected to be vice questore.

Paganini looked at his watch. "Good. We'll question him this morning. My deputy will take over the morning briefing."

"I would like to be in the interrogation room with him," Marco said. "He's very nervous. I had to talk to him several times last night to make sure he would come this morning. He was having second thoughts after telling me about the incident. I told him I would be there when you question him."

Paganini narrowed his eyes. "I understand. Witnesses and suspects often freeze when we question them. Having you there should help; he can't lie or hide facts if you're in the room. He's your brother-in-law?"

"Yes, he's married to my sister. Yesterday he confessed to me that he took a bribe to let shipments pass inspection without being examined. The person who bribed him threatened his family last week."

"We could have questioned him last night, but you know how it is with summer. I was diving on a boat when you called yesterday, and we didn't get back until nine o'clock. I called prosecutor Marmori immediately, but he was in Rapallo for a family wedding and couldn't come back until late last night. He's coming to my office so we can get more information before we question D'Imporzano."

He took Marco's arm and led him down the hallway. Paganini removed a key from the keychain on his belt and unlocked the door to his office, motioning for Marco to enter. He then gestured for him to sit at a chair in front of his desk. Paganini picked up his phone and punched a number. "Agent Molinari is in my office. Can you come down? Grazie."

Paganini put the phone down, logged in to his computer, and checked messages. Marco sat silently, listening to an antique clock ticking. He let his eyes roam around the office as he listened to the clock and waited for Marmori to arrive.

Paganini's office was like a library with artifacts he had collected: leather-bound books, antique clocks, and watches. The walls were covered with daguerreotype photos of the La Spezia and Genoa harbors in the late nineteenth century; fleets of three-masted wooden ships with huge sails and long lines; sailors rolling barrels up gangplanks; rows of wooden warehouses; crates of Italian olive oil, food, clothing, and machinery; and pallets of granite bound for ports around the world.

Two minutes passed. A knock at the door. Marmori entered, Marco rose, and they exchanged formal greetings.

"Buongiorno, dottore," Paganini said, turning away from his computer. "We need to hear from agent Molinari before we question his brother-in-law, who was bribed about material that came into the port. Marco, tell us what he told you yesterday."

"Yes, dottore. Gianni says that a man named Mimmo bribed him. The name is probably phony. Gianni took two bribes of five thousand euros earlier this summer. Last week, Mimmo threatened his family if he didn't let the shipment go through this week."

"Is it drugs?"

"I don't know."

Paganini nodded. "We've seen more heroin and cocaine coming from Pakistan and Afghanistan recently. This could be a big shipment. We've got to act fast and get whoever is behind it."

Paganini glanced at his watch. "Start from the beginning, Marco. I want to know everything before we question your brother-in-law. Leave him in the interrogation room; it's good to let witnesses sweat while we're talking about them."

An hour later, Marco joined Gianni in the interrogation room, an austere, windowless room at the Questura. Two overhead light bulbs emitted harsh cones of light onto the table, the five chairs, and what looked like minimalist brush strokes on the worn linoleum floor. The light didn't fully illuminate the corners of the room, which looked an eerie gray. But the light did reflect off a two-way mirror, making the room look like a carnival haunted house. In one corner at the ceiling, the black bulb of a video camera stared into the interrogation room like a silent spy.

Gianni looked around the room suspiciously, as if the walls had eyes and ears and were watching and listening silently, hearing his rapid heartbeat, and seeing the film of sweat on his forehead. After he had surveyed the room several times, he focused on a gray electronic console with dials, buttons, and LED lights on the table near Marco's arm. He shuddered, his arms shaking. Marco said, "It's okay. Don't worry. I'm here with you."

Gianni emitted a loud sigh and leaned back, looking only slightly less apprehensive. The lighting, stale air, and metal chairs were not supposed to put suspects at ease; they created a sinister atmosphere to generate tension while detectives let suspects "cook" for an hour or so before their interrogations.

Even with Marco next to him, the room unnerved Gianni. He couldn't relax. His dark eyes shifted around, again focusing on the dimly lit corners, the empty chairs across the table, and the two-way mirror. He chewed on his fingernails, which were raw and swollen, and glanced at the mirror. He knew detectives were staring at him from behind it. He wasn't so much breathing as panting in the stale air, his heart pounding against his ribs. Gianni was claustrophobic and became fearful and anxious if there wasn't an open door or window that he could see through.

Marco put a hand on Gianni's forearm, which was damp with sweat. The move startled him. "Take your time when they ask you questions," Marco advised him. "Don't try to bluff. Don't be evasive. Be honest and give details. If they suspect you're lying, you'll be here all day and night. You're not here as a suspect; you're not being investigated. You're here as a witness, that's why you don't need a lawyer . . . yet."

Gianni nodded, his eyes still darting around the room. He was especially unnerved by the two-way mirror. "Y-y-yes . . . yes, of course," he stammered. "I'll tell everything."

"It won't be pleasant, but you're doing the right thing. We have to get to the bottom of this."

"I know . . . I know . . . but I feel so . . . bad. I didn't mean to do anything wrong, it's just that—"

"Don't say any more. They'll be here soon."

"They're watching, aren't they?" Gianni said, staring at the two-way mirror.

"Don't worry. It's fine. Try to relax. I know this is hard. But I'm here."

Gianni reached for the Marlboro Rossa tobacco pouch in his shirt pocket, clumsily dropped flakes into a Rizla cigarette paper, lit the stump, took two quick puffs, and flicked the ashes into the metal ashtray, scored from thousands of squashed cigarette butts and mounds of tobacco ash. Gianni faked a smile, but the gesture looked painful. "I'm glad you're with me, Marco. I couldn't do this alone. I'd break down and cry or do something bad."

"Don't worry. I'm here," Marco repeated, worrying that Gianni might have a breakdown if they had to wait much longer.

Gianni smoked aggressively, squirming in his metal chair like a nervous schoolboy, raising one buttock and then the other to ease the discomfort of the hard surface. With his nubby fingernails, he scratched the back of his hands, leaving streaks of white on his tanned skin. Circles of sweat stained the armpits and collar of his shirt, which looked like he'd picked it off the floor that morning.

A loud click. The door opened, letting fresh air into the room, which smelled like a musty closet. Gianni flinched and his head jerked toward the door.

Three men carrying file folders entered the room and sat on padded chairs across from Marco and Gianni. Paganini pressed buttons on the electronic console, turning on an audio recorder. In a flat voice, Paganini recited the date, time, and names of everyone in the room.

Then he looked at Gianni. "*Signor* D'Imporzano, I am Vice Questore Riccardo Paganini."

He gestured to a tall man on his right, who sat erect as a hawk on his perch. He looked to be in his sixties, with thin white hair and the bearing of a judge. "This is public prosecutor dottor Stefano Marmori."

Paganini looked past Marmori to a broad-shouldered man seated next to him. "This is detective Angelo Carbonara." Carbonara looked like a bulldog, with a thick chest and forearms that stretched his suit coat. His dark, hooded eyes examined Gianni as if he were a dead fish splayed on a mound of ice at an outdoor market.

The file folders lay unopened on the table in front of the interrogators. Gianni's eyes shifted nervously from one to the other, fearful that the brief, official beginning of his interrogation might lead to physical threats or even torture; he hated pain and knew he would not last long if he was slapped or beaten.

Paganini asked the first question. "*Signor* D'Imporzano, we need to hear the story you told your brother-in-law yesterday."

"Yes, dottore. I'll tell you everything. I know I have to, it's j-just that I—" Gianni stammered, his eyes shifting from Paganini to Marmori, avoiding the reptilian stare of Ispettore Carbonara.

Paganini raised a hand. "Start at the beginning. Take your time. Don't leave anything out."

"Yes, yes," Gianni said, wiping a film of sweat from his brow. The cords on his neck were taut as a rope. "I . . . I was coming home from work one evening in May . . . around the eighteenth," he began, struggling to get each word out. "I think it was a Thursday, before I took the family to the Farinata Festival in Portovenere. My kids are crazy for *farinata*, you know. I parked my car near my apartment and was walking along the sidewalk. A man was standing in my path. He greeted me by name . . . asked me how I was . . . like he knew me. . . . I'd never seen him before. . . . I didn't recognize him. He wasn't from our neighborhood.

He looked Indian or Pakistani—dark skin, black hair, dressed in nice clothes, a blue sport coat, tan slacks, expensive moccasins . . . like he lived on a yacht, maybe."

"Did he tell you his name?" Paganini asked.

"He said it was Mimmo, a funny name for an Indian or Paki. I think he was using an Italian nickname."

"Last name?"

"He didn't say."

"Go on. Take your time."

"He asked me how Betta and the children were. My wife's name is Elisabetta. My children are Anita and Davide. Betta is Marco's sister." He glanced at Marco, who was looking at Paganini.

"Yes, we know. Go on."

"I was surprised—shocked, even—that he knew their names. I asked how he knew. He said he saw them on his morning walks. I asked if he lived in the neighborhood. He said he didn't but that he had a friend who lived nearby who he often came to visit."

"What happened next?"

Gianni coughed, stubbing out his cigarette in the dirty ashtray. "We exchanged a bit of small talk on the way back to my apartment—it's at the end of the block—the weather, soccer, the neighborhood. He knew where to buy good bread, fresh meat, and the best coffee shop. It's like he wanted me to think he was a neighbor. He asked about my job, how it was going. . . . Then he asked if I would like to make some money."

"How did he express it? What words did he use?"

"Something like . . . could I use some extra money . . . to pay bills, you know, buy something nice for my children and wife. He said families with young children need extra money. . . . He was trying to be friendly. . . . He was . . . slick . . . like he knew what he was doing."

Paganini nodded. "Did he mention how much money?"

"No, not at that point."

"What else did you say?"

"I asked him what he meant. He said he knew customs agents are not paid well and families have needs that are more than our salaries provide. He patted his coat pocket like he had something for me. . . . I said I didn't need any money; our family was fine. He looked up at my apartment and gave me a smile like he knew I wasn't telling the truth. Our neighborhood . . . is . . . you know . . . not the best. It's noisy, with motorbikes and motorcycles going by at all times of the day, teenagers hanging out at night and making a lot of noise. It's a busy street with lots of families with children—"

"What neighborhood?" Paganini asked.

"We live in Quartiere Umbertino. On Via Firenze."

Paganini nodded. "I know it. Go on."

Gianni coughed again, cleared his throat, and continued. "He patted his coat pocket again and said, 'Betta and the children need new clothes.' I was insulted and was going to walk away. Then he said, 'I want to be your friend. . . . I can help you, Gianni.' He kept using my name. Then he said, 'I have a present for you.' He put his hand in his pocket like he was going to take something out."

"Did anyone on the street see you talking to him?" Prosecutor Marmori asked. It was the first time he had spoken.

Gianni shook his head. "Maybe. I really don't know. It's a narrow street . . . a busy neighborhood . . . children playing in the street . . . running and kicking soccer balls. The closest park is three blocks away, so the children play in the street when they're not in school or at home. Cars park on one side and on the sidewalk, so there's not much room to stop and talk. There's not even a coffee shop close by."

"Was there anyone who saw you talking to the man?" Marmori repeated.

"Ah . . . I don't know. It was a long time ago."

"What did he say next?" Paganini asked.

"He took out an envelope and handed it to me. I didn't take it. He slipped it under my armpit, like this." Gianni demonstrated, slipping a hand under his sweaty armpit. "Then he said, 'Here's a gift for you and a note inside. A ship is coming into port next Wednesday. The note has a container number. When you inspect that container, there will be a wooden box with a serial number that's on the note. Sign the customs authorization and get your supervisor to sign off. Tell him you've done your job. He won't know that you didn't inspect the box. Customs agents like you are busy. It will only take five minutes or so. Five thousand euros for five minutes' work. How many weeks do you have to work to earn five thousand euros?'"

"How did you answer him?"

"I don't remember . . . something like . . . 'That's a lot of money.' He smiled and said, 'You'll earn it by following instructions.' I asked him how he would know that I followed instructions. He didn't say anything for a moment, and then he looked around to see if anyone was watching."

"Was there?"

He shook his head. "Just children playing in the street, that's all. I don't remember anything else."

"Then what did he say?"

Gianni stole a quick glance at Carbonara, whose eyes were locked on him. "What he said upset me: 'If you don't follow instructions, I'll find out. Then I'll come and get my money back. But you don't want that; you really don't. The money's yours if you do as I ask.'"

Marmori asked, "What did you think he meant by that?"

Gianni was still nervous, his eyes blinking. "It was . . . like a threat. It meant someone at the dock was watching me."

"Do you know who could be watching you?"

Gianni shook his head, twisting the tobacco pouch in his hands. "I never noticed. . . . Hundreds of people work on the dock every day— customs inspectors . . . dockworkers . . . police. Some I know. Many people, not always the same ones."

Marmori opened his file and scribbled on a notepad. He looked up at Gianni and said, "Keep talking. What happened next?"

"The envelope fell to the ground. We stood there. He didn't pick it up. I looked down at it . . . I didn't know what to do . . . I felt uncomfortable . . . it was . . . an uneasy feeling, just standing on the street . . . looking at each other. He never took his eyes off me." Gianni sighed, took a deep breath, and continued. "I . . . I picked it up . . . tried to give it back to him . . . but he put up his hand and said, 'It's yours, Gianni, a gift from me to you and your family. It's not polite to give gifts back.' He was smiling . . . like he had given me a Christmas present or something. It felt . . . so . . . strange . . . like in a Mafia movie."

"Did you put it in your pocket?"

"No. . . . I held it in my hand. . . . Mimmo smiled and touched his forehead like this." Gianni made a gesture like a quick salute. "He said to have a good evening with my family . . . that I was lucky to have a pretty wife and children. Then he turned around and walked away."

"What did you do?"

"I . . . I was shaking, not sure what I should do. I wanted to run after him and give the envelope back, but I felt almost . . . paralyzed. . . . I couldn't believe what had happened. It was like it was happening to someone else, not me. Someone I didn't know had given me money on the street. . . . It was like a dream. . . . That's the truth. I mean it." He opened his cigarette pouch to roll another cigarette, then stopped and put the pouch back on the table.

"Why didn't you follow him and tell him to come back?" Carbonara asked.

"I was going to . . . but I felt like I was dreaming, like I told you, and when I woke up, he was gone . . . around the corner."

The three officers looked at each other, blank expressions on their faces. Then they looked at Gianni, and Marmori asked, "What did you do after you woke from . . . this dream?"

Gianni's face drooped. He looked down at the table, his hands gripping the tobacco pouch. "I wasn't thinking right. . . . I was in shock. . . . I went up to my apartment . . . kissed my wife . . . hugged my children. . . . I just wanted to be home with them."

"What did you do with the envelope?"

Gianni looked at Marco before he answered. "I . . . I put it in my dresser."

"Did you open it?"

A wave of anxiety washed over Gianni's pale, sweaty face. He looked at Marco as if he wanted him to answer for him. "Tell him, Gianni," Marco urged. "Tell them the whole story."

"I didn't open it right away. . . . I was too frightened. . . . I waited until after dinner. . . . I was upset. . . . I couldn't eat. . . . All I could think about was the envelope and . . . what was in it."

"What was in the envelope?" Marmori said.

Gianni looked at Marco, then back at them. "A stack of fifty-euro bills, a hundred of them, with a clip around them."

"And the note?"

"A typed note. Short, just four lines: the date of May 28; the ship name, Oceana; the number of the container; and the serial number of a box in the container. I put everything back in the envelope and shut the dresser."

It was quiet for several moments. Paganini, Marmori, and Carbonara stared at Gianni, who looked nervously from one to the other, not sure if he should say anything more.

"Did you follow his instructions?"

Gianni looked down at his hands in his lap. In a trembling voice, he said, "Yes . . . yes, I did."

"What did you do with the note?"

He looked up but avoided their eyes. In a low voice, he said, "I . . . I tore it up and threw it away."

It was silent in the dank, smoky interrogation room. The legs of Gianni's chair squeaked as he twitched, his hands clutching his tobacco pouch.

Marmori broke the silence. "What did you do with the money, Gianni?"

Gianni squirmed and lowered his head. "I . . . I spent . . . some . . . I'm in debt . . . never get ahead . . . so many bills . . . rent . . . medicine for my children . . . food . . . car repairs. . . . I drive an old Audi. . . . It needed new brakes, a transmission, tires. I pay child support for my twelve-year-old son. Every month I end up deeper in debt." He looked at Marco, tears welling in his red eyes. "Marco knows my . . . situation. . . . He's lent me money. . . . I hate being in debt. . . . I just don't know what—"

"Did you spend the money to pay bills?" Carbonara asked.

"Yes! Yes, I did! I got the car fixed. . . . That was expensive. . . . I had to get a new alternator; a new muffler; new upholstery in the backseat that was torn; a new car alarm—that was broken. All that cost more than two-thousand euros. . . . I wish I could have bought a newer car, but I had other bills. I paid my landlord our back rent. . . . I owed my ex-wife child support I couldn't pay before."

"Did you spend any money on yourself?" Carbonara asked.

Gianni said, "Well, I—I bought a dress and a purse for my wife . . . and a few things she likes . . . perfume . . . soaps . . . a scarf. . . . I gave her money to have her hair styled. She looked so nice afterward," he forced a smile that lasted a second and then disappeared. "She doesn't dress up much. I was glad I could make her happy. I took her to dinner one night . . . a neighbor took care of the children. . . . We hadn't had dinner out . . . alone . . . in a long . . . long time." Gianni stopped abruptly. His face sagged like he was about to break down and cry. He sniffled, pinched his nose with two fingers. Marco put his hand on his arm. "Are you okay? Do you need a break?"

Gianni sniffed. "No . . . I'm okay. . . . I just felt this . . . sick feeling in my stomach. . . . I don't know what else to say. I'm sorry."

The officers waited, letting Gianni recover. Then Paganini said, "We'll take a break in a few minutes."

"Yes . . . yes . . . thank you."

"Did your wife ask how you could afford these things?"

Gianni nodded. "She wanted to know. I said that I had gotten a raise at work, and my mother had given me some money. She does sometimes, but not much. Just enough to buy toys and books for my children, that's all."

"Did you spend any on yourself?"

Gianni looked down at his hands again, avoiding their eyes, and mumbled something unintelligible.

"Speak up. We can't hear you," Marmori said.

Gianni looked up, cleared his throat, and spoke louder. "A pair of shoes. A belt. A hat to go to the beach. I took my family to Genova for a weekend to take the children to the aquarium and the pirate ship." He smiled weakly, remembering the weekend. "We hadn't had a vacation since Davide was born."

The officers looked at each other. "Let's take a break," Paganini said. "Gianni, we'll be back in ten minutes. I'll have someone bring water. Get yourself together; we have more questions."

The three men left the room and followed Paganini to his office. Seated in a chair across from his desk was Giuseppe Magnani, Gianni's supervisor, who'd been briefed about the situation by Paganini.

Paganini sat behind his desk. Marmori and Carbonara sat next to Magnani. "Dottor Magnani, we've questioned D'Imporzano about the incident I told you about," Paganini said. "It has grave legal consequences for him. Before we go back and continue our questioning, we'd like a little information from you. Later we'll need an official statement."

Magnani looked around nervously, unsure of how to respond to senior police officers. "Of course, I'll cooperate. I'll tell you anything you want to know."

"Thank you. We appreciate your cooperation. Tell us about D'Imporzano."

"What can I say?" he said, his voice nervous. "He's a good agent, not a great one. Shows up on time, works overtime when necessary. He doesn't have a strong personality; other agents tease him. He takes it and doesn't talk back to them. He's quiet. Does his job and goes home. I had to discipline him once for taking too long to do his inspections. He seems bored sometimes, not focused, and keeps to himself. He's not a team player; doesn't play on the soccer team or talk about sports like the other men. He seems to be daydreaming when he isn't working. I never know what he's thinking. But he's a decent man with a young family. A good father, I believe, but I've only met his family at holiday office parties. They don't stay long; his little boy has some kind of emotional problem. It's hard on Gianni, I know. Maybe that's what he's thinking about."

Paganini said, "He apparently has taken bribes and will face criminal charges by the time we complete our investigation. Because of the sensitive nature of the case, we must have complete silence about our investigation."

"Why, yes, of course. I understand. I'll cooperate any way you want."

"Thank you. A ship is coming into the port in three days. We need to inspect it for contraband. Probably drugs. We need the inspection to appear routine. Someone may be watching. We don't want to alert them that Gianni has confessed. We'll need to determine what is in the shipment and who it is intended for."

"I understand. You'll have my full cooperation."

"We will have plainclothes officers at the wharf when the ship arrives and is off-loaded. They'll need badges. If anyone asks who they are, say they're government bureaucrats from Genova doing a routine visit."

"That happens often. Sometimes announced; other times they just show up and spend a few hours."

"Good. Now we have to ask Gianni more questions. You can go now. Thank you for cooperating."

Magnani left. When the door was shut, Paganini said, "We need to turn the screws on D'Imporzano. We need to know everything. Do you think he's hiding anything?"

Carbonara shook his head. "Too early to tell. But he's cooperating. I don't think he's lying. Yet. I can spot a lie as easy as tying my shoes. It's second nature for me."

"It's obvious he's scared," Marmori said. "He's a weak character. Probably poor self-esteem. Criminals often have poor self-esteem; they do things to feel good about themselves, things that get them in trouble."

"We need to find out if he still has the notes. He had another encounter with the Mimmo character last week when he was threatened by him."

"So who is Mimmo working for?" Carbonara asked.

Paganini shrugged. "We don't know. Some drug operation, probably connected to illegal North African immigrants who supply hashish and cocaine all the way from Tuscany to Milano. The ship docked at several ports in the Mediterranean and North Africa. Five thousand euros isn't a lot of money for those people. He came cheap."

The men smoked as if each cigarette was fortifying them for the next round of interrogation. They took deep drags, exhaling clouds of smoke out the window, and then stubbed out their cigarettes.

"We need a better description of the Indian or Paki," Carbonara said. "He was dressed well, probably a front man who doesn't get his hands dirty, just greases palms so they can get their drugs into the country and spread around. We'll have D'Imporzano look at photos of local drug criminals."

They returned to the interrogation room. Gianni rose slightly from his chair, like a condemned man meeting his firing squad.

The three officers resumed their seats. Paganini pressed the button on the tape recorder. Gianni related the second meeting with Mimmo, which was almost a repeat of the first meeting. When he had finished, Marmori said, "Tell us about the meeting last week."

Gianni sighed and took a breath to collect his thoughts. "It was Wednesday, after work again. He gave me another envelope, but I refused. I could not live with myself. I was overwhelmed with remorse. I said no. He turned on me; he stopped being polite and became almost rude. His voice changed. He asked if Betta had been sick. He had missed seeing her at the market. Then he said, 'Do you think Anita is safe at her summer school? The playground has a crack in the wall where someone could snatch a child, drag her into an alley, and do something bad to her.' Gianni shuddered, his eyes moist. 'Your children should be safe. You shouldn't have to worry about them when you're at work. Do you?'"

Gianni wiped a tear from his eye with a shaky hand. "I was shocked. . . . I didn't know what to say. . . . I was afraid . . . of what he was saying. He had a scary look in his eyes . . . a cold stare, like a snake or something. He said instead of a payment, my reward for helping him would be the safety of my children. It was up to me. A shipment was arriving this week, Thursday. He handed me an envelope, but it was thin. There wasn't any money, only a note."

"Where is the note?"

"In my desk at the office."

"We need it to check for fingerprints," Carbonara said.

"Yes. Yes, of course," Gianni said, eager to show he was cooperating.

Ten minutes later, Paganini and his colleagues were back in his office. A police official had taken Gianni into another room to prepare an official statement for him to sign.

Paganini said, "We have only three days until the ship arrives. We don't want to tip off anyone at the wharf that we have interrogated D'Imporzano. He has to go to work every day and act normal."

"He's not our target," Carbonara said. "The Indian or Paki, Mimmo or whatever his name is, is our target. We have to identify him."

Paganini said, "Of course. We'll inspect the container and find out what's in there."

"It has to be drugs. What else could it be?" Carbonara said.

Paganini said, "I'll have D'Imporzano followed in case this Mimmo character shows up. We'll have undercover agents at his home to see if Mimmo is around the neighborhood. If we're lucky, we'll find Mimmo and bring him in."

Carbonara shook his head. "I doubt it. He probably has one or two people following Gianni every day to keep watch on his apartment and family. Mimmo only shows up to put the screws to him. We're dealing with professionals."

"You're right," Paganini agreed. "It might be one of the vicious drug gangs we know about. Let's find out and bust them."

CHAPTER THREE

Three days after interrogating Gianni D'Imporzano, Vice Questore Paganini was in La Spezia's harbor command center scanning through binoculars. Plate-glass windows allowed sweeping views from the sunny hillsides of Lerici to the south and picturesque Portovenere to the north.

La Spezia's horseshoe-shaped harbor was carved from the Ligurian granite mountains on Italy's northwest coast between Genoa and Pisa. Since Roman times, the deep harbor protected by a narrow entrance had provided La Spezia with a commercial port, strategic military base, and tourist resort. La Spezia was also known as the Gulf of Poets. Dante, Byron, Shelley, D. H. Lawrence, and Gabriele D'Annunzio and Eugenio Montale had written about La Spezia's romantic charms, sunny weather, coves, sandy beaches, and villages clinging to the granite mountains.

Although Paganini had lived his entire life in La Spezia, he never tired of the harbor's panoramic views. He lived in a hillside villa near the home where he had been born sixty-two years ago. Every morning, he enjoyed the scenic drive down winding roads to the Questura's waterfront *lungomare* office on the palm-lined Viale Italia.

But La Spezia's history and beauty were far from Paganini's mind as he scanned the harbor, following two rubber-bumper tugboats escorting a blue container ship into the gulf. The 250-meter-long Panamax ship had white letters CMA—CGM on its hull and was gliding low in the water like a giant crocodile. Its deck was stacked with containers in the distinctive colors of their owners; silver for Danish Maersk and Chinese Cosco, red for Korean Dong, and blue for Korean Hanjin. Inside the containers were goods destined for world markets: machines, engine parts, clothing, building supplies, consumer goods, foods, fertilizers, and chemicals.

Paganini scanned the massive ship from its bulbous red bow to its stern bridge, a white, multistory structure that looked like a block-house. Three figures inside the blockhouse manned the control panel: the captain, the first mate, and the pilot from one of the tugboats. The roof displayed an array of electronic gear: radio antennae, radar dishes, and navigation gear, along with telemetry, wind, and weather gauges.

Below the bridge were decks for crew housing, galleys, the communications center, the recreation room, the first aid station, and the engine room.

Sailboats, ferries, fishing boats, and yachts had been sailing in the gulf since daybreak. A massive white cruise ship that had docked the previous evening was sailing through the narrow passage to the Ligurian Sea. Small ferries were departing from the marina, with tourists headed for the Cinque Terre villages of Monterosso al Mare, Riomaggiore, Corniglia, Manarola, and Vernazza along the Ligurian coastline.

Paganini slowly turned to scan the working area of the wharf, where towering cranes hoisted containers off anchored ships and lowered them to safety-helmeted dockworkers. The cranes looked like industrial praying mantises, with bowed heads, elongated metal arms, and spindly steel legs bolted to the wharf. Engineers in the crane's belly worked at consoles to guide the steel cables that hoisted containers from ship decks to the wharf.

Paganini pivoted 180-degrees to survey the storage yards enclosed by security fences behind the command center. Stacks of red, blue, yellow, green, white, and silver containers, each twenty-meters long, awaited trucks that would deliver them to destinations in northern Italy.

After Paganini had scanned the full harbor, he lowered his binoculars and looked over the shoulders of the men working at computers and CCTV cameras, monitoring the dockworkers, warehousemen, truck drivers, security guards, and stacked containers around the wharf.

The harbormaster was seated in an elevated chair with padded armrests and a platform to rest his feet. Decades of piloting ships and working on the docks had given him the appearance of an ancient mariner: a ruddy complexion, wrinkles near his eyes and mouth, and a mane of white hair.

"Thanks for letting me see your operation, Tino," Paganini said. "It's impressive to see it all from your command center."

"Anytime, dottore. Always want to help out the police," the harbormaster said. He pointed to the tugboats nudging the CMA - CGM ship toward the wharf, where dockworkers were standing by to toss towlines to the ship's crew. "It'll be tied up in ten minutes. They'll start off-loading containers after that. It will take half an hour or so to get them into warehouses for inspection. You probably want to be there for that."

"Yes, I do," Paganini said. "One container has suspicious cargo that we want to inspect. How long will the ship be in port?"

"Two hours, maybe three. There's only fifteen containers coming off. After inspection, they'll be trucked for temporary storage in the yard until they're picked up by delivery trucks."

"Where does the ship go after La Spezia?"

The harbormaster looked down at an electronic panel with columns of red, green, and blue lights listing ships' data: registration numbers, size, weight, cargo, and departure and arrival times.

"Genova this evening . . . tomorrow Marseilles . . . then Barcelona. Next week it's in the Atlantic, stopping in Southampton, Copenhagen, Hamburg, Kaliningrad, Helsinki, and St. Petersburg."

"Busy schedule."

The harbormaster shook his head. "No, routine," he said, lighting a pipe and leaning back in his chair. He crossed his legs and puffed on his pipe. "Ship owners are greedy bastards. Tyrants. They don't make money unless their floats are moving day and night while they enjoy life in villas in Monaco or mansions in London. Most of them inherited their companies; they learned from fathers, grandfathers, and uncles that they rule the seas and never have to get their hands dirty. They fly around the world in private jets, sail on yachts, dine at expensive restaurants around the world, and treat their employees like slaves—except ship captains. They pay them well to keep crews in line."

"It's dangerous work on a ship."

"It is, but not for the pilots and their staff. Most of them are Danish, German, or Greek. They're paid well, but crews make only a few dollars a day: uneducated Filipinos, Arabs, Russians, Koreans, and

Chinese. They live in cramped, windowless rooms in the belly of the ship, trying to sleep with the banging and clanging of the engines and the stench of diesel fumes. The air's so foul, you want to puke. With no alcohol to drench their sorrows, they play cards when they're not working. They can't get off the ship when it's in port. Every day's the same: long and boring. Most of the time they're in sweltering tropical heat or freezing rain and ice in the north countries. When seas are calm, it's so boring you want to jump overboard to end your misery. Then there are storms. Nothing's scarier than being on a ship during a cyclone or a squall. They can last for days. With the ship rolling day and night, you can't walk without falling down, can't keep food down, and sleep is impossible."

"Miserable, I'm sure," Paganini said. "I have been seasick; it lasted a few hours until we were back on land. I can't imagine being on a ship during a storm."

"I'd rather die than get on another container ship," the harbormaster said, tamping the tobacco in his pipe. "I feel sorry for those poor souls. For many, it's the only work they'll ever have. Most won't live long; if they don't fall overboard or get crushed by a container, they'll die from drugs, alcohol, stabbings, or car accidents back on land."

Paganini handed over the binoculars to the harbormaster and said, "Thanks again. I'd better go. They're going to start off-loading."

"Come back anytime, dottore. Help us keep the harbor safe and secure."

"That's our job. After listening to you, I'm glad my sons didn't pursue careers in maritime shipping. They shuffle papers in air-conditioned offices, attend boring meetings, and go out for lunch every day. The only time they get near the sea is when they vacation with their girlfriends at Forte dei Marmi or some other fancy place."

"Lucky boys. You raised them well."

An hour later, Paganini was with customs supervisor Magnani in a warehouse with four plainclothes Polizia di Stato officers, including

Marco. Standing next to Marco was Gianni, who nervously looked around as he watched the customs agents getting ready to inspect the container.

The men stood in a semicircle at the sealed doors of a red metal container. The twenty-meter-long container showed the wear and fatigue of traveling on decks of container ships; its frame bore scars from the grip of metal cables and exposure to hurricanes, cyclones, the beating sun, freezing rain, and ice.

Magnani pointed to numbers stenciled on the doors while a police photographer snapped photos. "ABFU 0008976-4 is the BIC registration for the container, a sort of identification code," he told Paganini. "The four letters represent the code of the owner, called the alpha code. Standard code for shipping."

When the photographer finished, a customs agent sheared through a metal cable looped through the doors and let it fall to the ground. He lifted bars to unlock the doors and swung them open.

Magnani said, "Most of the cargo on this container is from China—clothing, shoes, purses going to Zara department stores. The suspicious one was loaded in Karachi, shipped to Port Klang in Malaysia to get insurance, and then reloaded for delivery here."

Magnani thumbed through the manifest paperwork and showed it to Paganini. "You see here, the sender is al-Haquib Mettalfabric in Karachi. Address is 63125 Khayabhan-e-Hafiz. The recipient is Vestburo Supply, in care of Massimo Cinti, Milano. Here's the company's address: via Guido Ucelli di Nemi 23, Milano, and a cell phone number. The manifest says the shipment is veterinary tools identified only with serial numbers. Not unusual; we see similar declarations. I immediately asked the Guardia di Finanza to check it; it is an S.n.c. company, a partnership between two people with equivalent shares. One is Massimo Cinti, and the other is Gazmim Saraci, an Albanian immigrant with a regular permit of stay who died last year in a car accident. The Chamber of Commerce register says the VAT number is used by a 'Nonoperative company.'"

When the doors were secured, the men could see cardboard and wooden boxes, barrels, and crates stacked near the top of the container.

Customs agents began removing boxes and setting them on the warehouse floor, matching the manifest with invoices inside clear plastic envelopes stapled to the boxes.

When they had removed about half of the goods, the agents cleared a corridor so they could inspect without moving cargo into the warehouse.

Paganini and Carbonara followed Magnani into the container.

Magnani maneuvered through the narrow corridor while agents inspected invoices with the manifest. In the far corner, Magnani scanned stapled invoices. He placed his hand on a wooden box shaped like a coffin. It was one meter high, four meters long, and one meter wide.

"This is the one," he said.

Paganini looked over the box, running a hand along the surface and reading the invoice. He motioned to the police photographer waiting outside the container. "Get some photos before we open this one, especially the invoice."

The photographer entered and quickly snapped pictures of the box and the invoice stapled to its side, his camera flash lighting up the dim setting. When he finished, Magnani motioned to one of his agents. "Open this."

The agent pried open the box with a crowbar, raising the top to reveal a layer of paper tarp. Magnani lifted the tarp. Paganini, two Polizia di Stato officers, and Carbonara moved closer to look inside. Three articles: a wooden box with Cyrillic writing, a silver metal case, and a metal container. Cardboard blocks between the items kept them firmly positioned in the box.

Paganini frowned, bending over to examine the contents. "Doesn't look like drugs; no bulky plastic bags. Let's open the wood box first. Is it locked?"

Carbonara leaned down to examine. "Doesn't look so." He lifted the box and set it on the floor. He flipped the latches and opened it.

Four stubby black pistols lay in a metal tray with etched Cyrillic writing. "Russian nine-millimeter Glocks," Carbonara remarked. He picked up one, turned it over to examine it, and ejected the magazine. "Not loaded. No shells in the magazine. Serial numbers erased. Looks new." He handed it to Paganini.

Paganini turned it over in his hands, examining the barrel, magazine, and trigger action. "The Mafia and Camorra use these. They erase the serial numbers. Looks like it's right from the factory, maybe never fired. You can get these any day on the black market in Pakistan. What's under the tray?"

Carbonara lifted a metal tray and set it on a corner of the box. Four cardboard boxes each had Cyrillic letters and the number 200 stamped on the top. Carbonara took out a box and opened it.

"Ammunition. Two hundred rounds in each. Four boxes, eight hundred rounds. Street criminals would love to get their hands on these," he said. He took out a bullet, rolled it around in his fingers, and put it back in the box. "This is a small shipment. Illegal weapon shipments have more than a few pistols. We usually find automatic rifles and pistols, grenades, grenade launchers, and sometimes explosives."

"What's in the silver briefcase?" Paganini asked.

Carbonara lifted it out and set it on the floor. "It's not locked, either." He unzipped it and lifted the lid. Clear plastic sheets were bundled around stacks of one-hundred-euro and fifty-euro bills.

Paganini whistled. "That's a lot of cash." He lifted the plastic sheet and picked up a stack wrapped in adhesive paper. He thumbed it; the bills were crisp and clean. "More than a million euros, probably two or three. We'll take it to the Questura and count it. It might be counterfeit."

The men stood over the box, shaking their heads in puzzlement. "A cache of illegal weapons . . . millions in euros," said Paganini. "What's in the metal case? I can't imagine."

"So far I don't understand why D'Imporzano was bribed. Certainly not for weapons and cash," Carbonara said.

Paganini said, "I agree. The fellow who bribed him sounded like a Mafia man. I was expecting a huge drug shipment worth thirty- or forty-million euros. This isn't much."

Carbonara grabbed the case and lifted it out. The top was sealed with thick black tape. "Should I cut it?"

"Yes." Paganini motioned to a PdS officer. The officer took a knife from his belt, slipped the blade under the tape, ran it around the lid, and lifted it off.

Inside were four black, plastic, one-liter bottles packed with Styrofoam blocks so they wouldn't spill. Their bulky, twist-top lids were secured by pieces of heavy tape in an X pattern.

The officer picked up one bottle. A white label taped across the middle described the chemical contents. Below the white label was a typed red warning label in Russian, Italian, Spanish, and English: Dangerous chemicals! Handle with care. Use protective gear when handling.

"This bottle says it's sodium fluoride," said the officer.

"What the hell is that?" Paganini said.

"Don't know, sir. Some chemical. Should I open it?" the officer asked.

"Hell, no! Anyone here know anything about chemicals?"

Paganini looked around at the others. All the men shook their heads.

Paganini said, his voice quivering, "We've got to get forensics out here! These could be dangerous chemicals. We need someone to tell us what they are."

He reached for his cell phone and called the Questura. "I need a forensic team at the port immediately. We have bottles with chemical warning labels. Urgent."

Paganini motioned to the others in the container. "Let's get out of here. I don't want to be in here if one of these bottles explodes."

Fifteen minutes later, an unmarked minivan drove into the wharf and parked in front of the open warehouse. Two uniformed officers got out, retrieved a metallic briefcase from the trunk, and followed Paganini and a Polizia di Stato officer into the container.

"We've got chemical bottles with warning labels in a shipping container," Paganini said. "Tell us what they are. We don't know anything about chemicals."

"Yes, sir," one officer said. Magnani and Carbonara joined the others in the container. One officer set the briefcase on the floor, and both officers knelt by the cardboard container. One opened the briefcase, exposing trays of nitrile plastic gloves, calipers, gauze tape rolls, micrometers, pipettes, and cotton-tipped swabs. The officer slipped on a pair of plastic gloves, picked up one of the bottles, and held it up so the others could see it.

"These were packed and labeled by a chemical supply company. There's a warning label."

He pointed to the tape: *Danger!* with a red exclamation point. "This one is dimethyl methylphosphonate."

Above the chemical and *Danger!* labels was a glossy, diamond-shaped, vinyl, scratch-resistant decal. Inside the diamond were four squares in red, yellow, blue, and white, with numbers in each square.

The officer pointed to the diamond shape with his gloved finger. "These are international warning signs for hazardous chemicals. Blue is a health hazard . . . red is flammable . . . yellow is combustible in air . . . white is special hazard. The numbers go from zero to four: zero for less harmful, four for most dangerous."

He set the bottle back and picked up the second one. "Phosphorus trichloride. This is bad stuff. Same warning labels." He set it back and picked up the third. "Sodium fluoride. Very volatile, I know that." He picked up the fourth bottle and read, "Ethyl alcohol, the least dangerous." He put the bottle back and secured the four bottles in the case. Both officers stood and moved back a step.

"These are dangerous chemicals," said the officer who had picked up the bottles. "We're in a warehouse, a confined space. They could explode. We need to get these to the lab for analysis. I don't like what we've found. Looks like those bottles are ready to prepare a chemical weapon. We're done here."

Paganini shuddered. "And they were on their way to Milano. I need to contact DIGOS and tell them dangerous chemicals were being shipped there. I know the chief, Giorgio Lucchini, an old friend. He's not going to like this."

Later that evening, a cell phone rang in a La Spezia apartment not far from Paganini's villa. A man answered. "Yes?"

"Sir, you told me to contact you after the inspection today."

"That's right."

"The police were at the wharf with customs agents inspecting one container."

"Go on."

"There were plainclothes Polizia di Stato officers. One of them stood next to D'Imporzano. He was very nervous, his hands shaking as he smoked one cigarette after another. He didn't participate in the inspection; he just stood next to another officer who was watching from outside the container."

"What else?"

"Supervisor Magnani went in the container with the police officials, maybe a prosecutor. They stayed inside about fifteen minutes, came out, and got on their cell phones."

"Then what happened?"

"Half an hour later, another unmarked minivan showed up, probably a Scientifica team. Two officers got out and took a metal briefcase inside. They were only there a few minutes, then everyone left. The Scientifica team carried out some small containers, put them in their van, and left also."

"What else?"

"They cleared the warehouse and locked it. Two officers were guarding the container after they locked it."

"Did anyone notice you?"

"I don't think so. I carried tools into the warehouse and talked to dockworkers, some are friends. I left and came back two more times. When I wasn't in the warehouse, I could watch from my truck."

"Good. You did your job well."

"Anything else, sir?"

"Throw this cell phone away. Drop it in the harbor when you go to work tomorrow. Don't let anyone see you."

"Right."

"I'll bring another phone for you tomorrow. You did well. I'll give you a bonus."

"Yes, sir, thank you."

After the man hung up the phone, he left his apartment, took the elevator to the street, and strolled around the neighborhood like he was out for an evening walk. But he was looking for garbage containers set out at curbs for morning pickup. In an alley, he found a row of green plastic rubbish bins overflowing with cardboard, plastic bags, paper coffee cups, wine bottles, and dirty paper plates. He lifted the lid on one, rummaged below the debris, and dropped in his cell phone.

He walked back to his apartment, whistling the aria "Nessun Dorma" from Puccini's *Turandot*.

CHAPTER FOUR

Giorgio Lucchini was terrified that his wife, Giulia, might die. In a few hours, she would undergo her first chemotherapy treatment at Ospedale Maggiore to treat an aggressive form of breast cancer.

Since receiving the diagnosis, Giorgio's life had been in turmoil. He had consulted with Giulia's doctors, researched therapies for breast cancer, and talked with men whose wives had been diagnosed with breast cancer. Some wives had died; others had survived. Giulia's tumor had been surgically removed, but she now had to face chemotherapy.

Giulia was the mother of their sons, Daniele and Vittorio, and Giorgio's closest confidante and best friend. She was the only woman he'd ever truly loved. In sixteen years of marriage, Giulia had given his life purpose. Without her encouragement, he might have stayed mired as a midlevel police bureaucrat instead of being promoted to the DIGOS capo at the Milan Questura. Giulia was one of the reasons he was one of the most respected police officers in Italy.

Giorgio's evenings at home had changed since Giulia's surgery. After warming up the dinner their maid, Maricelle, had prepared, he would spend a quiet hour with Giulia before escorting her to their bedroom to prepare for bedtime. Then he would spend time with Daniele and Vittorio, asking about their homework and what they expected at school the next day. He would urge them to get to bed early. After tending to fatherly duties, he'd load the dishwasher and do minor house chores.

After telling the boys good night, Giorgio would go to the master bedroom and sit on the bed with Giulia. They would share quiet conversation about her diagnosis and treatment, and he would reassure her that the chemotherapy would be successful and they would resume their busy social life in a few months. He would kiss her good night, quietly close the door, and shuffle down the hall to his study.

The rest of the evening, he would listen to opera, sip Moroccan mint green tea, and read DIGOS reports. Then he would pick up Umberto Eco's *The Name of the Rose*—his third attempt to read it—hoping the medieval mystery would be a pleasant escape for an hour or so.

Since receiving Giulia's diagnosis, Giorgio had spent many lonely late nights worrying about her, often falling asleep in his chair, bolting awake in the middle of the night. He would then tiptoe into the bedroom and gently slip under the covers so as not to disturb Giulia.

Her condition was not the only grave matter on his mind. Over the weekend, Giorgio had received disturbing phone calls from a colleague and longtime friend, Vice Questore Riccardo Paganini in La Spezia, and from the DIGOS chief in Genoa. Both men had alerted him that the Polizia di Stato in La Spezia had intercepted a contraband shipment destined for Milano that contained automatic weapons, a cache of three million euros, and toxic chemicals used to make sarin gas.

After half an hour of trying to concentrate on Eco's novel, Giorgio gave it up, left the study, and went down the hallway into the kitchen to pour another glass of Moroccan mint tea and nibble on mozzarella, *grissini*, and cherry tomatoes. This took another ten minutes, but it was still too early to go to bed, as he knew he would toss and turn for hours with dark thoughts running through his mind.

Giorgio returned to the living room to stare at family photos and reminisce about happier times. He had rarely dwelled on mortality or death, subjects he considered morbid. He faced a possible future as a widower. Could he raise their sons without Giulia? Could he survive without the comfort that she had given him for sixteen years?

He retreated to his study again and put on one of his favorite operas, Puccini's *Madame Butterfly*. He sat in his comfortable chair, leaned back, and closed his eyes. But after hearing Maria Callas sing "Un Bel dì Vedremo," he became even more melancholy with the haunting libretto. He turned off the CD and continued his solitary wandering, ending up in the dining room, sitting next to the balcony where he and Giulia had shared morning coffee and sipped *passito* wine after late-night dinners.

Giorgio stared through rain-spattered windows at the lights of Castello Sforzesco. Beacons of floodlights were shining on construction cranes for the new UniCredit Tower. Giorgio stared at the taillights along Via Ponte Vetero. Inky dark skies and the summer rain intensified his depression.

Raindrops streamed down the window, pooled on the sill, and fell on the apartment awning below. The raindrops reminded Giorgio of tears. He hadn't cried since the death of his father five years ago. He knew that he would have tears in the future; he was at that stage in life.

At midnight, he yawned, rubbed his tired eyes, switched off the lamp, and walked around the apartment, extinguishing lights in the kitchen and dining room. He cracked open the boys' bedroom door; the hallway light fell on two heads with tussled hair buried in pillows. The boy's blankets rose and fell with each breath.

Giorgio eased the door shut, crossed to the master bedroom, and put a hand on the doorknob. Giulia would be asleep. A stressful day was hours away. Two crises would consume him for days, weeks, months. How was he going to manage a health crisis that he had no control over and an unknown crisis that could endanger lives? Never before had he felt so uncertain about his future.

He mouthed a silent prayer. "Oh, God . . . please don't take Giulia. I need her. . . . The boys need her." Giorgio had been an altar boy at San Marco, reciting prayers for joy, peace, and thanksgiving. But all that he could manage now was a silent, feeble prayer as simple as a child's: "God . . . please don't take Giulia. . . . Please let her live. . . ."

Giorgio slept restlessly and arose at six fifteen, easing out of bed so as not to wake Giulia. He showered, dressed, and went out to hug his sons as they departed into the hallway and the elevator to catch the bus to the American School in Noverasco. Ten minutes later, Giorgio took the elevator to the lobby to begin his ten-minute walk to the Questura.

Milan's streets were slick and black from the summer storm. Rainwater puddled on sidewalks and gushed in gutters to storm drains. Pedestrians huddled under umbrellas as they dashed across streets or sought shelter at bus stops. Buildings were streaked with sheets of rain, looking as though they had been painted on.

Giorgio paid scant attention to traffic or remnants of the storm on his walk. He was tired and preoccupied. When he walked through the arched entrance to the Questura on Via Fatebenefratelli, he realized how little he remembered from his walk. He had been in a daze, weary and anxious, worrying about Giulia's first chemo in a few hours and the new crisis about dangerous chemicals bound for Milan.

Giorgio took the elevator to his third-floor office behind a vaulted door at the DIGOS command center. He got his coffee, greeted agents who had arrived early, and slipped into his office.

He sipped his coffee, turned on his computer, and scrolled through messages until he found the report the Genoa DIGOS had sent to the Ministry of Interior in Rome with copies to all DIGOS offices in Italy.

Giorgio scribbled notes on a pad and then logged in to the DIGOS secure database to read about sarin and terrorists groups known to have experimented with it. He checked Italian and international police databases for the name of Massimo Cinti, the recipient of the shipment, but found no criminal records. Strange. Not even a parking ticket.

He picked up one of his desk phones and buzzed his deputy, Antonella Amoruso. "Glad you're in early. Come down, please?"

A few plainclothes DIGOS agents had gathered outside Giorgio's office, hoping for a few minutes to discuss current investigations. Male DIGOS agents typically dressed casually, in jeans, running shoes, soccer jerseys, and T-shirts with logos of Lacoste, Abercrombie & Fitch, and Armani. A few sported goatees or beards to melt into crowds while conducting surveillance.

Female DIGOS agents dressed casually as well, wearing chic blouses, casual slacks, and sandals. Some of them wore their hair tied with bandannas. When DIGOS agents left the office, they wore sunglasses and loose sweatshirts or jackets to cover the Glock pistols holstered on their hips.

Giorgio went to the door to greet the agents lingering outside. "Sorry, fellows. I'm tied up this morning. Anything urgent you need to discuss?"

"No, sir. No, no," they reassured him. "We'll come back later."

"If it can wait until tomorrow, I'll have time then."

The agents drifted down the hall as Amoruso came around the corner and bumped into them.

"Buongiorno . . . dottoressa," they greeted her respectfully with a hint of manly charm.

Amoruso was the second-ranking officer at DIGOS, as well as an attractive, dark-eyed woman who dressed fashionably. This morning she was wearing a beige linen pantsuit and white blouse with a necklace of stones and polished teak. Her black hair was cut with a wave that swept over her ears, highlighting her pointed nose and prominent cheekbones.

The agents moved aside to let Amoruso pass, bowing slightly. A young agent known for having several girlfriends smiled and said, "Very attractive outfit, dottoressa. I think it's new?"

"You're observant. Thank you for noticing," she said, turning around to the officer. "Did one of your girlfriends buy you that new Abercrombie T-shirt? You look like a high school student."

The other officers snickered, poking the young officer in the side. "Which girlfriend was it, Alfredo?" one asked.

"Do you wear it when you're with your other girlfriends?" a second officer teased.

Giorgio overheard the gentle banter in the hallway. It had become a morning ritual at DIGOS. He enjoyed hearing friendly teasing among his officers; he found it preferable to enforcing a mood of seriousness and tension. DIGOS agents dealt with terrorists, violence, and maintaining public order every day. He wanted them to feel that they could let down their hair and enjoy their colleagues' humor before hitting the dangerous streets.

Giorgio rose from his desk. "Come in," he said to Amoruso, closing the door after her.

Giorgio motioned to the informal conference room adjoining his office. When high-ranking politicians and police officials visited DIGOS, he held meetings in his book-lined office with the trappings of an important police official: four telephones, a police radio, two computers, and file cabinets. On the walls hung his law diploma, letters of commendation from the Ministry of Interior, photos with the president of the republic and the mayor of Milan, and plaques from the FBI, the CIA, and Homeland Security.

Giorgio's conference room reflected his personal life: framed photos of family vacations, his parents' wedding, and DIGOS agents posing with the A. C. Milan soccer team at San Siro stadium. Giorgio had four season tickets to A. C. Milan games, which he handed out in the office as rewards for long hours and dangerous work.

"You look tired, Giorgio," Amoruso said, relaxing on the sofa across from him. "Giulia goes to the hospital today, right?"

"Yes. I was up most of the night. Couldn't sleep. The rain kept me awake. I'm taking her to the hospital at eleven this morning. I need a couple hours in the office, since I won't be back the rest of the day."

Antonella reached over and squeezed Giorgio's hand. In the eight years they had worked together, their relationship had become more than professional. They shared personal information and had developed a deep level of trust and friendship.

"Please tell her Carlo and I are praying for her recovery. I'll send flowers to the hospital."

"No, no. She's not staying in the hospital. She insists on coming home after her treatment."

"Then I'll send them to your apartment. If she wants visitors, I'd like to stop by."

Giorgio smiled. "You know, she'd like to see you. I'll let you know when she feels ready for visitors. Come for dinner. I've asked our maid to shop for groceries and prepare meals. The boys have promised to keep the apartment clean and run errands for Giulia. You know how messy teenage boys can be. When they left for school this morning, their beds were made, clothes hung up. And they wrote a note to their mother."

"They're good sons. I know how proud you are of them."

"We are. As I told you, I'll have a light schedule for the next few days. You'll assume more responsibility until things get back to normal . . . whenever that will be."

"Of course, as I agreed. This week I may be in court. The prosecutor wants me to stay in the office and not be in the field. I don't like being a prisoner of the courts, even on big cases like this one."

Two years ago, Antonella had broken the case of the Cecconi brothers' Brigate Rosse–style assassination of a financial official in Berlusconi's government and had freed the American, Sylvia de Matteo, who had been taken hostage at Milan's Stazione Centrale train station. Antonella had shot and killed the group's leader, Fabio Cecconi, and had been wounded in the shoot-out.

"I've been there before," Giorgio said. "It's frustrating, not only the time, but the slow pace of trials, and then the never-ending appeals. It takes years for the simplest case to get adjudicated."

"It's a byzantine melodrama," said Antonella. "No one knows what's happening, everyone genuflects to the judges, the prosecutors play games, and witnesses wait for hours to testify. But I shouldn't get on my soapbox; we've got work to do."

Giorgio smiled. "Thanks for your editorial on our courts." He cleared his throat. "So, something came up over the weekend. I was going to call you, but I was preoccupied with Giulia and the news that we'll have a new investigation."

Antonella frowned. "A new case? We're swamped with investigations. We started two new ones last week: the propane bomb at the RAI tower and the threatening letters received by the councillor for welfare at the Comune."

"Add one more to your list."

"What is it?"

Giorgio picked up a remote from the table and turned on the computer monitor linked to the DIGOS database. He scrolled through the reports until it displayed the Genova DIGOS report and Paganini's investigation.

Antonella recognized the name. "Paganini. You're friends, aren't you?"

"Yes. We met years ago while taking scuba lessons in Portovenere. Giulia and I have visited him and his wife in La Spezia, and we hosted them last summer."

"I remember you telling me."

"Paganini called to alert me about contraband cargo off-loaded at La Spezia from Karachi. They intercepted Russian Glocks with no serial numbers, eight-hundred rounds of ammunition, more than three-million new euros, and chemicals to make sarin."

Antonella blinked. "Sarin? That's deadly. Aum Shinrikyo used sarin to kill people in the Tokyo subway back in the nineties."

"The weapon of despots and terrorists. Saddam Hussein used sarin to kill five thousand Kurds in the eighties. We know that Assad has sarin gas and could use it against rebels. Russia, Iran, Egypt, and North Korea have stockpiles. It's not hard to get the ingredients, and it's easy to make and transport. La Spezia estimates that the chemicals in the shipment could kill or seriously injure hundreds if released in a confined area."

Antonella looked puzzled. "But what does this have to do with us? La Spezia isn't in our jurisdiction."

"The shipment was coming here."

Her eyes widened. "Really? Sarin coming to Milano? Who was it going to?"

"That's what we need to find out. The anti-Mafia DIA has just reported that they don't have any information about the Mafia or the Camorra using this kind of stuff. And one of the suspects involved looked Indian or Pakistani. My fear is that it could be someone with ties to Islamic radicals."

"Oh, God, I hope not. We have several investigations already with Muslim imams preaching violence at mosques, recruiting Muslims to go to Syria and Iraq, harboring criminals, and selling forged passports. Our cell phone logs are full of scary things they're doing."

"Let's hope it's not them," Giorgio said. "For now, we'll treat this as a potential terrorism case with unknown suspects."

"That's all we can do until we learn more."

"Nevertheless, the Ministry of Interior is scheduling a conference call this morning with DIGOS offices tracking Islamic terrorists. The shipment is coming here, but its final destination could be Bologna, Venice, Torino, or Rome. We're tasked with the initial investigation."

"What do we have to start investigating?"

Giorgio scrolled through the report. "Here's what we know: The shipment is going to a freight warehouse at CAMM, outside the ring road. Massimo Cinti is listed as the recipient. He doesn't show up in our database: no criminal record, never been arrested, no car registration, not even a driver's license. It's probably a phony name. Send a team to the warehouse and find out what they know about Cinti."

"What about the sarin? Is it being shipped here?"

"No. They quarantined it in La Spezia for a thorough analysis by the Scientifica. The shipment is coming here with the original contents removed. The chemicals were replaced with four identical bottles with the same labels but full of harmless liquids. The weapons were replaced with fake pistols, and the cash with bundled paper. They also installed a GPS monitor. They declared the contents "ready for the import" and issued the customs document IMZ4T so it can be transported from La Spezia to Milan. We need to let this Cinti person think that his goods have arrived safely and then question him or whoever comes to pick it up."

"When will it arrive?"

"It's being processed routinely. La Spezia will let us know when it's been loaded on a truck. Go to the CAMM warehouse, question people there, examine documents, and find out what they know about Cinti. Then go to the address on the shipping manifest and see what you find."

Frowning, Amoruso folded her hands on her lap. "Are you sure, Giorgio? That could be dangerous. If we show up and start asking questions, looking for Cinti, it could get nasty. There could be bad guys ready for a shoot-out if cops show up. Chemical weapons are risky to handle; they don't get shipped to a one- or two-man operation with no experience in dealing with them. This could be a new group we don't know about. None of the groups we're tracking would know what to do with sarin. Weapons and bundles of cash are routine. Chemical weapons designed for mass killing—that's more dangerous. We need to investigate before tipping off Cinti or anyone else that we know about the cargo."

Giorgio leaned back and raised his reading glasses to his forehead. "You could be right. Let's proceed more cautiously. Send a team to the warehouse and see what they can find out without arousing suspicion. Since you can't leave the office, who will you send?"

In her mind, Antonella went through the roster of agents and their assignments. "Our experienced officers are working multiple cases that are time-sensitive. I'll assign our new officer, Ispettore Simona De Monti, and agent Dario Volpara, who recently finished an investigation. De

Monti did well in training, I've observed her in interrogations. She's tenacious; going to be a good agent."

"You've mentioned her before. And Volpara has experience."

"Yes, a good match. Their first case as a team. We'll assign other agents as we build our case. By the way, how did La Spezia learn about the shipment?"

"A customs officer was bribed to let two other shipments pass inspection before coming here. Then he reported it to the police."

"Sarin's already here?" Antonella said, raising her eyebrows.

"Possibly. La Spezia doesn't know the content of those shipments. That's what we have to find out."

"I don't like this at all. We're really starting off in the dark. A likely phony name and other shipments that could be dangerous. We don't have much to go on."

"Precisely. One more detail . . . Paganini told me the person who bribed the customs agent hinted that someone at the wharf was watching him, which means this is not a small operation. The cell has operatives in La Spezia, one on the wharf, another who bribed the agent, and Cinti and his group, whoever they are. So we're talking about six, eight, ten, and probably more."

"It would have to be. I'll check with our IT team to see if they picked up any recent chats or messages that might have hinted about a shipment of chemicals. They could be using a code—a name, a reference to a sports event, or a movie. We have a database of vague terms, names, and references we've intercepted."

"Call me when you learn something. We need to get on top of this immediately."

CHAPTER FIVE

Afternoon rain had drenched Milan just before Inspector Simona De Monti and agent Dario Volpara drove out of the Questura in an unmarked police Fiat. Simona turned left on Via Fatebenefratelli and drove straight on Via Senato, passing the 1608 Palazzo del Senato and the luxurious Carlton Hotel Baglioni.

Commuters peeked out from covered shelters while waiting for buses snarled in traffic from the summer rain. Elegant pedestrians dashed across Via Senato, dodging puddles like they were running through a soggy minefield, worried that their Gucci and Armani attire might be soiled by splashes.

When Simona turned left on Corso Venezia, the rain suddenly stopped, as if the hand of God had turned off the faucet. The clouds parted. Slivers of radiant sunshine bathed Milan in the glow of a glorious, humid summer afternoon. Pedestrians, commuters, and drivers looked up at sunlight reflecting off the mists of the last shower. Water still streamed down buildings and dripped from awnings, trees, and lampposts. Pedestrians closed umbrellas, shook off rain, and strolled along the damp sidewalks.

When Simona and Dario reached Via dei Cappuccini, she had to stop the car while a stylish, tanned blonde lady was trying to park her convertible Mercedes SLK 200 in a space that was big enough for a Fiat 500. Dario laughed, mocking the clumsy maneuver, while Simona gazed at the elegant, private, fenced park of Villa Invernizzi, where a flock of pink flamingos were dipping their cupped beaks to sip water from puddles in the lush grass, their spindly legs like straws. Simona turned off the Fiat's wipers, cracked open a window, and felt a cool breeze moisten her cheek like a baby's kiss.

"Mmm, I love the smell after a rain," she said. "Reminds me of childhood . . . running barefoot in the wet grass . . . squishing my toes in the mud . . . my mother yelling for me to come inside and get dry."

She stopped before she said anymore. She was a cop, not a gushing teenager swooning over a summer storm. What would Volpara think? In her short career at the Milano Questura, Simona had maintained a no-nonsense profile. But for a brief moment, a change in the weather had elicited a childhood memory that she'd shared with a colleague she barely knew.

Dario hadn't noticed. When they turned right onto Viale Majno, he was absorbed in *La Gazzetta dello Sport,* reading a front-page story of an F.C. Inter striker—a renowned bully—who'd been arrested the previous night after an argument with his girlfriend at a nightclub in Formentera.

Dario flipped to the center page to see cell phone photos of the striker lunging toward his girlfriend, being pushed away, and getting slammed to the floor by her defenders. When the bully got off the floor, his face was bloodied, his shirt torn, and his hair mussed like he'd slammed into a brick wall. Dario loved reading about the tawdry episodes of sports heroes acting like fools. Such men made millions of euros a year but were as immature as rutting goats.

"Yeah, the rain stopped, but we're still stuck in traffic," Dario said, still scanning the photos almost a minute after Simona's comment about her childhood.

Simona was relieved that she hadn't embarrassed herself, but she felt irritated that Dario was preoccupied by the sports newspaper.

"You know the CAMM area?" she asked. "And what does CAMM mean?"

"If I remember, it's Consorzio Autostazione Merci Milano. It was built in the sixties to gather together the shipping companies and the carriers to direct heavy truck traffic to one location near the motorway to Bologna and destinations to the south."

He finished reading the article and tossed the newspaper into the backseat like it was trash. "The Linate Airport is nearby, so cargo from there goes there, too."

"No wonder I didn't know about it. Is it just a bunch of warehouses and trucks?"

"No, there's a city park where nobody goes. Monluè."

"What's Monluè?"

"You don't know Monluè? Oh, that's right, you're new in Milano."

"I've been here six months. I know the city center but not the suburbs and industrial areas."

"You should go to Monluè. Interesting place. A Cascina historic farmhouse and an old medieval abbey. Have your boyfriend take you there sometime and have dinner at the old restaurant, one of the first in Milan when the area was old farms and villages. That was in the old days, when every little village raised milk cows, sheep, pigs, ducks, and chickens."

"Really? Interesting. I'd like to go there."

"My wife and I went to a wedding in the old abbey once. A buddy from Moncalvo we knew when we grew up there. He married a Milanese, and her family wanted the wedding in Monluè, where their ancestors were from. Geez, that was a long time ago, before our second son was born and things got crazy between us."

Dario reached into a jacket pocket and pulled out a pack of cigarettes. He lit one and opened the window. He needed a nicotine fix after satisfying his sports pornography fix.

"You're not supposed to smoke in police cars," Simona said.

He took a quick puff and exhaled out the window. "Don't worry. I keep the cigarette out the window."

"It's against regulations," she said, regretting right away that he might think she was a pest.

"Everyone does it. Don't worry about it."

Simona simmered. He was lying. During training, she'd been on details with officers who smoked, but they never in police cars. However, she didn't want to argue with a partner on their first assignment. The last thing she wanted was to be known as a nag. In her few months at DIGOS, she had learned there were enough whiners at the Questura, and most officers avoided them.

Dario rested his hand with the cigarette out the window, flicking ashes, sneaking puffs, his eyes hidden behind wraparound sunglasses.

"Where'd you go in training?" he asked, changing the subject. "No TAV protests? Security for deputies giving speeches?"

"A few of those," she said. "I worked a couple of San Siro soccer matches in the 'anti-hooligan' squad, keeping drunks in line. It's like a zoo, where you have to keep the wild beasts from killing each other."

"Yeah, San Siro duty is standard for new agents," he said, exhaling smoke out the window. "You get to watch soccer free, but it's not the same as being there with friends, having a good time, drinking a few beers."

Simona detested men's obsession with soccer, a silly sport that glorified young men with little education and few social skills running after a ball around a field. "I don't like being around drunks in crowds. Not my idea of relaxation," she said.

Dario said nothing.

"I'm not a soccer fan," she continued. "My boyfriend is. He never misses a match of his beloved Atalanta. But he watches matches on TV rather than going to the stadium unless he's invited in the VIP box seats. When you're on duty, you don't see much of the matches; you have to keep an eye out for the angry *'minus habens'* fans who only go to the stadium to get drunk and make a mess."

Dario took another puff, exhaling out the window. "Not all fans are *'minus habens.'* Didn't you play soccer in school?"

"No, I preferred volleyball."

They stopped at an intersection at Corso XXII Marzo, named after the five days in March 1848 when Milan revolted against the detested Austrian occupation. A black-and-white street sign directed traffic to Linate Airport. Dario took a last puff on his cigarette and flicked it into a gutter, where it hissed in puddled rainwater.

They waited for the green light in silence. Simona wanted to learn more about CAMM. "I spent two months near CAMM at Ponte Lambro doing surveillance on that Croatian gang bringing weapons from Albania for the No TAV," she said. "You remember that?" She accelerated when the light changed and drove through the intersection.

"Yeah, everyone gets Ponte Lambro duty sooner or later," Dario said. "They usually get assigned there before rotating to other investigations. It's one of the worst *quartieri* in Milano, infested with petty criminals who make their living smuggling drugs, selling stolen goods, and shoplifting. But apartments are very cheap, and lots of good citizens live there. They don't dare to go out at night; they stick at home and watch TV."

"Yeah, it is pretty bad," she said, driving along Viale Corsica under the three bridges. "I worked a couple of shifts there. Didn't enjoy it much."

Dario reached for his cigarettes and then put them back. Simona had made it clear she didn't like smoking in the car. He didn't want to antagonize her, even if she was a newer agent with DIGOS.

Dario had met Simona during a joint operation between the Bergamo and Milan DIGOS teams for the rescue of hostage Sylvia de Matteo and the shooting of terrorist Fabio Cecconi. Simona had been recruited by Lucchini and Amoruso to join the Milan DIGOS team a few months later. At thirty-four years old, she was one of the younger inspectors, attractive and smart. People on the street wouldn't suspect that she was DIGOS; she looked more like a fashion designer: good-looking and slim, with reddish-blonde curls that brushed her shoulders.

Dario looked like a street cop. He had a wiry, athletic frame with ropelike arms and firm shoulders from weight lifting and practicing martial arts at the gym. His face looked almost feral: a knife-narrow nose, a sharp chin, and small ears. He used his looks to intimidate suspects. He'd lean toward them, take off his sunglasses, and stare; his small dark eyes, set in bony eye sockets, looked menacing. When he aged, he would look like an old boxer, with folds of wrinkles sagging over bony cheekbones.

They drove toward the northeast *quartiere*, passing industrial parks, blocks of apartments, auto repair shops, and plumbing and electrical service companies. Simona stopped at a traffic light while a tram crossed Via Mecenate, where an old factory had been turned into a red-brick compound of RAI production studios and venues for events, gala dinners, concerts, and fashion shows.

Dario glanced out the window, watching two young mothers in short skirts wheeling prams across the intersection, where another mother waited on the other side. An icicle stabbed his heart. The mother with long black hair and wide hips looked like his wife, Valeria, who had deserted him nine months ago and taken their two sons to Moncalvo, where he and Valeria had grown up, dated steadily as teenagers, and married when Valeria got pregnant during their last year in high school. Their son, Andrea, was born before they were nineteen years old.

He didn't miss Valeria; he did miss Andrea and their younger son, Filippo, joking with them at dinner, chatting with them, helping with homework. It had been two months since he'd seen his sons, but he thought about them every day. He had felt lost since Valeria had left, being separated from his sons and enduring criticism from his parents and in-laws that he was responsible for the fractured marriage.

Since Valeria had abandoned him, Dario had been sharing an apartment on Via Melchiorre Gioia with two DIGOS officers who were recently divorced, Maurizio Baraldi and Enzo Esposito. It was a typical male den: a big flat-screen with loudspeakers and Sky Sports channels, a fridge with a never-ending supply of beer, three big bedrooms, a poorly equipped kitchen filled with dirty pizza cardboard boxes, and a terrace where the ashtrays were emptied twice a month by their *portinaia*, Teresina. She charged them fifteen euros per hour in cash to mop their floors, clean their bathrooms, and tidy up what she called "your boys' pigsty."

Dario stretched and yawned. "Amoruso wanted to be with us today. She doesn't like to spend all day at the office; she'd rather be on the street with us."

"Yes, she's told me that before," Simona agreed. "She started as a street cop in Rome. Said it was the best job she ever had."

"A tough cop," Dario said. "I watched her interrogating a No TAV protestor we arrested in Ponte Lambro. The guy was squirming like a pig in a slaughterhouse. She caught him in one lie after another until he blurted out a confession to get her off his back."

They arrived at the CAMM, a fenced industrial park east of Milan near two main transportation hubs: Linate Airport and the six-lane ring road that carried heavy traffic south to Bologna, Florence, Rome, and Naples, and east toward Venice. The business center of Milan was a few kilometers in the distance, mere specks of high-rise corporate needles on the horizon.

Simona drove through the gates into the compound, which was devoid of lawns. The only vegetation was plane trees spaced far apart and occasional flower boxes in front of office buildings. CAMM consisted of three paved streets lined with warehouses, office buildings, service bays, a gas station, and parking lots for heavy trucks. Trucks were parked along the streets, off-loading cargo at docks facing the street, or at warehouse internal docks.

In the distance, commercial aircraft were descending through clouds, lining up to land on Linate's runways.

Simona found Via Gaudenzio Fantoli 115. "There it is," she said. "I want to check out the area." She drove to the end of the compound, turned around, returned, and parked across from the warehouse under a sign with the logo of a freight company.

"Let's see what we can find out," Simona said.

They got out, observing forklifts on the street and in warehouse lots loading and off-loading crates and boxes from trucks.

"Not a busy place anymore," Dario said, looking around. "The crisis hit hard here, too. Once all those buildings were busy with trucks going back and forth. Now look how many *To Let* or *To Sell* signs are here. Many shipping companies have closed or moved elsewhere in the last five years."

"Yeah, it looks almost deserted," Simona said, heading toward the warehouse. "But here is ours. The gate is open, so we should find someone in the office."

They entered a warehouse with a cracked pavement floor blotched with oil stains, dust, and debris. A forklift was unloading crates from a truck parked at a loading dock. Open bays around the warehouse contained crates, containers, and mechanical equipment stamped with logos of shipping companies.

Three men were standing beside an idle forklift and smoking. They watched Simona and Dario suspiciously. None came over; they resumed smoking and turned away.

Simona pointed at a wooden shed in the corner of the warehouse. "Could be the office." Through an open door, they saw a woman working at a computer. Simona knocked. "Police. May we come in?"

The woman was thin with gray hair, wearing a cheap dress. She looked up from her computer. "Police? What's wrong?"

"Just routine," Simona said, entering and holding out her badge.

The woman squinted at it. "This is a warehouse. What do you want?"

"Who's in charge, please?" Simona asked, glancing around the windowless office, which was heavy with the smell of cigarette smoke, mold, and disinfectant. The cramped space was cluttered with paperwork and files stacked on metal desks and file cabinets. Tacked on the walls were posters of soccer teams, a sexy calendar with scantily dressed women, No TAV bumper stickers, and a diagram of the warehouse. Dusty bottles of brandy, grappa, and gin were on one of the file cabinets.

The woman motioned over her shoulder. "You want Ernesto."

A man in the corner looked up. He was smoking an unfiltered cigarette and tapping ashes into a full ashtray. He looked to be in his sixties and had a nose like a stubbed toe.

Simona showed him her badge. "Ispettore De Monti, DIGOS. We have a few questions."

"What about?" he asked. "We don't do nothing illegal."

"Your name, please?" Simona took out a notebook from her purse.

"Ernesto De Cambio."

"Are you the owner, signor De Cambio?"

He shook his head. "Naw, I run the warehouse. What is this about?" His hooded eyes shifted from Simona to Dario.

"A container is coming to your warehouse in a few days from La Spezia."

He shrugged. "Containers come here every day."

"I have the serial number." She took out her notebook and read it to him.

"Hmm, La Spezia. . . . Let's see." He shuffled through file folders on his desk, picked up one, and opened it. He leafed through invoices. "Here's the T1 shipping document. Be here Friday."

"Who is the recipient?" Simona asked.

He read down the invoice. "Several. Zara Home . . . Imaginarium toys . . . Carpisa handbags . . . Vestburo Supply . . . truck batteries for Volvo Trucks . . ."

"Could I see it, please?"

He handed Simona the document. She compared it with her notes. "This is the one we want: Vestburo Supply, going to a Massimo Cinti. Can you make a copy, please?"

Ernesto took the document to a copy machine, laid it on the glass, and punched a button. After a whir and a whish, two sheets spit onto a tray. He handed them to Simona.

"Have other shipments gone to the same recipient, Massimo Cinti?"

"Name's not familiar. You know how many shipments we get every week? I can't keep up with all of them."

"No, but you keep records of them, don't you?"

"Of course. We keep copies for a year, box them up, and store them in the back."

"Can you check your files, please? We're interested in shipments to Massimo Cinti."

Ernesto went over to the file cabinets, searched through two drawers, and finally located a thin file near the back. He opened the file and said, "Two shipments: May 10 and May 24." He showed the file to Simona.

"Could you make copies?"

He took the file to the copy machine and returned with four pieces of paper.

"Do you know Massimo Cinti?" Dario asked.

Ernesto shook his head. "No, I only deal with big retailers, department stores, plumbers, electronics. This is a small order."

"Do you call Cinti when his shipment arrives?" Dario asked.

Ernesto nodded toward the woman. "Cristina calls when small shipments come in."

Simona walked over to Cristina and handed her the documents. "Do you know Massimo Cinti?"

Cristina made a face like she'd bitten into a lime. "I do recall him slightly, although it's hard to remember the people who come here. They show up and give paperwork to the men in the warehouse. They check it and load the goods. I get copies at the end of the day. File them. Every day the same."

"So Massimo Cinti did come into your office?"

"Mmm, once. Everyone in the warehouse was busy. He brought his invoice. I signed. He went back and waited to load his stuff into his van."

"Can you describe him?"

"I donno. Forty years old, maybe. Drove a small van or truck. Don't remember."

"Was he alone?"

"Someone was with him and stayed in the warehouse. Younger guy. Didn't get a good look at him."

"Could you describe Cinti?"

Her eyes narrowed as she tried to remember. "He looked Middle Eastern or maybe from the south. Dark skin, short hair, beard. Don't remember his clothes. He was clean. No calluses on his hands—probably works in an office."

"Did he have a foreign accent?"

"No. His Italian was good, like he's educated. Polite. No swearing or dirty talk."

"Did he say what he was picking up?"

She shook her head. "Why should he tell me? We just give them their stuff."

Simona handed her card to Cristina and Ernesto. "Call me when Cinti's shipment arrives. If he comes before, call me immediately. Don't let him leave or tell him we've been here."

"Is he . . . in trouble?" Cristina asked.

"We just want to talk to him. Routine. Nothing to worry about."

CHAPTER SIX

Simona was two steps ahead of Dario when they left the warehouse. She stopped before they reached the car as if she'd slammed into a wall.

Dario bumped into her with an ooomph. "What the—"

"*Cazzo*! Pigeons shit on our car!" she cursed.

Dario looked over her shoulder and saw a white blotch of pigeon excrement running down the roof and onto the driver's side windscreen. Their black Fiat had been washed that morning, looking shiny and new like in TV ads.

Except now it had a splotch of pigeon excrement the size of a *panino*.

They simultaneously looked up. A row of cooing pigeons were roosting on a metal sign above their car, wings fluffing, heads bobbing, beady eyes following other pigeons swooping over the compound like feathered dive-bombers.

"We can't drive back to the Questura with pigeon shit on the car!" Simona squealed. "I'll look like an idiot! How the hell do we clean it off?"

Dario stifled a laugh, but stopped when Simona glared at him, fire blazing in her green eyes. "It's not funny, Dario! We have to clean it off! Get rags or something. We've got to get rid of this . . . this crap!" she exclaimed, waving her arms.

Dario dashed back into the warehouse, waving at the men seated by the parked forklift. "*Scusi*, we need something to clean pigeon crap off our car."

The men stood and leaned out to see Simona pacing in front of the car, hands on her hips, like she was furious that the car had attracted the excrement. The men snickered, one covering his mouth so he wouldn't burst out in laughter. Two others snuffed out cigarettes on the floor and pointed toward a metal sink against a wall with sponges, towels, paper cups, and solvents.

"Take what you need," one said. Then he turned toward Simona. "Want help, *signorina?*"

"No, no," Dario said, waving him off. "We can take care of it. Thanks." He went to the sink, tore off sheets of paper towels, grabbed paper cups, and filled them with tap water.

He went back outside and handed a cup and some paper towels to Simona. They sprinkled water on the spreading splotch, wiping the windscreen with the paper towels.

Dario was grinning at the comical interlude. He hadn't had much to laugh about in a long time. Simona was dutifully scrubbing the windscreen, dropping soiled paper towels on the ground, and splashing water to wipe off the hazy white film that remained.

The warehousemen had walked over to the entrance, grinning at the DIGOS officers performing Operation Pigeon Crap Removal. Water spots blotched the front of Dario's white shirt; a soiled towel had dropped onto the toe of Simona's designer shoe. Simona glared at the men, not saying a word but conveying hostility that a blind man would have detected.

Dario splashed the last of his water onto the windscreen, picked up the soiled towels with his fingertips, and headed back into the warehouse, tossing the paper towels into a trash bin. He tore off more paper towels, poured two more cups of water, and hurried to bring new supplies to Simona, who was cursing as the white smudge spread while she frantically tried to scrub it off.

Dario splashed more water on the white haze and wiped it with towels, spreading the smudge even wider.

A *plop* noise sounded, like cookie dough falling on a floor.

Simona screamed, "Cazzo! Another one shit!"

A fresh white smudge on the roof was smearing down the windshield on the passenger side. Dario's side.

"Damn pigeons!" Simona swore, shaking her fist at the pigeons above them. "Get more water!"

"Watch out," Dario warned, "you're standing almost under the pigeons. In fact, you'd better move the car out of the way."

Another *plop*. Simona screamed again. "My shoe! Pigeon crap on my shoe!" She stepped back, looked up at the pigeons, and cursed once more.

One pigeon flew off the sign, then another, and a third, making room for other pigeons to waddle down the sign to fill the vacant space. They cooed, ignoring Simona's frantic gesturing.

Dario stifled a laugh, turned so Simona wouldn't see his grin, and went back into the warehouse for more supplies. He flashed a smile at the warehousemen, who were enjoying the comic scene.

Dario kept a straight face as he came back outside with more water and paper towels. Simona was out of the pigeons' bombing range, staring at her soiled Hogan shoe. Dario bent down and wiped it off, leaving a hazy film on the suede finish. Simona squatted, grabbed a towel from his fingers, and feverishly scrubbed it some more.

"Cazzo! Cazzo! I want to kill those pigeons!"

Dario returned to clean his side of the windshield. The harder he scrubbed, the wider the milky haze spread. "Better move the car before another accident," he suggested again. He returned to the warehouse to toss the soiled towels and paper cups into a trash bin.

He washed his hands with soap, dried them, and went back outside. Simona had started the car and moved it forward a couple of meters. When he opened the car door, he noticed a new, fresh blotch of white that had plopped onto the trunk. Without acknowledging the latest bombardment, he got in and buckled his seatbelt, deciding to keep the matter to himself. Simona was driving; she didn't need another reminder of the Pigeons Attack DIGOS Incident.

Simona jammed the accelerator hard. The car leaped forward, tires squealing on the asphalt. She was staring straight ahead, her face crimson, jaw tight. She turned on the wipers and sprayed water to remove the remaining haze from the windscreen. She turned the wipers off after a few strokes, leaving clean glass with a white border on both sides of the windscreen.

"Cazzo!"

"Ease up, Simona. It's not a crisis, just a silly thing that could happen to anyone," Dario said, trying rather unsuccessfully to conceal his amusement.

"We're in a DIGOS car! Damn it, it's not funny!" She reached the security gate, and Dario waved at the guard as they pulled out onto the street.

"Calm down. Problem solved. No one will know. It's only a car."

Simona sped down an empty street, cut corners, accelerated, and hit the brakes hard at intersections. It was a couple of minutes before she responded to Dario. She avoided looking at him. "Okay. I'm all right. I got carried away."

Dario didn't like it when people overreacted to a trivial incident—especially if it was hilarious. He felt that it was a sign of immaturity or a short fuse. Simona wasn't immature, but she had a lightning temper.

"You're too uptight, Simona. Relax."

She drove, eyes straight ahead. "You don't understand. This is my first important assignment. I want to do a good job. I want Lucchini and Amoruso to respect my work. I don't want them to think I make foolish mistakes."

"Like getting pigeon shit on their car," he chuckled.

"Stop it. It's not funny!"

"You're overacting, Simona. We didn't do anything wrong. Pigeons shit on our car. We cleaned it off. It's over. Settle down."

"They shit on my new shoes!"

"Scrub them when you get home tonight. They'll be good as new."

He reached into his coat pocket for a cigarette. As far as he was concerned, the incident was over. "I'm going to smoke. Don't get angry. I want a cigarette. That's how I relax. You need something to calm down. If it wasn't so early, we'd go for a drink."

"We're on duty."

"After work, I meant."

"No."

"I wasn't asking you out for a drink. I just thought you needed something to relax."

"I relax at the gym. I do yoga. That's how I handle stress."

"Good for you. Whatever works."

They drove in silence, Dario smoking and exhaling out the window. Simona slowly loosened her grip on the steering wheel. Natural color returned to her cheeks. She resumed breathing normally.

"So . . . ," Dario said slowly, "we got what we needed at CAMM. We learned about Cinti. We'll return when his shipment comes in. Amoruso will be satisfied with what we learned."

"Yes. A good start." When she glanced over at him, Dario cracked a smile to break the tension. "Hey, what do you think the warehouse crew thinks of DIGOS? We're supposed to be crack investigators, and we didn't even notice we parked under pigeons." He laughed. "Even children know what pigeons do."

Simona smirked. "We failed at public relations, that's for sure."

Dario laughed again, lightening the mood. "The joke was on us. They'll have a funny story to tell their friends. DIGOS are good at arresting terrorists but fail at pigeon surveillance."

He chuckled some more and reached over to pat her hand on the steering wheel. Simona forced a smile. "Thanks. Sorry if I overreacted a bit back there. I'll be more careful where I park next time. Don't tell Amoruso; she'll think I'm a rookie."

"Don't worry. She has a sense of humor. We'll wait until we have good news to tell her and then mention it. She'll get a good laugh. She's not judgmental."

"No, you're right."

"I've had my share of pompous pricks for bosses," Dario said. "Lucchini and Amoruso are cool. They motivate us to be good investigators and don't take all the credit for themselves."

They drove through Milan as the summer sun was high in the west. The billowing rain clouds had evaporated, leaving horsetail wisps high in the sky.

Dario looked out the window, watching the traffic as they headed to Via Vittorini. He took a last puff, tossed his cigarette out the window, and said, "What did you think about the workers at the warehouse?"

"What do you mean?"

"Just thinking out loud. They're working people in low-paying jobs with no future. I feel sorry for them."

"Why?"

"They reminded me of my childhood. My father and uncle worked in a fertilizer factory. It was always dirty and noisy. I was scared the first time I went there, when I was about four years old. My mother packed lunches, and we walked to the factory to take them to my father and uncle. They only had a half hour and had to hurry back to the factory. They hated their jobs—smelly, dirty. That experience was one reason I studied in school, so I wouldn't end up working at a boring job in a factory. I wanted to work in an office, wear nice clothes, and be around good people."

"Where did you grow up?"

"Moncalvo, in Piemonte. It's a small town; you probably haven't heard of it."

"No, I haven't. Do you go back often?"

"Now I do . . . when I have time off. My wife left me and took our sons to Moncalvo, where our families live. She didn't like living in Milano—too many people, too expensive, too much traffic. She was miserable and didn't have many friends. She took it out on me, blamed me because she was so lonely and unhappy."

"I didn't know that. I wasn't prying."

He shrugged. "Don't worry about it. My friends at the Questura know. Word gets around. I'm moving on with my life. But I miss my boys."

"I'll bet you do. How old are they?"

"Andrea is sixteen; Filippo is ten. We talk on the phone every day, but it's not like being with them. I hear about their day at school, their friends, and if they might have a girlfriend."

"Yes, children go through so much every day."

"Do you have children?"

"No, I've never been married."

"I thought you had a Bergamo boyfriend when we broke the Cecconi terrorist case in Cornalba."

Simona shrugged. "Sort of. We haven't seen much of each other since I came to Milano. He wanted to get married and live in Bergamo. I wanted to join DIGOS. He wasn't happy about it, but he's getting used to it."

It almost sounded callous, the way she said it. Dario was curious about how the boyfriend would have described their relationship. Had he moved on, or was he coming to terms with the new situation? No way was he going to ask. Wrong time, wrong conversation. "So, how is single life in Milano? Do you have a lot of friends?"

Simona felt nervous. She avoided sharing her private life with colleagues. She kept her personal life and professional career separate. During training, she had shied away from personal conversations and hadn't gone to have aperitivo after work with Questura colleagues, which often led to romantic relationships. She had turned down invitations to parties and had even declined having coffee before work. She had rented a small apartment in Isola and hadn't shared her address with anyone at the Questura except the human resources department.

"I like it here. I'm meeting interesting people," she answered and said no more. She wasn't dating anyone locally but didn't want word to get around the office. She changed the subject. "Call Amoruso. Tell her we're on the way to Cinti's shipping address."

"Good idea." Dario reached for his phone and left a message on Amoruso's voice mail about their visit to the CAMM warehouse.

When they turned right on Via Parea, they entered a blighted neighborhood of two- and three-story apartment buildings in need of restoration, with pockmarked walls and boarded-up windows. Overflowing trash bins were everywhere

Diverse people were on the streets: immigrants from North Africa and South America, idle men smoking cigarettes with arms covered in tattoos, old ladies lugging shopping bags, old men staring in silence at workers behind a construction fence where a new primary school was scheduled to open in mid-September.

Ponte Lambro had been a neglected area of Milan for years. Police cars rarely ventured there after it had been taken over by drug dealers, squatters, illegal immigrants, petty criminals, and knife-armed gangs from South America. The Comune di Milano had considered plans to revitalize Ponte Lambro with redevelopment, construction of a college campus, and a city park, but the area was still blighted by neglect.

Simona turned onto Via Guido Ucelli di Nemi, looking up at the numbers on the front of buildings. "This is number 19. . . . Next buildings should be 21 and 23. . . . There's 23, look!"

Number 23 was an abandoned five-story apartment with boarded-up doors and windows. No scaffolding, no workers, no restoration under way.

"Number 23 is deserted, just like we suspected," Dario said.

Simona pulled over to the curb and parked. "Let's check out the area. Even if it's a phony address, there's a reason Cinti used it. Maybe he lives nearby and used 23 as a smoke screen."

A breeze was blowing down the street as they got out of the car, fluttering plastic and paper debris. They walked to Via Parea, a hundred meters from the abandoned building, and came upon a tobacconist shop. Signs in the window advertised that it sold lottery tickets, bus and tram tickets, cigarettes, sandwiches, soft drinks, cheap wine, and beer.

"Let's check out the tobacconist," Simona said, crossing the street. Dario followed, noticing two young men in worn dungarees in a narrow alley between two buildings. They moved out of shadows and stared at Simona, who ignored them. Their blank stares didn't change when they turned their attention to Dario as he followed Simona inside the store.

The shop's interior was semidark even though it was late afternoon. A man with a mustache and a bush of facial hair was behind the counter, resting against a wall, arms crossed over his chest. He looked like he was from the south. His face reflected that he was wary; well-dressed people, especially attractive young women, weren't his typical customers.

"Can I help?" he said.

"We're looking for an address, Via Guido Ucelli di Nemi 23. We don't see a building with that number."

The man shrugged, his eyes shifting from Simona to Dario, who was standing behind her. Dario looked down the aisle, where three boys who looked like they were South American were smoking in front of the beer and wine cooler, a violation of regulations banning smoking in public places. Their T-shirts were old and soiled, their hair long and uncombed. One mumbled to the others, and they moved to another aisle and made their way to the door, avoiding Simona and Dario.

"Punks," the counterman said. "They think I'll give them beer even though they don't have money. Like other kids on the street, they don't have jobs and don't go to school. All they do is smoke pot and get in trouble."

"Are you the owner?" Simona asked.

He shook his head. "I just work here. What do you want?" The man moved away from the wall and sat on a stool between the cash register and a rack of cigarette packets and rolling papers. His eyes shifted from Simona to Dario, not knowing what to expect from these official-looking customers.

"DIGOS," Simona said. "We're looking for the person who used that address." She pulled out her badge and held it toward him. He leaned forward to examine it.

"DIGOS," he said, looking relieved. "Why are you here? I haven't broken probation. I obey the law. I pay my traffic fines."

"This isn't about traffic fines or your probation," she said. "We want to know what you know about the deserted building, number 23. How long have you worked here?"

"Almost four years, since I got out of prison."

"What was the charge?" Dario asked, moving closer to the counter.

The man's nervous eyes shifted from Simona to Dario and back again. "Robbery. I served six years at San Vittore. I was young and stupid. I have a family now. A three-year-old boy. My wife is pregnant. I work to support them. I don't look for trouble no more."

Simona turned and pointed outside. "Your security camera has a view of the intersection."

He shrugged. "So?"

"We're looking for someone who drove a van to a building near here."

He flinched. "Do you know how many cars and trucks drive by every day? I don't care who they are or what they're doing. I just work here until 8:00 PM"

"How long do you keep the security tapes?"

"A week. Then we reuse them."

"So you don't have tapes from the last couple of months?"

"No."

Dario looked at Simona. "Let's step outside a minute."

They walked out onto the street, out of range of the video camera. The two boys had melted back into the narrow alley.

"Where are you going with this?" Dario asked. "He's a small-time crook who works in a shabby tobacconist store. He doesn't know anything. What can you learn from him?"

"We have to start somewhere. Maybe there's nothing going on here, but there's a possibility that Cinti lives nearby and used the phony address because he knew that building was deserted."

"Slim chance. We're wasting our time."

"Could be, but we make a contact or two and move on. We might learn why Cinti used the phony address."

She turned and went back into the store. "Where do you keep your CCTV tapes?"

The man motioned to the back of the store. "In the office. The boss changes them every morning before I come to work."

She took out her notebook. "How do I get in touch with him?"

"I'll give you his number," he said. Simona wrote it down.

Simona handed him one of her business cards. "Give him my card. I'll call him in the morning. I want to know more about the tapes."

CHAPTER SEVEN

G iorgio Lucchini was weary from lack of sleep, worry, and an aching molar. Giulia had had an allergic reaction to her first chemo treatment. Her blood pressure was very low, and the doctors had insisted she remain in the hospital for observation.

Giorgio stayed by her bedside, going home to shower, change, return to the office, and spend a couple hours there before returning for the evening vigil. The Filipina maid, Maricelle, was looking after the boys while he was at the hospital.

Antonella was keeping him informed during his absence, passing along Simona and Dario's report on their CAMM investigation. She had scheduled a meeting for all of them in Giorgio's conference room at 11:00 AM. He arrived at 11:20 with rings under his eyes. His wavy black hair, normally neatly combed, looked like he'd just gotten out of bed. The knot on his blue silk tie was slightly twisted.

Simona and Dario stood when he entered the room. "Please, no formalities. Let's get to work," he said, waving them to be seated. "Dottoressa Amoruso told me about your investigation at CAMM."

Simona and Dario briefed him on their visit to the forwarding company. When they finished, he said, "We're in a blind alley: a suspicious cell phone number and a shipment going to an abandoned building addressed to a nonoperative company whose partners are a Massimo Cinti and a young, deceased Albanian. It doesn't make sense. Whoever we're dealing with is covering their tracks. These aren't amateurs."

"All we have so far is the phone number on the manifest," Antonella said. "Prosecutor Bassanini signed off on the subpoena to tap Cinti's cell phone. We received records from the telco this morning."

"What have you learned?"

"He used his phone rarely," Antonella replied. "The last call was the day the La Spezia police inspected the container. I think Cinti was tipped off and got rid of the phone. It might be a dead end now."

"What about earlier calls?"

"His calls were limited, a few each month, short, and to numbers we haven't traced yet. We'll get authorization to tap them. But I'm suspicious; we don't know who this Cinti is. No criminal records, and the Automobile Club doesn't have a driver's license in his name. He's a phantom. Something isn't right."

"Are you sure there *is* a Cinti person?" Giorgio asked. "You can't get a cell phone without an ID."

"We've checked. Tax records have three *codici fiscali* for the name Massimo Cinti: one is a fourteen-year-old boy who lives in Macerata and goes to Liceo Classico; another is a fifty-one-year-old pastry chef who emigrated with his family from L'Aquila to Melbourne, Australia, after the earthquake in 2009. The third is a pensioner from Desio, a ninety-year-old disabled veteran who's been collecting a disability pension since 1946. None of them sound like terrorists. De Monti and Volpara are going to Desio today to see the disabled veteran to see why the suspicious cell phone is connected to his name."

"He's not our guy," Giorgio said. "Desio could be a connection. It has a large population of Pakistani émigrés. The shipment came from Karachi. Check with the Desio police."

"I called them," Amoruso said. "There's a mosque where a fundamentalist imam is suspected of stirring up a few radicals. We keep an eye on them. Other than that, there's not much crime. Routine drug problems, standard robberies and burglaries, few violent crimes. Pakis who live there generally work as waiters, mechanics, DHL deliverymen, or Web developers for software companies in Milan."

"Find out what you can," Giorgio said to Simona and Dario. "Keep dottoressa Amoruso informed."

"Yes, sir," Simona said. "Tomorrow we'll go back to the CAMM warehouse to be there when the shipment from La Spezia arrives. Let's hope the person using Cinti's phone shows up."

"I doubt that will happen," said Giorgio. "He was likely tipped off and warned that we'd be there if he showed up." He looked at Antonella. "Tell them what we learned yesterday."

"We were briefed by forensic scientists about sarin," said Antonella. "It's deadly, as you know. Too dangerous for amateurs. We're looking for suspects who are well educated, likely with a science background, maybe chemical engineers. You need special training to handle the chemicals. Accidents can happen; innocent people can get killed. We have to find the people behind this, neutralize the chemicals, and save lives. We're depending upon you to find them before a lot of people die."

Giorgio stood and the others followed. "The Ministry of Interior considers this the most serious terrorist threat in the country. We have their support to assign as many agents as we need to this case. We're briefing all the agents next week." He nodded at Simona and Dario. "You'll lead the investigation."

Simona and Dario left the Questura an hour later, driving north on the SS35 highway to Desio, forty-five kilometers away. When they crossed the ring road, Dario reached into the backseat and picked up *La Gazzetta dello Sport*, which was reporting another episode about the F.C. Inter striker.

The drive to Desio would take an hour in traffic. He'd have time to taunt Simona a bit. Her reputation at the Questura was that she was eager to succeed, exhibiting the serious, unflappable attitude that was typical of new DIGOS agents. But after a few cases, DIGOS agents tended to loosen up, share personal details with colleagues, and build relationships critical for teamwork.

Agents were fiercely supportive of their colleagues, sometimes jeopardizing their own safety to protect each other. Dario and Simona were a new team starting a critical investigation; he wanted to know her better and show her what he was like. He believed that a little gentle teasing was part of becoming a good team.

Dario held the paper up so Simona could see he was reading the cover story about a press conference arranged by the striker's attorney the previous day, which had been one of the leading stories on TV news the previous night and on the morning shows. The striker's girlfriend stood proudly next to him, wearing a short skirt and a tight blouse that revealed a baby bump. The striker was holding his four-year-old son from an earlier girlfriend. He tearfully begged for forgiveness, wiping his eyes on his sleeve and then putting his arm around his girlfriend, whose makeup barely hid the bruise on her cheek.

Before TV cameras, she accepted his teary marriage proposal. Their wedding would be the following month at the Basilica di Sant'Ambrogio, followed by a party at a villa near San Siro stadium. The wedding party would include his teammates, coaches, and team owners. His four-year-old son would be the ring bearer. The headline quoted the striker's tearful pledge: "I'll be the best husband and father in the world."

"How can you read that trash?" Simona asked Dario as he devoured the mawkish photos spread across the inside pages.

Without looking up, he said, "He's one of the best on the team. Scored the winning goal a week ago against Juventus."

"He's a creep! His girlfriend has his baby when he's nineteen years old. He didn't marry her. Dumps her and has another baby with a new girlfriend two years later. Now he's going to marry his latest girlfriend. She's a tramp! Pregnant like his other girlfriend. Don't these girls know about birth control?"

"Yeah, he's a real Don Giovanni. Handsome, with that curl of hair falling over his forehead."

"Pfff," she hissed. "He's a *tamarro*—a pretty boy, rich, spoiled, and rotten."

"Mmmm, you're being a bit hard on him, Simona. He looks more like a model for Dolce & Gabbana or Versace: wickedly gorgeous with tattoos on his arms. Young girls swoon at good-looking bad boys."

"Yeah, then they fall in bed with him, get pregnant, and he's out the door. Who would want to marry that creep? It makes me sick that people admire scoundrels just because they can kick a ball and run fast."

"I'm surprised you know so much about him. He's certainly not your type."

"Of course not! But I was at a club last night, and every TV in the bar was playing the story. The guys were whooping and hollering; even their girlfriends were. It made me sick. I eventually left. I couldn't take it."

"Yeah, TV loves scandals about sports heroes' reckless behavior. It brings fans into the stadium to see the bad boys."

"It's not about sports," she fumed. "It's people's lives. Poor children who will be pampered and then discarded when the next girlfriend shows up. His latest girlfriend—soon to be his wife and a mother—slept with half of his teammates before he got his turn."

"Oh, you know about that."

"It's been front-page on all the online newspapers, even *Corriere*, *La Repubblica* and *La Stampa*. You can't miss it. He's the poster boy for spoiled sports brats. He gets paid millions of euros to kick a ball! Never finished high school and had a child with a teenage girl he didn't marry. Yet everyone's thrilled that he's going to father another child and marry the little tart he beat up in a bar when he was drunk. Really . . . it's a pathetic soap opera."

Dario closed the paper and flipped it into the backseat. "It's a touching story, human interest and all. Everyone was talking about it this morning at work."

"What's touching about it?"

"He's marrying the mother. Promised he'll be a better player because he'll concentrate on soccer and not hang out in bars. He's going to change his life." He looked out the window so Simona couldn't see the smirk on his face.

She scowled. "He's 25 years old! Acts like he's 17. He'll never grow up."

"He was twenty-five last week."

"Oh, big deal!" she said, as if she was listening to a criminal spin out a string of pathetic lies. "Right, he's a mature 'older man,' going to settle down, raise a family, send them to good schools. He's got the brain of a kindergarten brat."

Dario reached into his pocket for his cigarettes, enjoying Simona's ranting. "You clearly are upset, but I don't understand why. You don't like soccer and probably don't even watch it on TV." He lit the cigarette, opened the window, and exhaled a plume of smoke.

"I sat through a game on one of my first dates with my boyfriend. I was so bored. I couldn't believe how all the guys went crazy with every little move on the field—"

"Pitch. A soccer field is called a pitch."

"Whatever. Call it what you like. It's a cow pasture with bullies running around in shorts and thousands of people screaming their lungs out as if the world will explode if their team doesn't win."

Dario took another drag on his cigarette and exhaled into the breeze, barely able to conceal his enjoyment at Simona's tirade.

"You're funny when you're angry, Simona. I like women who have a temper. My wife goes nuclear when she's angry. We used to have arguments that lasted for days. I'd listen and try to calm her own, but it didn't work. You're not like that; you just don't like soccer. I understand. But you've never been outspoken at the office."

"Not my style. I keep things to myself. This is just between you and me. Got it?"

He shrugged. "That's fine. I won't say anything. I like a woman with strong emotions who's not afraid to share her opinions . . . even if they are overheated."

"I don't care what you like. We're DIGOS officers. Our energy goes into our work. It shouldn't be wasted on foolishness."

"Hmm, that's true. I think about my job day and night."

"Except when you're watching soccer on TV."

"Yeah, I do that once in a while," he grinned.

A road sign indicated that Desio was eleven kilometers away. "Let's change the subject. We're getting close," Dario said.

"Yes, please. We need to discuss our strategy. We're meeting a ninety-year-old pensioner. What do you know about Desio?"

"I've been there a couple of times. Not much to say. Pretty boring, like Lucchini said. No gangs or major trouble. I don't know how a disabled pensioner could be connected to a shipment of chemicals. Someone probably stole his cell phone."

Ten minutes later, they exited onto a ramp that took them through Desio's residential areas of tree-lined neighborhoods, middle-class homes, apartment buildings, and playgrounds. Traffic was light. They passed occasional cars, delivery vans, and motorbikes.

"Looks pretty quiet," Dario said.

"Quiet and safe, far from Milan," Simona said. "Families can raise children here without worrying that someone will snatch them off the streets."

As they approached the center of town, they passed through a neighborhood where men wearing white robes and white skullcaps were walking down the street. Behind them, women in black hijabs pushed strollers, surrounded by young children. On a playground, adolescent boys and girls were kicking a soccer ball, laughing, and gently pushing each other. The boys wore shorts and short-sleeved shirts. The girls had colorful head scarves, the ends of which fluttered as they chased the ball.

Simona and Dario stopped at an intersection. Middle-aged, dark-skinned men were sipping tea and smoking cigarettes at outdoor tables of a café advertising sandwiches, gelato, teas, and candy. Nearby were a halal *macelleria*, a call center, an Islamic bookstore, a money transfer place, a Laundromat, and a market with boxes of fresh fruit and vegetables on tables. Signs and writing on the windows were in Italian and Arabic script.

Simona and Dario crossed the intersection and turned on Via Garibaldi toward the center of town. After a few blocks, they passed the church of Saint Pio X. In the courtyard, pensioners in dark clothing sat on benches under shade trees, reading newspapers, smoking cigarettes, and watching boys kick a soccer ball across the stones. A bocce ball court was vacant in the heat of the day.

"Turn at the next intersection; that's the address," Dario said.

Simona turned onto a quiet street, passed a monastery, and pulled into the parking lot of an apartment building with a fence surrounding it. An open gate led into a courtyard with plane trees and a garden with blooming camellias, petunias, and geraniums.

Dario read the sign on the building. "Villaggio dell'Ospitalità Santa Cristina. Nice-looking retirement home."

"Cinti lives here with his wife in apartment 283."

Simona and Dario parked and walked through an arched entrance into a tiled courtyard with a fountain, flowering plants, and grapevines snaking over a wooden lattice. They studied a directory with a map of the stairwells, elevators, fire exits, administrative office, and an exercise room. Security cameras followed them as they climbed stairs to the second story and walked down a covered walkway to apartment 283.

Dario rapped on the door. No answer. They could hear the faint murmur of a TV. He knocked again.

"*Un momento,*" a woman's frail voice answered. Simona and Dario heard the rattle of locks being opened. The door opened a crack, and an old woman's wrinkled cheek appeared. One eye stared out. "Who are you?"

"*Buongiorno, signora,*" Simona said. "We're from DIGOS, Milan Questura. We'd like to talk to signor Massimo Cinti."

"Qu—Questura?" the old woman stammered. "Why do you want to talk to him? He's an old man."

"We just have a few questions."

They held their badges up to the crack in the door. "My eyesight is not good."

Simona extended her badge a bit farther.

"It looks official. What do you want?"

"Could we come in, please?" Simona asked. The woman opened the door, and they entered, their eyes adjusting to the dim lighting from a floor lamp in the dining room and a table lamp next to a blue armchair where an old man was seated. Hanging behind him was a framed diploma that read, *Medaglia d'Argento al Valore Militare per Attivitá Partigiana.* Dated 1948, it had been given to those Italians who fought to free the country from the Fascists and the Nazis at the end of World War II. Below the diploma were black-and-white photos of the Cintis' wedding day, he in a uniform and she wearing a white robe with fresh flowers in her hair. Another photo showed a young and gaunt Cinti in an Italian army uniform, holding a rifle. A third picture was of the middle-aged Cintis and a little girl with tight braids and ribbons.

The old man glanced at the DIGOS officers without saying a word and then returned to stare at the TV, which was blaring the sound of people giggling on a daytime game show while a buxom female hostess breathlessly chatted with contestants.

A blanket draped over the old man's lap reached below his knees. His feet were tucked into worn slippers, socks bunched above his ankles. The shirt sleeve on his right side was empty, pinned to his shoulder. His frayed pants and shirt showed years of wear, with washed-out colors. On a table to his left were a half-dozen medicine bottles, a pencil, reading glasses, and a copy of the left-wing newspaper *L'Unita*.

"Are you signor Massimo Cinti?" Simona asked, forcing a smile.

The old man squinted at her. A wrinkled fist contorted by arthritis lay on his lap.

"Who are you?" He was mostly bald, with a few strands of wiry white hair stretched over his scalp like threads on aging papyrus. Veins traced across his temples and forehead.

Simona held her badge in his line of vision. "Signor Cinti, we are from Milan Questura. We want to ask you a few questions. Someone used your name to register a cell phone."

Cinti looked confused. "Cell phone?" he said, more in a wheeze than a voice. "Someone stole my cell phone. Now I use the phone in the house," he said, pointing his arthritic hand toward a small table with a black phone, a worn phonebook, and a sewing machine.

"The person who stole your phone is using it. We want to find him."

Cinti looked up, teary eyes trying to focus. Simona was unsure if he had heard her. Then he said, "Stole my wallet, too." He looked over at his wife, whose arms were folded across her apron. "When was that, Isabella?"

"Remember? The Saverio wedding. You ate salami at the reception and got sick. You were in bed three days. Don't you remember? The doctor had told you not to eat salami."

He stared at his wife, his reaction slowly changing from surprise to recollection. "Meh," he mumbled. "I thought I was going to die. I can't eat salami anymore. It makes me sick to my stomach and . . ." His voice drifted off.

Simona paused. "Do you remember when the wedding was?"

His wife answered. "Saverio's son, Antonio, was married a year ago at the Chiesa di San Giovanni Battista in June. The reception was in a restaurant in Merate. All young people, drinking and smoking and dancing to loud music. Massimo went to the bathroom and left his jacket on his chair. I was at another table talking to my sister. Someone took his coat. The next morning, someone found it in the parking lot and recognized it as Massimo's. He brought it to us, but his wallet and cell phone were gone. We reported this to the police, but they didn't do anything. They don't care about pensioners. They just chase kids driving motorbikes and smoking those drug cigarettes."

"Did you recover the wallet or phone?" Dario asked.

She shook her head. "No, my husband lost about forty-five euros, family photos, a letter from a priest, and his card from the National Partisans Association. They're all gone."

The old couple looked at each other, her gentle eyes expressing sorrow and his expressing mild bewilderment. Simona felt pity for them. "We'll talk to the Desio police to see if we can find who stole your cell phone."

Cinti looked up at Simona with teary eyes, his hand twitching like a coiled spring. "I don't care about the cell phone. I just want my wallet back. I lost my partisans card. It's a treasure. . . . Those were terrible times. . . . So many died . . . freezing . . . hungry. Just boys from villages . . . saving our country from those bastard Germans!" he choked, coughed, and put his hand to his mouth to wipe off spit.

"My partisan friends were heroes. . . . They're dead now. So is Father Carlo, a man of God. Today, Italian boys don't choose the path of God. Priests in churches are from South America or the Philippines. They have terrible accents. You can't understand their prayers."

He cleared his throat. "Priests aren't like when I was an altar boy and sang in the choir and helped sick people. Now the church only wants money . . . for this . . . for that. Always asking for money. They don't care about souls. They beg for money for starving people in Africa, a new roof for the parsonage, a refrigerator at the parochial school, or fixing the parking lot." His chin sagged and he stared at the worn carpet.

Simona said, "A lot of changes in the church the last few years."

He shook his head, not looking up. "Those terrible priests . . . hurting children. Why did they do those bad things? I don't know why I go to church anymore, but it's the only place I feel at peace. Only old people go to church, waiting to die, feeling alone. It's terrible to be old."

Later that afternoon, Simona and Dario drove down Via Garibaldi after visiting the police station to inquire about Cinti's cell phone. They turned the corner near the shops where they had seen the Pakistani men sipping tea and smoking outside the café.

Through open windows they heard a wailing sound, a male voice ululating in a wavering high pitch, calling Muslim worshippers to Friday prayers. The wailing ricocheted off buildings as men and boys wearing skull caps carried prayer rugs to the mosque. Older women and young mothers followed, pushing prams, heads and necks covered in long scarves, keeping distance from the army of men ahead of them.

Simona stopped the car and stared at the crowds walking toward the mosque. The ululation rose and fell in a haunting cadence of tones and strange-sounding chants that mystified her.

"Have you seen the Muslim call to prayers before?" Dario asked.

"No. . . . No, I haven't. Amazing. . . . Strange."

"I have. When I joined DIGOS, I was on duty at the Islamic Center in Milan. They had a radical imam recruiting angry young Muslims to fight in Bosnia and Iraq. They provided them with forged passports, visas, and money to become martyrs."

CHAPTER EIGHT

Antonella studied the complicated diagram with capital letters, names, and a grid of dates on a blackboard in Giorgio's conference room for a meeting at 11:00 AM with him, Simona, and Dario.

She referred to her notes taped on the blackboard from work the previous day, when she had been interpreting the telco data with Gerardo Annichiarico, DIGOS's IT specialist. Annichiarico worked in the DIGOS communications center; a secure, windowless suite with racks of computers, servers, secure telephones, and communications terminals to the Ministry of Interior and other DIGOS offices. Annichiarico instructed DIGOS agents on using computers to listen to tapped conversations and interpreting technical data from the telco.

"When you click on a phone number, you'll see a list of calls made from and to the number, along with the dates and times," he had said. He had pointed to the number at the top of the list. "The first number is the stolen phone that belonged to Massimo Cinti from Desio. The second number is a phone booth in Corso Nazionale in front of the Esselunga supermarket in La Spezia. The third number is the forwarding office at CAMM."

"We knew the CAMM number before," Antonella had told Annichiarico. "The forwarding office called Cinti's number to report about the shipment. His name was on the manifest. The La Spezia phone booth from which calls were placed to Cinti's phone was likely used by the person linked to the shipment from Karachi addressed to a nonoperative company here in Milan."

Annichiarico had nodded. "I have to say, dottoressa, that your case is unusual. Only seven phone numbers have been called from Cinti's number. Also, none of the cells have been active in more than a week, Cinti's number included, so we don't have any conversations recorded. Most cases, as you know, show daily activity, often many calls a day, and we know the names of the people making and receiving the calls. Do you have any idea why there hasn't been any activity?"

"I'm not sure, to be honest, but that's not the only situation that makes this case unusual," Antonella had told him. "Five cell phones were obtained under suspicious circumstances, mostly stolen from old people who didn't report the loss to the police or the telco. I assume the individuals behind the thefts are connected to a clandestine group planning a possible bioterrorism attack."

The agent's eyes had widened in surprise. "Aah, I see. That would explain why they don't use them often. But when they do, we'll be able to plot their location by the cell phone tower that receives the call."

"That would be important. We have to pin down their locations. Also, I notice that the list of calls made in the last year isn't long. Can you print that list so I can review those calls?"

Annichiarico had clicked on each cell phone number and hit the print button. A printer in the corner of the room had hummed and printed pages.

That evening, Antonella had studied the data, flipped through the pages, scribbled notes, drawn arrows, and made circles. She had noticed interesting connections between two groups of phones and the dates and times of calls. She had taken a notebook, scribbled more notes, and composed a diagram and call grid, which she had drawn on the blackboard in Giorgio's office. She liked working on Giorgio's chalkboard, as it had a tray of different colors of chalk.

She had started with white chalk and made a column with the capital letters A, B, and C. Next to the individual letters she had written in blue chalk the names Massimo Cinti, La Spezia, and CAMM.

Then she had drawn a line connecting the letters and several names taken from the telco data. Below the line she had drawn a second column with the letters W, X, Y, and Z in ascending order. Next to those letters she had printed in blue chalk the names of the people whose cell phones had been stolen but not reported.

She had stepped back from the blackboard and surveyed her work, pleased with the results. She had studied her notes and continued her work, this time using red chalk to construct a spreadsheet grid across the blackboard. Next she had printed in the boxes the dates of calls made to and from Cinti's stolen phone to each of the other phones.

Antonella had stepped back again, studied her multicolored chart, and smiled. Yes, the different colors of chalk were a bit artistic, and she felt they would help Giorgio, Simona, and Dario to understand the patterns she had noticed from the data. Buried in pages of names, cell phone numbers, and dates and times of calls were two clues. Police lived for finding such clues and interpreting them.

She had left the Questura at midnight, tired but eager to share her work with her boss and her agents the next morning. She had done her job.

When Giorgio arrived at his office the next morning, Antonella was in his conference room, again studying her diagram on the blackboard. She held her notebook to her chest and rolled a piece of red chalk in her fingers.

Giorgio smiled. "Ah, I see you're diagramming again. Good for you. What do you have there, an equation?" he asked, scanning the grid of circles of capital letters, names, and dates of calls in different colors.

"Not an equation. Think of it as a key to our puzzle," she said, a confident smile on her face.

"I know the puzzle, the cell phone mystery. What's the key?"

"I'll explain it when De Monti and Volpara get here for our briefing." She fingered the red chalk, went to the grid, erased a date that was partially smudged, and rewrote it more precisely.

"Red chalk—is that significant?"

She smiled at him. "Yes, it is. You'll find out soon."

"Good." He stood next to Antonella, pointing at the columns of letters and names and then across the grid of dates and times. "Interesting . . . a puzzle. Do you have a name for it?"

Antonella pressed her lips together as she contemplated his question. Although she and Giorgio frequently shared similar thoughts, he was often a step ahead of her. "Hmm, hadn't thought of it. Maybe it needs one. Give me a minute, and I'll see if I can come up with one."

Giorgio could tell she was deep in thought, and it was best not to distract her. "I'll leave you alone," he said, going over to his desk and keeping an eye on her while she studied her diagram. He took a few minutes to rifle through the papers, files, and cables left on his desk by the evening DIGOS shift. He signed documents that needed signatures, skimmed through the rest of the paperwork, turned on his computer, and checked his messages.

Simona and Dario appeared at his door. "Buongiorno, dottore. Here for our meeting."

"Right on time," Giorgio said. "Dottoressa Amoruso has a puzzle for us to decipher. Let's see what she has."

The three crossed into the conference room where Antonella was standing by the blackboard, arms crossed, red chalk in one hand, her eyes moving across the diagram.

Simona and Dario sat on the small sofa, and Giorgio chose the cushioned chair where he conducted briefings. They all studied the diagram, craning their necks to read the dates, names, and letters in the circles.

Giorgio was the first to comment. "The puzzle is the mysterious cell phone issue."

"Correct," said Antonella. "I studied the data from the telcos with guidance from Annichiarico. We don't have any taped conversations yet, but I think we will. In the meantime, I found connections between two groups of phones and the dates of calls. Clues, I hope."

"What are they?" Giorgio asked.

"I'll get there," she said, rolling the red chalk in her fingers. "Let me start at the beginning." She drew a red circle around the letter A at the top of one column. "A is the stolen cell phone traced to the pensioner Massimo Cinti from Desio, who was questioned by De Monti and Volpara."

Next she circled the letter B with the red chalk. "Letter B is a public phone near the Esselunga in La Spezia, a busy place. Clever to use a public phone if you're trying to hide your identity. Few people use public phones anymore, and you can't trace who placed the call. Anyone could have placed the call from there—locals, tourists, or immigrants."

She circled the letter C in red chalk. "Letter C we know. It's the number of the forwarding office at CAMM."

She put the red chalk on the tray, picked up blue chalk, and underlined the dates and times in the grid for letters A, B, and C. "Notice that the dates and times for A's calls to and from B and C—La Spezia and CAMM—seem random. They're placed on different days of the week going back three months. The calls from La Spezia to A occur two or three times over a few days, and then nothing for several weeks. Then there are calls from and to A and CAMM over a few days, and then nothing for several weeks also.

"Those calls to B and C—I'm almost positive—relate to the three illicit shipments from Karachi off-loaded in La Spezia and delivered to Milan."

"I see," Giorgio said. "The calls from La Spezia happened first and the CAMM calls later."

"Precisely," Antonella said. "Person A learns from La Spezia about the arrival and then calls CAMM to arrange to pick up the goods from the warehouse. What appears to be random is the first connection I found."

She drew with blue chalk a line under the letter B. "The La Spezia caller is part of the overall plot linked to Pakistan. He probably knows about the plan for the chemical attack, if that's what we're dealing with. That's disturbing; a Pakistan connection possibly linked to Muslim terrorists . . . dangerous chemicals . . . and a sinister group in Milan hiding their identities behind stolen cell phones. We all know about Muslim radicals in Milan; some we've been following for years."

"That's been my worry from the beginning," Giorgio said. "The La Spezia phone is probably that Mimmo character who bribed and threatened the pathetic port inspector. I talked to Paganini yesterday. He told me the inspector is facing criminal charges. He was suspended from his job and has an attorney, but his trial won't take place for months. Without him confessing, we wouldn't have known about this plot. I expect he may get a reduced sentence because he cooperated."

Antonella nodded. "We're on the same page, Giorgio. That's why it's so important to resolve this cell phone issue. It's all we have so far."

She put down the blue chalk, picked up the green chalk and drew a double line between the two columns of letters. "Now let's look at the data for the other phones A called in the last few months. We see something different in A's calls to W, X, Y, and Z, all stolen or missing phones."

"Another pattern . . . a key," Giorgio said. "Good analysis."

"A second, different connection. I'm calling this the Milan phone tree. Annichiarico told me these phones operate from Milan and have rechargeable SIM cards."

Antonella drew a circle around the letter W. "W's phone was stolen from a wealthy old woman, Irma Brazzelli, from Rapallo. She died in February 2012 in a nursing home in Genoa. Someone probably stole her phone at the nursing home. No one reported it stolen."

Antonella circled the letter X. "Next we have X, an eighty-seven-year-old man, Benito Colasanti, from Tivoli. He was visited by burglars disguised as charity volunteers in December 2012, a few days before Christmas. They came inside his apartment, claiming they were collecting money for the orphaned children in Haiti. He was in a wheelchair and didn't see them snatch his cell phone when they went through his place.

"He was too embarrassed to tell his wife or report the event to the police. He admitted his phone had been stolen months ago when our colleagues from DIGOS Rome paid him a visit yesterday and scared him to death, saying that his mobile phone was being used for criminal purposes."

"Interesting," Giorgio said, nodding. "And Y and Z?"

Antonella circled the names next to Y and Z. "Y was an eighty-two-year-old woman, Agatina De Blasio. She had Alzheimer's and was moved from a hospital to a nursing home and then to her daughter's home in Bologna last summer. Her phone was never reported stolen. Her daughter said she could have lost it during the moves. The first call from Cinti's cell number to it was in February of this year.

"*Dulcis in fundo* [Last but not least], Z was a twenty-eight-year-old Albanian immigrant who worked in a bakery and was involved in a car accident in November 2012. He died from his injuries and had no family or relatives in Italy. We know his name. Guess who he is?"

"Gazmim Saraci!" answered Simona and Dario at the same time.

"Exactly! Cinti's ghost partner in the phony Vestburo company. This link shows that we're on the right track."

"Excellent work!" Giorgio said. "This group is clever. They came up with an ingenious way to get phones not connected to their identities. They want to remain hidden. Deeply."

"For now, let's assume there are five suspects," Antonella said, "all in Milan. That's not a fact, but with time and a more thorough investigation, we'll find out."

Dario said, "The stolen phones are rechargeable at any tobacconist shop without producing ID cards. Hand over cash, and they give you a recharge card, no questions asked. And they can use the phones as long as they're not reported stolen."

"The telco confirmed all are operative," Antonella said. "I instructed them that it's critical for our investigation that they all continue working. Telcos will cooperate as long as we have an order from GIP [Giudice per le Indagini Preliminari—Judge for Preliminary Investigations]."

Antonella underlined several dates in the grid. "Notice this next connection for phones W, X, Y, and Z: *when* the calls were placed. Most were placed the first Wednesday of the month around 8:00 PM Person A places a call to W . . . then to X . . . then to Y . . . and then to Z. The calls last only four to six minutes. Pretty short. Person A gets down to business— passes along a message. After the calls, everyone hangs up and turns off the cell phones. Their business is done in thirty to forty minutes." Antonella circled the calls in June. "Except for calls in June. Notice they are a bit longer, eight to ten minutes. Person A had something more complicated to tell them. In July, calls are again shorter, five or six minutes. Routine."

All of them were quiet for a few moments as they studied the dates and times of the calls to W, X, Y, and Z. Then Giorgio said, "If we follow your assumption that they are all in Milan, the calls could be to arrange a meeting. Suppose A tells them the time and place. They go someplace where they can talk in private, get business done in person, and don't take their cell phones with them because cell towers would follow them."

"The telco said cell phone towers haven't picked up signals from them between calls. They turn the phones off and take out the batteries so there's no link to cell phone towers between calls."

"Disturbing," Giorgio said. "They've been planning something dangerous and are taking precautions not to be detected. This group—your Milan phone tree—is going to be very difficult to locate and identify."

Antonella smiled. "Yes . . . but . . . we have less than two weeks before the next call."

"The first Wednesday in August," Giorgio said, nodding.

"We'll be ready, with all phones tapped. We'll hear A's instructions, track the cell phone tower location, and start to pinpoint where they all are."

"Let's hope," Giorgio said.

CHAPTER NINE

Giorgio had spent the day at the hospital arranging to bring Giulia home for the first time since her chemo had begun. Antonella was about to leave work on Monday evening when her cell phone rang; it was Giorgio.

"I'm glad I caught you. Are you still at the Questura?"

"I'm leaving in a few minutes. How is Giulia?"

"Sleeping. Her doctors authorized her release from the hospital after more tests. She was eager to come home; it's the best place to recuperate before her next treatment. Her sister is going to spend a couple of nights with us to help."

"Hospitals are dreary places. I don't even like going there to see friends."

"Can you stop by my place on your way home? I'm flying to Amsterdam tonight and won't be in the office for a couple of days."

"Amsterdam?"

"I'll explain later. Can you make it over?"

Antonella glanced at her watch: six forty-five. "I'll be there in twenty minutes."

When she got off the elevator, Giorgio was in the hallway holding the apartment door open. He was dressed in slacks and a sport coat but no tie. His suitcase and briefcase were inside the front door.

He ushered Antonella in, pointing down the hallway toward his study, where she could hear the overture to Verdi's *La Traviata*.

"How is Giulia feeling?" she whispered.

"Happy to be home. Her sister is spending a couple of nights here to help her while I'm away."

"Tell her Carlo and I hope for her speedy recovery."

They passed the formal dining room, decorated with works by Italian contemporary artists. A black chandelier designed by Philippe Starck was switched off. The Lucchinis usually had a vase of fresh flowers on the crystal dining table. But not this night. The only light came from a corner lamp.

They continued down the hallway, passing the beautiful set of lithographs called *Queen of the Night* by Emanuele Luzzati. A black marble diptych by Diamante Faraldo was displayed on an antique table. Paintings by Enrico Baj and Valerio Adami hung on the walls.

"The boys are staying with school friends while I'm gone. Giulia needs rest for a couple of days," Giorgio whispered.

"Good idea," Antonella whispered back.

Over the years they had worked together, Antonella and Giorgio had shared the joys and pains of their families. Antonella had been a confidante and friend during Giorgio's grief over his father's death and his mother's declining health. Giorgio had been sympathetic about Antonella's stepbrother, who had taken a wrong turn in his youth that had led to a life of crime and misfortune.

Giorgio's study was his refuge from the pressing demands of his work. His bookshelves were filled with law books, novels, histories, and biographies. On the walls were prints that reflected his love of Milan: two city plans, dated 1527 and 1640, and a set of scenes from Meyerbeer's *L'Africaine* at the Teatro alla Scala in 1867.

On a table were stacks of CDs: operas by Donizetti, Verdi, and Puccini; symphonies by Mahler, Beethoven, and Schubert; and Mozart's piano concertos. Giorgio hadn't made the conversion of transferring his CDs to an iPod. He still enjoyed the act of scanning his stack of CDs, opening the CD machine, inserting a disc, and pressing "Play." His routine on quiet evenings found him listening to music, sipping whisky, and reading the latest Andrea Camilleri Inspector Montalbano mystery.

Giorgio poured Antonella a cup of herbal tea as they sat on the sofa in his study. "As I said, I won't be in the office for a couple of days. I was on the phone all weekend with the Ministry of Interior and Dutch intelligence officers."

"About what?"

"Dutch intelligence has a terrorist in prison in Amsterdam. During interrogation, he hinted about a possible terrorist attack in Milan this winter."

"*Mio Dio*! Do you think it's our case?"

"I need to find out. The prisoner trained at a terrorist camp in Afghanistan, where he met a Paki-Italian from Milan. As you know, the sarin shipment came from Karachi. The guy who threatened the customs agent in La Spezia looked Paki. Pakistani immigrants live in Desio. One of the stolen phones was from the old man in Desio. The pieces are falling into place."

"Could be. We need a break."

"The Amsterdam terrorist was planning a bombing at Schiphol Airport, where he worked. They tapped his phone, inspected his home, and found explosives in his garage."

"That's scary. Schiphol is one of the busiest airports in Europe."

"He told Dutch officials that he knows about a possible plot in Milan, and he'll exchange information for a lighter sentence."

"Any idea about what he knows?"

Giorgio shook his head. "I don't have the details. That's why I'm going to question him. Jailhouse negotiations can be tricky. Criminals think they can trick prosecutors with information that turns out to be smoke and fog. I'll press him for details. We need to know if this is really connected to our case. No fairy tales."

"When are you leaving?"

He checked his watch. "At nine thirty, on the last flight to Amsterdam. A police car is driving me to Linate."

"I saw one of our cars at the curb. They're waiting for you."

Giorgio turned out the dining room lamp and tiptoed into the bedroom. He silently waved to Chiara, Giulia's sister, who was sitting in the armchair next to the bed, reading a book. He kissed Giulia. She opened her eyes and stirred. "I'll call you in the morning," he said softly. "Have a peaceful sleep, darling."

"I will. Thank you for bringing me home. Tomorrow night maybe Chiara and I will have a wild night on the town." She smiled and patted his hand. "It feels good to sleep in our bed. Have a safe trip."

He kissed her forehead again, brushed a hand over her hair, and left the bedroom. Antonella was by the door and handed him his briefcase. He picked up his suitcase, and they went down in the elevator and out onto the street.

An unmarked Polizia di Stato car was at the curb, with a driver and an armed escort in the front seats. The escort got out and put Giorgio's suitcase in the trunk. Giorgio and Antonella brushed cheek kisses. He got in the backseat, and the car sped off into the early evening. Twenty minutes later, the car dropped him at the *Partenze Internazionali* entrance at Linate.

Giorgio obtained his boarding pass, went through security, boarded the plane, and took his seat in business class. The plane was half full, with most of the passengers tired road warrior businessmen journeying to another round of meetings in another foreign city.

The plane departed on time, turned northwest, and climbed to cruising altitude. Giorgio leaned back in his seat, shut his eyes for a few minutes, and then opened them and looked out the window as the plane approached the snowcapped Alps.

Giorgio didn't read on flights. He relished the solitude of airplanes. No ringing phones, no computer screens, no meetings. A rare time in his stressful life with no distractions.

The hostess served him hot tea. He sipped it, looking out at the fading pastel pink, orange, and violet sky.

It had been a long and emotional day. Giorgio was eager to get to his hotel room and sleep. For the past week, his sleep had been episodic, interrupted by bizarre dreams and concerns about Giulia. He closed his eyes, dozed off, and then jerked awake. He rubbed his eyes and looked below at the lights of Aachen, Cologne, Düsseldorf, and Essen along the Rhine River. The plane crossed the Dutch border, and the pilot announced they were beginning their descent to Schiphol Airport.

The landscape was beads of car headlights and taillights snaking along highways, along with small towns on canals, rivers, dams, and channels that protected the low country from North Sea storms, floods, and high tides.

Giorgio's Alitalia flight approached Amsterdam from the west and came in on a runway that ran southwest to northeast. The plane touched down with gentle bounces, braked, then began a ten-minute ride to the gate. Giorgio got off the plane, retrieved his luggage, and proceeded through customs. He showed his DIGOS ID card and entered a brightly lit arrival lounge with kiosks selling coffee, pastries, pretzels, beer, and sausages.

Giorgio scanned an arc of people in the arrival lounge. A young man wearing a dark suit with short blond hair was holding a sign with *Lucchini* printed on it. He went over and said in English, "I'm Giorgio Lucchini from Milan."

"Welcome to Amsterdam, sir," the man said in clipped British English. "My name is Ruud Keizer. I'll drive you to your hotel. We have a room for you at the Renaissance downtown. Can I help with your luggage?"

"No, this is all I have. Please lead the way."

"Yes, sir. I'm sure it's been a long day for you."

CHAPTER TEN

The next morning, Ruud Keizer was in the lobby of the Renaissance Hotel, wearing the same dark suit. With a smile on his face, he greeted Giorgio warmly. "If you want breakfast, signor Lucchini, we have time; our meeting doesn't start until 10:00 AM," he said. "I already had breakfast with my wife and children at home. I can have coffee with you."

"That would be nice," Giorgio said. They went into the bar where the hotel served breakfast for guests. It was a tastefully modern design with a polished blond wooden floor, plush chairs, glass tables, and small sofas for intimate conversation. A selection of pastries, cheeses, breads, meats, fruits, cereals, and yogurt had been laid out on the bar. Giorgio chose traditional Dutch treats: a croissant with raisins, a soft bread with *hagelslag*, a slab of Gouda cheese, a slice of ham, and a nectarine. He joined Ruud at a window table looking out on a canal. A waiter brought a tray with a small coffee pot and a pot of tea with fresh mint leaves and honey, and then departed.

Giorgio sipped his coffee and glanced out at platoons of men and women riding bicycles along the Singel canal: professionals, students, teachers, and children, almost everyone with a backpack. They resembled salmon swimming upstream, maneuvering around other bikers on their way to work or school.

"It's refreshing to see people commuting on bicycles instead of being stuck in cars," Giorgio said. "You enjoy a more serene lifestyle in Holland, not the hectic pace we have in Milan. On my morning walks to work, I pass by buses and cars honking and trams clanging."

Ruud smiled. "What you see may look serene, but Amsterdam bikers are rude sometimes. Friends ride their bicycles together, crowding pedestrians along the canal, interfering with car traffic. They are a bit arrogant, thinking that since they're not creating pollution, they should have the right of way."

Giorgio glanced out the window, where bicycle riders seemed to be orderly. "Really? They don't look like a nuisance."

Rudd smiled. "I'm not condemning all of them, just those who aren't considerate. We are lucky to live in Amsterdam. My wife and I send our children off to school on their bicycles. Then we get on ours and head in different directions to our work. My wife is a teacher, and her school is only ten minutes from our home. My commute is fifteen minutes, biking along the canal and passing over two bridges to my office."

"I'll tell my boys about it when I get home. Maybe I'll encourage them to attend university here. I could bring the family for a vacation so they could experience Amsterdam themselves. I went to the Rijksmuseum one summer when I was in law school. Dutch art is superb—Rembrandt . . . Vermeer . . . van Gogh. I stood in front of Rembrandt's *Night Watch* for an hour. Such an amazing painting. I can still see it."

"Did you go to the Van Gogh Museum?"

"Aah, unfortunately, no. I was with law-school friends, and we had only two days here before we took the train to Copenhagen."

"Nice trip."

"It was." Giorgio smiled. "But I haven't been back since. I need to bring my family here."

They exchanged polite conversation about European politics, the hot weather, and Ruud's family vacation on Lago di Garda while Giorgio nibbled his breakfast and Ruud had a second cup of coffee. When Giorgio pushed his empty plates to the side, Ruud said, "My superiors prepared a briefing for you at our Amsterdam office. Our headquarters is in Zoetermeer, in Zuid-Holland, about sixty kilometers from here—too far to drive. Plus the prison is here.

"There are things you should know before we take you to the prison. We have extensive background, an intelligence assessment, and a psychological profile of the suspect. And, of course, his request to speak with you."

"I'm very interested in hearing from him. I have several questions about a possible connection to a case we're investigating."

They left the hotel at nine thirty and got into an unmarked police car that had been idling in the Renaissance valet parking. It was a ten-minute drive to the Amsterdam office of General Intelligence and Security Service (AIVD), a nondescript, six-story building near the local police headquarters.

Giorgio followed Ruud into the building to a security desk. Giorgio handed over his DIGOS ID and signed a form prefilled with his name and rank and the Questura address. A clerk stamped the form, put it into a folder, and gave him a visitor's badge. Ruud escorted Giorgio to an elevator, which they took to the top floor.

They exited the elevator, and Ruud led Giorgio down a hall to an office where the door was open. A short, thin man with wire-rimmed glasses stood and came around his desk to greet them.

"Good morning, signor Lucchini. I'm pleased that you could make it. My name is Cor Rijkaard. I'm deputy director with the General Intelligence and Security Service. Ruud is my assistant working on this case. Please take a seat."

"Thank you for letting me know about this case. I hope to find a link to an investigation we're working on."

"Signor Lucchini, it is our duty to inform immediately our European partners about these serious threats we're all facing. International terrorism does not respect borders."

Giorgio nodded and Rijkaard continued. "Let's dispense with pleasantries. We have serious work to do."

Giorgio nodded again, pleased they would not waste time.

"We monitor individuals who represent a security threat to the Netherlands. Like the rest of the European countries and America, we are greatly concerned about how terrorist elements in the Middle East have been infiltrating our country and planning dangerous attacks on our people. I'm sure you remember the Hofstadgroep, an Islamic terrorist group who murdered the director Theo van Gogh. He produced what they considered an anti-Islamic film. His murder was a national tragedy and a shock to the Dutch people, who consider us a tolerant nation.

"For the last two decades, we have noticed changes in how extremist groups organize and protest. In the past, our main concerns were activist groups protesting for animal rights, against fascists, for and against left-wing radicals, and against globalism, sanctuary, and immigration. Each of these groups was focused on one issue, but more recently they have joined forces to demonstrate. Some of these demonstrations are conducted within legal means, but 'Black Bloc' extremist groups calling themselves 'anarcho-extremists' have disrupted protests with vandalism, arson, and attacks against police.

"Most protest groups are young people in their twenties and early thirties who have a university affiliation or live near a university. They don't hold regular meetings, issue cards, or publish political tracts like the socialists and communist groups of the past. They keep in touch in quiet gatherings and via social media, texting, and webpages."

"We have similar groups in Italy," Giorgio said.

"We also have serious problems with immigrants who came here in the 1960s and 1970s from Surinam, Indonesia, Morocco, Turkey, and the Middle East. We expected them to work a few years and then return to their homes. But many brought their families, and some were radicalized by al Qaeda, the Taliban, AQAP. More than one hundred jihadi fighters who are second-generation Dutch citizens with dual passports are fighting in Syria now. Some have been killed."

Rijkaard paused and looked away. "This . . . was a shock to the Dutch people. We had opened our country to them. We gave them a chance to get an education, raise families, and get good jobs—to live a peaceful life as part of our country. Then . . . some repay our kindness by becoming terrorists.

"So now . . . we are concerned about recruiters who radicalize young men and women immigrants here or those who return from Syria who have already been radicalized. We've jailed many of them, but they try to spread jihad among other immigrants in prison. It's a dangerous situation for all of Europe."

Giorgio nodded. He admired Rijkaard. He was a professional police officer, a man dedicated to protecting his country from great dangers.

Rijkaard continued. "Our government this year increased funding for monitoring those who return or who express jihadist causes in mosques and on the Internet. That is how we came to the case of an individual, Farooq Mohammad, a resident of the Netherlands for ten years. He earned an engineering degree and worked at Schiphol airport handling baggage and cargo on international flights. His job gave him access to data on incoming and departing flights, and he had security badges to secure areas of the airport.

"Through cell phone taps and surveillance, we became suspicious of Farooq Mohammad. Information led us to a cache of explosives stored in his garage. We arrested him, charged him with terrorist acts, and interrogated him. He denied everything, of course. But when presented with our evidence and the serious charges he faced, including very long detention—thirty years at least—his attorney counseled him that if he cooperated with us and shared sensitive information, he might be eligible for a lighter sentence. During interrogations, he hinted about potential terrorist plans in Europe, specifically in Milan. We contacted your colleagues in Rome's DIGOS office, who informed us that you are investigating a potentially dangerous terrorist attack in Milan."

"That's right. A shipment of chemicals to make sarin arrived at the port of La Spezia from Karachi two weeks ago. But we have not been able to identify who the shipment was going to. The name and address on the shipping manifest were bogus, and the cell phone listed was stolen. We're very worried, because we have no idea about their intended target."

"Hmm, very serious," Rijkaard said. "That is what the chief of DIGOS in Rome told us when he referred us to your office. So, talking with Mohammad, you might learn something to help your investigation."

"That is why I'm here."

Rijkaard reached for a file on his desk that was three inches thick. "I have a file on the case I will turn over to you tomorrow, a full record of the Mohammad affair, including transcripts of his interrogations. It is too much to read now. We thought it was better for you to question him yourself. We'll have an initial briefing now."

"Thank you."

"Tomorrow morning our officials will give you a full briefing. You know enough to question him this afternoon and return tomorrow if there is more information. We have learned from past interrogations that

Mohammad is evasive and uses doublespeak. He contradicts himself and gives false information. Over multiple interrogations, we've pieced together the true situation from what he dribbled out a detail or two at a time, but not everything. It has been a trying experience to learn what he knows. He may give you some information today, and more tomorrow. He's a cagey and slippery fellow. He probably learned about interrogation tactics in a terrorist camp."

"I appreciate your guidance."

"Would you like to go and meet Mr. Mohammad now?"

"Yes, most definitely."

Bijlmerbajes Prison, along the Amstel River, did not look like a prison at all. It resembled apartment buildings, six fourteen-story towers, but with barred windows, a high fence, floodlights in the corners, and a security gate.

As the men approached Bijlmerbajes, Giorgio noticed a metro station near the entrance. Pedestrians walked past, oblivious to the prison. From the car, Giorgio could look through the fence at the towers, parking lots, and people walking between buildings.

Ruud stopped at the gate and extended his badge to the security guard. Their car entered the compound. Another AIVD agent, Willem van den Ende, rode in the front seat with Ruud.

Once they were inside the prison, a police officer wearing a bullet-proof Kevlar vest and armed with an automatic weapon walked around their car and motioned for Ruud to drive toward a parking lot where police vans and cars were parked.

They got out of the car, and van den Ende led them to a glass double door, where another officer gave Giorgio a temporary badge. The officer swiped an electronic card on a panel near the doors, and they swooshed open. A security escort met them inside the door.

"Our prisoner is in Demerluis Tower, near the end of this corridor called the Kalverstraat, which links all six towers," van den Ende told Giorgio. Their escort led them down a long corridor. "The prisoners named this corridor Kalverstraat, which is actually one of the main shopping streets in the center of Amsterdam," van den Ende added.

They proceeded down the Kalverstraat, stopping at a security desk in front of an elevator to the Demerluis Tower, where an officer was seated behind two computer screens. Van den Ende showed him his badge, the officer pressed a button on the desk, and the elevator opened.

They exited at the eighth floor and encountered another security checkpoint. They flashed badges again, and the officer waved them to a narrower corridor lit by overhead light bulbs in wire cages. The corridor was eerily quiet. They passed metal doors on both sides of the corridor. No doorknobs. Barred glass windows the size of a book.

At the end of the corridor, the escort swiped his card over a panel. The door whisked open silently. They entered a narrow, windowless room the width of a bus. Another metal door faced them. The escort opened it with his security card.

They entered a room ten meters square, with a table and three metal chairs facing a window into a bare room that was smaller than the one they were in. The window was half a meter wide and tall. A single, black metal chair was in the center. Empty.

"Please have a seat. We'll have the prisoner here shortly."

Giorgio glanced around the beige room, feeling claustrophobic. Not a speck of dust or scrap of paper. Antiseptic. No telephones or computers. On the ceiling, a bulb enclosed by a metal cage illuminated the cramped room. Two video cameras in opposite corners stared blankly down, one aimed at the glass window, the other at their table.

They sat in silence. Giorgio heard the muffled *whoosh* of metal doors opening and then an electronic ping, like from a child's toy.

A light came on in the smaller room. Two men in police uniforms escorted a thin, dark-haired man with a full beard to the chair and pushed him to sit down. He was wearing a gray shirt, dark pants, and sandals. His wrists were restrained in handcuffs linked to a chain belt around his waist. His feet were shackled by cuffs also connected to his waist restraint.

"Mr. Mohammad, I have an officer from the Italian police that you requested to speak to," van den Ende said. "He speaks Italian and English. Shall we proceed in English?"

"Yes," he said, his voice trembling and weak. "Could I have your name, sir?" Mohammad asked.

"He isn't required to identify himself," van den Ende said. "Would you like him to speak in Italian so you know where he is from?"

"Yes." His voice was soft, strained.

In Italian, concealing his Milanese accent, Giorgio said, *"Sono nato vicino a Firenze. Ho imparato l'inglese a scuola."* [I was born in a town near Firenze. I learned English as a student.]

"You can hear Italian is his mother tongue," van den Ende said. "He is affiliated with the Italian government. He fulfills your request to talk with an Italian official. Now, will you please share with him what you told us during your interrogation about an operation you learned about in Afghanistan?"

Mohammad's black eyes darted left, then right, and then stared into Giorgio's eyes. Next he looked down, twitching in the chair, trying to get comfortable. His fingers were stubby as pegs, with jagged fingernails. Wires of black curly hair poked from the collar of his jumpsuit into his beard.

He coughed and cleared his throat but still didn't speak. He looked anxious, as if he was expecting a jolt of electricity to surge through his metal chains. The room was silent. He took a deep breath. Another, and then he spoke.

"My name is Farooq Mohammad. I was born in Kabul. I am Muslim. I read the Quran and pray to Mecca five times a day. I have my prayer rug in my cell. I fast during Ramadan."

His voice was weak and slow, like that of a patient emerging from surgery.

"Mr. Mohammad, you are stalling," van den Ende said sternly. "Tell us what you said in interrogation, or we will end this meeting and you will go back to your cell. We will inform the judge that you refused to cooperate after we made the special arrangements that you requested."

Mohammad's eyes shifted around his cell. He squirmed, but the restraints limited his movements. He took another deep breath and then spoke softly once again.

"Mr. Italian . . . I don't know your name . . . I was in a camp in Afghanistan two years ago. Did they tell you?"

"Louder. We can barely hear you," van den Ende said.

Mohammad cleared his throat and repeated what he had said.

"Yes, they told me," Giorgio said. "You have information to share with the Italian government."

Mohammad nodded, squirming at his restraints. "In the camp, I met . . . Europeans . . . others from Afghanistan, Saudi Arabia, Yemen, Iraq, Pakistan . . ." His voice trailed off.

"Tell us about the man from Italy," van den Ende said.

Again, Mohammad's eyes shifted. "I met a man . . . he had been in Pakistan before coming to the camp. He lived in Italy. Milan, I think."

"You said Milan before," van den Ende said forcefully.

"Yes, all right, it was Milan. It was a long time ago."

"Tell us what you wanted to tell an Italian official."

Mohammad's eyes shifted, and sweat trickled down his forehead and his nose. He raised his shackled hands to wipe the sweat, but his fingers only reached his throat. A drop of sweat fell onto his jumpsuit. "He was a smart man . . . spoke Urdu . . . English . . . Italian . . . went to Italian university."

"Which university?" Giorgio asked.

He shook his head.

"What was this man from Milan going to do that he learned in the terrorist camp?"

Mohammad lowered his head as if he were trying to choose his words carefully.

"We could not give our names. I learned he was training for a mission. In Milan, he said. We learned about poisons, gases, and toxic chemicals. He knew about chemicals. He wanted to know how to make poison gases and use them in public places."

"We need details," van den Ende said. "His name. Where was he going to use these chemicals? When?"

Mohammad was nervous, squirming. His nose was running, he tried to wipe it off with the back of his hands, but couldn't. He lifted his shoulder and managed to brush it off.

"I did not know his name. He was educated. He wanted to wage jihad against the infidel. He was planning something during a holiday.

I wasn't sure what he meant. Our instructors told us not to talk about specific plans, only how to make weapons."

"What holiday?" Giorgio asked, rising from his chair. "A Muslim holiday? A Christian holiday? A national holiday?"

"He just said holiday."

CHAPTER ELEVEN

Ruud drove Giorgio back to his hotel after the meeting with Mohammad at the prison. Giorgio felt drained from the tension of interrogating Mohammad and sensing that he was withholding information. In his long career as a police officer and head of DIGOS, Giorgio had interrogated many criminals and terrorists, including alleged terrorists at the Guantanamo Bay Naval Base prison in Cuba. He found them defiant and lacking in morality; interrogating them was depressing.

Criminals and terrorists were reluctant to disclose critical information unless they got something in return. Mohammad was wily and untrustworthy, negotiating for a lesser prison sentence. It was not going to be an easy process.

Giorgio sensed that Mohammad was evil. Going to a terrorist training camp and plotting to use explosives at Schiphol were violent acts that would result in the deaths of innocent men, women, and children. However, Giorgio was not in Amsterdam to judge Mohammad's nature or motivation; he was there to learn about a possible terrorist plot in Milan.

When he arrived at his room, Giorgio undressed, put on a hotel robe, and went into the bathroom to take a shower. The prison had been claustrophobic and antiseptic, like being in a scientific laboratory. But after Mohammad's interrogation, Giorgio wanted to scrub off the negative aura of the experience.

After a shower, he felt refreshed, cleansed, and renewed. He sat on the bed, reviewed his notes from the day, and considered calling Antonella to tell her he was encouraged by what he was learning from the Dutch police. But he decided to call Giulia first to see how she was feeling and restore balance to his dark mood. He'd been thinking about her since leaving the prison.

"Ciao, *tesoro*. I'm so happy you called," Giulia said, her voice cheery. "How's your mission in Amsterdam going?"

"A long day, but I'm back at the hotel. Going out to dinner soon. Did you rest today?"

"Oh, yes. Chiara has been a blessing. She's such a good soul, cheering me up. She knows how to boost my spirits. She tells me juicy details about her friends, their love lives, and about her own latest boyfriend. She makes me feel as if I were her age. It's great to be thirty, pretty, single, and living in Milan!"

"Chiara certainly has an exciting single life in Milan. But so did we when we were young."

"We did, Giorgio. But we're older now, more mature, with active boys. I wouldn't change a thing."

"Me neither." It was reassuring to talk to Giulia. They had always been soul mates and treated each other with compassion, understanding, and support. "Are you getting enough rest?"

"Plenty. I napped this afternoon but was awake when Vittorio and Daniele came home from school. They brought me a surprise: a delicious strawberry *crostata* from Taveggia. I wanted to save it for dessert tonight, but it's almost gone."

Giorgio's spirits lifted, imagining the boys back at home, helping their mother, preparing for dinner. He'd join them soon. "Wonderful. They're glad to have you home. How do you feel?"

"Rested, but still a little weak. Chiara is working in your study, writing an article for the interior design website where she works. She listens to your opera CDs and lets me rest. We had tea this afternoon before the boys got home. Maricelle made risotto alla Milanese with saffron for dinner. The boys love it crunchy with Gorgonzola sprinkled on top."

"Your favorite meal, too. I wish I were with you." Giorgio could hear one of his sons in the background. "Is Vittorio or Daniele with you?"

"Daniele is next to me. He wants to say hello." She handed the phone over to Daniele. "Ciao, Papi. Where are you?"

"I'm in Amsterdam for work. I'll be home tomorrow night. Are you and your brother looking after *la Mamma*?"

"Of course, Papi. We're glad she's home. We're having risotto alla Milanese tonight. I'll stuff myself with Gorgonzola cheese—yummy! After dinner, Vittorio and I are helping Mamma write notes and e-mails to everyone who sent flowers. Papi, you won't believe this: The dining room is full of flowers for Mamma. She wants to thank them and tell them not to send any more. We've run out of vases!"

"That's great! A nice homecoming for her. But don't stay up late; your mother needs a good night's sleep. So do you boys. You have to study for your history test Friday. Don't disappoint your teacher."

"Don't worry, Papi, we know. Zia Chiara says we have to be in our rooms by 9:00 PM, like we're kindergarten children."

"Tell Vittorio hello. Let me say goodbye to your mother before you have dinner. I'll bet the risotto will be a masterpiece."

Giulia answered, "How was your day, Giorgio?"

"Busy. A man from their department picked me up at the airport and took me to the hotel last night. I'm at the Renaissance in a room with a view over the canal in old town. We had breakfast at the hotel, and then he drove me to a meeting. Later in the afternoon, we had another meeting away from their office."

"I hope they were successful meetings."

"We have more meetings tomorrow before my flight leaves at six, I should be home by ten o'clock. Don't wait up for me. I'll tell the boys good night if they're awake."

"They would like that. They miss you. So do I."

Giorgio ended the call and punched Antonella's cell number. She answered immediately. "I've been waiting for your call, Giorgio. I hope your visit has been productive. What did you find out?"

"The Dutch have done a thorough investigation that I'll tell you about when I return. We had a preliminary meeting this morning at their headquarters. In the afternoon, they had arranged another meeting with the person I told you about."

"How was that meeting?"

Giorgio sighed. "To be honest, it wasn't very helpful. The information exchange was tense. He was evasive, defiant. I'm going to probe more aggressively tomorrow."

"I understand."

"Anything new I should know about?"

"I had a morning meeting with De Monti and Volpara. We briefed others about your assignment in Amsterdam. You're coming back tomorrow?"

"Late. I'll be in the office the next morning to brief the Questore and Prefetto about the Dutch investigation. It's very detailed, and some information is relevant to our case. We'll have a conference call with Rome."

"We need hard data—more than what we have now."

"That's why I'm here."

After he hung up with Antonella, Giorgio dressed and went out to get fresh air before dinner. He was hungry; all he had eaten that day was a light breakfast at the hotel and a quick lunch before driving to the prison.

Midsummer in western Europe meant languorous, sunlit evenings that lasted until ten. Cafés and restaurants along Amsterdam's canals were crowded with customers who leisurely quaffed mugs of Heineken and Amstel lagers and ate buckets of mussels and fries, raw herring, pastas, and salads.

Giorgio chose a restaurant where two canals met. He ordered a Heineken; a platter of sausage, cheese, and mustard as an appetizer; and *bitterballen* meat croquettes for the main course. After dinner, he enjoyed a strawberry mousse and coffee, followed by a relaxing walk in the Jordaan quarter and Westerpark before returning to his hotel.

After a long day, a sumptuous dinner, a beer, and a refreshing evening walk, Giorgio fell asleep immediately when his head creased the pillow. He awoke in the middle of the night, disoriented, seeing the glow of streetlights through the shades on his left, not his customary view of streetlights to the right in his apartment. He thought about Giulia and hoped she was sleeping well. He missed her next to him in bed.

Ruud and Giorgio had breakfast at the hotel at 8:00 AM and then headed for the AIVD office, where Dutch intelligence officials briefed

Giorgio again and shared intelligence from the American CIA about Afghan terrorist camps, including the one Mohammad had been to.

After the briefing, Ruud and van den Ende drove Giorgio back to the prison for another interrogation of Mohammad. While they waited in the small room for the prisoner to be escorted into the interrogation area, Giorgio studied the notes he'd prepared for interrogating him.

Giorgio looked up when Mohammad was led by guards into the tiny room, manacled. The guards again put him in the metal chair. As before, Mohammad looked uneasy, his eyes darting around the cell. He glanced over his shoulders at the guards behind him and then stared into the small window where Giorgio, van den Ende, and Ruud were waiting.

The air was antiseptic, warm, and dry, like recycled air in a long airline flight. Giorgio could hear metallic pings and clangs outside their confined room, sounds of the guards opening and closing doors where prisoners were behind bars, along with a muffled voice over a loudspeaker speaking Dutch in a monotone.

Van den Ende asked the first question. "We want to learn more about the Paki-Italian you met in the camp. Do you have anything else to tell us?"

Mohammad shook his head. "I've told you all I know." His tone was blasé, dismissive.

"The Italian police official has questions for you."

Mohammad's jaw clenched. He narrowed his eyes and glared at Giorgio like he was trying to intimidate him.

"Farooq, have you had any contact with the Italian you met in the camp?"

"No."

"Do you remember his name?"

"No. I told you already. Why do you ask again?"

"Would you recognize him if I showed you a picture?"

Mohammad blinked. "Aaah, yes . . . I think so. Has he shaved his beard? His hair was long. Maybe he cut it when he returned to Milan. Do you have his picture?"

Giorgio ignored his question; he didn't have a picture but wanted to ask a nonconfrontational question to start his interrogation. "Did he say anything about a family? Children, wife, parents?"

Mohammad looked puzzled by the change of questioning. "We didn't talk about personal lives. Someone from the camp was always with us. We were told not to talk about anything except training. At night, we sat in tents, drinking tea and talking about jihad and how we would change the world, bring a new caliphate. It will happen. Islam is supreme. We will be victorious!"

Mohammad's tone rose in a defiant crescendo like he was back at the terrorist camp, not manacled by chains on his wrists and ankles, behind bars in a prison where he would spend years before he would be set free.

Giorgio and van den Ende exchanged glances, Mohammad's disturbing challenge lingering in the air like the stench of cordite, cement dust, and seared metal after a bomb explosion. Van den Ende nodded for Giorgio to continue.

"You haven't give me much information, only that you met someone from Milan. Are you making up your story?"

"I tell truth! I am Muslim! Don't say I make up story!" Mohammad held his head erect, again striking an arrogant pose.

Giorgio waited several seconds, letting Mohammad strike his pose until he lowered his chin. "You have given me nothing about the man from Italy. You know more."

Mohammad shook his head forcefully, his eyes glowing like burning coal. "The camp was for training . . . preparing for jihad . . . not recruiting. Don't you believe me?"

"No, I don't. You haven't told me anything more than I knew before I came here."

"What did you know?"

"I won't tell you." Giorgio paused, waited to see if Mohammad would react. "The man you met is in Milan. We know him. He went to a training camp in Afghanistan. I want to confirm we're talking about the same man."

Giorgio was dangling bait to see if Mohammad would take it.

Mohammad's eyes widened, a slight smile on his face, the first time he had done more than scowl or pout. Softly he asked, "What is his name?"

Giorgio answered immediately. "You said you didn't know his name."

"No . . . no . . . I didn't know his name. We used other names in camp. Mine was Suliman; his was Barraba."

"When did you first meet him?"

Mohammad blinked, his mood subdued, no longer defiant and angry. He was thinking, trying to recall memories from the camp.

"He was in camp before me," he began, his voice almost calm. "He was only there five or six days before he left. I stayed another week. Jihadists were coming every day into the camp . . . from Pakistan . . . Iraq . . . Libya . . . Syria . . . Africa. I would see someone for three, four days. Then they would be gone, their training over, or they went to another camp. It was not like you think, everyone arriving at the same time, leaving together. Recruits were coming and going every day."

"Do you know how long the man from Milan stayed?"

"No."

"Were other Italians in the camp?"

"I don't know," he said like they were having a normal conversation. Mohammad seemed less menacing, like he wanted to talk more. His personality could change on a whim, bitter and resentful, then compliant and open. "There were two or three from Germany, one from Denmark, more from Spain, France, Portugal. They were all Muslims, some born in the Middle East, others in Europe or Africa."

Giorgio recognized the mood change and wanted to keep Mohammad talking while he was more forthcoming: slow, methodical questioning, getting pieces of information he needed before he returned to Milan. "How many were in the camp when you were there?" Giorgio kept his questioning neutral, not raising his voice, not expressing irritation or any emotion.

Mohammad hesitated. "Let me think . . . some days twenty, twenty-five . . . other days . . . more. . . . I never counted."

Mohammad stopped talking, as if he were recalling memories from the camp. Giorgio waited. He didn't want to ask a question that might interrupt the prisoner's thoughts.

Mohammad continued. "We never had time to know each other. We were in groups, four or five from different countries training for jihad, learning about grenades, automatic weapons, suicide vests with explosives, IEDs for blowing up trucks or infidel armies, chemicals to make poison gases. One instructor was from Iraq; he had scars from fighting Americans. He had only one eye; the other he lost from an American grenade. He hated Americans. Said he would kill any he saw. He asked if we knew about chemicals to set off in public places to kill or injure many people. The man from Milan and I said we were educated at university; we knew chemistry, math, calculus. We wanted to know formulas to mix chemicals to make sarin, ricin, or anthrax. They didn't have chemicals in camps, only formulas. They said they would ship chemicals or explosives to us."

Giorgio held his breath. Mohammad was revealing details not in the Dutch intelligence reports. He needed to keep moving forward, learning important information. "How were they going to ship chemicals to you?"

Mohammad hesitated, chewing on his lower lip, eyes narrowed. "Container ships from Karachi. They would give us names of ships and dates they arrived. We had forged documents to receive them. We were to store them and wait for instructions on jihad websites."

"Which websites?"

"There are many. They put them up and take them down. They know police read them. We were told how to find them: look for the names we got in the camps—never our real names. We would search sites for our camp names. Then there was a ship name and date. That was all: no message, just the name and date. There were many names and dates, some probably fake."

"Where did your explosives arrive from Karachi?"

"Rotterdam."

Giorgio listened without taking notes. He felt Mohammad was telling the truth. He had confirmed that the container coming to La Spezia had been arranged the same way Mohammad had received his explosives in Rotterdam. He modified his questioning.

"How many times did you talk with the Paki-Italian?"

"Three or four times . . . maybe five times. I don't remember. He didn't associate with others, only Pakistanis and me a couple times. He spoke Italian. He knew English—his mother was English or Italian, I think. She was not Pakistani; he said his father was born in Pakistan. He said something about London once . . . someone mentioned England, and he said he had lived in London. That's all I know."

"Did he say when he lived in London?"

"No. He didn't say more. But he asked where I was from. I told him Amsterdam. He said he was from Milan. He had a job—a good job. He didn't go to mosques, because he said Italian police watch mosques and arrest Muslims."

Giorgio didn't respond. He was very familiar with DIGOS surveillance at Milan mosques. He didn't want to divert Mohammad from anything except talking about the Paki-Italian.

"He told you he had a job. What kind of work did he do?"

"He worked in construction. Or he was a security guard. Who knows? He worked at buildings in Milan."

"What buildings?"

Mohammad shrugged. "Big companies, I think. He knew about electronics. Heating. Computers. Things he learned at university. He was smart, knew a lot of things."

"Did he mention a university where he went?"

"No."

"Did he tell you names of companies?"

"No."

Mohammad looked away, up at the ceiling, then down to his manacled hands. Giorgio felt nervous. Mohammad's attitude was changing: He was again being slippery, wasting time, making up answers.

Van den Ende interrupted, speaking in a harsh voice. "Tell the truth, Farooq. You know more than you're telling us. Tell us where he worked. We need information, not bluffing. Everything you say will be told to the judge. Do you want him to think you're playing games, stalling? You're not helping yourself by being evasive."

Mohammad sighed, looking anxious. He seemed to be weighing how much he should say. "He . . . he said that he worked in Milan—jobs about engineering and entering buildings with special privileges. I don't know anything else."

"Tell me what he looked like," said Giorgio.

Mohammad shrugged like he was bored. "He was average, normal height, weight. Nothing else I remember."

"What color was his hair?"

"Brown."

"Was he older or younger than you?"

"Older."

"How much older? Two, three years or more?"

"Maybe four. Hard to tell."

"How tall?"

"He was taller than me, maybe two, three inches. Why?"

Giorgio ignored the question. "When did you last see him?"

Mohammad narrowed his eyes, either trying to recall or figuring out how he could make up a vague answer. It was a full minute before he answered. "I . . . remember. . . . Yes . . . it was at night. . . . He was finished training and was going down from the mountains in trucks with guards. There were U.S. Army patrols in the mountains, fighter aircraft bombing villages and camps. We traveled at night, one truck at a time."

"Where did you see him?"

"It was dark. . . . I was walking toward my tent. He was behind a truck, ready to climb in. He saw me . . . waved for me to come over. . . . We clasped hands . . . said goodbye . . . wished each other a successful jihad. . . . He smiled—I think the only time he smiled. He said someone was waiting for him . . . a woman. She wasn't Muslim. She might have been a Christian."

Giorgio again held his breath. This was new information, not what the Dutch investigators had in their reports. He was careful to keep his tone neutral, not wanting to let Mohammad know this was important. "What did he say about this woman? Was she in Milan?"

Mohammad paused. "I think so. She was waiting for him; she didn't know where he was. He told her he was going to Pakistan to see relatives, not go to a camp. I think she was Italian, but I'm not sure. If she was Pakistani, a Muslim, he would have said so. But he didn't."

"Did he mention her name?"

Mohammad wrinkled his brow and looked down, as if he was concentrating. "I think so, but it wasn't a Pakistani name. It was a Western name. He just said it once, that he would see her in a week."

"Was it Maria, Silvia, Anna, Cristina?"

"Something like that . . . it ended with an 'a.' But it wasn't Maria. It was a longer name."

"Was he married to this woman?"

"No. He wanted her to become Muslim. Then they could marry and have children. He said all men should have a woman . . . father many children . . . boys . . . boys for waging jihad! He was a good Muslim—a warrior for Islam!"

CHAPTER TWELVE

W hen Giorgio arrived at DIGOS the next morning, he went down the hall and signaled to Antonella, who was on her cell phone. "Come in as soon as you can. We need to talk."

She hung up and followed him down the hallway into his office. Giorgio put his briefcase on his desk, reached into his pocket, took out a key, unlocked a false-bottom compartment, and pulled out several folders.

Tabs in English and Dutch read:

Profile

Legal Documents

Surveillance Reports

Transcripts of Interrogations

Interrogation CDs

CIA reports

CIA photographs

Giorgio handed the top folder to Antonella. "Here is the profile the Dutch intelligence has on Farooq Mohammad, the Afghan terrorist in prison for planning an attack at Schiphol airport."

Antonella opened the file and skimmed the opening paragraphs, a summary that ran down almost to the end of the page. She flipped to the second page, background on Mohammad's life before coming to Amsterdam. She turned to the third and fourth pages. Antonella was a fast reader, even in English. Her eyes raced down the text, spotting key sentences, nouns, and verbs of the principal points she wanted to absorb as quickly as possible.

Her body was erect, no movement, as if she were in court during a trial. She was engrossed in the depth of information that police collect on criminals, their past, their weapons and training, their objectives, and their intent to commit a major crime.

"Amazing," she murmured. "What might have happened if the Dutch police hadn't arrested him? I hate to think. . . ."

"They do an excellent job of protecting their people."

Antonella continued reading, shaking her head, learning about Mohammad's early life events that brought him to Amsterdam when he was a teenager, his university attendance, his first job, and his second job at Schiphol airport. He was bright and motivated and had been radicalized by an imam at an Amsterdam mosque who inspired him to travel to Afghanistan with false documents and money.

"Mohammad went to a training camp in Afghanistan, where he met a Paki from Milan who could be the suspect we're looking for," said Giorgio.

"Yes . . . yes . . . I see," Antonella said, flipping through the pages until she reached a summary page of key details. "I'll read this carefully later. . . . I just want to get an idea of how he might be a link to our suspect."

"In another file, you'll find CIA photos taken by drones of the terrorist camp before they bombed it. They killed twenty people, all reportedly terrorists in training. The Dutch were given classified reports after they queried the CIA if they had information on the al Qaeda training camp."

"That will be interesting to read."

"After you've read the whole report, make copies for De Monti and Volpara."

"Right away," she said. "They need to know we may have an important lead on our suspect."

Giorgio reached into his briefcase and held up a computer thumb drive.

"On this pen drive you'll see videos of my interrogation with Mohammad. If he was telling the truth, the Paki works in some kind of construction in Milan. He didn't specify; he could be a security guard, a bricklayer, or even a civil engineer. Who knows what his profession is. He's university educated and speaks English, Italian, Urdu, and Arabic."

"So we'll have some leads to work on. Thank God. We knew none of this before you went to Amsterdam," said Antonella.

Giorgio leafed through a file and handed her a page of his interrogation. "Read this. . . . He has an Italian girlfriend!"

Antonella grabbed the page and read the section. Her head snapped back, and she read it again. "Italian girlfriend! Really?" She showed her surprise with a curl of a smile and raised eyebrows. "Very, very interesting."

"That could help us."

"I wonder who she is. Maybe she was a Catholic and now she converted. Or she could be a second-generation Italian who comes from a Muslim family of immigrants. Do you think she knows what he's planning?"

"No idea. We have to find her first."

"If they're still together, she could confirm he's the guy we want. De Monti will like this. She could do surveillance on her, identify her friends, find out where she works, and learn if she's involved as well."

"But first of all, we need our suspect's name," Giorgio said. "We won't get anywhere until we find out who he is."

"We'll work around the clock until we do."

"Have you chosen your team to assist De Monti and Volpara?"

Antonella nodded, closing the file. "I told them yesterday. They're ready to go as soon as you give the word."

"Who's on the team?"

"Cella . . . Baraldi . . . Morucci . . . Patruno . . . Ferrarin . . . Mastrantonio."

Giorgio nodded. "Good choices." He handed her the rest of the files, which she cradled in her arms, flipping through the tabs.

"They're all working multiple cases," said Antonella. "We'll assign them when we need them."

"Have them all in the chapel at 3:00 PM I'll brief them about Amsterdam."

Antonella smiled. "The chapel, an excellent choice. I haven't been in there for some time."

The DIGOS "chapel" had originally been an actual chapel at the Collegio Longone, a school operated by friars. Many Milanese elites from the Enlightenment, such as Alessandro Manzoni, one of Milan's most famous writers, had studied at the Collegio Longone. During the Allied bombing of Milan during WWII, the Collegio Longone had been evacuated and taken over by the City of Milan and converted into the Questura.

In recent years, the chapel had been used by DIGOS for delicate interrogations. It was in a remote area of the building, most of which was used for storage. But it had a separate private entrance on Via Montebello that could be accessed by DIGOS agents without using the Questura's main entrance on Via Fatebenefratelli.

Antonella returned to her office, read through the Dutch intelligence reports, and handed them to her agent to make copies. When the agent returned half an hour later, she set a stack of files on Antonella's desk. Antonella took them down the hallway to Simona and Dario, whom she had alerted after her meeting with Giorgio.

At 3:00 PM, Giorgio was in the chapel when Antonella's team filed in, taking seats in a semicircle of chairs, with Dario and Simona seated in the center. They were all experienced agents, bonded by years of working together on dangerous assignments.

Giacomo Cella, thirty-five, was tall and handsome with a firm, athletic body and long blond hair that touched his shoulders. He had had an earlier career with the NOCS (Nucleo Operativo Centrale di Sicurezza) SWAT team.

Maurizio Baraldi, thirty-eight, was a veteran DIGOS agent. He was also Dario's best friend and flatmate.

Febo Morucci, thirty-two, was rugged-looking and had the body of a weightlifter. He had olive skin and green eyes. He had given up a cushy job working at his family's luxury hotel in Versilia to become a policeman.

Franco Patruno, forty-three, was the most experienced agent in street surveillance. He had trained with international security teams, including the CIA.

Mirko Ferrarin, thirty, was thin and gaunt but had a youthful appearance. He was often assigned to cases involving the infiltration of street gangs.

Ruggero Mastrantonio, forty-five, was a mentor to many new agents in DIGOS. He was born in Tripoli and spoke Arabic as his mother tongue.

Giorgio was standing on a riser, arms crossed, leaning against a table on which he had placed a copy of the Dutch reports. When everyone was seated, he straightened up, cleared his throat, and began, dispensing with formalities.

"Let me give you a report about the last two days I spent in Amsterdam at the Dutch intelligence headquarters. They briefed me on the case of Farooq Mohammad, a terrorist arrested before he could set off a bomb at Schiphol airport, where he worked."

Every eye in the room was on Giorgio. No one moved. They wanted to hear every word, every nuance, every inflection. Giorgio had a reputation for speaking calmly even when he was discussing serious criminal matters. It was rare to hear him raise his voice or express anger. He led others with his demeanor and intelligence.

"The Dutch authorities took me to the federal prison so I could interrogate Mohammad about a possible connection to the chemical shipment that arrived in La Spezia last month. Videos of the interrogations are in the file. Mohammad revealed bits of information that could help us identify the prime suspect we believe is responsible for the chemical shipment. This case is the top priority of DIGOS."

Giorgio's eyes scanned the row of agents, eyeing each one for a second, letting his statement and the following pause dramatize the importance of their assignment. "You can expect to be assigned to work on this case at a moment's notice. You're all working other cases; coordinate with other officers and be prepared to hand off your assignments to them. Does everyone understand?"

They nodded in unison, sitting stiffly in their chairs, grim faced.

"Forensics determined that chemicals to make deadly sarin gas came into the port at La Spezia. The cargo included Russian Glocks with erased serial numbers . . . ammunition . . . and three million euros. An informer said that two other shipments had arrived in La Spezia earlier but were not inspected. We presume they arrived in Milan, possibly with similar cargo—weapons, cash, chemicals. This group is well funded. They have weapons and a possible stockpile of dangerous chemicals. We presume they have a plan to use them . . . and kill many people."

Giorgio looked at the agents, letting the gravity of the situation continue to sink in. "Our information at this point is slim. We need to identify suspects and build a case. When we have a lead, you will be assigned to conduct around-the-clock surveillance—identifying and tailing suspects, listening to phone taps, reviewing criminal records, determining where suspects work and live, establishing their associations with others, and building profiles for all of them."

Heads nodded around the room.

"Our biggest challenge is that we are in the dark about who we are up against. We suspect one of them possibly trained at an al Qaeda camp in Afghanistan."

Giorgio held up a copy of Antonella's Milan phone tree diagram. "All we have now is one cell phone listed on the shipping documents and a list of phone numbers he called. That's all. To make matters worse, we don't know who has the phones. They were all stolen and not reported."

He set Antonella's document on the stack of files and looked around the room. "Any questions?"

No one raised a hand. Giorgio nodded and turned to Antonella, who was standing next to the riser. "Dottoressa Amoruso will brief you about her analysis of the stolen phones."

He stepped aside. Antonella passed down the row, handing out copies of her Milan phone tree diagram. She then stepped up on the riser next to Giorgio.

She gave the agents time to study her diagram and then explained her analysis of the stolen phones and the patterns of calls from Cinti's phone to the others. When she finished, she turned to Giorgio.

"As you can see," he said, "we have the barest of information and no names to connect with the tapped cell phones. We assume this is a potential terrorist network hiding in Milan—possibly Muslim. This group is using extreme measures to remain secret. It's one of the best schemes I've ever seen."

He gestured to Simona and Dario. "De Monti and Volpara have been working on the case, number H24, and are handling the day-to-day investigation. You'll join them when they have a break in the case. Ispettore De Monti is team leader."

CHAPTER THIRTEEN

Simona left the DIGOS office at 7:00 PM and took the green underground in front of the red-brick Teatro Strehler to Gioia station. She exited five minutes later for the ten-minute walk to her apartment on Via Confalonieri, in the Isola district, north of Stazione Centrale.

Isola was isolated from the more traffic-clogged center city; it was a neighborhood that retained nineteenth-century features of the former working-class section of Milan. Since 2004, Isola had begun evolving into a bohemian neighborhood with trendy shops selling antique jewelry, designer furniture, and ceramics. The area had designer floral shops, art galleries, and hip restaurants. Young Milanese professionals came to Isola to shop, sample the cuisine at specialty restaurants, and party at posh nightclubs and hip bars. Weekends were especially noisy, when late-night partygoers roamed Isola's streets until early morning, leaving empty bottles, trash, cigarette butts, and odd bits of clothing in their wake.

Simona felt lucky to have found a cramped but charming studio apartment in a *casa di ringhiera*, a former public housing building. To decorate her place, she had sought out weekend markets, where she'd acquired contemporary art, ceramics, and black-and-white photos of early twentieth-century Milan and the northern Alpine lakes.

Simona loved it that her kitchen and bedroom windows faced west. She typically arose early in the mornings, showered, dressed, and sipped coffee before rushing out the door to work. But when she returned home in the early evenings, she would fling open the shutters and let the last rays of sunlight bathe her apartment in splashes of bright yellow and gold.

This day had been a long one: meetings with Amoruso and Dario, reading the Dutch intelligence reports, and attending Lucchini's briefing with the new agents assigned to their team. Lucchini and Amoruso's briefing had lasted two hours, including the discussions afterward.

Simona was eager to return to her Isola oasis, change clothes, and have a cup of tea. She was debating between going for a thirty-minute run around the neighborhood or out for a quiet dinner and a glass of wine at the nightclub restaurant Deus, where she could see someone she knew and have a pleasant chat before returning home and going immediately to bed.

Simona had met interesting people after she'd moved to Milan: artists, fashion designers, professors, and writers. She had many acquaintances but no close friends yet; she knew that would come in time.

When meeting new people, Simona didn't admit she was a DIGOS agent at the Questura. She told them she was a researcher at a law firm specializing in international patents and trademarks. She made the job seem boring, so few asked more about her work. Simona steered away from personal conversations, instead asking acquaintances about their work and interests. She was enthusiastic about her yoga class, her favorite antique stores, and the cooking classes she was going to take over the winter.

When she arrived at her third-floor apartment landing, she reached into her handbag for her keys.

"*Ciao*, Simona. *Come stai?*" said a familiar voice.

She was startled; it was her old boyfriend, Alberico, standing by her door, leaning against the wall, arms crossed in a relaxed but posed position. Although he was three years older than Simona, he could pass for a man in his twenties. He had an almost boyish face, pale skin, curly blond hair, and clear blue eyes.

Alby always dressed stylishly in the latest fashions. His top-quality, expensive clothes were not a problem, since he came from one of Bergamo's oldest and wealthiest families. He was wearing a Caraceni suit, a tailor-made white shirt with his monogram on the left wrist, a shiny Gucci silk tie, and black Church's shoes that likely cost around seven hundred euros. His watch, which peeked out of his left cuff, was a limited-edition, platinum Patek Philippe.

Simona opened her mouth to speak, but nothing came out. *What is Alby doing here?!* She didn't want to see him. She didn't want to see anyone! She just wanted to be alone and go out for a quiet dinner and a glass of wine.

"What are you doing here, Alby?" she said at last, her voice brittle.

Alby fluttered a hand like he was swatting away a fly. "Simona . . . aren't you glad to see me?"

"Why are you here?" she repeated.

"Aah . . . I had a meeting this afternoon at the new office on Via Laghetto with a top client. I thought I'd come over and surprise you. Surprise!" he joked, trying to sound spontaneous.

"Alby, why didn't you call first?" she said, her jaw tense. "You know I don't like surprises."

He lowered his arms and moved to embrace her, but Simona stepped back. "No," she said curtly.

Alby frowned. "Why are you upset, *pasticcino*? I wanted to see you. It's been three weeks since you were in Bergamo. I miss you. Can we go inside and talk?"

Simona made a growling "rrrrr" sound in her throat that came out more harshly than she intended. "Alby," she said, hanging on to the "y" like she was scolding a child who had spilled his milk, "this is not a good time. I'm tired. I've had a long, stressful day. Tomorrow will be the same. It's almost 8:00 PM I just want to be alone."

"What's wrong?" He frowned, wrinkling his brow like a boy who'd been admonished by his mother about a smudge on his shirt.

Simona stepped back, gripping her key in her fist as if it was a weapon. "It's just . . . you—you've upset me," she stammered. "You've come at a bad time." She slipped the key into the lock and opened the door. She wanted go in, shut the door, and not deal with Alby. But she pushed the door open, and Alby followed her inside, catching the door and closing it so it wouldn't slam.

Simona hurried down the narrow hallway past her favorite black-and-white photos of Milan. She dropped her purse on the hall table, turned into the kitchen, opened the refrigerator, took out a bottle of water, and tipped it back. She was thirsty. The afternoon briefings with Amoruso and Lucchini had drained her energy. She needed liquids.

She drank the water, her back to Alby, wishing he was not there. Having him in her apartment—uninvited—made her want a glass of wine instead. But not with Alby there; he'd want a glass and would possibly get amorous. She was *not* in the mood.

Alby stood in the kitchen doorway, sensing that Simona didn't want him closer. Her brittle comments made him feel more like an intruder than a former boyfriend who had slept with her in the apartment two months ago. He loosened his tie, removed his jacket, and set it on the back of a kitchen chair. Simona's morning coffee cup and breakfast plate with bread crumbs and a pat of melted butter were still on the table next to a bowl of fruit.

Simona went to the window, unlocked it, and swung open the shutters. Evening sunlight bathed the kitchen in a warm, yellow glow. Her spirits lifted a bit. She leaned out the window, took a deep breath, and struggled with how she was going to deal with Alby. She was furious that he had come to her apartment without calling ahead.

Alby's timing was atrocious. He would be excited to talk about some business or legal meeting that she didn't want to hear about. She had enough on her mind without having to endure a long-winded tale of Alby's brilliant legal strategizing to impress clients. She just wanted to be alone, get mentally prepared for the next day, and ponder the responsibility Amoruso and Lucchini had given her and Dario.

She turned to face Alby, who now was standing frozen like an iceberg by the kitchen table. "I need a shower, Alby. It's been a long day. I'm very tired."

She walked around him and left the kitchen without looking at him.

"Wouldn't you like to go out for dinner?" he begged as she headed to her bedroom. He knew he wouldn't be welcome in there.

"I don't know. Let me have a shower," she said, slamming the bedroom door behind her.

She sat on the bed, took off her clothes, and went to the bathroom to take a shower. A long one. She turned the knobs, adjusted the temperature, and stepped inside. As streams of hot water flowed over her, Simona recalled the eventful day at DIGOS and how Alby's unexpected appearance had interrupted her train of thought. He was a distraction from how she wanted to spend the evening. She could send him away, back to Bergamo. But the more she thought about her reaction, the more she realized she might have acted rudely.

She still had feelings for Alby, but not as a current lover. He was a relationship from her past. During the months in Milan, she'd grown distant from him. She'd embraced her new life and her small, but comfortable Isola apartment. She was enjoying meeting new people, especially a couple of men who were interested in her. Never would she tell Alby about them.

But most of all, Simona loved her work with DIGOS. She loved the challenge, the excitement of the current investigation, liked her colleagues, even Dario, who was a difficult but interesting partner. They were worlds apart in temperament and background, but their chemistry was good for a partnership. She was critical and quick to judge; Dario was methodical and slow to react, but he had a sharp, inquisitive mind. They would learn from each other, become better officers, better investigators. Dario irritated her with his smoking, his breezy manner, and his fawning over loutish soccer players. But he was a smart and experienced officer. She liked smart and crafty.

So what about Alby? She couldn't send him away; that would be rude. She would cool down, have a quiet dinner with him, and then gently tell him she wanted to go back to her apartment alone because she needed rest before her next day at work.

She had no interest in having sex with Alby. Facing him in the morning would be painful, faking being nice and courteous, when her brain would be stimulated by the intriguing case she was working on. Tomorrow would be her first full day as team coleader with Dario. The challenge was exciting.

She left the shower, wrapped a large towel around her, ran a comb through her wet hair, and went into her bedroom. She rummaged through her closet, grabbed a soft gray-and-white, sleeveless, cotton summer dress and a pair of strappy sandals. She put on lipstick, mascara, and a touch of perfume on her wrists and temples. She looked in the mirror and flashed a smile. Then it vanished. Her natural look was one of unemotional concentration. Being a police officer required you to look neutral, not signal emotions with facial expressions.

Granite face. Don't mess with me. I've got your number.

She checked her profile in the mirror. She was slim, attractive, seductive, ready to go out for a quiet evening, even if it would be a brief one. In an hour or so, Alby would be on his way home, not spending the night. She felt more relaxed after the shower, a change of clothes, and being in her bedroom. Alone. The spat with Alby had gotten rid of the day's tension. She'd swapped professional anxiety for intimate drama. Not her choice.

Seeing Alby had repressed her appetite, but now she was hungry. She wanted a glass of wine. Maybe two. When she walked out of the bedroom, Alby was eating an apple from the bowl of fruit on the table. He looked up, eyes widening. He smiled, a fake, forced smile. He was good at that.

"Simona, you look beautiful! Is that a new outfit? It's stunning!"

She shrugged, avoiding his eyes, and drank from the water bottle she had taken out earlier. "Oh, something I picked up last weekend at the market," she said casually, as if talking to a flirtatious man seated next to her on the metro. She looked into the hallway mirror, fingered her earrings, pivoting slowly to let Alby admire the slim cut of her dress, which dipped low in the back, almost to her waist.

"Very nice, even if you bought it at a market," he said with a seductive smile. "Your taste is great, even if you shop for bargains. Your darling dress is perfect for a summer evening. Where would you like to go?"

"I know a place," she said, moving down the hallway and picking up her purse and keys from the table. Alby followed like a puppy going for a walk on a leash, catching the door and closing it so Simona could lock it.

As soon as they were on the staircase, Alby started talking about his meeting that day with a business client, eager to divert Simona from disparaging him any more about his surprise visit.

Alby worked in his father's law firm, which represented wealthy landowners, politicians, and corporate leaders, striving to protect their business ventures against the government's attempts to tax them heavily. The company's clients liked the tax gifts that had been handed out to them by Christian Democrat leaders in the past; Alby liked to impress his clients with his skill in protecting their financial gains.

A year ago, Alby had been a vibrant part of Simona's life. They had met long ago as teenagers at a music event, had seen each other occasionally, and had started dating at university in Bergamo where they were both law students at the Giurisprudenza facility. Alby was being groomed to inherit his family's estate in the hills above Bergamo and take over his father's prestigious law firm. For a while, Simona had enjoyed being the girlfriend of the wealthy and famous son of a noble family.

But Simona's new and intriguing life in Milan had made her former life seem quaint, old-fashioned, and irrelevant. She was building a new career; meeting new, exciting people; and becoming Milanese. Her new life was more fulfilling than what was offered in Bergamo. If she had married Alby when he had asked a year ago, she would have become a social prisoner tied to a wealthy family with no chance to explore what might await her in Milan.

They walked down two floors onto Via Borsieri. She took Alby's elbow and guided him around the memorial to Italian partisans at Piazzale Segrino, a busy roundabout with speedy Fiats, noisy *motorinos*, and taxis exiting onto quiet Isola streets.

In the early evening dusk, fashionable young men and women were strolling on the tree-lined street, peeking into café and restaurant windows and scouting a spot for happy hour *aperitivo*. Cigarettes hung from their lips. They wore posh clothes and shoes like they were walking down a runway during Milan's Fashion Week.

Outside tables were filling up. Isola was coming alive on this warm summer evening. It felt like a time to be with someone special.

"So how is your mother?" Simona asked when Alby paused after telling her about his meeting. Simona liked Alby's mother. She was a kind woman, and they had shared confidences about marriage and relationships. She was the only person Simona felt close to in Alby's family. His father was arrogant and bragged. His sister was vacuous, interested only in fashion, TV soap operas, and parties. Even with his privileged background, Alby didn't have the polish Simona wanted.

"She's doing fine. Her birthday is two weeks away. She sent you an invitation to her party, but you haven't answered. Did you receive it?"

"*Mio Dio*. Yes, I did. Sorry I haven't replied. I've been so busy the last couple of weeks. I'll let her know I can't make it."

Alby didn't respond. Simona had said the same thing when he'd called her to arrange dates in Bergamo or Milan that summer.

They walked down Via Borsieri past the Blue Note jazz club, where Simona had spent several evenings, staying past 1:00 AM on weekends, feeling a bit like a New Yorker in the only European outlet of the famous American jazz club franchise.

Simona pointed down a narrow street at a sign. "That's the gym where I take yoga classes and Pilates. I sometimes have tea at that little café on the corner," she said, turning to point at another sign.

They walked farther without talking until she saw the sign for Deus. Some young men, a few of whom looked like teenagers, were standing on the curb, smoking and ogling women passing by.

One of them called out, "*Ciao*, Simona. *Come stai?*"

Alby jerked his head to glare at him. He looked like a twenty-five-year-old kid with new sneakers, a spiked haircut, and tattoos on one arm. *How does he know Simona?*

She waved and smiled at the men, ignoring Alby. They walked under the arch at Deus into a courtyard. Couples were sitting at tables under umbrellas, drinking wine, nibbling antipasti, and enjoying the mellow sounds of the Miles Davis Quartet over a speaker. Deus's balcony, which overlooked the courtyard, was crowded with couples enjoying a late happy hour *aperitivo* while bartenders reached for liquor bottles on three shelves that were attractively backlit.

Simona and Alby sat down at a small table and looked around for a waiter.

"Nice place," Alby said, observing the crowd of young, attractive professionals drinking wine, eating salads, and enjoying each other's company in a casual setting. "Why didn't you bring me here before? Do you have a secret lover here?"

"Alby, please don't be rude," she said, raising a hand at a young waiter who had watched them sit down in the courtyard. He nodded, picked up drink menus, and gracefully moved toward their table like a ballet dancer.

A man across the courtyard glanced over, winked at Simona, and then turned away. Alby fumed, feeling like he was not part of the insider crowd.

The waiter greeted them warmly, handed them menus, and took their drink orders. When he walked away, Alby looked around the courtyard and at the long bar a few steps up. He saw a man at the bar excuse himself and walk down the steps, carrying a wineglass, on a direct line to their table. *Who is he? Why is he coming over?*

Simona cringed. It was Gianluigi Marinoni, nicknamed Giangi, a flamboyant Deus regular. He was a blogger in the fashion industry and a frequent guest at parties publicized in Milan's gossip sheets and magazines.

Giangi made a theatrical entrance into the courtyard, stopping a few feet before Simona and opening his arms like he was about to smother her in a mushy embrace.

"Siiiiiimoooo! Where have you been?" the man squealed, shocking Alby.

Giangi was wearing a tan summer suit and a pale blue shirt unbuttoned to midchest. Overhead lights shined off his bald head, damp from the summer heat. Giangi took off his red-framed eyeglasses and let them fall to his chest, where they were caught by a silk cord with Japanese designs. He exchanged cheek kisses with Simona, his light beard feeling like a soft brush.

"Simona, so nice to see you!" he gushed. I haven't seen you in days!" His voice was a chirp, like a violin being plucked.

"I've been busy, Giangi. How are you?"

"You look ravishing, *amore*! Such a nice outfit. So chic!" he flirted, slightly slurring his words.

Simona smiled without responding. Giangi's dark eyes darted toward Alby and back at Simona. "Is this . . . a friend?" he asked, lowering his voice to a purr. "I don't recognize . . . him. Are you new?"

Alby was stunned. They had been on the street ten minutes, and two men had greeted Simona by name.

"Giangi, this is a friend from Bergamo, Alby."

Giangi theatrically offered his hand, his mouth curled in a grin. Alby hesitated, took the man's hand, pumped once, and dropped it.

"Alby? Is your name Alberto?" Giangi said with a hint of sarcasm.

"No, Alberico."

"Ooooh, Alberico. That's a rich name. Are you from a famous family?"

"What difference does it make?" Alby hissed. "My family has lived in Bergamo since the Renaissance."

Giangi flinched, leaning backward. "Aah, I see . . . hmmm," Giangi said, winking at Simona. "One of the old royal families? Are you involved in politics?" It was a question that sounded like a challenge.

"No. I'm an attorney."

"Oh, that's nice," Giangi said, wrapping his fingers around his wineglass in a flamboyant gesture. "Heaven knows Italy needs good attorneys. I'm sure you're one . . . if you're a friend of Simo's."

Giangi smiled down at her, inching closer. "In my *humble* opinion," he said, raising his eyebrows provocatively, "most lawyers are corrupt. Even judges! What a pity. But I'm sure you're one of the honest ones. You look like you are. And friends with Simo. She knows the nicest people." His smile radiated like he was posing in front of a TV camera.

The waiter delivered two glasses of prosecco to the table. Simona and Alby took polite sips. Giangi smiled, turning to look at her and then at Alby. The moments of silence were awkward for Simona. How was she going to handle Giangi during this strained conversation with Alby, who was clearly angry at the intrusion?

Alby finally spoke. "Giangi, I don't know you. Simona and I came here for a quiet dinner. Would you mind leaving us alone?"

Giangi stepped back and fluttered a hand in a defensive gesture. "Excuse me, your lordship! Simo, I would never be rude; you know me. I just wanted to know who your friend was. You simply disappeared from the face of the earth, darling. It's been *weeks* since I've seen you."

"I've been working late, Giangi. I don't go out much during the week."

"Of course, of course," Giangi said, grinning like a child. "There was a gallery opening last week. . . . I wanted to invite you. So *many* interesting artists and writers were there. I thought you'd like to meet them. Can I have your phone number so I can call next time?"

Alby flared and jerked his head to glare at Simona. "Simona, let's go to some other place. I'm not comfortable here."

Their waiter returned and handed them dinner menus. *"Buona sera.* Would you like to hear our specials this evening?"

Alby pushed back his chair to stand. Giangi said, "Maybe Simo would like another prosecco? I'll have another merlot," he said, raising his empty glass to the waiter. "How about you, Alberico? Would you like a cognac?"

"No!" said Alby. "Simona, can we go? Now."

Rather than risk a quarrel in a public place, Simona said, "If that's what you want, Alby, we can leave." She looked up at Giangi. "We'll be going, Giangi. It's late. I have a busy day tomorrow."

The waiter was confused by the drama. "So, does anyone want dinner?"

Simona sighed, disappointed that the evening was over before it started. No dinner. An embarrassing encounter with Giangi. An unpleasant walk back to her apartment with Alby fuming. The evening had become painful.

"No, thank you," she said to the waiter. "We're leaving."

She stood up. Alby dropped a fifty-euro bill on the table and escorted Simona out of Deus, leaving Giangi standing next to the waiter, who snatched up the euro bill, cleared the half-filled wineglasses off the table, and scurried away.

Simona clutched her purse as she followed Alby down the street, neither one speaking. He stepped briskly, moving ahead, not reaching for her hand, putting distance between him and the disgusting Giangi at Deus. *How could she know such a detestable person?*

Simona followed behind, letting Alby escape an embarrassing scene he never would have encountered in Bergamo, where every waiter knew him and his family. But this was Milan; nobody knew him here. Bergamo was like a remote village in Ireland as far as people in Milan were concerned.

Nothing had gone right since Alby had shown up unannounced: a strained conversation at her apartment, her decision to go to dinner with him, the unfortunate encounter with Giangi. The evening had become such a dreary soap opera, when all she wanted was a peaceful night to relax and unwind.

"Alby, slow down. You're walking too fast," Simona said at last. She took brisk steps to be beside him as he continued walking quickly, not turning his head around, fleeing from Deus.

Then he turned to her, his face crimson. "What was all that about?" he snarled. "Who is that pathetic person? He's gay . . . flamboyant! Why are you friends with such a . . . a . . . disgusting creature?"

"I don't care about that, Alby. I'm not prejudiced against gay men or women. But Giangi can be a bit much sometimes, especially when he's been drinking. I don't know why he came over. He didn't know you. Maybe he thought he could create a scene and you'd walk out—which you did."

"I had to! Don't you understand? I felt humiliated!"

"Look, I barely know him. We've only talked a couple of times. He works in the fashion industry as a journalist of some sort. He's a name-dropper, knows a lot of people, moves with the party crowd."

"Where they do drugs . . . and other things. Pathetic!"

"I don't know about that, Alby. I've never been to one of those parties."

"Yeah," he snapped.

"I'm sorry it happened, Alby. It wasn't my fault."

Alby began walking at a normal pace, calming down now that they were some distance away from Deus. Simona slipped her arm around his, trying to appear like an ordinary couple out for the evening.

"People know you at that place. You must go there often."

"I meet people every day, Alby. Don't be offended. It doesn't mean anything. You know me. I'm serious . . . responsible . . . not a party girl. Don't try to make this into something that isn't so."

They reached a seafood restaurant and stopped to look at the outdoor menu. "Do you want to go here for dinner?" Alby asked.

Simona pretended to study the menu but had no interest in dragging out the evening. "Alby . . . I don't think so. You're angry and I'm tired. I don't want an argument. Would you please walk me home?"

"You said you were hungry." His face sagged like a deflated basketball.

"I'll have a bite at home. I can't stay out late. I'm tired and don't want a long evening. Tomorrow is a very important day for me. I need rest."

They stood outside the restaurant, looking at each other. Couples walked around them on the sidewalk, sensing a standoff that looked like it might break out into a lovers' quarrel.

Alby looked at Simona, his lips pressed tight, his eyes darting to her left eye, her right eye, and then back to her left without saying a word. He couldn't speak. He was embarrassed and infuriated by what had happened at Deus: encountering a dreadful, gay man who acted like he was a dear friend of Simona's and treated Alby like he was a shabby messenger boy.

When Alby had been driving to Milan that day, he'd been excited, anticipating that he would surprise Simona and they would have an amorous evening together. But now he was shattered. Simona had changed.

She was not his Bergamo girlfriend anymore. She acted like she was trying to forget her life in the small, provincial town and was pretending to be a classy Milanese professional woman, on the job 24/7, while in truth she was not much more than a country girl. *Who does she think she is?*

Simona looked away and then back at Alby. Her face was blank. The abbreviated evening had been torture, starting poorly and getting worse by the minute. She didn't want any more emotional conflict. She felt exhausted from the stressful day at DIGOS and the unpleasantness at Deus.

She touched Alby's arm with her fingers, a gesture to end the stalemate. Her words were soft. "Let's not have dinner, Alby. I need to go home. Now."

CHAPTER FOURTEEN

Simona and Dario were in Gerardo Annichiarico's office in the DIGOS IT center. His office had desks with computers linked to servers monitoring cell phone taps approved by the prosecutor. On Annichiarico's desk were two computers and stacks of file folders, loose paperwork, cell phones, and a framed family photo.

It was 7:45 PM, the first Wednesday in August, a time when Simona and Dario anticipated that they could monitor monthly calls from Cinti's phone to the other stolen phones.

A desk next to Annichiarico's was littered with a pizza box with two uneaten pieces, paper plates with leftover salad, plastic utensils, napkins, and water bottles. Although it was early for dinner, Simona and Dario had brought food, preparing for a possible late evening.

Simona and Dario sat alongside Annichiarico so they could see his desktop computer. On the monitor was a data folder labeled:

Amoruso Milano phone tree

Caso La Spezia

AT 7865

Below the folder name and case number were separate files designated by the cell numbers of the stolen phones.

"They're a cagey group," Dario said, scratching the stubble of a four-day beard on his chin. "The last few months, their monthly calls have been brief, a couple of minutes each. They're probably suspicious that their phones could be tapped."

"Let's hope we get lucky," Simona said, "and someone says something important on a call. Luck is always a factor in investigations."

Annichiarico was slouching in his swivel chair, arms crossed over his chest, slowly swiveling. Most of his career at DIGOS had involved sitting in soft chairs working on computers for long hours, day after day, with few opportunities to join other agents on patrols. Annichiarico's sedentary duty—and a distaste for exercise—had molded his body into a paunch bulging at his belt, flabby arms, and sallow skin. But his attention was focused on his work, which meant scanning the computer and muttering to himself.

When the digital clock on his computer changed to 7:54 PM, he said, "You ready? I think we're going to get a call soon. Their previous calls start right around 8:00 PM"

"Let's hope we don't have to wait long," Dario said.

At 7:56, Simona began tapping her pen on her notebook. *Tap-tap-tap-tap-tap-tap.* The tapping sounded like a lab rat pressing a pedal for water in a science lab. *Tap-tap-tap-tap-tap-tap.*

"That's distracting, Simona. Stop it," Dario said.

"Sorry," she said. "I'm nervous. My heart's pounding like a hammer." She put the pen in her mouth and started chewing on the plastic end.

After a minute of listening to her grinding her teeth on the pen, Dario sighed. "Will you please stop it, Simona? . . . It's bugging me."

She stopped. A telephone ringing on the computer monitor startled them at 8:01 PM.

Bdddrrring! Bdddrrring!

"Right on time," Annichiarico said, sitting erect, his eyes just inches from the monitor.

Simona gasped. "First call! Here we go!"

It was Cinti's phone calling W's phone. Both numbers lit up on the monitor. A click as the call was answered. "Pronto. I'm here." Male adult on W's number, an eager tone in his voice. Middle Eastern accent.

"Can you talk?" The voice on Cinti's phone was brusque, perfect Italian, no accent.

"Yes . . . I've been waiting."

"Change of plans," the caller from Cinti's phone said, the words spit out. "Next meeting, Thursday night, not Tuesday."

A pause. "Umm, okay. Why?"

"Don't ask." Like the question was an insult. "Will you be there?"

A pause. One of them cleared his throat followed by a cough.

"Yes, of course."

"Eight o'clock. Don't be late."

"Same place as before?"

"Yes. See you then. Leave your cell phone home."

Two clicks. The callers disengaged. The lit numbers on the monitor dimmed. No one spoke for a few seconds.

"Well, we know the phone tree is active tonight," Dario said.

"A little under a minute," Annichiarico said, checking his digital clock: 8:02. "Not much information. They're disciplined."

"The Cinti voice speaks flawless Italian. Perfect elocution, almost like an actor," Simona said, looking down at her notebook, where she had scribbled *Time change . . . Thursday . . . 8:00.*

"No names, no greetings, just a message about changing a meeting time," Dario said. "We might not get any information if all the calls are as short as the first one."

"Where do you think they're meeting?" Simona asked.

Dario shrugged. "No idea. We might learn something on other calls, but I doubt it. They know the place; no reason to mention it."

They sat in silence, sipping water from plastic bottles, staring at the monitor. Simona underlined the scribbled notes on her notepad.

Dario reached down, pulled out the bottom drawer of the desk with the pizza box residue, and propped his feet on the edge. "Think we'll have to wait longer for the next—"

Ringing from the computer monitor interrupted him. *Bdddrrring! Bdddrrring!*

Two numbers lit up, Cinti's phone and X's. "It's 8:07. X's cell phone," Annichiarico said.

"Pronto," X answered. Another accent. A heavier, deeper voice, possibly an older man.

"Time change," the voice on Cinti's phone said. "Next Thursday, not Tuesday."

"Hmm. OK. What time? I work until seven thirty." He pronounced his "T"s hard, like many foreigners who hadn't learned Italian in school.

"Same time, eight o'clock."

A pause. Neither voice spoke. Simona held her breath, pen scribbling in her notebook . . . *X off at 7:30.*

"I can make it," X answered. "I'll come from work, maybe a couple minutes late. It's not far. Can everyone else make it?" His accent was not Italian, possibly North African or Middle Eastern. Hard to determine with short, choppy sentences.

"I'm calling them now."

"See you Thursday," he said, mashing the consonants in *Thursday* so it sounded like *Trrzzdy.*

Two clicks. The call ended.

"Crude accent," Simona said. "He hasn't spent much time in Italy."

"Or his work means he doesn't have to speak much," Dario said.

"It's 8:08. One minute again," Annichiarico said. "They don't waste time. Short and sweet. Routine, brief calls. No names. They're disciplined."

Simona looked at her notes: *Bad accent . . . X work not far . . . Where? Late maybe?*

The air in the small office was warm, rank with the aroma of pizza, oily salad dressing, and three bodies in a confined space.

"Two down. Who's next?" Dario said impatiently. He squirmed in his chair, moving his feet from the desk drawer to the floor and then back again. He reached for the cigarette packet in his shirt pocket, took it out, and tapped it on his thigh. It had been an hour since his last smoke. He wanted a cigarette, but not in the office.

A siren wail broke the silence: *Weeeooo . . . weeooo . . . weeooo . . . weeooo.* A police car leaving the Questura, the wailing weakening as the car drove in the direction of Piazza Cavour. Any time of the day and night, police cars raced from the Questura, sirens shrieking, speeding to a burglary, a fight, a car accident, or worse. The sound was routine, almost unnoticed by those working in the Questura.

It was 8:16 PM. *Bdddrrring! Bdddrrring! Bdddrrring!*

Cinti's phone calling Y. *Bdddrrring! Bdddrrring! Bdddrrring! Bdddrrring! Bdddrrring!* Five rings. Cinti's phone clicked and hung up.

"No answer," Simona said, a frown on her face. "What does that mean? Someone's not answering. What happened?"

Dario said, "Maybe Y forgot. Let's wait and see."

Cinti's phone called Y again at 8:19 PM. *Bdddrrring! Bdddrrring! Bdddrrring! Bdddrrring! Bdddrrring! Bdddrrring!* No answer. Click. Cinti's phone hung up.

"Hmm, a second call to Y, right after the first," Simona said. "Y's not answering. Where is he?"

Dario put the cigarette pack back in his shirt pocket and leaned back in his chair. "Has this happened before? If someone doesn't answer, what does the Cinti caller do?"

"No way to know," Annichiarico answered. "We have records of calls made and received, not when no one answers."

"Too bad," Dario said.

Simona glanced at the clock and scribbled: *8:21. No answer from Y. Two calls.*

They waited in silence. A rumble of thunder from a summer rainstorm broke the silence. A crack of lightning. A louder thunder rumble. Dario looked across the IT center to a window where he could see street lights glowing on Via Fatebenefratelli. "Look at the rain . . . supposed to keep raining all night."

It was 8:28 PM. Two numbers lit up on the screen, Cinti's phone and Z's. *Bdddrrring! Bdddrrring!*

"Pronto, I'm here," Z answered quickly. Foreign accent, softer, possibly a younger man.

"Date change," Cinti answered. "Next Thursday, not Tuesday. Same place."

"Hmmm, okay. I can make it. Anything else?"

"No."

"It will be good to get together again."

"Yes."

"See you then."

Two clicks. The lit numbers on the computer dimmed.

"Another short one, less than a minute," Dario said. "We're not getting anything. Three answered calls, one no answer. Same message. Is that it?"

"All we have are four phone numbers," Annichiarico said.

"Are we done, then?"

"No way," Annichiarico said. "We keep listening and see what happens. I've spent hours waiting for calls, sometimes long into the night. Then one comes at two thirty in the morning, and you get good intelligence."

"Yeah, I guess you're right. Maybe Cinti's phone will call Y again."

They leaned back in their chairs, sipping water and staring at the phone numbers on the computer monitor. Five minutes. Ten minutes.

Dario pushed back in his chair, stretched, and yawned. "I should have gone to the gym today. My muscles are cramped. Break time." He stood and walked around Annichiarico's desk into the main IT center. He raised his arms over his head, twisting his torso and stretching stiff shoulder and back muscles.

Simona was also stiff from sitting in a hard chair. "I wish I could do yoga," she said, rotating her arms, flexing her fingers, pressing her palms together in an isometric exercise.

"Go ahead," Dario said. "You need a rug or something?"

"It's a yoga mat, not a rug."

"There's a rug in Lucchini's conference room."

Simona shook her head. "I don't have the right clothes. You can't do yoga in a few minutes. You need to stretch, loosen your muscles, do exercises. What if Lucchini comes back to his office and I'm splayed out on his rug? I'd be doing traffic patrol on the *autostrada* in a week."

Dario went back into Annichiarico's office. Simona picked up her notebook. Dario ran his hand over the cigarette pack in his shirt pocket. He wanted a cigarette. How much longer would he have to wait? "*Che palle*. I'm feeling claustrophobic," he said. "I'm used to being out on the street, driving around, talking to people, working a case."

"Waiting is part of our job," Simona reminded him.

"Yeah, I know. I'm not good at waiting for something to happen. I want action . . . something to get my juices going. How do you spend every day listening to tapped conversations?" Dario asked Annichiarico. "Don't you get bored . . . just sitting . . . waiting? I'd go nuts."

"I don't mind waiting. I think about the callers and why we're tapping them. I get into their psychology . . . wondering why they commit crimes, why they made bad choices in their lives. Bad childhoods? Pressure from shady characters? I've listened to a thousand phone taps, but nothing like this group. Usually it's a couple of guys talking like they're in a bar, bitching about something or somebody—angry, pissed off, spilling information we didn't know about. But this group is disciplined . . . secretive. They suspect that their calls are tapped, so they don't use names or mention details. They're up to something—"

It was 8:54 PM. *Bdddrrring! Bdddrrring!* Cinti's phone called Y again. Seven rings. Hung up.

"That's three times Cinti's called Y," Simona said. "Why isn't he answering?"

"Cinti's pissed. I'll bet his blood is boiling," Dario said with a smirk on his face. "I'd want to wring his neck if I was Cinti. He's trained them to expect a call; they're expected to answer at the appointed time. Maybe something happened to Y. An accident? Got in trouble and can't use his phone? Hey, Gerry, I'm getting into your psychology. Who are these characters?"

Annichiarico smiled. "See? It's a little game we play. We're snooping on them . . . they don't know. Use your imagination . . . fantasize what they look like . . . where they're calling from . . . where they work . . . who their girlfriends are."

"Girlfriends?" Dario said. "Hey, Gerry . . . I was thinking about that, too. Terrorists have girlfriends, don't you think? All that testosterone, plotting something dangerous. They'd need a girlfriend so their pants wouldn't explode."

Annichiarico roared. "Yeah, Volpe! If they didn't have girlfriends, they'd be a hazard just walking down the street."

Dario guffawed. "I can see it. . . . You're in a park. You see a couple of Muslim men. One bends over, his pants catch fire . . . he runs . . . his friends chase him . . . their pants explode . . . they run screaming, smoke coming out of their pants."

They both roared, high-fiving at their low attempt at humor.

"Stop it, boys," Simona said groaning. "You're both sick. You're acting like teenagers!"

Dario and Annichiarico snickered, making faces at each other like they'd been caught being naughty.

Simona shook her head and sighed. "Men. Pitiful. No, you're just horny boys. Why do women put up with you? Maybe you'll grow up one day . . . although some boys never do."

"Ow," Dario said. "She's right, Gerry. Some of us never do." Annichiarico nodded and made a hand gesture that translated into "What can you do?"

Ten minutes passed. Dario stood. "This boy needs a bathroom break," he announced, leaving the IT center. He was back in five minutes. Simona and Annichiarico were standing by his desk, staring at his monitor.

Dario grabbed the last plastic bottle of water and sat down.

"It's nine fifteen. How long do we wait?" he asked.

"Let's wait another hour," Simona said. "I don't want Amoruso to think we left early."

Dario sipped his water, took out his cigarette pack again, and tapped it on his leg. It had been more than two hours since he had had a smoke. He wanted one. Now.

At 9:25 PM, a new phone number flashed on the computer monitor calling Cinti's number.

"What's this?" Simona blurted. "Who's calling Cinti?" She scribbled the new phone number on her notepad.

Three rings. Cinti's phone picked up. A click, no "pronto."

"Hey, listen, *amico*, I'm sorry," a male voice said in a casual tone. An American accent. "Uh, I'm in Sardinia . . . with friends on the family yacht. No cell phone coverage. I left your phone at home. I just found your number I wrote down—"

"*Vaffanculo!*" the voice barked from Cinti's phone. "You're calling from a personal phone? Hang up!"

"Well, okay, but when—"

"Call on the phone I gave you! Don't ever call this number from your phone!"

One click. Then a second. The brief call was over.

"Whoa, what was that?" Simona exclaimed, her voice excited. "An American accent! I thought we were investigating Pakistanis."

"Maybe our assumptions are wrong," Dario said. "No doubt, that was an American accent. He violated their procedure and called Cinti's number from his personal phone. Who's the caller?"

"No idea. That number hasn't been used before," Annichiarico said. "We'll have to get the name from the phone companies."

"When can we get it?" Simona asked.

"At this time of night, we're not likely to," Annichiarico replied, shaking his head. "Technicians are on duty at night. They don't have the authority to give us names. They'll pass it off to someone who works days."

"Should we call Amoruso?" Dario asked.

"Yes," Simona said. "There was a breach in the calls. We have a new, unknown caller."

"No, wait until morning," Annichiarico suggested. "This isn't urgent, just something we weren't expecting. I'll come in early tomorrow, call my contacts in the phone companies, and get Amoruso a name and address first thing."

The next morning, Simona and Dario briefed Antonella on the previous evening of listening to the tapped phones and the one unknown caller.

"Annichiarico got me the caller's name: Alessandro Boni," Antonella said, handing Simona a slip of paper with the name and address.

"An Italian name, but he had an American accent," Simona said.

"Yes, he did, no mistake," Dario confirmed.

"An American. That's a surprise."

"We thought so, too," Simona said.

"And look at his address . . . in Piazza del Carmine, around the corner from here," said Antonella.

"Piazza del Carmine!" Dario exclaimed. "I had lunch near there yesterday."

"Well, you might have seen Boni. Get a photo of him and pass it around the office. Anything else you heard on the call?"

"Just a little," Simona said. "He sounds like he's in his thirties or forties. And if he lives in Brera, he's got money. What the hell is an American doing getting involved with Middle Eastern terrorists?"

"That's what we have to find out," Antonella replied. "I'll get approval from the prosecutor to tap his phone. In the meantime, find out everything you can about this signor Boni."

"We'll check our databases right away," Simona said.

"Come back when you have something. I'll brief Lucchini when I give him the paperwork for the prosecutor."

"Let's go, Dario," Simona said, motioning to him with her head. They left Antonella's office and returned to theirs. They searched police databases for arrest records, auto registrations, and tax and immigration records. They learned that Boni had a string of parking tickets that went back for years. He had frequently traveled around Europe and to the United States. Four cars had been registered under his name in the last five years. He'd wrecked a BMW M5 in 2011 while speeding on the Milano–Bologna *autostrada*. A woman with him had been injured and had spent three days in a hospital. Boni had been given a speeding ticket and another ticket for dangerous driving. He had lost ten points, and his license had been suspended for six months. He was a dual citizen of Italy and the United States.

After Simona and Dario had completed a search of government records, they put his name in web search engines.

At noon, they were back in Antonella's office with notes from their searches.

"So, what did you find out?" Antonella asked. "I told Lucchini you'd give us background on this signor Boni."

"We learned quite a bit, dottoressa. As far as police records, he's never been arrested, but he has enough parking tickets to fill a box. He's probably paid a few thousand euros for those, plus three speeding tickets on the *autostrada*, including a car accident in which a woman with him was injured and had to go to the hospital."

"Reckless, isn't he?" said Antonella.

Simona nodded and went on. "Boni's father is Italian, and Boni has dual citizenship. He was born in the U.S. but traveled here often before he became a resident in 2008. He's thirty-seven years old and works at his father's architecture firm. Sometimes he drives his stepmother's Mini Cooper with Swiss plates, but he owns a new Audi Q5. Those cars cost about seventy thousand euros. The Audi is his fifth new car in six years. He spends a lot of money on travel, entertainment, and dinners, according to social media posts.

"He lives in a nice apartment in Brera, paid for by his rich daddy. He's a spoiled brat with no sense of responsibility or maturity," Simona said.

"Married?"

"No, nothing about a wife . . . current or past," Simona answered.

"A rich, spoiled, single man in Milano," said Antonella. "I'll bet most of his friends are well off, too. How about his father?"

Dario looked down at his notes. "His name is Guglielmo Boni; he goes by Ghigo. His company website has bios on both of them. Ghigo's family emigrated to America from Calabria in the 1950s. His father was a tailor in New York's Little Italy. Ghigo got a business degree at NYU and then attended Yale architecture school. He got scholarships and did well. He won a competition to study in Rome, after which he returned to New York and had a job before he came to Milan and started his own architecture firm in the 1980s. Impressive background. He's well connected, is friends with the mayor, and goes to *salotti buoni* with judges and professors."

"I know about him," Antonella said. "His photo has been in the newspapers with his wife. They're active on the social scene. What else about Alessandro? He's the one we're interested in."

Simona read from her notes. "He has a blog and is on Facebook, Twitter, LinkedIn. He blogs some about work, but mostly it's social, travel, and good times. He's a party animal—photos with friends at restaurants and parties, on sailboats with women in bikinis, at concerts and soccer matches. I've just started; it will take time to complete a report on him."

"Any photos with Middle Eastern men? Or anything political?"

Simona shook her head. "Nothing so far. But we've just begun."

"Dig deeper. I want everything you can come up with on Alessandro and his father. I'm taking paperwork to Lucchini to get emergency authorization right after his two o'clock appointment. I'll pass along what you've found so far."

Later that afternoon, Giorgio was reading the request to the prosecutor for legal authorization to tap Alessandro Boni's cell phone. He picked up a pen, signed it, and pushed it across to Antonella. "Deliver this to his office right away. In the meantime, start surveillance on Boni. Follow him, see where he goes, who he associates with. Get photos."

"I've assigned Cella to follow him home from his office this afternoon."

"Good. Set up twenty-four-hour surveillance as soon as you can."

"We will. De Monti and Volpara have done a quick database and web search on him. Boni is very active on the social media scene—dinners, parties, vacations. Can you imagine . . . a terrorist suspect on social media?"

"Terrorists used to be like alley cats lurking in dark alleys, but times have changed. They use social media for recruiting—chat rooms, blogs, Twitter, all of that. But I'm leery about this. Why is Boni so visible if he's involved with terrorists?"

Antonella handed over Simona's brief profile. "Is his father Ghigo?" Giorgio asked, flipping through the pages.

"Yes."

"Interesting. He's a friend of the questore. I'm sure the prosecutor will tell him about this. We'll get authorization."

Antonella nodded.

Giorgio continued reading through Simona's and Dario's notes. "I met Ghigo Boni at a reception at Palazzo Marino last year. The mayor had a reception for corporations and politicians involved in the Milan Expo."

"I remember you telling me."

"Half of the Comune's bureaucrats were there, along with politicians, contractors, and developers who got big contracts for the Expo."

"Boni's father's architecture firm is probably designing Expo pavilions."

"A hotel by the Expo, too, I think. You know what? I think I met Alessandro."

"You did?"

"Yes. I was talking with Ghigo Boni, his friends, and some developers. Alessandro came over. His father introduced me, and we shook hands. He looked about forty—decent looking but not movie star looks. A young woman was with him."

"He's a busy boy, all over Milan at parties and dinners."

Giorgio picked up the notes again. "I'll tell the questore tomorrow. He knows Boni as well."

"Tell the questore that Alessandro Boni is your neighbor. He lives in Brera."

"Really? What's his address?"

She told him.

He raised his eyebrows. "A neighbor, huh? Quite a posh place for a potential terrorist. I wonder what he's up to."

CHAPTER FIFTEEN

At 7:30 PM, Giorgio stopped by Simona and Dario's office before going home. It had been a long day, spent mostly with the Alessandro Boni development, preparing the request for authorization for the prosecutor to approve a phone tap, organizing a surveillance team, and talking to the questore and his staff about Ghigo Boni's son.

Simona and Dario were still on their computers, researching and writing a profile for the DIGOS staff.

"I wanted to tell you how much I appreciate your research into our new suspect," Giorgio said. "With luck—and a few phone calls—we'll have the judge's authorization to tap Alessandro Boni's phone in a couple of days. In the meantime, we start surveillance tomorrow, following him from his apartment to work and wherever he goes at night. Good job on the phone tap last night. We finally have a break in the case."

Simona and Dario nodded at Giorgio, appreciating his comments. Receiving a compliment from their boss was a reward in what had been a frustrating investigation that had led them into blind alleys for weeks.

"Thank you, dottore," Simona said. "We're going to finish our work tonight so we can post a profile of Alessandro for tomorrow morning's briefing. In the meantime, we have more information about him."

"Good. Can you share with me? I'm in no rush; my wife is doing better."

"Nice to hear, sir. We wish her the best," Simona said. The news of Giulia Lucchini's cancer diagnosis was known at DIGOS, but not the details about her surgery and chemotherapy.

Giorgio moved a chair so he could sit between Simona's and Dario's desks. They both swiveled their monitors so he could read along with them.

"We've divided up our research," said Simona. "My responsibility is writing a profile on Alessandro. Volpara is working on his father. We started with a search of police and government databases."

"Dottoressa Amoruso told me what you found out about Alessandro's parking tickets and dual citizenship."

"It will all be in the final report. We've also searched widely on the Internet, starting with Ghigo Boni's company's website. He is mentioned in newspapers and business journals in connection with his many projects, including the Milan Expo. He and his wife, Lucrezia, are prominent on the social scene, mentioned in articles about charity fundraisers, benefits, premieres, and that sort of thing."

"I met Ghigo Boni at a reception the mayor had promoting the Expo last year," said Giorgio.

"You know Ghigo Boni?" Simona asked.

"Just one meeting. He might not even remember. I also met Alessandro at the same reception. Just shook hands, really, nothing more than that. He was with a younger woman. It was a year ago."

"I wonder how someone like him can be connected to our investigation," Dario said.

"Yes, it's odd. That's what we have to find out. What's the latest on your research on Alessandro?"

Simona clicked an open document on her computer. "Quite a bit, starting with his family. Alessandro's mother is American. Her name is Louise. She and Ghigo were living in New York. She's an architect, too; maybe they met at university. They had two sons, Alessandro and Giacomo. They divorced—I'm not sure when—and both sons stayed with their mother after the divorce. Ghigo Boni moved to Milan twenty years ago and started his architecture firm. He married an Italian woman, Lucrezia Carminati de Fleury, in 1997. She's a Swiss resident. Her family has a villa at St. Moritz, where they travel in the winter. They had a daughter, Allegra, in 1998. She is a teenager, just fifteen."

"How did you find out so much about the family?" Giorgio asked.

"It's amazing what you can find on the Internet," said Simona. "Both Alessandro and his father are active on social media. Ghigo has a press office that promotes the company and gets its name in the media at social and charity events. One article in an architectural magazine had a story about Ghigo's Central Park West home, which he's trying to sell. The real estate agent is using Ghigo's celebrity status to promote the property. He has photos of Ghigo, Lucrezia, and Allegra at the home. Alessandro wasn't in the photos, by the way. He posts on his own blog and Facebook—childhood photos with his mother and brother, birthdays, holiday photos. Not a bit shy or private, I'd say."

"Good work. You like research."

"Yes, sir. Want to see a bit?"

"Of course. I'm learning a lot from you," Giorgio said, inching closer to her desk to read her monitor.

"Alessandro is boastful. He talks about himself most of the time," said Simona. "He doesn't blog every day, sometimes not for weeks. Most of the comments he makes are boring. Lots of name-dropping, like he wants people to think he has a very exciting life."

Simona opened a document with several photos. "Here's something typical: photos he took in Sardinia two years ago on a yacht. They're anchored at Porto Rotondo; you can see the sign on the dock."

"A popular vacation spot for wealthy travelers," noted Giorgio.

Simona scrolled through photos. "People on the yacht are probably Alessandro's Milanese friends. The women are young and pretty, sunbathing in bikinis on the deck, as you can see. The men pose like athletes or movie stars." She scrolled through more photos. "Here they are at a seaside restaurant in Porto Cervo: lots of champagne bottles, lobster, pasta and seafood platters. They're certainly enjoying themselves."

"The women look like they're in their mid- to late-twenties, the men a few years older."

"Typical," Dario said.

Simona clicked on a document file with a list of names that ran a full page. "I'm collecting the names of Alessandro's friends. I'll run them through our databases to see if any have police records or arrests."

"Good. Let me know what you find. What else?"

Simona scrolled further, stopping at photos of Paris landmarks. "Here he is in Paris last year with another couple . . . at the Louvre . . . at the Jules Verne restaurant on top of the Eiffel Tower . . . on the metro . . . at the Sorbonne . . . in front of the Chanel boutique on Rue Cambon . . . in the Cristal Room Baccarat in Montmartre . . . Sacré-Coeur, looking over Paris . . . at the Salvador Dali exhibition in the Musee d'Orsay."

"Hmm, they're pretty busy. They know how to get around," murmured Giorgio.

Simona nodded. "The couple they're with is married; they're on my list. Alessandro's girlfriend, Marina Cellini, was also on the yacht. She's a fashion photographer; she freelances for magazines and has a small studio. On her website, she posts photos from fashion shows, parties, and such. Alessandro was in her photos a year ago but is not in recent ones. Maybe they're not together anymore."

"He's single. Probably has several girlfriends," Giorgio said.

"Typical," she added.

"So, what about politics? Did you find anything relevant to our investigation?" Giorgio asked.

"No, nothing related to Italian politics or terrorists. He doesn't write about politics, maybe so he won't offend any of his or his father's politician friends. Just an opinion . . . I don't have any reason for saying that. But he is critical of American politics, especially former President George Bush and the invasion of Iraq."

"Can you show me?" Giorgio inched closer to her desk.

Simona closed one file and opened another while she talked. "Yes, but first of all, let me give you background. As I mentioned, the Bonis had two sons, Alessandro and Giacomo. Giacomo, or Jack, was the older, and it seems he was a favored son. He graduated from the army military academy of West Point. He was commissioned and went into special training to become one of the Green Berets, the elite commandos."

"I know West Point," Giorgio said. "I was taken there when I was at an FBI meeting in New York a few years ago. West Point graduates serve in the Pentagon and at high levels of government. They're smart, politically conservative, and believe in a strong U.S. military presence around the world."

On her computer, Simona displayed a photo of a young army officer with rows of ribbons on his chest and an American flag behind him. His name and rank were printed on the bottom. "Giacomo Boni was a captain who was killed in Iraq in 2003. His armored Humvee was blown up by an IED; he and six other American soldiers were killed."

"Sad," Giorgio said, shaking his head. "I can only imagine how that affected the family. I didn't know Ghigo Boni had lost a son in Iraq."

She opened another document. "Here's what Alessandro posted about his brother, whom he called a war hero. Alessandro wrote two entries the last two years on March 23, the anniversary of Giacomo's death. Last year he posted photos of his West Point graduation." She clicked on a photo of Giacomo in his army officer uniform, holding his diploma over his head in a sea of new West Point graduates.

"Handsome soldier. Resembles his father."

"This year Alessandro posted a photo of his brother's grave at Arlington National Cemetery in Virginia." She clicked on a photo of a white marble cross with Giacomo's name, rank, and birth and death dates. In the background were rows of similar white crosses and American flags planted on graves in the rolling green hills of Arlington Cemetery.

The three of them looked at the photos in silence. Giorgio said, "Sad . . . many American soldiers died in Iraq and Afghanistan."

Simona scrolled down to a text box under the Arlington Cemetery photo. "Read this," she said. "'Giacomo was one of 4,500 American heroes, men and women who lost their lives because of George Bush and Dick Cheney's failed foreign policy. They belong in jail for their war crimes.'"

"Harsh. He's very bitter," Giorgio said. "Alessandro has a grudge against American foreign policy in the Middle East. That could be why he connected with possible terrorists."

Simona leaned back, taking her hand off the computer mouse.

"Sir, if I may, I could tell you what I think about Alessandro from studying his posts."

"Please, yes. I want to know."

"Reading between the lines, I think Alessandro was envious of his brother. He didn't go to West Point; he didn't even graduate from college. He also doesn't have an architect license, even though he works at his father's firm."

"Really?"

"Yes. On Ghigo Boni's company's website, senior people have degrees—M. Arch, PhD Arch—with specialization in landscaping, technology, and regional and urban planning from Harvard, the University of Pennsylvania, Yale, the Politecnico."

"I'm sure he hired well-educated architects. But Alessandro isn't even an architect?"

"No. Alessandro attended college but didn't graduate. He went to the State University of New York in Binghamton. He doesn't say what he did after college, but he came to Italy in 2005 and started working for his father in 2009. Nothing about what he did before he was hired. He didn't start his blog or have a Facebook page until 2010. There are several years during which we don't know anything about him. Maybe he had dead-end jobs before his father put him on the payroll. He certainly has a less distinguished career than his older brother, and he ends up working for his father even though he's not an architect."

"An obvious case of nepotism," Giorgio said. "Alessandro could be resentful of his father's success . . . a classic father-son conflict as old as the Bible."

A little before 9:00 PM, Simona was exhausted from ten hours at her computer, scrolling the Internet and writing a profile for her DIGOS colleagues on Alessandro Boni. Although she had finished writing the profile, she wanted to read a few more posts before she went home.

In the last hour, she had found Alessandro mentioned in websites of Milan's well-known restaurants, galleries, celebrity parties, and social events. She had put Alessandro's name in the search bar, and occasionally a photo or a mention of Alessandro Boni in the text would pop up.

One website considered mildly provocative featured Milan's party crowd of hustlers and opportunists, some with shades of scandal or intrigue. Suddenly she stopped: a photo of Alessandro at a party in a restaurant. Almost every inch of the table where he sat was covered with dinner and salad plates, cutlery in disarray, soiled napkins, water bottles, wine bottles, and champagne flutes. In the background, a crowd of inebriated people filled the restaurant.

She gasped. She recognized the restaurant: Deus in Isola. Minutes from her apartment.

Alessandro was with a young woman, two couples, and a man without a woman. The men were Milanese fashionistas, wearing designer shirts and sport jackets. The women, years younger, wore sleeveless mini-dresses, earrings, and gaudy necklaces. The woman next to Alessandro looked Nordic, staring at the camera with the stony stare of a fashion model on the runway. She wasn't more than twenty-two or twenty-three, with spiked blonde hair and imperceptible breasts. She looked bored, ignoring the others at the table who were aglow in blissful inebriation. The other women looked Ukrainian or Russian. Thin and pale, with heavily mascaraed eyes. Also bored.

The man without a woman was next to Alessandro, shoulders touching. It was Giangi, the fashion blogger who had embarrassed Alby at Deus a few nights ago. Giangi and Alessandro had glassy, heavy-drinking eyes, lips curled in surly smiles. Alessandro was wearing a crisp, white Ralph Lauren shirt, with his arms around the Nordic woman and Giangi, whose blue jacket was open. Giangi's yellow silk shirt was unbuttoned, revealing a silver neck chain. A Rolex Submariner watch on one wrist, a platinum band on the other.

Simona was stunned. She wanted to call out to other DIGOS agents and tell them someone she knew casually was linked to a possible terrorist. But no one was left in the office. Dario had left a half hour earlier. She had to contemplate her discovery in isolation, a crucial connection in the most important case DIGOS was working.

She would brief Amoruso first thing in the morning. She knew the first question Amoruso would ask her: What was the connection between Alessandro and Giangi?

Simona had no idea. But she was going to find out.

CHAPTER SIXTEEN

Kareem Hussain lived in two worlds, cosmopolitan Milan and the tribal lands of northwest Pakistan. He lived in one but dreamed about the other. At times, Kareem felt he was two people, a blend of two cultures: his Italian Catholic mother, Elsa, and his Pakistani Muslim father, Hamid. Kareem held two passports, Italian and Pakistani.

Kareem's parents met in 1974 when they were students at the University of Reading in the United Kingdom. They fell in love and married in 1975 at a Reading mosque. To please her husband, Elsa converted to Islam but resisted the restrictions of being a Muslim wife: wearing a veil in public, being subservient to her husband, not being alone with another man, and avoiding alcohol.

In the early years of their marriage, Elsa adapted to Hamid's dark moods, volatile temper, and strict observation of his Muslim faith. He went to services at the campus mosque, attended Muslim meetings, fasted during Ramadan, and participated in the *iftar* breaking of the fast. He prayed five times a day and never touched alcohol. As a nonpracticing Catholic, Elsa respected his devotion to Allah. She also read the Hadith and the Quran, stories told by Muhammad, although she found them less inspirational than Jesus's parables in the gospels.

After obtaining his engineering degree, Hamid was hired by the British national railway's Great Western Main Line in Reading, where his father had worked after emigrating with his family from Pakistan in the 1960s. Hamid was one of four children. The family lived in a strict Muslim environment enforced by Hamid's father. Hamid's mother was a typical subservient Islamic spouse, obedient to her husband and devoted to her children.

Kareem's mother, Elsa, worked as a receptionist at a four-star hotel until she took maternity leave for Kareem's birth in 1977. When Elsa was eight months pregnant with him, she returned to her hometown of Verona, Italy, for his birth so Kareem could have an Italian passport. Hamid remained in Reading, angry about her decision. In 1979 and 1981, Elsa returned again to Verona for the birth of their daughters, Amira and Laila. Hamid remained in Reading, furious that his wife had defied him three times.

Raising three young children with Hamid was hard for Elsa. Hamid wanted his only son to grow up to be a devout Muslim. Elsa wanted Kareem and the girls to spend as much time as possible with their Italian relatives in Verona. Hamid become emotionally abusive and sometimes slapped Elsa in front of the children. He frowned on her maintaining friendships with English women she had known before their marriage.

Elsa never felt accepted in the Muslim community. Muslim women were polite but formal, inviting her to tea and playtimes with their children. Elsa felt isolated and friendless raising her children. She longed for her family and friends in Verona.

Kareem's relationship with his father was strained. Hamid schooled Kareem in his heritage, sharing stories of growing up in the tribal lands of northwest Pakistan. He taught Kareem Urdu and Pashto, telling him that a well-educated man must speak many languages. In addition to two Pakistani languages, Kareem spoke perfect British English and Italian.

Elsa protected her children from Hamid's moods, nurturing them and teaching them kindness, empathy, and respect for others. Kareem was tall, like his Italian grandfather, and athletic, with the graceful stride of a cat moving around a room. His appearance was a blend of his father's olive features and his mother's alabaster complexion.

Kareem inherited his father's intelligence and aptitude for technology. From his mother, Kareem inherited a calm demeanor and almost feminine features: small hands, a petite nose, gray eyes, and a warm smile. With his handsome appearance and gentle manner, Kareem never lacked for girlfriends.

When Kareem was nine, Elsa told Hamid that she wanted to return to her Catholic faith. For weeks, he lashed out at her, calling her an unfit mother who was not worthy of raising his Muslim children. He accused her of being an infidel and made veiled threats that she should be punished. After months of emotional abuse, she packed up the children one morning when Hamid was at work. They took a taxi to a friend's home in a London suburb, and three days later flew to Verona. Elsa never returned to the United Kingdom.

Kareem was upset about his parents' breakup. He missed his father but felt relieved to be away from the tension in their Reading home. He and his sisters did well in Verona schools and easily made Italian friends. Their lives were freer than they had been in the sheltered domesticity in Reading.

Kareem's teachers recognized his aptitudes in math and science and encouraged Elsa to enroll him in after-school courses in computer and information technologies, math competitions, and chess. When he graduated from high school with honors, his teachers wrote recommendations for him to receive a scholarship to attend the University of Bicocca in Milan. He enrolled in 1995, studied hard, and made excellent grades.

Although Kareem had been raised Muslim, he wasn't devout. He was secular and ambitious, interested in pursuing a technical education and having a career with the rewards that came with a high-paying job.

After Kareem moved to Milan, he visited his father annually in Reading. He attended Friday services with him but confessed he did not go to a mosque in Milan. Hamid badgered him and told him he must become more devout, marry a Muslim woman, and raise his children in Islam.

Kareem was disappointed that Hamid did not remarry. After the divorce, his father became withdrawn, had few friends, and lived alone, with no interests outside of work, where he was awarded patents in designing navigation gear for railroads. His sole hobby was building small railroad trains. Kareem's relationship with his father remained fragile and distant.

After Kareem graduated cum laude from Bicocca in 2001, he passed national tests to become a certified electrical engineer. He was hired by Carefull Services, an Italian company that had maintenance contracts around Milan. Kareem's job involved maintaining technological infrastructure at Milan's most important landmarks: the Pirelli Tower, Teatro alla Scala, Teatro degli Arcimboldi, the Triennale palace, Malpensa and Linate airports, Palazzo Mezzanotte (Milan's stock exchange), and Palazzo Marino (Milan's town council headquarters).

Kareem's security badges allowed him access to Carefull's clients' sensitive infrastructure: computer servers, electrical systems, emergency generators, security surveillance, data transmission, and heating and air conditioning. He knew how buildings breathed, communicated with the outside world, provided security for employees, and eliminated wastes.

Kareem enjoyed the rewards of being a successful Milanese professional. After he was promoted to project manager with a generous salary raise, he bought a late-model Audi and a two-bedroom apartment in Città Studi at Piazza Ferravilla. His eighth-floor terrace provided views of the Politecnico, the Duomo, the Torre Velasca, and skyscrapers in Porta Nuova and Isola.

Kareem furnished his apartment with the latest technology and hired an interior decorator, who installed Cargo&HighTech furniture, a double sink and Bisazza tiles in the bathroom, and a Boffi kitchen.

Kareem was a weekend athlete. He played striker on a soccer team and was an avid mountain biker. Parked on his balcony was a nine-hundred-euro, handmade, Lombardo Sestriere 350 racing bicycle, which he rode during summer races around Lago di Como.

Kareem's TV was mounted on the wall between diplomas from Politecnico and Bicocca and certificates of excellence from Carefull Services. Framed photos on his bookshelves showed him vacationing with friends at Lago di Como and Alto Adige, often with his Italian girlfriend, Francesca, a petite, attractive beautician with curly black hair, piercing dark eyes, and a buxom figure.

Francesca was pretty but barely literate. She came from a poor family that lived in a village outside Milan. She was immediately attracted to Kareem when they met mountain biking. She was seduced by his wit, handsome appearance, and prestigious career. She flirted, said he looked like a Gucci model, and asked if he had a girlfriend. He said no. Their first date was dinner and dancing at a Milan nightclub the next weekend. She slept with him that night at his apartment and moved in a month later.

Francesca loved Kareem's elegant apartment and his vibrant social life. He was a gentleman. He paid for dinners, vacations to Sardinia and Ligurian resorts, and mountain biking around Lago di Como. Francesca's previous boyfriends had never lavished her with so much attention or bought her expensive clothes, jewelry, and a mountain bike. She didn't tell her girlfriends that he was Pakistani; instead, she bragged that he was from London.

Before he met Francesca, Kareem had lived a carefree life, drinking and dancing in nightclubs with friends and sleeping with women he picked up. He wasn't proud of his decadent lifestyle but rationalized that he was merely going through the hedonistic phase that attractive single men in Milan experienced. He enjoyed pleasures of the flesh with little interest in searching for a deeper meaning in life. He was happiest when enjoying good food and wine, vacationing with friends, and pursing beautiful young women—even if he didn't remember their names after occasional one-night stands.

After he turned thirty-three, Kareem began examining life's meaning, questioning his materialistic life, and feeling outrage about the never-ending wars in Iraq and Afghanistan. He believed the wars were a clash of civilizations between Christianity and Islam; a conflict that went back to the Crusades and the sixteenth-century wars between the Ottoman sultan Suleiman the Magnificent and the Holy Roman emperor Charles V. Kareem's allegiance in this titanic struggle was with his Muslim faith and his father's heritage.

As a boy and a young man, Kareem had been proud of Italy's history, art, and lifestyle, but he had increasingly felt like a foreigner living in a country that was no longer his home. He identified with his father's homeland, the tribal regions of northwestern Pakistan.

Kareem's struggle with his identity was complicated because of his love for Francesca. After a year of living together, they casually discussed marriage and raising a family. But it never reached the stage of talking about it with her family, who lived in a dingy apartment in Carate Brianza, north of Milan. The reasons were not complicated; her family disliked Kareem's ethnicity and religion. Her father, Daniele, was poor, a part-time carpenter who often humiliated his wife at family gatherings. His conduct infuriated Kareem, who remembered how cruel his father had been to his mother. Daniele was a conservative Catholic and opposed his daughter marrying a Muslim. The few times they visited her parents, Daniele avoided talking to Kareem, even ignoring him when he asked questions.

A bigger obstacle was Francesca's older brother, Antonio, also a poorly paid carpenter. When Kareem and Francesca drove in Kareem's Audi to visit her family, Antonio was bitter, complaining that he didn't know how a Pakistani could have such an expensive car while he drove a twenty-year-old Fiat with rusting panels and a broken side window. Antonio was rude to Kareem and warned Francesca that her family would shun her if they married. One night when Kareem and Francesca were saying goodbye to Francesca's parents, Kareem heard Antonio in the kitchen, where he'd been drinking all afternoon: ". . . filthy Arabs migrate to Italy . . . steal jobs from hard-working Italians. Get rid of the filthy bastards!"

Antonio's behavior and appearance were offensive to Kareem. Antonio smoked constantly, drank heavily, and carried a paunch that hung over his belt like a pillow. Although two years older than Kareem, Antonio looked ten years older. His gray hair and beard were rarely trimmed. He had poor dental hygiene, tobacco-stained teeth, and bad breath.

In Kareem's eyes, Antonio was a vindictive, heartless man whose personal life was a disaster. He had always been a mama's boy and was still living with his parents. He never married but had a teenage son who insulted him to his face. His latest girlfriend was an ill-mannered woman who dressed like a whore and talked only about TV soap operas and reality television shows.

The deterioration in Kareem's relationship with Francesca began when he started attending Muslim Friday services. He had gone to the mosque rarely when he was a student. But a Muslim colleague at Carefull encouraged him to go to the Islamic Cultural Center on Viale Jenner, telling him it was his duty as a Muslim.

The Islamic Center was a political hotbed with imams preaching fundamental Islam to Muslim immigrant men from North Africa and the Middle East who had sought political asylum from repressive regimes. Imams at the ICC aroused them with incendiary sermons railing against the evils of decadent Europe, thundering about Italy's moral decline: a Catholic nation that was now blatantly secular and materialistic, and ignored the church on issues such as abortion, contraception, and divorce.

"Italians don't attend mass," an imam preached. "They worship at their TVs, watching RAI and Mediaset idiotic game shows and pornographic soap operas, as well as teleshopping shows with scantily clad women flaunting implanted breasts as they peddled cheap consumer goods—shampoos, expensive shoes, jewelry, lingerie." These infidel women were referred to as blasphemous among devout Muslims.

Kareem was conflicted but also inspired when one imam preached, "European democracy and capitalism are in their death throes, buried under mountains of debt from corrupt governments and decadence! America and Canada are islands that may survive the first waves of jihad, which will sweep across Europe. One day, jihad will invade North America! A thousand years of Christian oppression since the Crusades will be avenged; we will bring down the foreign infidels that mock Islam! Islam is the future! Prepare for that glorious day! Rise up and join jihad!"

Kareem came away from the sermons dazed and confused. How could he justify his good fortune, living in a nice apartment, and having a new car and a good job? Could he risk giving up his privileged life to follow the imam's call for jihad, a path to certain danger? He struggled every day with the dilemma, at work, at home, and especially when he was with Francesca at her family's dingy apartment.

It was August, the traditional vacation month when Italians go to the beach or mountains. Kareem would be leaving in a few days for a trip to Pakistan. Francesca was unhappy about his upcoming trip, resentful that he wouldn't be taking her for a relaxing vacation on Ibiza or Sardinia.

Kareem's conflict about which life was right for him coincided with a traumatic experience at the thirtieth-birthday party he arranged for

Francesca at a nightclub on Lake Como: dinner, drinks, dancing, and expensive gifts.

When Antonio heard about the party, he crashed it, driving from Carate Brianza with his trashy girlfriend, who chose for the occasion a cheap dress with a slit up the thigh and a neckline that exposed the sides of her breasts and plunged to reveal tummy rolls.

As guests were being seated at a long table, Kareem and Francesca were shocked to see Antonio and his date stroll from the bar out to the patio, drinks in hand. Antonio came up behind Kareem and Francesca, slapped Kareem on the back and reached down to kiss Francesca's forehead. "Hey, guess who's here! My little sister and her Paki boyfriend!" He winked at his date, who rolled her eyes, trying to pull him back into the bar.

Antonio ignored her and waved his meaty hand to a waiter pouring wine for the guests. "Hey, waiter! Waiter! Two more chairs at the table. I can't miss my sister's birthday party."

The waiter looked at Kareem, who looked at Francesca. She shrugged a "what can you do?" gesture and whispered, "He's drunk, honey. He'll get ugly if he can't stay."

Kareem was furious about Antonio's brash intrusion but nodded his approval. The waiter added two more settings at the end of the table, forcing other guests to make room for them.

Antonio proceeded to get more and more drunk, talking loudly and embarrassing the guests. After dinner, the band began playing popular 1980s tunes, guests started dancing. Kareem and Francesca went to the dance floor, mixing with friends and staying away from Antonio and his date.

Later in the evening, Kareem excused himself to go to the bathroom. When he entered, he was disappointed to see Antonio in front of a urinal, a cigarette dangling from his lips, bracing his hands on the porcelain partitions to support his bloated frame. Kareem walked to the urinal farthest from Antonio.

"Kareeeeem . . . I love parties . . . especially my sister's!" Antonio slurred, squinting through a cigarette-smoke haze. "I dunno why Francesca is wasting her time with you."

"You're drunk, Antonio." Kareem said, not wanting to antagonize him. "I love Francesca. She loves me."

"Hah!" Antonio fumed. "Love? Does she love you? She loves your apartment . . . your fancy car!" He coughed, spit into the urinal, and flushed the handle violently. "She's nothing but a . . ." Kareem heard him start to say "putta."

"Stop it! Don't talk about your sister like that. You're vulgar." Kareem was shaking with rage fearful that Antonio was working himself up to hit him.

Antonio coughed and spit again into the urinal. "Kareeeem . . . you know I don't like you? You notice you're the only towel-head here? Francesca's friends are from northern Italy. You're the only one from Pakistan."

"I'm not from Pakistan. You know that. I'm Italian. I have lived in Italy since I was nine years old. Want to see my passport?"

"Which one?" Antonio slurred, the ash from his cigarette falling into the urinal with a hiss. "You have a Pakistani passport, right?"

Kareem didn't answer.

"Your father is Paki, right?"

"Yes. But he lives in London."

Antonio's disheveled, gray-haired head bobbed side to side, trying to keep cigarette smoke from his squinting eyes. He reached into a back pocket, pulled out a wrinkled napkin, and blew his nose, a nasal honk that made Kareem sick to his stomach.

Jutting his jaw toward Kareem, he drawled, "Whoooo . . . carrrrz-z-z-z . . . e'zz Muzzlim . . . you're Muzzlim. Everyone knows about Muzzlims . . . suicide bombers . . . blowing up planes . . . subways. Jihadists kill Christians . . . if you don't kill each other first . . . call us infidels. Your religion is crazy. . . . Muhammad was a pedophile . . . marrying a nine-year-old girl! He's not holy; he's a pervert!"

Kareem was stunned; Antonio had made racial slurs before about immigrants, but this tirade was blasphemy, a crime that called for beheading in Muslim countries. He stepped away from the urinal and walked behind Antonio to one of the sinks. Antonio let his cigarette drop from his lips into the urinal. He spit again, zipped up, grunted, and shuffled toward the sinks, where Kareem was washing his hands.

Kareem was nervous with Antonio next to him as he gazed into the mirror while he turned the faucet and ran his hands under the water. Should he ignore Antonio and return to the party? Or should he confront him? He surprised himself by what he said: "How often do you attend mass, Antonio?"

He wanted to take back the words, but it was too late. He feared that in Antonio's drunken state, he might slap him. How disgusting, at Francesca's birthday party, to be assaulted by her slovenly brother, drunk in the bathroom, spitting in a urinal. Disgusting.

Antonio shrugged, checked himself in the bathroom mirror, turning his head left and right to admire his profile. He lifted his wet hands and stroked his beard. He burped, a crude guttural blast.

"Duzzn' matter . . . Kareeeem," he slurred. "I was an altar boy . . . damn good Catholic. Italy is Catholic. Even if we don't go to church, we're still religious. We like the pope . . . what the church does for the poor. You go down on your knees on dirty rugs with your asses in the air and no shoes. Your feet stink. Catholics don't humiliate women like Muzzlims do . . . treat them like dogs . . . make them wear burkha. If you want to live like that, go back to Pakistan. You don't respect our laws. *Ciapa el camèl e la barchèta e te turnet a cà fòra di ball!*" [Take your camel and your boat and go back to where you belong, never to return!]

Kareem stammered. "You—you're making racist, insensitive—"

"I don' care what you think, Kareeeemmm!" Antonio snarled, ripping off one . . . two . . . three sheets from the towel dispenser. He wiped his hands and tossed the damp towels toward the trash bin but missed, stepping on them as he grabbed the door and flung it open.

Antonio turned, making a snarling face at Kareem, eyes narrowed. "Our family . . . Francesca's friends . . . are Italians. We're patriotic. We love our country. We don't want it to be a sewer with illiterate Africans, Polish prostitutes, Russian criminals, fanatic Muzzlims. Think about it. . . . Are you really wanted here?"

The door closed, leaving Kareem at the sink, shaken by Antonio's vicious attack. He was so stunned that he stayed in the bathroom, trembling and distraught. Should he return to Francesca's party, which was winding down on the patio? The band was playing slow music;

the laughter was muted. No, he couldn't go back and pretend nothing had happened. Kareem left the bathroom and took the elevator to their room.

Maybe Antonio had been right; he didn't belong there. Francesca's friends were cordial with him but kept their distance. They were polite because he was Francesca's boyfriend but none had become close friends.

Kareem undressed in the dark, got into bed, and tried to fall asleep. He couldn't. Sometime after two in the morning, Francesca returned to their room and turned on the light, uttering, "Hullo? Hullo? You here, Kareem?" He feigned sleep, not wanting to talk. "Oh . . . you're in bed. I couldn't find you. What happened to you?" He rustled but didn't answer, not wanting to bring up what had happened.

Francesca kicked off her shoes, unzipped her dress, and sat on the bed. She reached over and ran her fingers through his hair. "Hey, sleepy . . . you okay? What happened? I missed you."

"Something I ate," he mumbled, not wanting to tell her about the bathroom encounter with Antonio.

She went into the bathroom, undressed, and brushed her teeth. When she returned, she turned out the light and slipped naked into bed. She nestled up to him, her breasts against his back. She slipped a hand around his chest, letting her fingers stroke his stomach. "Thank you for the wonderful party, honey. I really enjoyed it. Everyone had a wonderful time," she said, planting wet kisses on his neck and ears. "Want to fool around? My little birthday present for you?" Her breath reeked of alcohol and nicotine.

"Mmm," he mumbled.

"Too tired to have fun? Ssss my birthday. We should celebrate," she whispered, nibbling on his ear.

"Tomorrow. . . . I don't feel good . . . stomach . . . something I ate." He hated to turn her away, but his anger overpowered any sexual feelings he could have called up. Francesca was puzzled. He had nibbled at his fish dinner and had drunk a small glass of wine, followed by orange juice the rest of the night. How could he be sick?

She pulled back her hand and rolled over, their naked backs together. Something happened, she thought. Kareem had been mixing with her friends earlier that night, talking and laughing like normal. Then he had gone to the bathroom and hadn't returned. What happened?

Sleeping restlessly, Francesca recalled the many times they had slept together without making love in the last few months. *What's going on with him*, she wondered. He's going to Pakistan next week but hasn't talked about it, other than wanting to visit relatives. I wish he'd talk more. Is he bored with me? His moods have changed. He's distant, quiet, rarely happy like before. He hasn't initiated sex often, maybe once or twice a month but without passion. He goes to that damned Islamic Center every Friday night instead of taking me out. Could that be it? He talks about men he's meeting, but he's secretive, like he's hiding something. Why is he pushing me away?

On the drive back to Milan the next morning, Kareem told her about the encounter with Antonio in the bathroom and the nasty things he had said.

"Oh, honey, I'm sorry," she said. "I suspected he'd do something like that when he was drunk. I've told him to leave you alone, keep his nasty remarks to himself, and not be rude. He can be so obnoxious. I hate it. Don't worry; I'll tell my parents. They're mad at him already. He's rude to everyone. Forget about it."

They drove in silence until they reached Milan's ring road. Francesca knew he would be concentrating on driving once they entered the city. She wanted to change the subject, knowing that when they were back at the apartment, he'd be on his computer until late at night while she watched TV.

"Kareem . . . what are you going to do in Pakistan?"

"You know I have relatives in Pakistan, cousins I haven't seen in six years."

Nothing more. Why so secretive? She wanted to know more, not just that he was seeing relatives. "I'd like to go there sometime. Could you take me?"

"Sure . . . sure," he said, not taking his eyes off the road. "Good idea. Next trip."

CHAPTER SEVENTEEN

Kareem first visited Pakistan with his father in 1986 when he was nine years old. His mother was not happy about him traveling to a remote, unsettled part of the world, but Hamid was insistent, telling her his son had to meet his relatives. She agreed, relieved that she and their daughters would have a respite from Hamid's strict rules and dark moods around the home.

After landing at Islamabad Airport, Kareem and his father boarded a regional bus crammed with a cross-section of Pakistan: babies and young children, middle-aged parents, old couples, cats, cages with parrots—nothing like Kareem had experienced in England. The people resembled him and his father, dark-skinned with black hair. Their heads were held high.

The bus crawled in heavy traffic through suburbs of tall apartment buildings and busy street markets. Every road was a jangle of trucks, buses, noisy motorbikes, garishly painted vans, and minibuses all dodging potholes and ruts.

Pakistan was not the paradise his father had bragged about, but a cacophony of honking horns, noxious diesel fumes, and swirls of dust and debris kicked up by vehicles. Motorbikes weaved between trucks and buses. Pedestrians walked inches from speeding vehicles along the crumbling shoulders of roads, carrying shopping bags, pushing carts, and holding children's hands.

Kareem's initial shock at this loud and raucous country turned into curiosity. He loved the excitement and chaos. It was nothing like England! The bus eventually moved into the countryside, with rural villages and small farms. The villages had one- and two-story, stone and concrete homes, weedy gardens, fields of grain, and fruit trees. Kareem stared out the window at farmers tilling fields behind yoked mules. Ditches were filled with polluted water and raw sewage. Mangy dogs and skinny cats searched for scraps of food in empty lots and along fetid canals.

By the time they arrived at his father's village of Mansehra three hours later, Kareem's curiosity had become fascination. Mansehra was waiting for them. A mob of relatives and curious neighbors cheered when they got off the bus, calling out: "Hamid, welcome home! Kareem, welcome to Mansehra!"

The mob embraced Hamid and Kareem, gave them sweets and plastic cups of tea, and led them along dusty streets to an uncle's home, a concrete hut with a wooden fence decorated with ropes of flowers and handwritten banners of greetings. Tables were set with traditional foods: chicken biryani with rice, tomatoes and peppers; plates of yogurt and vegetable salads; lentil soup; naan breads; and pretzels. There were pitchers of tea and sweet fruit drinks for the children.

Kareem's aunts and other women all wore mandarin-collared kurtas. The men and boys wore *shalwar kameez* and sandals.

Kareem was introduced to his relatives, first to uncles and aunts in their fifties and sixties, then to younger men and women, teenagers, children his age, and finally three-year-old twin girls and more than a dozen babies. He tried to count—thirty-five, maybe forty relatives—until he gave up and ran with other boys to play soccer in a dusty empty lot.

Over the next two weeks, Kareem developed friendships with three cousins close to his age: Hashid, eight; Abdul, ten; and Mohamed, twelve. They played cricket with other boys and rode bikes through the village, along river banks, and into the rocky hillsides. Every day, they walked through local markets, sampling nuts, fruits, vegetables, and sweet drinks served in plastic glasses. Kareem struggled to communicate in Pashto, picking up some of the local dialect. Everywhere he went, Kareem was showered with affection and kind words.

He joined with family members, prayed five times each day, ate simple meals in their homes, and talked late into the night.

Pakistani boys were initially shy around Kareem. He tutored them with elementary English, and they taught him slang in the local dialect. They peppered him with questions about English cricket teams, cartoons, TV shows, school, and toys. Almost everyone had relatives who had emigrated to Europe, returning for visits wearing fashionable clothes and sharing tantalizing stories of life in England, Germany, and France.

These were his father's people; now they were his.

When he returned to Reading, Kareem and his father spoke only Pashto and the local dialect, making Elsa and the girls uneasy, as they were excluded from conversations. Kareem had no brothers, just two younger sisters. Hashid, Abdul, and Mohamed were like his brothers. He hoped they could come to England one day so he could introduce them to his friends, take them to his school, go to movies, visit London, ride double-decker buses, and watch cricket on TV.

Kareem returned to Pakistan with his father when he was fourteen after the school term finished in June. He was excited to reunite with Hashid, Abdul, and Mohamed and to renew friendships with boys he had met before. As a teenager, he was beginning to like girls. He helped a few pretty Mansehra girls with their English. They coyly flirted with him and asked if he would like to have a Pakistani wife. Kareem felt loved, appreciated, and blessed. Pakistan was his second home.

During this second visit, Kareem saw more of Pakistan's tribal lands along the Afghanistan border. One of his uncles arranged excursions for him, his father, and several cousins. They all traveled in a van to the Karakoram Highway, the KKH, linking China and Pakistan; and to the Indus River, where three mountain ranges merged: the Hindu Kush, the Himalayas, and the Karakoram.

Kareem was thrilled with the natural wonders of Pakistan: eight-thousand-meter-high snowcapped mountains, glaciers in steep valleys, turbulent rivers roaring through the mountains, and treacherous roads. On one excursion, they parked on a cliff road to see centuries-old petroglyphs carved with stone tools on rock walls by invading armies, pilgrims, and traders traveling on the ancient Silk Road. The boys brushed their hands over the primitive symbols of birds with spreading wings, the sun, the moon, stars, and men with spears hunting wild animals.

When he returned to Italy, Kareem was obsessed with learning more about his father's homeland. He wrote letters to his cousins and sent them photos of his Verona friends, his school, and his mother and sisters. He devoured books about the Silk Road from the time of Alexander the Great to Mongol invasions, the Ottoman Empire, and the British Army building forts during World War II to prevent the Nazis from invading India over the Khyber Pass.

Kareem wrote school reports about Pakistan's history, from Marco Polo to the wars in Kashmir with India after the British granted independence to India in 1947. He impressed his classmates and history professor, who listened in rapture to his stories. Kareem used tools from art class to draw a colored map of the tribal areas where his relatives lived: Bajaur, Mohand, Khyber, Orakzai, Kurran, North Waziristan, South Waziristan, and the six frontier regions of Peshawar, Kohat, Bannu, Lakki Marwat, Tank, and Dera Ismail Khan. He daydreamed about the tribal lands, fantasizing what it would have been like to grow up there and know all the customs, traditions, and legends. Although he lived in Italy and had spent his childhood in England, Kareem felt his soul was Pakistani.

When Kareem had traveled to Pakistan as a boy, he'd cared only about playing with his cousins and their friends, learning local customs, and exploring the borderlands between Pakistan and Afghanistan. In his late teens and early twenties, Kareem devoured books about Pakistan's contemporary politics, the turbulent history of the wars with India over Kashmir, and the Federally Administered Tribal Lands, or FATA, where his relatives lived.

Even as a boy, Kareem had witnessed the Pakistani Army providing police services along the border, which was notorious for lawlessness, violence, tribal hostilities, and danger. Opium was the largest crop in the

FATA, grown in remote mountain valleys and smuggled into Europe. The dangers were exciting for a young boy.

Kareem made a third trip to Pakistan in 2004. Carefull Services's HR office had told him that he had accumulated too many holidays and it was time to take a long leave. He booked the plane tickets to stay in Pakistan for over a month. He packed light—one set of Italian clothes and shoes—planning to buy traditional clothes as soon as he arrived. When he left the airport, he was dressed like a Pakistani, wearing *shalwar kameez*, sandals, and a black cap. He had grown a beard, and he melded in on the street like a native Pakistani.

Kareem's cousins were now married and working. Hashid was a regional bus driver. Kareem rode with him as Hashid picked up riders at dusty bus stops and dropped them off in villages or along the roads among weedy pastures, simple huts, and grazing cattle and goats. He spent a day with Mohamed, who was now a laborer at an apartment construction site where workers scaled bamboo scaffolding and hoisted pails of cement and stone. Kareem joined Abdul, who was teaching Muslim boys at a madrasa Islamic school about the Quran, sharia law, and strict adherence to the Hadith, the homilies of Muhammad.

But in 2004, Northwest Pakistan was a war zone. The United States and its allies had invaded Afghanistan in October 2001 to hunt down Osama bin Laden and al Qaeda terrorists after September 11, 2001. American bombers, fighter aircraft, and cruise missiles were bombing al Qaeda camps in North and South Waziristan, across the border from Pakistan. Taliban forces were recruiting young men from madrasas to fight American forces and their allies. Abdul, Mohamed, and Hamid talked about the dangers of living in the tribal areas. They sympathized with the Taliban ideology, wanting to rid Afghanistan of foreign infidels and restore Taliban rule in Kabul. They all said they would join the Taliban one day.

A jarring memory for Kareem was seeing women in Pakistan's tribal areas wearing head-to-toe burkas, not the head-covering hijab scarves they had worn before. Everything had changed.

Kareem was disturbed about how war had disrupted the lives of his relatives. After he returned to Milan, he searched for news on Islamic websites about the lingering wars in Iraq and Afghanistan. Letters and e-mails from his cousins alarmed him, hinting in vague terms that they were being recruited by the Taliban. Hashid didn't own a computer but wrote occasional short letters. Abdul had a cell phone but didn't use e-mail. Mohamed e-mailed that his madrasa had sent young men to Taliban training camps in the mountains.

Kareem responded, asking for more information. It was weeks before Mohamed replied tersely, ignoring his queries. Then e-mails to Mohamed were kicked back by the server with the message "Service suspended." Hashid wrote a postcard with one sentence: "They have gone to the mountains."

Kareem attempted to find out more from his father, but Hamid knew nothing. He was only in touch with an eighty-six-year-old aunt who was terminally ill in a hospital. Uncles and aunts Kareem had met as a boy were all dead. He had lost contact with other cousins and friends he had met. Only Hashid remained in Mansehra.

Late at night, after Francesca was asleep, Kareem watched YouTube videos of Anwar al-Awlaki, the American-born imam preaching about jihad against America and its allies. Kareem had viewed Sheikh Anwar's DVDs of the life of Prophet Muhammad, learning more about the Islamic faith than he had at mosques.

Kareem was stunned in October 2011 when Italian newspapers reported that American drones had bombed a convoy carrying al-Awlaki in Yemen. Two weeks later, an American drone killed al-Awlaki's American-born, sixteen-year-old son. Americans were killing their own citizens in foreign countries because they were Muslims. This was a religious war.

Kareem returned to Mansehra in 2012. Hashid was his only living cousin. Abdul had been killed by an American drone in March. Mohamed had died in a battle with American special forces in 2011 at a remote outpost in South Waziristan.

Kareem met Abdul's widow and two sons, ages six and eight. Abdul's oldest son told Kareem, "I can't wait to be fourteen so I can join the Taliban, fight Americans, and bring sharia law to Pakistan."

Abdul's wife shook her head and said in tears, "I lost my husband . . . I don't want to lose my sons, too."

Mohamed's widow was raising their five-year-old son at the home of her parents. Kareem was allowed to see her only if her father was in the room. She wore a burka, allowing Kareem to see only her dark eyes through a narrow slit between her forehead and nose. She spoke guardedly, nervously eyeing her father across the room, and answered Kareem's questions with simple, vague replies. Kareem left after ten minutes.

After a week, Kareem went to an al Qaeda safe house in Mansehra. The address and instructions had been given to him at the Islamic Cultural Center in Milan. He introduced himself with a code name and a quote from the Quran to two men wearing prayer caps and long tunics. They checked his passports, verified his contacts from the ICC, and instructed him to take a bus the next morning to a mountain village near the Afghan border.

The bus ride took three hours over a dirt road that ran through a valley. The last hour was spent climbing up a switchback road to the village. When he got off the bus, Kareem was greeted by three men in long beards wearing robes, turbans, and dusty sandals. The men questioned him by asking him to recite passages from the Quran to verify his identity.

When they were satisfied with his answers, they escorted him to a stone building outside of the village. They were greeted by an older man who invited Kareem to come into the building, sit on a rug, and sip tea under the watchful eyes of the three men who had escorted him there. The older man questioned Kareem about his reasons for coming to the village as well as his personal, political, and religious beliefs. He also asked Kareem if he had ever been in trouble with the police. One man scribbled notes of Kareem's answers, staring at him with a look that made Kareem anxious and afraid. Kareem knew that what he was doing was dangerous, but he didn't want to return to Mansehra. This was a mission he wanted to pursue.

He spent the night on a cot in a small stone building after being served a meal of rice, boiled vegetables, and tea. The next morning, he was awakened by one of the men, who drove Kareem on the back of his motorbike higher into the mountains. After an hour-long bumpy ride along a dirt trail that wound through narrow valleys of dried river beds, Kareem was stiff and sore when they arrived at a concrete hut across the Afghanistan border.

They were met by two bearded men wearing long robes, turbans, and dusty worn boots. They led him into the hut, sat on a dirt floor, and drank tea from a metal pot over a stone fireplace. They also questioned Kareem about his background and asked for code names, passwords, and passages from the Quran. When they were finished with the interrogation, they invited Kareem to go outside to kneel on prayer rugs and bow toward Mecca for *isha,* the evening prayer.

The next day, Kareem filled out a questionnaire about his career, friends, education, and skills, as well as his contacts in Milan who had provided him with the code names and addresses in Pakistan. He handed over his passports. One of the men took them, along with the questionnaire, and left the village.

Kareem spent three days walking along mountain trails, admiring the raw beauty of the snowcapped peaks of the Karakoram mountains. The altitude was greater than he was used to, and he had to stop several times to sit on a rock and catch his breath. One of the men walked with him, asking about Italy, his life, his friends, his faith. The man had never lived outside Afghanistan and expressed a desire to travel but had no money. He did odd jobs in construction, acted as a courier, repaired motorbikes, and herded goats.

The man who had taken Kareem's passports and questionnaire returned after three days. That night, three men put Kareem in a truck and drove after dark with headlights hooded to avoid being spotted by airplanes or drones. The journey took three hours, ending at midnight among circles of tents in front of a cave. A campfire inside the cave revealed men in dark robes holding automatic weapons. One man left the cave, approached Kareem, and spoke a dialect he didn't understand. He flashed a light in Kareem's eyes, asked through an interpreter for his identification papers, peppered him with questions to verify his identity, and asked him about passages from the Quran. When the man was satisfied with his responses, two armed men led Kareem to a tent where six men sat on a rug on a dirt floor. They greeted him like a lost brother, praising him for his courage to join other recruits at the al Qaeda terrorist training camp.

Kareem spent three weeks in different camps, transported by trucks at night with armed guards. When they arrived at a camp, they were secluded in tents with other recruits inside a walled compound with guards armed with automatic weapons, pistols, and curved daggers. Recruits were given aliases to use in the camp and warned not to reveal their real names or home countries. Kareem's jihad name became Barraba.

During the first week, instructors trained recruits in using automatic weapons, grenades, and knives. The next week, they were taught codes and learned about conducting counterintelligence, surveilling targets, and recruiting other Muslims to join their cells. They were warned that, once they returned home, they were to avoid attracting the attention of the police. In addition, they were not to use cell phones to pass messages or talk with other members of their cells. They were told to avoid mosques or places where Muslims gathered, to not dress like a Muslim, and to have a cover story if interrogated or tortured.

During the third week, Kareem was driven at night to a valley where caves had been dug into steep mountains. When they arrived, Kareem was led by hand to a tunnel and put in a room with a dirt floor and walls. He was scared; he could hear men talking in the dark about warplanes bombing villages and drones killing innocent people. In the morning, a man took him to a tent where recruits were having morning tea, fruit, rice, and naan bread.

After morning prayers, the recruits were escorted through a tunnel that led to a hotel, a mosque, a clinic, a radio station, a kitchen, a gas generator, and rooms with automatic weapons, ammunition, and wooden boxes. The recruits were led outside for a training session of shooting automatic weapons at targets of American soldiers. The training was conducted under a camouflage tarp stretched over a compound of cement huts, tents, open fields, and a parking lot with trucks.

The first morning on the target range, they heard a plane fly overhead. Everyone froze, fell to the ground, and covered their heads. Voices shouted, "A bomber! . . . No, a jet! . . . It's a drone! . . . No, a bomber . . . drones are quiet . . . bombers are loud!" They remained on the ground until the sound of the plane diminished, flying over a mountain range into the next valley. Then they heard bombs falling, explosions, machine-gun fire. It was an hour before Kareem and the other recruits were told to continue training. They rose, dusted off their robes, and continued shooting at targets.

That night, the recruits stood at the mouth of the cave, staring at the stars and a crescent moon, speaking native languages, smoking, and drinking green tea. They scaled down from the cave in almost total darkness, holding onto a rope mounted on stakes that led to the entrance of the tunnel. The only light came from the stars and moon.

The next morning, Kareem was escorted by an armed guard through the tunnel and under the camouflage tent to a cement building. Three other recruits were waiting: a Libyan, an Egyptian, and a Syrian. Speaking Arabic, Urdu, and Pashto, they exchanged greetings and said they were members of rebel groups opposed to their governments and were training to learn about using explosives and chemical weapons.

There were two rooms in the cement building, the smaller one with sinks, tables, and cabinets containing plastic bottles, metal canisters, filters, plastic pipes, tubing, and measuring instruments.

The larger room was for instruction. A half-dozen wooden chairs surrounded a table near a crude chalkboard. On the table were notebooks for making, transporting, and igniting explosives, along with well-worn university chemistry textbooks in English, Arabic, and Pashto. Scribbled on the chalkboard were formulas, calculations, and diagrams.

Walls in both rooms were plastered with posters of Osama bin Laden, Anwar al-Awlaki, the Abu Ghraib prison in Iraq, Muslim prisoners in Guantanamo Bay, banners with quotations from the Quran, photos of bomb-damaged subway cars in the London metro, twisted wreckage of trains in Madrid, and hijacked commercial jets crashing into the Twin Towers in Manhattan.

One of Kareem's instructors had trained with Abu Musab al-Zarqawi and Abu Khabab at the Darunta training camp near Jalalabad, which specialized in chemical and biological weapons.

Kareem lived for a week in the village under the camouflage roof. He made a few friends there but didn't know their real names. One had been in training with him at the firing range where they used automatic weapons and grenade launchers against targets of American and British soldiers. He was from Amsterdam, his nom de guerre was Suliman.

CHAPTER EIGHTEEN

Kareem was disappointed but not surprised when Francesca was not at Malpensa airport to meet him when he returned from Pakistan. She had promised she would be there, but doubts had surfaced when she hadn't returned his texts from Mansehra. Or from the Peshawar airport before he boarded his return flight. Or from Istanbul on a layover.

When he returned alone to his apartment, he discovered that Francesca had removed her clothes, shoes, toiletries, cosmetics, and laptop computer. A note on the dining room table read: *Dear Kareem, I moved in with a girlfriend. Please don't call or look for me. I'll call you when I feel ready to see you. Love, Francesca.*

Kareem was troubled; the woman he expected to marry was out of his life. Repeated phone calls went to her voice mail. Text messages went unanswered. He didn't know where she was living. Her beauty parlor supervisor told him she had quit and no one knew where she was working.

He even tried Francesca's parents' landline number, but her mother, who always had seemed to be the friendliest of the family with him, answered angrily: "Finally she has dumped you. I will never tell you where she's gone. Forget about her and don't call anymore!"

It was a month before Francesca called Kareem. She apologized for not returning his calls, claiming she had been ill. She asked to meet at an outdoor bar in Parco Solari the next Saturday. He agreed, and the call ended. It lasted less than two minutes.

That Saturday, he walked to the bar, hands sweating, exhausted after a night of little sleep. His heart skipped when he saw her seated at an outdoor table sipping coffee.

She looked up when he stood by her table. They exchanged cheek kisses, and she asked if he would like coffee. He caught the attention of a waiter and ordered. They stumbled through uncomfortable small talk about work and the weather. Then Francesca said, "You look like a skeleton, Kareem. You lost weight in Pakistan?"

He patted his flat stomach. "I caught a bug there, but I'm fine now, eating pasta and bread every day. I missed Italian food."

"I've heard that from people who travel," she said. "But I wouldn't know. I would never leave Italy to go to such a dirty and poor country. Let's walk in the park."

An order, not a request.

They finished their coffees and crossed the street into the park, neither one speaking. Their initial conversation had been brief but polite. Kareem had a flicker of hope that they could have a pleasant talk and get back together. Francesca snuffed out that flicker immediately. "I'm sorry, Kareem, but we can't be together anymore."

"Because I went to Pakistan?" he said, his voice trembling.

They continued walking. She kept her arms folded across her chest so he couldn't hold her hand. "Something isn't right, Kareem. You've changed. . . . You're not the man I fell in love with."

"I'm the same as when you met me," he protested, sensing the futility. "I have the same job, I live in the same apartment, I still love you—"

She cut him off. "I don't know, Kareem. You say you do. I'm sorry. . . . I don't know what else to say. You've changed. . . . It started months ago. I thought it was because you were working long hours and getting home late. I tried to talk to you, but you wouldn't listen, said it was nothing. Something was going on. You were shutting me out."

"But maybe . . . in time," he pleaded, "you can like who I am now."

She shook her head. Even the way he was acting was not like the old, carefree Kareem. He was a stranger, like he had been over the last few months. "No . . . I can't. I'm sorry. We have to stop seeing each other."

They sat on a park bench. He reached for her hand and looked into her eyes, hoping to see something that would give him hope.

She pulled her hand away and stood up. "I have to go, Kareem. Please don't call. . . . I need to be alone for a while." She reached into her jeans pocket, took out his apartment key, and placed it on the bench gently, as if it were a bird's egg. She waved her fingers like a child leaving a parent and walked off, crossing the playground, disappearing behind a hedge.

Kareem was stunned; he had hoped they would reconcile. But Francesca had brushed him out of her life with the indifference of a passenger exiting a taxi. He stared at boys playing soccer on the grass, mothers chatting on park benches, children biking on a path. He no longer felt a part of this life.

Francesca was right. He had changed. He had been distant. For months before he'd left for Pakistan, he'd been meeting Muslim immigrants at backstreet cafés, where they talked in low voices so no one could overhear their conversations. It was too dangerous to meet at mosques; undercover police were lurking in alleys, following men after Friday services, tapping cell phones, and questioning neighbors.

With Francesca out of his life, Kareem spent evenings surfing websites of fundamentalist imams preaching from Pakistan. He lurked in chat rooms of Muslim refugees in North Africa and the Middle East.

He rearranged the room where Francesca had kept her magazines, workout clothes, and computer. He moved articles he'd kept in closets into the room. On the walls, he tacked maps of Pakistan and the tribal lands; photos from visits to Mansehra and Khyber Pakhtunkhwa; photos of Hashid, Abdul, and Mohamed dressed in traditional *shalwar kameez*; and women in mandarin-collared kurtas.

In the only picture from his latest trip, he was dressed in traditional clothing, wearing a white skullcap, a long white robe, and a full beard, standing with Abdul's wife and her two sons, who wanted to join the Taliban. That photo was taken the day before he took the bus ride that led to his three weeks in the training camps.

CHAPTER NINETEEN

K areem returned from Pakistan determined to fulfill a commitment
made at the terrorist camp. He had gone through a conversion
in the past year—a religious conversion that conflicted with his past life
of living in an elegant apartment with a prestigious job, a good salary,
and an Italian woman he'd thought he would marry.

He had sensed his relationship with Francesca was over when she
hadn't met him at the airport and had moved out of his apartment. Her
treatment when they'd met for coffee had been rude and offensive, most
likely influenced by her ignorant father and racist brother.

Kareem felt isolated after he returned from Pakistan. People he loved
and admired were out of his life; cousins Abdul and Mohamed, killed
in Afghanistan. And now Francesca. He went through the motions at
work, showing up on time and managing his projects but avoiding conversations with colleagues except about work responsibilities. In time,
his colleagues recognized his desire to be private.

Over the winter, his isolation increased. He spent lonely nights in
his apartment, his rage growing about the wars in Afghanistan and
Iraq and his cousins dying in battles with American and allied forces.
He read the Quran daily. At night, he watched Al Jazeera news about
drone attacks and suicide bombings, scanned Islamic websites and read
sermons by radical imams.

His phone calls to his father were brief, superficial, and difficult. Hamid invited him to Reading, but Kareem was evasive, telling him he was busy at work but might be able to come in the spring.

His calls to his mother were rare and tense. She was angry that he had traveled to Pakistan and that he had not visited her or his sisters in two years. Elsa bragged about her grandchildren and asked when Kareem was going to get married and have babies. She assumed he was still living with Francesca, and he didn't tell her their relationship had died. Elsa invited him and Francesca to Verona for the baptism of his sister Amira's twin five-year-old boys in June. Kareem listened in silence as Elsa pressured him to attend and insisted, "You're coming, right?" He hung up without saying goodbye.

He was sick over the winter, with colds, flu, indigestion, and severe headaches. He lost weight, missed a few days of work, stayed home, and read the Quran and Hadith, the Prophet's exhortations that Muslims must fight all enemies of Islam and live in an Islamic state with strict laws forbidding other religions. He became more convinced that his duty was to become an Islam warrior, first in Italy and later in Pakistan.

He relived his training at the terrorist camp and the weapons he had used: automatic rifles, pistols, and grenades. He recalled making small bombs with household chemicals. Recipes for making bombs were all over websites. He studied them, knowing he could make a chemical bomb. But that would be an isolated act, one of desperation. He wanted a bigger challenge. He wanted to make a chemical weapon that would express his outrage about the continuing wars in the Middle East and his anger at the Western world, including Italy. After all, he had made a commitment to carry out a terrorist act, backed by swearing an oath from the Quran.

In a private chatroom on a website dedicated to jihad, he met a man who said he lived in northern Italy. Kareem took it as a sign that the Prophet was going to guide him to fulfill his plan. The man, who called himself Mimmo, said they should meet secretly. On a cold, rainy night, they did so, at a service station on the road between Parma and La Spezia. They greeted each other in Urdu and went to Kareem's car to talk. Kareem listened while Mimmo recited passages from the Quran that were commonly used in the terrorist camps about the urgency to wage jihad. Mimmo had fought in Iraq and said his contacts in Pakistan were shipping weapons, money, and material to Europe. Kareem felt Mimmo was a messenger from the Prophet and pledged to follow his instructions. Mimmo gave him a stolen cell phone with a Swiss SIM card and said he would pass messages to him about "special materials" that would be delivered to Milan.

When they departed, they shook hands and exchanged salaam.

"Assalamu Alaikum Warahmatullahi Wabarakatuh."

"Peace, mercy, and blessings of Allah descend upon you."

Kareem returned to Milan, convinced that he would organize a terrorist attack with Mimmo's guidance. He was convinced Mimmo had the connections to provide money and support, the kind of support to commit a terrorist attack. Mimmo stressed he could arrange it all. Kareem needed two or three other men to join him, all fanatics who would swear to secrecy in the name of the Prophet.

Kareem's first recruit was his oldest friend in Milan, Tariq "Tito" Gajani, whom he had met at the Politecnico. Tito was wiry-thin with intense dark eyes and long hair combed over his head like a lion's mane. Tito had invited Kareem to his home in Desio for dinner, to watch football matches, and to celebrate *Eid al-Fitr* at the end of Ramadan. Kareem felt like a member of Tito's family. Tito also introduced Kareem to Pakistani immigrants who worked as truck drivers, warehouse workers, department store clerks, and carpenters.

Kareem trusted Tito. He shared about his breakup with Francesca and his experiences at the terrorist training camp. Tito asked many questions, vicariously reliving the experience with Kareem.

"Kareem," he told him, "I knew you would become a jihadist when you went to Pakistan. I'm happy that you finally see that Francesca is nothing but a stupid cow. You would have been miserable if she had pressured you into marrying her. Even the thought that that prick Antonio could have been a brother-in-law would have turned me into a terrorist!"

Tito laughed and slapped Kareem on the back. "Yes, I'll join you, brother. Anything so I don't have to spend the rest of my life making kebab sandwiches for my father. Let's do this, and then take me to Pakistan. I'm fed up with Italy."

Tito had shared with Kareem the frustrations of working at his father's kebab and pizza café in a Milan suburb since he was twelve years old. Tito had worked nights while he was pursing his architect degree at the Politecnico, but he'd had to drop out when his parents couldn't continue paying for his studies. He resented that his family was poor and that he had to work twelve hours a day in a menial, dead-end job.

Since Tito had arrived in Italy as a preteen, his school career had always been promising. He'd had excellent grades, but his Italian classmates had isolated him and other foreign kids. His anger had grown even more when he was eighteen and discovered that, having lived there most of his life, he could not obtain Italian citizenship because his parents hadn't been born in Italy. His radicalization started when he had to leave university and work full-time without any other chance to improve his life. He needed something to believe in that would give him hope and a future. That hope was in Islam.

Tito suggested a third member, Kalil Khan, who had lived in Desio as an Egyptian refugee until he received a residency permit. Kalil was thirty-three years old and stocky, with thick glasses. He walked with a limp from injuries when he was tortured as a political prisoner during the Mubarak regime. Prison guards had beat him with clubs and poked his genitals with electrical prods. He had become impotent, a condition that frustrated and angered him. Kalil was nervous and clumsy around women, fearing they would learn about his condition.

After Kalil was released from prison, he fled to Libya, where he paid three thousand dollars to board a rickety boat with desperate African refugees seeking new lives in Italy. When the boat capsized off Lampedusa Island, Kalil was one of a handful of refugees rescued by the Italian Coast Guard. Eighty-four others perished in the frigid waters.

Kalil spent six months in a refugee camp in Sicily and then made his way north on buses and by hitchhiking until he reached Desio, where an uncle lived. His uncle was a bitter, paranoid man who told him lurid tales about sexually promiscuous Italian girls. He pressured him to avoid sex, since his reward would be virgins in the afterlife if he sacrificed his earthly life for Islam. Kalil was too embarrassed to tell his uncle he was impotent, fearing he would mock him. His uncle urged him to read the

Quran daily, eat only halal, and take lessons from a radical imam at the mosque. The imam preached verses exhorting the slaying of nonbelievers, beheading, lashing, amputation, and slavery. A true believer's rewards would be delivered in Paradise with eternal life and the joys of sex with seventy-two virgins waiting to fulfill his erotic desires.

When Kalil received his residency permit, he found a job as a dishwasher in a Lebanese restaurant near Stazione Centrale. He left Desio and moved into a grimy apartment in a run-down, public housing building in Milan at the end of Via Giambellino with other African refugees, an experience that made him even more frustrated and angry. He was arrested for harassing a woman jogging in Parco delle Cave and given four months of house arrest. After serving his sentence, he received an expulsion order but was saved by an Egyptian entrepreneur who owned a company cleaning sewage tanks in Rho, an industrial park north of Milan.

Kareem's third recruit was Esman Bilal, thirty-four, a Syrian chemist and former officer in the Syrian military unit developing chemical weapons. After the Syrian civil war broke out, Esman was fired for questioning the brutality of the Assad government, and he joined the resistance.

Esman's parents, wife, and son were killed when their Homs apartment was bombed while Esman was fighting with rebels on a Damascus barricade. Esman escaped across the Turkish border and hitched rides on trucks and freight trains through Bulgaria, Macedonia, and Slovenia until he crossed the border at Trieste.

He arrived in Milan with eighteen euros in his pocket and lived in a dark, musty basement of a Muslim he met on a bus. After he got his first job, he moved to a cramped apartment with five Muslim refugees. When he received his residency permit, he was hired at Amsa to ride on garbage trucks, dumping trash, recycled paper and bottles into compactors. He was frustrated with what fate had dealt him; he was a university-educated chemist forced to work on a garbage truck from 5 AM to 3 PM six days a week.

When Kareem brought them all together one night at his apartment, he insisted they agree to strict conditions to maintain secrecy. "We must never contact each other on our cell phones. Leave them at home when we meet. The police track SIM cards on cell phone towers even if you don't make calls. That's why I told you to leave them at home tonight."

The others nodded.

"Never discuss anything we talk about outside of this group. Not with friends or with people you work with . . . even if they are Muslims and you suspect they support jihad."

He looked at Kalil. "Kalil, I know you had a problem with police once. Never . . . ever . . . get involved in anything—a dispute on a bus or at work, a traffic accident, shoplifting, a fight in a café where police might show up. Leave immediately. Never trust police. Stay out of trouble."

Kalil nodded. "I despise police. I always have. I hate to see them even writing a traffic ticket or riding in a car. They're evil and cruel. They beat Muslim immigrants just for the fun of it. I stay as far from them as I can."

"Just be very careful. Your temper can get you in trouble. Don't take any risks."

"I promise. I swear an oath on the Quran."

"Good. Meet your friends in apartments, not in public. The police might be watching. Trust no one. Police have informers everywhere." He instructed them how to exchange messages on a Gmail e-mail account he had opened. He gave them the password and said they could leave messages by writing a draft but never sending the e-mail. They could read the draft e-mails, which could never be traced.

"We need another way to communicate without being detected by police." Kareem pulled a shoe box out of a cloth bag, opened it, and handed each of them a phone.

"We communicate on stolen phones Tito bought in Desio from a gang of thieves." From the shoe box he took out slips of paper, handing one to each of them. "Here is a list of cell phone numbers. Open the phone when you get home tonight. Put in the phone numbers along with numbers 1 through 4. I am number 1, Tito is 2, Kalil is 3, and Esman is 4. Never use names on calls, only numbers."

They pressed buttons to turn on the phones. None of them worked.

"Your phones need to be charged. I didn't want their SIM cards tracked here. Use them only in your apartments, not on the street where you could be tracked. I will call once a month to confirm our meetings.

After our call, turn off the phone and take out the battery. At our meetings, I'll tell you the next time I'll call. Keep batteries out of the phones until the day when I'll call. Understand?"

"I think so," Kalil said. "We only turn them on the day you tell us you'll call."

"Yes. We can't meet at my apartment. Video cameras are everywhere, and my neighbors would get suspicious if you came here often. Most of them are old people or young parents with children. Instead, we'll meet Thursday evenings at Tito's father's kebab café near Turro metro station. The café has a private office where our conversations won't be overheard or recorded."

"We'll buy everyone a meal, a drink, and a sweet," Tito said. "My father doesn't care. All he wants me to do is work."

"Where's the café?" asked Esman.

"You know Via Padova?"

Kalil and Esman shook their heads.

"Take a bus to the M1 Metropolitana Red Line," said Tito. "Travel north, get off at Turro, and walk to Via Padova. It's a typical Milan neighborhood—apartments and offices with retail shops and cafés on the ground level. When you reach Via Padova, you'll see a *tabaccheria* on the corner. It's always busy with people buying bus passes, cigarettes, SuperEnalotto, and instant lottery tickets."

"I don't know the areas on the north," Esman said. "I haul garbage from Porta Romana south to Corvetto."

"One block from the *tabaccheria* is our café, the Pizzeria Kebab Mingora, between a barbershop and a children's shoe store. People from our neighborhood come to the café, mostly Filipino teenagers, Pakistani boys, Bangladeshis. My father and I work behind the counter; my brother makes pizzas in the back. Just the three of us. We're there every day. I hate it. It's boring, same thing every day. I'd do anything to get out of there."

That summer, Kareem, Esman, and Kalil met at Tito's father's kebab café as the evening sun was settling behind apartment buildings. They greeted each other with handshakes, saying "Assalamu Alaikum" [Peace be unto you]. They waved at Tito and his father behind the refrigerated counter filled with salads, garbanzo and pinto beans, bowls of couscous, creamy hummus, tabouli, hard cheeses, artisan salamis, marinated olives, and goat cheese in a milky brine.

Tito's younger brother, Farooq, toiled in the cramped kitchen, sprinkling slices of pepperoni, sausages, green peppers, olives, sun-dried tomatoes, and basil on pizza dough, and then shoveling trays on wooden platters into an open-flame oven to let the pizzas bake.

When the group arrived, they ordered iced teas and diet sodas and retreated to a corner table to watch the soccer match on a wall-mounted TV. It was noisy in the low-ceilinged cafe, with customers speaking Pashto, Arabic, and Spanish; Italian pop tunes streaming from the kitchen radio; the clatter and clang of kitchen ware; and boys sipping sugary sodas while cheering the soccer match.

Posters of Pakistan were pinned on the plaster walls, along with a handmade rug in faded green and gold; calendars with photos of snow-capped Himalayas; posters of snow leopards, blue sheep, and Tibetan wolves; and ads for flights to Pakistan and international cell phone service.

"How's work going, Esman?" Kareem asked. "Did you get that promotion?"

"Finally, I get to drive a truck as soon as I get my license and pass the safety exam. I earned a chemistry degree at university when I was twenty-five and was an officer in the Syrian army. I'll reach a new high in my career by getting a commercial truck license. Driving garbage trucks. Pitiful. Life can be cruel." He shook his head in disgust.

"It is, brother. It is," Kareem said. "Life has been strange for all of us. Don't worry. You'll pass your test and get a raise."

Esman recoiled. "Not from my boss. He's a tight bastard and a racist. Been in the same job for thirty years, warming his fat ass in a comfortable chair in his office. Filthy dog. He'd be the first I'd kill if I could."

The others looked at him with sympathy.

"Kalil, what happened to your hand?" Kareem asked.

Kalil cursed, holding up a hand with a cloth bandage attached with clips. "Bad day. I stuck my hand between a container and a hoist and almost crushed it." His hands and arms showed the damage of working in dangerous surroundings: scars, scratches, bruised knuckles, fingernails blackened with dirt and grease. "You can get killed working around sewage tanks."

"I know how hard you work, Kalil. I'm sorry. Maybe you can get an office job one day."

"Aaach," he growled. "Impossible. Only Italians get the easy jobs. The rest of us don't stand a chance. The system is rigged against immigrants."

Kalil's sour attitude squashed the conversation for a few moments.

Kareem glanced up at Tito and his father preparing kebabs: sliced slabs of roasting lamb and beef spiced with onion, lemongrass, and mint. They stuffed them in pita bread sleeves wrapped in a thin foil, spooning in lettuce and sour yogurt.

Tito nodded at them and lined up plastic baskets on the counter with their sandwiches. Kareem, Kalil, and Esman went to the counter to pick up their meals, returned to their table, and ate without talking. When they finished, they dumped their refuse in a trash bin and slipped through a glass-bead curtain into a hallway with four closed doors: a bathroom, a storage closet, the kitchen, and a locked door marked *Private*.

Tito came around the counter, wiping his hands on his apron, and met them. He unlocked the door marked *Private*. They followed him into a windowless room. Tito's brother was in there on a break, munching a slice of pizza, sipping lemon soda, and watching a Pakistani website on an old HP desktop computer.

"Farooq, back to the kitchen," Tito said, waving his hand. "We need the place." Farooq stuffed the last slice of pizza into his mouth, grabbed his soda can, and left. Tito lingered in the hallway to check that no one was watching. He shut the door, turned the lock, and turned off the computer. Above the desk, a Pakistani flag was pinned on the wall between photos of mosques in Islamabad, Mecca during the Hajj, and banners in Urdu extolling the virtues of Islam.

The group pushed the clutter of Pakistani magazines and Italian sports newspapers to the side. They emptied an ashtray and put soda cans, paper cups of tea and coffee, and plastic forks and spoons into a waste can. Tito moved a cardboard box stuffed with bills, ledgers, receipts, and invoices off a chair and set it on the floor.

Kareem didn't waste time. "Bad news. The last shipment from Karachi was intercepted by the police."

"No! What happened?" Kalil said. "Who messed up?"

Kareem held up his hand. "Not so fast. I'll tell you. Last month, a shipment arrived in La Spezia: two million euros, weapons, and the final shipment of chemicals."

"Damn!" Tito swore.

"What about the guns? And the money?" Kalil asked. "We need them. How do you know the police stopped them?"

"I got a call from La Spezia from our sponsor."

"Who is he?" Esman asked.

Kareem shook his head. "It doesn't matter. He uses a code name. He keeps me informed of shipments. I don't ask questions; I only listen to his messages. His spies at the port watched police inspect the container, remove our shipment, and take it away in a van."

"How did they find out?" Kalil asked.

"We don't know. The other shipments went through without being inspected. This was our last before we execute our plan."

Tito asked, "Do the police know about us? Are we going to be arrested?"

"I doubt it. No way they could," Kareem said. "They intercepted a shipment with a phony manifest, a bogus phone number and name. We're invisible. Let's keep it that way. Stay away from people you don't know. Never discuss anything we talk about."

A rowdy cheer and applause erupted from the café, penetrating the thin plaster walls like gunshots. Kalil flinched. Whoops and hollers, more applause.

"A.C. Milan scored a goal," Tito said with a grin. "I wish I could see it. I was watching the match."

"No more distractions, please," Kareem cautioned.

Esman raised a finger and spoke. "Kareem is right. Listen to him. This is serious business, deadly serious. Soccer's a stupid game, like a religion worshipped by Italian infidels."

"Thank you, Esman. You understand how important our plan is. It's unfortunate the shipment was inspected, but we won't let that stop us. We will still go ahead with our plan. Agreed?"

Kalil raised his bandaged fist. "Yes!" The others nodded.

"I didn't go to the warehouse after our brother called to warn me," Kareem continued. "Police would be waiting. They would ask questions, take me to the station, and get my fingerprints and cell phone. I'd end up in their database as another Muslim with suspicious activities. If my boss found out, I'd be fired."

The air was stuffy and warm, reeking with the odor of pizza, stale cigarette smoke, and neglect. Tito turned on the desk fan, which stirred warm, humid air around the room. Kalil wiped sweat from his brow and brushed it onto his pants.

A police siren shrieked, a high-pitched wheeooo . . . wheeeoo . . . wheeeooo, shearing through the thin walls as if the police car was in the hallway.

They all held their breath, eyes wide, looking around at each other. Kalil jumped, his leg pushing magazines and newspapers across the floor. "Damn police!" he swore.

After a few tense moments, the siren faded into an eerie whine that eventually stopped, leaving the room in temporary silence. "Cops! I hate them," Kalil said. "They scare me. Wherever you go, police are there."

Tito said, "Someone ran a red light . . . made an illegal turn. Don't get upset."

Kalil squirmed in his chair and wiped more sweat off his brow. "That fan's worthless. Can we open the door? We need fresh air."

"Stop it, Kalil!" Esman said, pointing at him. "Let Kareem talk! I didn't come here to listen to you bitch."

"Let's settle down. Nothing to worry about," Kareem said to calm the nerves in the room. "I hate to waste time."

He put a hand on Kalil's shoulder. "I want to tell you about the plan Esman and I are working on. You know he was a chemist in Syria. The army taught him how to blend chemicals into sarin gas. We did a small test at a lab at the Bovisa campus last week. We wore masks, took safety procedures, mixed the chemicals in a covered beaker, and released the vapor through a tube into a ceiling ventilator."

"Sarin dissipates quickly in open air," Esman said. "After our test, we went outside and saw the vapor spread and blow into the trees."

"Wasn't that dangerous? Someone could have seen you," Tito said.

Kareem shook his head. "We knew when the guards make their rounds and check the doors. They don't bother the scientists and students working at night. Don't worry. No birds died; none of them fell to the ground. In a couple of minutes, the gas was diluted by air."

"I'm scared of gas," Kalil said with a snarl. "They used it in prison. I could smell it. I don't want to be near any gas."

"Don't worry. You won't have to," Kareem said. "Esman and I will handle the chemicals. We'll mix them, set a timer so we can escape before alarms go off. You will be in a vehicle not far away and drive us out of Milan."

"What is our target?" Tito asked. "Is it one of the buildings where you work? The stock exchange, Palazzo Mezzanotte? Linate Airport? Teatro alla Scala?"

Kareem shook his head. "I rather not say yet. I'm checking out several places where Esman and I can get in, set up the chemicals, and leave without suspicion."

"Okay," Kalil said, nodding his head. "You're good at planning. We don't need to know now."

Tito looked at his watch. "I have to get back to work." He reached for a pouch of tobacco and rolling papers and rolled a cigarette but held back from lighting it.

"But how do you know we can get away?" Kalil asked.

"They taught us evasion and escape networks in Afghanistan," said Kareem. "There are brothers in Italy and Eastern Europe who will hide us, get us passports and papers to cross the border, and pass us on to brothers in other countries. I have code names and contact information that I don't want to share now. Our plan is a high priority. Milan is a key target for jihad actions. Weapons and explosives are also being shipped to Paris, London, Frankfort, and Brussels for more attacks."

"When do we execute our plan?" Tito asked.

"December. Italians are shopping for their Christmas holiday and going to restaurants and parties."

"Good!" Kalil said, raising his bandaged fist. "But I'm still afraid. I can't get arrested again. I'd be deported, sent back to Egypt, end up in prison and tortured."

Kareem reached out to cover his hand. "Trust me. I wouldn't do anything to endanger you. You're a brother."

Kalil lowered his eyes. "I still worry. I'd rather die than go back to prison. I would kill myself first."

The others nodded, understanding the gravity of their plan.

"Trust Kareem, Kalil. I do," Tito said. "He was trained by experienced jihadists, *mujahideen* who drove the Russians out of Afghanistan . . . Saddam Hussein's Republican Guard who fought the Americans in Iraq. They're preparing for jihad in Indonesia, Somalia, and the Philippines. We're not alone."

"I trust Kareem; we all do," Esman said. "But I'm a scientist. We're trained to prepare for every possibility, good or bad. I'm confident we can execute our plan, but we need money and more weapons. None of us have any money except pitiful payment from our measly jobs."

Kareem held up his hand. "I have a plan. Don't worry. As soon as I heard about the intercepted shipment, I found a temporary solution. We need money to get out of Italy. It's coming from a rich American I know. His father is very wealthy. Carefull has a contract to provide security and infrastructure maintenance at their building. This fellow's mother is American, his father Italian. He has radical political ideas and hates the American government for the wars in Iraq and Afghanistan. He despises his father and his politician cronies, and he says Italy is full of criminals and corrupt judges."

"We all hate corrupt politicians and judges. Everyone does," Esman said.

"But this man is different. He's politically motivated to show his radical views. One time he asked if I knew any terrorists. Absurd. Imagine that. He thinks he can meet a terrorist just because he knows a Muslim. That, of course, opened up the opportunity to let him know how he could help some friends of mine." Kareem looked at each of them and smiled. "You're those friends."

"Do you trust him?" asked Esman.

Kareem held up his thumb and first finger, showing a gap of an inch. "This much . . . just enough to get us what we need."

"He'll give us money?" Tito asked.

"Yes, and soon. He's offered more than once. I push back, tell him not to rush and that there will be a time. We're meeting next week. He said he wants to go to a mosque and learn about Islam. One time at lunch, when he had drunk half a bottle of wine, he said he'd consider converting to Islam. He hadn't been to mass in years—only goes into a church for weddings or funerals. I don't know about psychology, but I think he's in turmoil about his life, his beliefs. He asked me to take him to Pakistan. I told him it was dangerous for Westerners to travel there. I've shown him pictures of Pakistan—but not from my last visit. He's angry about drone attacks and wants to know what al Qaeda and the Taliban will do next."

"He is . . . a little bit crazy?" Kalil asked.

"Maybe not crazy, but unstable," Kareem responded. "He has strong emotions, a lot of anger. I'm careful about what I say to him, but I've hinted I have a plan, and he wants to be part of it even if he still doesn't know about it. I'm going to invite him here next month. We'll keep him in the dark but excite him that we have a secret operation he can help us with."

CHAPTER TWENTY

"**L**et's get started," Amoruso said, speaking from a platform in the DIGOS command center. Seated around the room were her agent team, sipping water and fruit juice as she began her briefing. Mounted on the wall behind the platform was a row of TV screens linked to CCTV surveillance cameras around Milan; similar ATM monitors at subway, bus, and train stations; a monitor with a Google map of the Brera area; and a muted TV screen tuned to the RAI News24 channel.

"Tonight is when we expect that Alessandro Boni is meeting the Cinti stolen phone group."

"Let's hope he does," Lucchini said from the back of the room. "Find out who they are, what they're planning, and stop them. This case is top priority. The Minister of Interior wants updates at every step."

"Precisely," said Amoruso. "So far, Boni's been an easy surveillance target . . . going to work at 10:00 AM . . . lunch with colleagues near his father's office . . . home around five thirty . . . out for dinner, usually with male friends, once with a woman. His favorite restaurant is L'Estro Armonico on Viale Monte Nero, designed by his father's firm. Pretty classy place, wouldn't you agree?"

"That's for sure," one agent snickered. "Can't get out of that place for under a hundred euros per person—wine not included, of course."

Snickering, a guffaw, and muted laughter rippled from his colleagues, whose dining experiences tended more toward fast food, panini cafés, and bars.

"After dinner, they cruise bars and nightclubs," Amoruso continued. "Let's hope that's not what he's doing tonight. But we're ready for him, whatever his plans are." She turned to look at the Google map, which

194

was zoomed in on the Brera area and highlighted with street names, restaurants, apartments, hotels, and the Pinacoteca art museum. "Cella and Baraldi are outside Boni's apartment, about here." She pointed with a laser at two locations. "And three cars are parked around the corner in case he takes his Triumph motorbike or Mini Cooper."

She looked at Lucchini, standing in the back. "Anything you'd like to say to our team in the field, sir?"

The agents in the room swiveled around to see him. Lucchini shook his head. "No, they're ready to do their jobs. You're in charge."

"All right, let's check in," she said into her secure police radio. "Three cars, four agents in each. Volpara at Piazza del Carmine."

Volpara answered, "Loud and clear. Volpara ready."

"De Monti at Via Cusani?"

De Monti said, "We're ready."

"Ruggeri at Via Brera?"

"Ruggeri here," he answered.

"On the street, Cella and Baraldi at Boni's apartment?"

"Cella here."

"Baraldi. Ready."

Amoruso had chosen two of her most experienced surveillance agents, Giacomo Cella, thirty-eight, and Maurizio Baraldi, forty-three, to follow on foot if Boni walked from his apartment instead of driving his car or motorbike.

Giacomo Cella was across from Boni's apartment, sitting on a bench under a tree, wearing a tracksuit, running shoes, and sunglasses. The *Gazzetta dello Sport* newspaper was open on his lap so he could use it to hide his face, if necessary.

Maurizio Baraldi was at a bus stop a block away with a view of two intersections and Boni's apartment. Few would think he was an undercover police agent; he looked more like a reclusive composer or painter, with a frizz of graying hair, thick glasses, and a four-day beard he wore when on street surveillance. His clothes were disheveled: baggy pants, worn sneakers, and a long-sleeved shirt with frayed cuffs and missing buttons. His scruffy appearance was so effective that he had once been questioned by a rookie police officer when he was on duty near a school yard where children were playing. Baraldi had reached into his baggy pants, flashed his DIGOS badge, and shooed away the young officer. He had become a Questura legend.

"All teams ready," Amoruso said. "Boni should be arriving in a few minutes."

It was quiet in the command center as the agents watched the CCTV monitors in Brera. Each monitor had multiple screens showing pedestrians, taxis and cars passing on streets, and people sitting outside cafés drinking wine and chatting.

"I think that's Boni," Amoruso said, pointing with her laser pen at a monitor showing men and women in business suits walking in pairs or alone. "Sport coat . . . sunglasses . . . Musella and Ricci are following." She pointed the laser at the two agents who had been assigned to Boni during the day. One agent was behind Boni, the other across the street.

The figures moved from one screen to another as they walked down the sidewalk. Amoruso's laser pointer followed Boni as he turned at an intersection and walked along a hedge of bushes behind an iron fence. Baraldi said into his lapel microphone, "Got him . . . just turned the corner."

Cella lifted his *Gazzetta dello Sport* so his eyes could follow Boni approaching the gated entrance to his apartment. He reached it and pressed a key code, and the gate opened. Cella stood and tucked the paper under his arm, signaling the team assigned to Boni during the daytime that Boni had passed to him and Baraldi.

Amoruso said, "Musella and Ricci relieved." She glanced up at the clock: 5:35 PM

The agents in the command center, who had been sitting silent and immobile, squirmed in their chairs, sipped drinks, and whispered to each other. They knew the routine; surveillance would resume when Boni left his apartment. Lucchini strolled through the chairs to the platform. "Good start," he said to Amoruso. "Boni looks like has no idea he's being followed."

"He's an easy target. Let's hope he doesn't disappoint us tonight."

"He's all we have, our only link to the Cinti group, whoever they are. We need Boni to lead us to them."

"You have a meeting, don't you?" she asked.

Lucchini nodded. "With the Prefetto and Questore. Call if something comes up. I'll come back when the meeting is over."

"Yes, sir."

Amoruso's team in the command center talked in low voices as they watched the CCTV monitors while the agents in cars called in periodically as they waited for Boni to come out of his apartment. The screen that was tuned to the RAI station broke in with news of a fire near the Rho fairgrounds. For a few minutes, agents read the running scroll on the muted station as police and fire departments moved crowds away from a burning building.

A half hour later, Cella broke in. "Boni coming out . . . changed clothes . . . black sweater . . . running shoes . . . dark pants."

Boni opened the gate, which shut behind him, and walked down the street. Cella lifted his newspaper and waited for Boni to come into view to his left, which he did while waiting for a light to change at an intersection. Boni crossed the street. Cella tucked the newspaper under his arm and crossed to the same side of the street.

"I'm on him," Cella said quietly into his lapel microphone. He lowered his eyes, following Boni's running shoes. If his shoes turned right or left, he could alter his path.

Baraldi followed on a parallel route across the street, watching Cella keep pedestrians between him and Boni.

The team in the command center followed on the CCTV monitors. "Boni at Via Cusani," Cella said ". . . turning toward Largo Cairoli." Cella turned onto Via Cusani several steps behind Boni, merging with people enjoying *aperitivo* at outdoor cafés and shoppers browsing at windows displaying shoes, purses, and clothing. Rush-hour commuters waited at bus stops as traffic whizzed by on the congested urban street: hornet-buzzing motorbikes, honking buses, clanking trams, and speeding cars.

Boni stopped at the intersection of Foro Buonaparte and Largo Cairoli, waiting for the light to change, mingling with tourists on their way to an overpriced meal and bottle of wine at tourist-trap restaurants on Via Dante. Across the intersection, tour buses disgorged tourists who hurriedly snapped photos of the Garibaldi statue in the piazza before walking to the fountain in front of the Castello Sforzesco.

"Crossing the street . . . headed for the tram or subway," Cella reported.

Amoruso: "Cars to Cairoli." Volpara and Ruggeri put their cars in gear and drove toward Largo Cairoli, which was always clogged with gawking tourists and *Milanesi* rushing for a tram, subway, or bus.

When the light turned green, Boni crossed and hurried down the steps of the Cairoli metro station.

Cella: "Entering Cairoli subway." Boni disappeared down the steps, with Cella and Baraldi several steps behind. Boni swiped his metro smart card on the turnstile and pushed through the bar, turning to his right for one of the stairways to the underground platform.

Cella and Baraldi swiped their smart cards on the turnstile, turned right, and followed. They knew the Cairoli station; no reason to rush, as there was no screech of an approaching subway train. Boni would be waiting on the platform below.

Cella: "Heading to Cordusio." This indicated that Boni was taking the north line.

Amoruso: "I see him." She checked the ATM monitors on the Cairoli platform. "All cars, head north on the Red Line. Let's hope he doesn't get out at the Duomo. We could lose him in all the crowds and underground passages. It's always chaos there."

Volpara's car left Piazza del Carmine, stopped at the traffic light on Via dell'Orso, and turned left. De Monti's car turned around on Via Cusani and slipped into traffic headed toward Piazza della Scala and Via Manzoni. Ruggeri left Via Brera for San Babila, four stations down the Red Line.

Cella and Baraldi separated and walked to opposite ends of the subway platform. Boni was in the center between teenagers talking on cell phones and women carrying Carrefour shopping bags.

An LED screen above the platform flashed subway arrival times.

Cella: "Train in three minutes."

Amoruso: "I see you both: Boni behind the yellow line, like he's supposed to be."

DIGOS cars racing to stations along the Red Line called in with their positions.

Amoruso: "Let's hope he goes beyond San Babila. Be extra careful if he gets off there. Always big crowds from the shopping centers and offices at this time of day. And with three exits, he could slip away unless Cella and Baraldi are right behind him."

The LED monitor flashed a train arriving in one minute. Cella and Baraldi walked toward the center of the platform, which was crowded with boisterous teenagers, men and women lugging briefcases, and gypsies holding paper cups and handwritten signs begging for money.

The approaching train screeched as it emerged from the tunnel. It slowed and braked to a halt with a final jolt. The six-car, red-and-white ATM train was slashed with gaudy graffiti and crude slogans about politics, the environment, and sports teams.

"Cairoli, fermata Cairoli. Treno proveniente da Cadorna diretto a Sesto F.S." [Cairoli, station Cairoli. Train travels from Cadorna direct to Sesto F.S.] the station loudspeaker droned. The doors whooshed open, and passengers spilled out like mice leaving a sinking boat, elbowing through the crowd waiting to board. After the last person exited, passengers hurried in and scrambled for seats in open compartments already crowded with commuters staring at cell phones, reading newspapers, and hanging on straps, their faces glazed with fatigue.

Boni entered a middle car; Cella entered one car behind, Baraldi a car ahead. The brightly lit compartments were crowded with commuters. Monitors in each compartment displayed the subway route; next station Cordusio, in one minute. The doors slammed shut. The train jolted forward, accelerated, and entered a curved tunnel lined with lights along grungy walls. The cars rocked side to side, lulling passengers into a semicomatose state as the train sped along. The tunnel straightened for a hundred meters as the lights of Cordusio station appeared ahead.

When the train slowed, Baraldi moved to the door in case Boni exited. But he doubted he would; Cairoli and Cordusio stations were only blocks apart. If his destination was Cordusio, he could have walked from his apartment.

DIGOS agents followed a drill when tailing someone on public transportation. One agent would step onto the platform in case the suspect bolted at the last second. At the next stop, the other agent would follow the same drill.

Boni remained in the aisle, hanging onto a strap as the train continued north from Cordusio to Duomo, toward San Babila. Cella and Baraldi took turns eyeing Boni, who was staring blankly at advertisements for cheap cell phone rates to the Philippines, miracle products for impeding baldness, private acting schools for children, and cheap funeral services with the slogan "Feel at home at our funeral home."

When Boni didn't exit at San Babila, Cella passed on the news. Amoruso updated her team.

Amoruso: "Departed San Babila. . . . Keep driving . . . one car at Palestro . . . Porta Venezia . . . the third at Lima. Step on it."

Cella and Baraldi continued to take turns on the platform to see if Boni was getting off. When the speaker droned that the doors were closing, they stepped back inside and resumed traveling. Boni was squeezed between passengers who'd entered at Duomo and San Babila; he moved into Baraldi's compartment and reached for a strap near an exit, his back to Baraldi.

Cella moved into the car where Boni had been, positioning himself so he could see the top of his head in case he exited.

The police cars sped through traffic along Corso Venezia, Corso Buenos Aires, and Viale Monza toward stations at Palestro, Porta Venezia, and Lima.

Cella, Baraldi, and Boni remained in place through the next stops until the metro approached Turro. Boni craned his head to look at the platform, the first time he had done so since he'd boarded. Cella and Baraldi braced themselves, anticipating that this was Boni's stop. The train braked coming into the station, and Boni inched toward the door.

Cella: "Turro." He whispered the word into his microphone, a signal that this was Boni's destination.

Cella and Baraldi were ready to exit, standing close to the doors. Baraldi's back was to Boni until the train halted and the doors opened. Boni stepped off the train and walked toward the escalator. Cella and

Baraldi followed several meters behind, giving Boni space as the metro departed for the next station. Boni had only one place to go: the escalator to the station exit.

He walked onto the escalator, rode to the ground floor, and headed toward the turnstile. Cella and Baraldi surveyed the area, saw no places he could disappear, and gave him more distance. Boni exited the station on a street with a bus stop and an intersection. Two cars and a van drove through the intersection. An older woman who had gotten off at Turro was the only person waiting with Boni for the light to change.

Cella and Baraldi waited until Boni had crossed the intersection before they left Turro. Baraldi crossed the street to follow on a parallel surveillance route.

Cella: "Moving on Via Valtorta. No suspicious moves." He waited until Boni was fifty meters ahead before he began tailing him. The three walked two blocks without diversions, passing apartment buildings, a café, a dry cleaner's, and a *tabaccheria*. Boni didn't look back. He walked purposefully as the evening sun cast shadows over the quiet neighborhood. Two boys on skateboards raced by on the street, dodging cars driving toward them. Boni didn't notice, with eyes ahead.

Boni reached an intersection with a traffic light. A bus drove through, along with cars, a taxi, and motorbikes. When the light changed, Boni crossed the street, melding in with pedestrians walking in both directions.

Cella: "Via Padova . . . walking north." Cella walked down Via Padova, now across the street from Boni. A blue *polizia* Fiat passed in front of him; the two uniformed officers didn't look his way.

Baraldi reached the intersection. The light had changed. He waited on the corner for it to change again, watching Boni walk down Via Padova, passing news agents, a TIM cell phone store, real estate offices, a Penny discount supermarket, and an Eni gas station.

The two agents followed on opposite sides of Via Padova until Boni disappeared into a pizza and kebab café in the middle of the block. Middle Eastern boys were eating pizza and kebab sandwiches and drinking sodas at outdoor plastic tables.

Baraldi: "Boni entered a kebab place on Via Padova." He gave the address and stepped into a *tabaccheria*.

Cella: "I'm going into a Vietnamese café across from the kebab place." He ducked into the noodle shop and looked around: plastic tables and chairs; a woman singing in high-pitched Vietnamese over a speaker; a middle-aged Asian couple eating fried fish, rice, and steamed vegetables at the only occupied table. They ignored him.

The stuffy, humid air in the noodle shop reeked of frying vegetable oil, boiling tea, and fish. Cella was starved; his stomach growled at the smells. His last meal had been a ham-and-cheese panini, salty chips, and a soda he'd gobbled down at his desk hours ago. He checked the kebab entrance across the street and saw no one entering or exiting. Could he risk taking a few minutes to ease his hunger? The aromas in the noodle shop prevailed.

Cella went to the counter and checked a menu written in chalk on the wall. A Vietnamese teenage boy wrapped in a grease-stained apron looked up from behind the counter filled with platters of steamed and fried rice, steaming broths, mixed vegetables, fried fish, and boiled chicken.

Cella ordered a bowl of pho and an iced tea. The Vietnamese boy shook his head, said something in Vietnamese, ending in *"scusi, non Italiano."* Cella pointed at a tureen of steaming pho with slivers of green onions, carrots, crabmeat, and rice floating on top. The boy reached for a bowl and spooned in several helpings. Cella salivated, inhaling the warm aromas, feeling almost dizzy.

The boy slid a tray across the counter with the bowl of pho, a ceramic spoon, napkins, and a bottle of iced tea. Cella paid, left a euro coin tip in a jar, and took the tray to a table with a view of the kebab café. No sign of Boni in the café or on the street.

Cella: "Across from the café. Clear view." His empty stomach was anticipating the bowl of steaming pho.

He stirred the broth with the ceramic spoon, blowing gently as steam rose from the bowl. He sipped, swallowed, and closed his eyes, having a moment of ecstasy that rivaled sex.

He opened his eyes, looked out the window, and spooned another delicious mouthful.

Back to work. Senses alert. He was on duty after a few moments of pleasure. Foot traffic passed by the window: Arab mothers wearing hijabs pushing prams, Chinese men smoking hand-rolled cigarettes, and Filipino parents walking hand in hand with children.

He noticed a bit of action at the kebab café. He put down his spoon.

Cella: "Two Middle Eastern men entered . . . a boy came out, a teenager . . . people ordering . . . two men serving food over the counter. No sign of Boni."

Cella enjoyed his meal, his eyes never leaving the kebab café. A greasy residue of cool broth and onion slivers was all that he left in the bottom of the bowl. He pushed back the tray, sipped his tea, and heard Amoruso in his earpiece.

Amoruso: "All cars in Turro . . . Volpara at the station . . . De Monti on Via Padova a block from the kebab shop . . . Ruggeri on a side street. We've checked . . . the owner of the kebab shop is from Desio, where the cell phones were stolen. We're at the right place."

Volpara: "Ah, Desio. Is that a coincidence?"

De Monti: "We might have to go back."

Amoruso: "I want replacement teams when Boni comes out. Morucci and Ferrarin, take over from Cella and Baraldi."

Morucci and Ferrarin got out of their cars at Turro and walked toward Via Padova, checking their earpieces and microphones. They were rookie agents. Febo Morucci, thirty-two, was a handsome Tuscan who loved the theater and took acting classes, the skills from which he applied on surveillance, modifying his voice and body movements to adapt to the environment.

Mirko Ferrarin was thirty but looked younger. He wore baggy pants, a sweatshirt, and a baseball cap. He could easily pass for a high school student, a backpack slung over his shoulder.

Morucci and Ferrarin reached Via Padova and separated. Morucci walked toward Baraldi outside a *tabaccheria*. He walked by him, caught his eye, and stood in front of a TIM cell phone store. Relieved, Baraldi crossed the street to return to Turro and a waiting DIGOS car.

Ferrarin passed the noodle shop and saw Cella inside, sipping tea. Without acknowledging each other, Ferrarin stopped at an *edicola* two doors away and scanned racks of magazines and newspapers. He took out a pack of cigarettes, lit one, and looked left and right, as if he was waiting for a date.

Cella took his tray to the counter, left the noodle shop, and walked down Via Padova without looking toward the kebab café. He joined Baraldi at Volpara's car, parked at Turro, five minutes later.

Amoruso: "Patruno, take three agents from the cars. I want one agent on each corner nearest the kebab place. We don't know how many Boni might be meeting. Go!"

Patruno and three agents left their DIGOS cars and hurried toward Via Padova. In five minutes, they were in place, all with views of the kebab shop.

A half hour passed. Forty-five minutes. The surveilling agents made periodic sound checks, waiting for Amoruso's next order.

The door to the command center opened. Lucchini entered, surveyed the room, and took a seat at the rear, not wanting to distract anyone. Amoruso glanced over and nodded. He acknowledged with a raised hand.

"It's been almost an hour," she said to her surveillance team. "I assume they're in the meeting, discussing whatever they are doing. Let's hope Boni doesn't come out alone. We need to know who he's meeting."

It was getting dark. Street lights flickered on, and retail stores were closing. Teenage Asian and Middle Eastern boys were roaming the streets, smoking, talking on cell phones, joking, and pushing each other around. The agents watched with concern, hoping they wouldn't break a window or start a fight, bringing police cars to the scene.

At 9:45 PM, four men came out of the kebab café, Boni the last.

Ferrarin: "Leaving the café . . . Boni with one man . . . two behind . . . walking away . . . coming toward Morucci."

Ferrarin snapped photos with a telephoto lens as the four men walked down Via Padova.

Amoruso: "Where's the fifth? There are five phones; where is the other one?"

Ferrarin: "No one else coming out."

Amoruso: "Stay behind . . . might be someone in the restroom. Let me know if anyone else comes out and follows Boni. Morucci, track Boni and the three. Patruno, you and your three follow Morucci. Pick them up. Don't lose anyone."

Morucci: "They've turned off Via Padova, going toward Turro. Four . . . no sign of a fifth. One has a limp, walking slower, stooped over."

Amoruso: "Stay where you are, Ferrarin. I want the fifth."

Volpara aimed a camera with a telephoto lens at the four walking toward Turro. He snapped pictures, focusing on headshots, and then zoomed out to get all four together.

The man with Boni glanced over his left shoulder. Morucci turned to look into a shoe store window, counted to ten, and saw out of the corner of his eye that the man had turned and resumed walking with Boni.

Morucci: "Boni's companion looked back. Didn't see me. Tall . . . Middle Eastern . . . thin. Black hair and beard. Tan pants, gray shirt, boots. I'm on the other side of the street. Parked cars . . . trucks . . . trees between us."

The five agents used diversion tactics, stopping to look in windows, checking cell phones and watches, and melding in with other pedestrians.

Morucci: "Approaching Turro. No evasion attempts. They're talking . . . taking up most of the sidewalk."

Volpara: "I've got photos of them all . . . crossing street to Turro . . . a minute away." He snapped more photos through the car's windshield.

Amoruso looked at the ATM monitor showing the Turro platform.

Amoruso: "Careful in Turro . . . eight people on the platform. Spread out . . . keep your distance. Buy a newspaper . . . fake a cell phone call . . . look distracted."

The team moved toward the entrance from different directions, not approaching each other.

Boni and the others entered the station single file through the turn-stile and headed toward the escalator to the platform. No trains were approaching the station.

The agents entered Turro, a few meters between each other. They lingered in front of a vending machine. One by one, they bought sodas or bottled water and took the escalator to the platform, keeping distance from each other. No rumbling of a train approaching. They took their time spreading out on the platform, looking toward the streets and apartment buildings, their backs to the bench where Boni and the others were seated and talking in low voices.

A rumbling down the tracks indicated that a train was arriving from Gorla. A minute later, a four-car train braked to a halt at the platform. The doors opened. Boni and the three entered the second car. Morucci and Patruno entered the first and third cars, sitting apart from each other. The three other agents split up, entered adjoining cars, and sat alone. They pulled out cell phones and opened newspapers.

The metro jolted forward, leaving Turro on its way back into central Milan.

Morucci: "Leaving Turro . . . all on board." He was sitting alone, a car away from Boni. "Green light on return."

Amoruso: "Cars to Rovereto . . . Pasteur . . . Loreto, in case any get off. We're covered on the train." The tension in Amoruso's voice had softened. She took a deep breath, sighed, and nodded at the agents in the command center. They smiled, poked each other in the ribs, and raised their arms in celebration.

Amoruso: "Got 'em! Follow Boni's friends when they get off. . . . We need addresses and license plates if they have cars. Don't worry about Boni; we have a car at Cairoli when he gets off. He delivered what we wanted. Good job, everyone. Good job!"

In the back of the room, Lucchini pumped his fist and walked over to congratulate Amoruso. "Great work," he said. "I think we'll have names by tomorrow. We'll know who we're up against."

CHAPTER TWENTY-ONE

The streets near Brera were quiet except for taxis returning tourists to hotels and the buzz of motorbikes and scooters moving through the neighborhood. A gentle evening rain had left puddles in the cobblestone streets and gutters, slowing couples returning from bars and restaurants in the chic area bordering Via Brera, Via dell'Orso, Via Madonnina, and Via Pontaccio.

Raindrops slithered down Giorgio's apartment windows as he and Antonella enjoyed a glass of Barolo Chinato and nibbled Venchi dark chocolates in his library two nights after the surveillance of Boni.

Giorgio was reading Antonella's notes on the surveillance of Hussain, Khan, and Bilal and the information retrieved by DIGOS from security databases of driver's licenses, tax records, residency permits, and passports.

"This is a very suspicious bunch that Boni is associating with," Giorgio said, scanning photos taken by DIGOS agents. "Not his crowd of Milanese professionals who hang out in nightclubs and bars around town. These men all have Middle Eastern or African backgrounds. Only Hussain has a professional job and lives in a middle-class area. Think he's the leader of the group?"

"I expect he is," Antonella said. "An engineering degree from Politecnico. He has dual citizenship and works with a company called Carefull Services, which has maintenance contracts with major corporations throughout Lombardy. An apartment in Città Studi . . . good salary . . . no police record or connection to any of the mosques or radical Muslims . . . a spotless record. We'd never have found him without the Boni connection."

"Not your typical terrorist suspect. He's lived in Milan, what, fifteen years or so?"

"Right. His mother, Elsa Zanin, is from Verona. She married a Pakistani in England. They started a family but divorced. She moved to Italy with the children, our suspect and his two sisters. She hasn't remarried but lives with an entrepreneur, ten years younger, by the way, in an apartment behind Juliet's house."

"Juliet? You mean that Juliet?"

Antonella smiled. "Yes, that one, Romeo's sweetheart. I had to laugh when I read that report from the Verona police. Anyway, Hussain has traveled to Pakistan, last trip a year ago. He was gone five weeks in August and September. His father's hometown is Mansehra, near the Afghan border."

"That's disturbing. There are terrorist training camps along the borders of Pakistan and Afghanistan. The Taliban are a big problem, recruiting young men, attacking villages in hit-and-run operations. Dangerous place."

"It certainly is, but we don't know if Hussain has dangerous political or religious beliefs. I've asked the Pakistani intelligence service for information on him. He's not on their terrorist watch list or anyone else's. They're contacting local police and the military in the borderlands area. It's a lawless place, with tribal warlords, a high crime rate, opium growers, and smuggling of drugs and weapons. The military handles most police functions."

Giorgio nodded, his eyes narrowing. "We need to know more about his politics and what he did when he went there. He could be a sleeper, the most dangerous type."

"He drove to Malpensa Terminal 2 this morning with two other employees. They were there all day. Carefull has a maintenance contract there and at Linate."

"I flew out of Linate when I went to Amsterdam," Giorgio said, raising his eyebrows. "Thousands of people go through Malpensa, Linate, and Orio every day—big targets for terrorists. But we haven't received any alerts from our sources about possible terrorist threats at any of those airports. We need to track Hussain's every move when he's working there. Airports are always potential targets."

"I called the Carefull Services HR director today. He's coming to the Questura for a meeting tomorrow. I told him we'd like updated background checks on every Carefull employee who works at the airports. He said it's not a problem and they're always willing to help us. There might be others Hussain works with at Carefull that we want to keep an eye on."

"What about Kalil Khan? He works in Rho."

"Yes, cleaning sanitation tanks," Antonella said. "The company is AmbroSana srl. Thirty-two employees, many of them immigrants. He's an Egyptian refugee. Received his residency permit in 2010. Lives in the Quartiere Stadera, where a lot of African and Middle Eastern refugees live. I don't see him as a leader, more of a follower.

"Esman Bilal is from Syria. His residency permit says he was in the Syrian army and has a chemistry degree. He's one we have to watch. But he drives a garbage truck for Amsa, not a likely place we could expect an attack from. His address is . . . let me check my notes . . . yes, Via Amoretti, Quarto Oggiaro."

"Amsa picks up trash from every building in Milan," Giorgio said. "Employees don't have access inside buildings, but they could have someone inside who lets them in, perhaps another refugee. We'll watch him carefully."

"Volpara and De Monti are working with security at Amsa and AmbroSana, getting employment records on Khan and Bilal and questioning supervisors about them to see if there's anyone else we should be following."

"That's just three. We're still missing one," Giorgio said. "There were five on the stolen-phone tree."

"Right, but no one else came out of the kebab place who looked suspicious. I'm betting the fifth is the owner of the kebab café, who lives in Desio. It makes sense; the others left with Boni, but he stayed at work."

"Start surveillance on him."

"We have. He might show up when we're surveilling the others. The judge approved cell phone taps on Hussain, Khan, and Bilal. We'll start intercepting their calls tonight."

"Do you need more agents for surveillance?"

"Not yet. We're following four suspects around the clock, six on a team. That's twenty-four, plus three in the command center coordinating with surveillance teams. Eight-hour shifts for everyone. I'm briefing four new agents about the case. They're assigned to other investigations, but we might need them as backups if we turn up new suspects."

"If they're planning something for Christmas, like Mohammad said in Amsterdam, we need to get evidence to arrest them. The Questore wants daily updates."

"I have my report for you to brief him tomorrow."

"Good. Anything else?"

Antonella smiled and sipped her wine. "I approved for Ispettore De Monti to go to Deus in case this Giangi character shows up with Boni. But not alone, like she's looking to get picked up. She'll be with Emanuela Rossi from the immigration office."

"Aah, Maurizio Baraldi's girlfriend."

"You knew about them?"

Giorgio smiled. "We're in intelligence . . . on terrorists as well as our agents. I like to know everything."

"It's not much of a secret. I hear Cella and Volpara teasing Maurizio about her. Volpara lives with him. I think you knew that . . . DIGOS bachelors living the wild single life, even though they're divorced with children."

He nodded. "But with De Monti . . . she's single, young, attractive— a target for a lot of men out there. I get nervous when agents mix their personal and professional lives. I don't want to put her in a bad position."

"She won't be. She and Emanuela are both savvy. I trust them. Emanuela might make a good DIGOS agent if she weren't so attached to the idea of getting married and starting a family soon."

Giorgio put down the file and rubbed his eyes, stifling a yawn. "You've done a good job while I've been out the last couple of days. Thanks for taking over." He looked over her shoulder at the raindrops splattering the windows and running down in squiggly streams, making a gentle patter in the library.

Antonella waited until he looked back at her. "Giorgio, you're tired. You should go off to bed. Giulia's sickness is taking a lot out of you."

He nodded, stretching his arms. "You're right. It's been a rough couple of days. Her latest treatment was hard on her. She's nauseous, has sores in her mouth, and feels exhausted all the time. She lost weight since it started. Can't eat. Sleeps most of the time."

"I understand. So sorry she has to go through this. And I know how hard it is for you." Antonella swirled the wineglass in her fingers, watching Giorgio. His eyes looked like he was in a trance, absorbed in deep thoughts. "Giorgio . . . ," she said, her voice soft. "I hope you don't mind me saying, but you look like you've aged in the last couple of months."

He blinked and looked up, his face gray. "It shows that much? The last few days have been stressful. I worry all the time . . . feel tired and listless, with no appetite. I don't let Giulia know. I try to be positive and encouraging. She has enough to worry about. I don't want her worrying about me."

"It's natural. I've been through it with friends before. It's like they lose a year or two of their lives. Is there anything I can do for you and Giulia?"

"No, just keep me up to date and let me take a little time off when I need it. Thanks for coming tonight. You're handling everything well; you know how to lead a team. If I didn't have you, I'd have more to worry about."

"Thank you. Everyone is giving it their best. You don't have to worry about that."

Giorgio sipped his wine, put it down, and looked over at her. "As long as we're on the subject . . . you look weary as well. I'm not the only one under stress. You've been working around the clock on this case."

Antonella made a motion with her hand like she was swatting a fly. "Don't worry about me, Giorgio. I'm fine. I don't get a lot of sleep, but I manage. I get strength when I need it."

He nodded. They were quiet for a few moments. The soft patter of rain on the window and the ticking of a wall clock were the only sounds in the library. Giorgio looked up, widening his eyes. "I just remembered—wasn't this the week you and Carlo were taking a vacation?"

Antonella managed a smile. "You remember. It was to be our first major vacation in years. He and colleagues from work were awarded a working vacation in Los Angeles, San Francisco, and Las Vegas with their wives. He called from Las Vegas this morning and joked that he's the only single man in the group. Everyone asked why I'm not there. He can't say, of course, just that work came up last minute."

"You talked about this months ago. You were so excited, buying new luggage, new clothes."

"I've never been to California. I wanted to see Disneyland and Hollywood, take a cable car in San Francisco, go to the wine country in Napa. Carlo will enjoy the vacation, but without me. We were going to celebrate our anniversary; it's this Saturday."

Giorgio was quiet, wanting to let her keep talking. She needed to lament being apart from Carlo on their anniversary. She confided in few people, and never at the Questura. Her women friends had drifted away after she had canceled too many dinner or lunch appointments, blaming work demands. He was probably one of the few friends she confided in.

A truck passed on the street below, sounding like a dog growling at a strange noise in the house. Antonella sipped her last drop of wine and set the glass on the table. She reached for another chocolate but then changed her mind.

"But I won't be alone this weekend. My sister Marianna is coming from Bologna on Friday night. An old friend from Naples, a magistrate, is joining us for a girls' weekend—shopping . . . the Modigliani exhibit at Palazzo Reale . . . lunch in the Naviglio, and Massimo Ranieri's recital at the Teatro degli Arcimboldi on Sunday. I'm treating them to dinner at Al Garghet on Saturday night."

"Al Garghet—one of our favorite restaurants! Fabulous food and cozy rooms with wonderful art. We always enjoy the drive there, too, out in the country with farms and fields of corn, rice, and hay. Whenever we go there, I fantasize about giving up the city, living a peaceful life in the country, and opening a little restaurant. We get so caught up with our busy lives and work; people living just a few miles away seem to have a better, more peaceful life without all the stress."

Antonella shook her head. "No, thank you, Giorgio! I had that life growing up. I'd never go back. When I was about twelve, I wanted to leave our small town outside Napoli, move to Rome, Milan, or even Paris, and have an exciting life."

"You have that, no question," he said, gratified that she was reminiscing, talking about her younger life, something she rarely did.

"My parents are gone, and I don't go back often," she added, "but whenever I do, I get an anxiety attack. I worry that something awful will happen and I will have to live there. I didn't mind so much when I was young and carefree, but as I grew up, I saw so many things that I didn't like. I belong right here . . . right now . . . working with you."

"And I appreciate you."

"Thanks. I love living in Milan . . . all the history, art, music, culture. And the food is not as bad as southern Italians believe. My sister brags about how special the food in Bologna is. Our friend from Napoli says their local cuisine is the best in Italy. But this weekend I'm going to spoil them with the best Milanese cuisine. I want to see their faces when I order the elephant ear veal cutlet and the waiter delivers it to our table. The meat covers the entire plate." She smiled.

"Nice idea. But I don't order the elephant ear anymore; the last time I did, my sons had to finish it. I always have my favorite now: saffron risotto with osso buco. Giulia is crazy about the Nepenta pasta, the creamy *maccheroni* with tomato, bacon, and *peperoncino* cooked in vodka. It's so 1980s, when we all believed we'd be rich and happy."

"Oh, yes, the eighties. Everything was so special—the food, the music, and the crazy hairstyles!" Antonella laughed, the first time all night. Giorgio was pleased to see the evening ending pleasantly.

"I have an idea. Giulia and I will take you and Carlo to Al Garghet when he comes back."

"Splendid! I'll tell Carlo. He'll love it . . . maybe it will make him homesick. But then, he's in California, and he's been looking forward to that."

"Maybe we'll have something else to celebrate besides your anniversary."

Antonella frowned. "What do you mean?"

"We apprehend those fellows from the kebab shop, wrap up the investigation, make arrests, and save Milan from some terrorist act."

CHAPTER TWENTY-TWO

"Hi, Simo. What a lovely walk from the Gioia metro station," Emanuela said as Simona opened the door to her apartment that evening. Emanuela was dressed like she was going to a party: stiletto heels, a white linen skirt above her knees, a sleeveless blouse in bright red and blue, and hooped earrings. Her light brown hair was styled in a high ponytail, and her makeup looked like she'd just come from a beauty appointment.

"Welcome to my Isola mansion, Manu. It's sooo big, I hope you don't get lost," Simona said as they exchanged cheek kisses.

"You're lucky to live here. It's a beautiful building, so old Milan style."

"I am lucky. All my neighbors know me, almost too well. We're one big family in the building. I'm not used to that."

"I wish I lived here. It's so fashionable—the restaurants, cool people, so many cute shops."

"Come in. Let me show you my little home." She took Emanuela's bulky Michael Kors purse, set it on the hall table, and led her down the hallway, letting her peek into her small bedroom, sitting room, and kitchen. "It's small, but I love it. Easy to clean and just enough room."

"Lovely, lovely. Nice touches . . . posters in your hallway . . . all the books. Where did you get that antique table where you have your laptop?"

"I picked it up at the antique fair at the Naviglio a month ago. I didn't bring anything from Bergamo, only some clothes. I wanted a fresh start in Milan. Come in the kitchen. Let's have a glass of juice before we go out. Do you prefer orange or pineapple?"

"Pineapple, please."

"Fine. We'll probably have wine at Deus if Giangi and Boni show up, but for now, we're on duty. Let's be good girls."

Simona led Emanuela into her kitchen, opened the refrigerator, and took out a pineapple juice carton and a plate of Sicilian olives, prosciutto, and Asiago cheese slices she'd picked up on her way home.

Simona put the plate on the café table she'd set with glasses, plates, napkins, and tiny forks. She poured the juice. Emanuela sipped and reached for an olive and a slice of cheese.

"Lovely view. Your courtyard is so nice and quiet," Emanuela said, looking out the kitchen window. "My kitchen faces a parking lot. All I hear are rowdy boys skateboarding and teenagers goofing off, smoking, talking crudely. Ugh."

"I like the evening sun when I get home from work," Simona said. She took a sip and nibbled on a piece of cheese. "I sit here, read a magazine, take something from the refrigerator, and unwind with a little prosecco."

Emanuela picked up an interior design magazine from a corner nook table and leafed through it. "When do you have time to read these?"

Simona laughed. "Hardly ever anymore. I devoured them when I lived in Bergamo, four or five a month at least. But not since I came to DIGOS. I take a book or magazine to bed, but I fall asleep after a couple of pages. In the morning, the book or magazine is on the floor."

"DIGOS is a pressure cooker, isn't it?"

"Yes, but I love it. I was thrilled when Amoruso recruited me. My job in Bergamo was okay but not challenging. I was looking for something more interesting, exciting. I certainly have it now. I'm just a rookie, but everyone treats me like I've been around."

"You're lucky. DIGOS had only a few women until a couple of years ago. Your team needs more women and people who speak different languages to reflect how society has changed."

"Indeed. We need Arabic, Urdu, Pashto, Mandarin, and Russian speakers, with all the immigrants here. Lucchini and Amoruso did a great job recruiting at Accademia di Polizia recently. They're wonderful bosses. Fair, open, no playing games."

"I'd love to join DIGOS, but it wouldn't be compatible with my dream to have a family—if I can talk Maurizio into it. The immigration office is a perfect fit for me now."

"I wouldn't recommend DIGOS if you want to have kids. The job consumes your life; never time for anything—or anybody. That's tough on families."

"Oh, I know that. You can count on one hand the DIGOS agents who are still married to their first wives."

They sipped juice and nibbled on the olives and cheese. A warm breeze blew in the window, fluffed the curtains, and fluttered the table napkins as well as Simona's and Emanuela's hair. "Mmm, I love olives," Emanuela said, building a small mound of pits on her plate, "and this wonderful breeze. But I didn't come to Isola to sit around and talk like old ladies."

"Of course. We have an assignment. We should leave soon."

"I'm ready. Amoruso briefed me about it. Word has gotten around the Questura, not details, just that DIGOS has many agents assigned to this case."

"It's a major case. Some nasty characters we need to watch before they do something bad. We got a break a couple of nights ago."

"That's what Maurizio said, but he can't tell me about it. You know how it is."

"We're bait tonight, hoping to spot someone DIGOS is following. An American, Alessandro Boni. His dad's an architect, very wealthy and politically connected."

"Is he cute?"

"Not particularly. Why are you asking?"

"Deus is the club where you and your Bergamo boyfriend had an argument, isn't that right?" Emanuela picked up more olives, ate them, and added to the mound on her plate.

Simona nodded. "*Former* boyfriend, Alby. That was ages ago, two weeks at least. He wanted to spend the night, but I sent him back to Bergamo. I wasn't in the mood."

"Ouch, I'll bet he didn't like that."

"He was pissed. But I didn't want him to stay. He surprised me when he showed up at my door without calling beforehand. I don't like it when people make assumptions."

"I don't blame you."

"I wanted him out of the apartment. We went to Deus and ran into Giangi, that flamboyant gay I told you about who flirts with me. Alby's not used to that behavior in Bergamo; he associates only with wealthy political people, not artists or fashion people, God forbid."

"It probably scared Alby that gays flirt with you."

"Alby's from my past. We're still friends, but I don't need a boyfriend now."

Simona went to the open window, pulled back the curtains and closed the wood blinds. "Enough gossip. I don't want to bore you with my personal life. Let's have fun tonight, maybe meet someone interesting."

Emanuela's face lit up. "I hope it's packed with gorgeous, single men! It'll make Maurizio jealous. He takes me for granted. He knows I want to get married and have kids. When he saw me go out the door in this outfit, I thought he'd have a heart attack. 'Where are you going, looking like that?' he asked. I grinned and said, 'To Deus . . . with a friend.' 'Who?' he asked. I told him you. He pinched my cheek and said, 'It better be Simona . . . not some Sicilian Lothario you met at the gym.' 'Oh, no,' I told him. 'No one could ever replace you, Maurizio!' I pinched his cheek and gave him a kiss. I wish you could have seen the look on his face."

Both women roared with laughter, enjoying the humor about a colleague they both knew and admired.

"Consider yourself a chaperone, Amoruso doesn't want me going to Deus alone. Tonight, we're just two girls out on the town. Maybe we'll see Boni, maybe not. But we'll have a good time anyway."

"There's a connection between the gay who flirts with you and the American?"

"Yes, but we don't know what it is. We need to know more about Boni. Giangi could be the link. So, once we leave, we're on the job. You okay with that?"

"Of course," Emanuela said, stabbing the last olive and finishing her juice. "We'll have fun even if neither Boni or Giangi show up. Amoruso gave me a cover story. I'm a personal assistant to a marketing director for a pharma company. Sounds boring, doesn't it?"

Simona laughed. "For a reason. It will stop most guys from wanting to know about your professional life. Let's go!"

It was eight thirty by the time they were on their way to Deus. Early evening crowds were on the street, window shopping at the boutiques and the furniture and crafts stores. Outside tables at cafés were full of couples drinking wine and nibbling *aperitivo* servings of cheeses, fresh berries, rice with grilled vegetables, pizzas, and pastas.

The fashion styles were eclectic: hip, sporty chic, bohemian, floral appliques. Women wore trendy gladiator boots, impossibly high heels, sandals, or flat slippers. They carried vintage handbags with ethnic designs. The men were stylishly dressed as if they were auditioning for a fashion magazine: perfectly cut trousers and jeans, cotton sweaters, boat shoes, and sneakers. They sported trim haircuts and a few days' growth of beards.

Simona and Emanuela strolled down the streets, relishing the warm summer breezes and the relaxed social atmosphere. They turned the corner between Piazzale Segrino and Via Thaon di Revel and saw the neon *DEUS* logo in blue lights. A queue at the entrance snaked down the sidewalk, and they joined the line. They stood in line five minutes before a young man in black pants and a black shirt with a Deus logo walked down the queue and stopped.

"Do you have a reservation tonight?" he asked.

"No, just coming for a drink and *aperitivo*," Simona said.

He flashed a reflexive hospitality greeting. "Yes, I remember you came with a friend recently for dinner."

"That's right."

"Well, then, we like to accommodate regular customers. Would you follow me? There's room at the bar if you don't mind waiting a few minutes."

Emanuela's eyes widened. "I'm impressed, Simo. Do you always get the VIP treatment here?"

Simona groaned as they followed the greeter into the patio dining area. "Hardly. He probably remembers Giangi flirting with me."

The patio tables were full. Busy waiters were serving drinks and carrying platters of pastas, pizzas, grilled fish, and fresh salads. The atmosphere was lively with laughter, the tinkling of plates and glasses, and the sounds of jazz playing inside near the bar.

Simona and Emanuela weaved through tables to the tiled steps that led to the bar and a shop selling designer sportswear, bicycles, motorcycles, helmets, watches, and skateboards. The line at the bar was two deep; a crowd was waiting in an adjoining room with small tables. The decor was chic, with modern art prints of gambling tables, rolling dice, horse racing, sports cars, motorcycles, surfing, mountain climbing, and skydiving.

The bar was noisy with laughter, lively conversations, the tinkling of glasses, and a trumpeter playing a Miles Davis tune from *Kind of Blue* on a tiny stage in a corner. The music was too mellow for the boisterous crowd. No one seemed to be watching a muted soccer game on TV.

Deus's logo was painted on the tinted mirror at the bar behind shelves of Italian and imported liquors: Gilbey's, Beefeater, Bombay, Macallan, Hennessy, Grand Marnier, Courvoisier, Captain Morgan, Smirnoff, Jameson, Jack Daniel's, and Old Kentucky.

Attractive young women and a husky bartender poured drinks; served platters of cheeses with honey and nuts, and wooden trenches with razor-thin slices of prosciutto, pancetta, and bresaola; collected credit cards; and carried glasses to a window connecting to the kitchen.

Thin, blonde waitresses in short skirts and tight blouses picked up drink trays from a serving station at the end of the bar to deliver to the patio.

In five minutes, Simona and Emanuela snagged two empty bar stools before they were snatched away. A bartender cleared the empty glasses, soiled napkins, and *aperitivo* plates and dropped a menu on the bar.

Simona and Emanuela scanned the menu, taking their time. Emanuela waited until she caught the eye of a bartender. "Hello, could we order please? I'll have a club sandwich and a glass of Roero Arneis wine."

"The *nasi goreng* for me, same wine," Simona said, ordering her favorite Deus specialty with pilaf, chicken, shrimps, julienne vegetables, and eggs.

"Deus is quite the place," Emanuela said, raising her voice above the noisy bar. "If I wasn't seeing anyone, this would be my favorite place to hang out. Look at all the handsome men . . . like movie stars or models. I'm sure they have good jobs and money to spend on sexy girlfriends."

"Who they probably picked up here last week," Simona said with a laugh.

The bartender brought a wine bottle and two glasses, poured a couple of inches, and departed to wait on a couple who had just taken bar stools. Simona and Emanuela sipped and looked around the bar. "This certainly is not the kind of place where you'd find anyone from our office," Emanuela said. "They drink in sports bars and talk about soccer or working out at the gym. Oooh, Simo, look at that hunk at the end of the bar! He's gorgeous. Tanned, hair like wheat, gelled, combed back."

"I see him. . . . His date must be at most nineteen. Hungarian or Russian, probably. She's not letting him or his bulging wallet get away tonight."

Simona and Emanuela looked around the bar and the adjoining café area, enjoying the music and the lively conversations. They finished their small serving of wine, and the bartender poured more when he brought their meals. They ate leisurely, soaking up the party atmosphere. It was too loud to have much of a conversation, but they would be able to talk more on the walk back to Simona's.

It took only a few minutes to finish the modest servings of their meals. Simona pushed back her plate, finished her wine, and turned around to look at the patio.

Her heart skipped. She gasped, spotting Giangi and Alessandro Boni in the queue outside Deus, a dozen or so people in front of them. She leaned toward Emanuela. "They're here. . . . Don't turn around. Play it cool."

Simona turned back and looked in the bar mirror. She watched Giangi and Boni as they advanced in the queue. When the maître d' waved them inside, they strolled through the patio. Giangi mocked a celebrity entrance, smiling, waving, blowing air kisses, almost stumbling once. He followed Boni, who avoided the bar crowd spilling down the tiled steps. Boni detoured into the sports shop and made his way to the *aperitivo* buffet table at the end of the bar. He was certainly familiar with how to navigate his way through Deus.

Giangi continued his flamboyance, waving, laughing in a high-pitched bray, annoying people at the end of the bar. His mildly raucous behavior worked; a couple left their bar stools and headed toward the café room where the jazz group was returning to play another set.

Simona kept her eyes on them through the bar mirror. "Giangi's the short one. Boni's taller, with the blue Ralph Lauren shirt. Don't look at them."

The jazz group returned to the stage, blew warm-up notes, and sipped complimentary drinks delivered from the bar. The musicians set down their drinks, blew a few more notes, and started up with another Miles Davis piece.

Simona and Emanuela were turned toward the café area, Simona occasionally glancing up at the mirror.

Without warning, she heard a familiar squeal from the end of the bar. "Siiimooo, amooooore!"

She whispered to Emanuela, barely moving her lips. "Giangi. He spotted me. Coming over. Play it cool."

Simona ignored him. He squealed again, elbowing through the crowd behind the bar stools. "Permesso . . . permesso. . . . Siiiimooo . . . permesso . . . Siiimooo, hellohellohello! It's me!"

Simona turned her head and felt a moist hand on her shoulder. She greeted Giangi with a curt nod.

"*Ciao, tesoro. Come stai?* I've missed you!"

Giangi had reached over a man's shoulder to touch her. The man turned to Giangi, swore and pushed back. "*Guarda dove vai, coglione.*"

"*Coglione a me.* Suck my cock, darling, I know you'd love it," he squealed. "Simo, it's been ages! Where have you been?"

"*Imbecille!*" the man said, grabbing his girlfriend's hand and moving his bar stool so Giangi could squeeze next to Simona.

"Giangi, you're a prince like always," Simona said with a grin. "No need to be obnoxious all the time."

"Obnoxious? It's not me who drags around a fat-assed cow like that! Anyway, I'm so excited to see you!" He was drunk, slurring his words. "Who's this, a new girlfriend?" he cooed. "She's beautiful—almost like you. What's her name?"

Simona took her time answering. "This is Emanuela. Emanuela . . . meet Giangi . . . one of the Deus regulars."

"*Ciao*, Elena. A friend of Simo's, how lovely!"

"It's Emanuela, not Elena," she corrected.

"Oh, sorry, sorry. S-sorry, my mistake," he stammered. "Two beautiful ladies and no gentlemen with you? You were waiting for us, maybe?"

"Nice shirt, Giangi. Bright turquoise, very chic," Emanuela said, ignoring his comment.

He fluttered a hand like he was waving away a mosquito. "Oh, it's just something I got from a designer. Actually, it's Etro, given to me by Kean—yes, that Kean. It's part of their summer collection. It costs five hundred euros, but I got it free before any of the glamour boys strut on the runways wearing it. By that time, I'll probably give it away; it will be too common. I don't like common. I like new styles, shoes, new everything. Don't you? You should always wear the latest fashions." He was talking fast, slurring his words and releasing sprinkles of spit. His cologne was lime and lavender, more feminine than masculine.

A hand on Giangi's arm pulled him back a few inches. "Slow down, Giangi. You're getting in these ladies' faces. Anyone going to introduce me?"

"Alex, look who I found!" Giangi said, gripping Boni's hand. "This is my dear friend Simo and her girlfriend, Elena."

"Emanuela, Giangi, not Elena," she corrected him again.

"Ppfff, sorry, sorry," he snorted. "I forget so easily. I blame the cheap champagne we drank tonight. Right, Alex? We were pouring it down like we were dying of thirst."

"Hi there . . . I'm Alex." He held out his hand and shook theirs.

"Nice to meet you, Alex," Simona said. "This is my friend, Emanuela."

"Excuse me, do you mind if I move your stools a bit?" Boni said to the women. "There's room on both sides."

They nodded. Boni gently pushed their bar stools a couple of inches apart so he could stand between them.

Simona made quick observations. Boni's eyebrows were long, curly. She smelled a wisp of minty aftershave. He wasn't handsome, but he was a pleasant-looking man, someone she might share a few words with at a party or café who wouldn't leave a lasting impression. She'd looked at many photos of Boni already and had been curious what he was like in person. Nothing threatening or uncomfortable. He was average, like many men she'd met and forgotten about. But he was polite, and she liked polite men.

Giangi picked up where he had left off when Boni showed up. "Tonight's been a *disaster* until we met you lovely ladies. I took Alessandro to the Guido Restelli's VIP preview for next spring's collection at Superstudio, and what did we get? Horrible champagne—as tasty as sparkling water—grapes, and cheese chunks. That's it! I was invited because they want me to write about it on my blog. But the models were pitiful . . . like they'd run a race. Tired, bored, hating the clothes they were modeling. They were dreadful! None of my favorite colors, even! All yucky gray—I hate gray. I absolutely hate gray in clothes, like they dragged the clothes through ashes. Awful! Awful! Awful! No freesia yellow or hemlock green or placid blue—those are trending colors for next spring and summer. Even children know it.

"The dresses—or whatever you call them—were more like sacks hung on the girls, like they'd ripped cloth off a shelf and just threw it at them! Can you imagine? No style whatsoever! What are they thinking? No one's going to wear those clothes! Ship them to Africa or Somalia or Lebanon and give those wretched people something to wear instead of the ugly things they throw over camel humps. Those countries need fashion! Maybe I'll write about that sometime, start a crusade to dress people in those horrible countries where women wear drab sack things that look awful and hide their faces like there's something wrong with them. Dreadful! Dreadful! They should go modern and wear nice clothes, like us! I love, love, love that idea! What do you think, Alessandro?"

"Slow down, Giangi. You sound like you've been drinking jet fuel. No more champagne for you tonight."

"Oh, Alessandro, don't be mean! Don't you like Simo? And Elena—sorry—Emanuela?" Emanuela rolled her eyes and nodded.

"Aren't they gorgeous, Alex? I love beautiful women, *absolutely love them!*"

"Okay, Giangi, slow down a bit," Alex repeated. "You're going to scare them. Be nice . . . a gentleman." He grinned at Simona and Emanuela. "Don't mind Giangi. He gets carried away when he's had too much champagne, preaching like Papa Francesco that fashion will save the world." He laughed, patting Giangi on the shoulder.

"But fashion is important, darling! It's important that people dress right! They must! It can change the world!"

"Take a break, Giangi. Let me talk to the ladies. They look like decent people. The conversation at the premiere wasn't exactly interesting, for me at least."

"You have an accent, Alex?" Emanuela said.

"A little. I'm American but learned Italian very young. My father is Italian, my mother American. I grew up in New York but spent summers in Tropea with my grandparents."

"That's nice," Simona said. "Do you live in Milan?"

"Yes, I work with my father. He's an architect. But I travel to the U.S. and around Europe."

Giangi raised a hand and waved to the bartender. "Yoo-hoo, waiter. Waiter, can we get drinks over here?" he shouted over the noisy crowd. "I'm going to faint if I don't get a drink!"

Alex looked at Simona. "Would you like another drink?"

"Alex is treating tonight, ladies," Giangi said. "He *loves* to buy drinks for pretty women. Isn't that right, Alex?"

"Giangi, why don't you go outside and get some fresh air? Let me talk with these ladies in peace."

"But you drank that awful champagne, too!"

"A glass, maybe two. It was pretty dreadful. At least I wasn't grabbing the waiter every time he came by."

"But I was depressed . . . forced to look at those awful clothes!"

"Do you go to fashion shows often, Alex?" Simona asked, looking for a way to cut him away from Giangi.

"Yoo-hoo, wine here, please!" Giangi cried out again, waving at another bartender.

"That's Giangi's job. I'm learning about the fashion industry. We have clients in fashion—important ones—and I need to know more about their business. We design stores for them."

"That's interesting. Sounds like a great job," Simona said. "You must enjoy it."

"Oh, I do. It's creative. We design buildings—apartments, hotels, villas—not just in Italy. We have projects starting soon in Moscow, Nice, and Istanbul."

"Fascinating. Have you designed anything I'd recognize?"

He shrugged. "Not really. We work in teams. The lead architect gets all the credit—he's my father, actually. The detailed work is done by others who help out on various parts of the job: foundations, materials, working with contractors, laying out floors, services, special features for the client. Most of our work is with the government, foreign corporations, or private companies, like in real estate."

"I didn't know that. Makes sense."

"How about you, Simona? Where do you work?"

Simona reverted to her DIGOS cover story. "It's nothing important, like your job. I work at a law firm, researching patents, getting permissions, preparing documents for clients and courts. It's boring legal stuff. I don't know why I stay with it. I'd love to open a yoga studio, but you can't make money in that. So I stick with my job, go to the gym, and just take it easy."

"Where's your office?"

"Near the Giardini Pubblici, a small office on the seventh floor."

"My father's apartment is on Corso Venezia."

"Really? What a great place to live."

The bartender delivered four wineglasses, napkins, and a tray of finger food. "Finally! Our drinks!" Giangi squealed. "Service tonight is horrible . . . and the bartender is rude! A piranha in a bidet. I'd fire him if Deus was my place."

Alex took out a hundred-euro note from his wallet and waved at the bartender to keep the change.

"Thank you, Alex. You're a prince," Giangi said. "I love to come here with you. You spoil me."

Simona and Emanuela thanked Boni. They each reached for a bowl-shaped glass with a couple of ounces of red wine.

"This wine is delicious!" Giangi squealed. "I love this! So much better than the rainwater we had earlier."

"Take it easy, Giangi. This is your last for tonight," said Boni.

They all sipped and looked around the room. The conversations and laughter were getting louder as the wine flowed like a waterfall, drowning out the jazz combo. Raising his voice, Alex said, "Deus is packed tonight. Do you come here often, Simona?"

She nodded. "Yeah, a couple of times a week. Deus has good vibes, and the people who come here are interesting. Good jobs and very social."

"Yes, Isola is quite the place to live. My apartment is in Brera. Good restaurants there. You should come over sometime."

She shrugged, sipped her wine, not picking up on his offer.

Giangi said, "I'm starved, Alex! All I've had to eat tonight were those pitiful *parmigiano* chunks and grapes. I swear, I thought the designer was going bankrupt when I saw what looked like real food but wasn't. Awful! He deserves to go out of business with his horrible new collection." He guffawed, laughing at his own attempt at humor.

"Go to the *aperitivo* buffet and get something there," said Boni.

"Be right back!" Giangi took his almost empty wineglass and moved through the crowd to the buffet with its remains of rice salads, pasta, cheese, olives, prosciutto, breads, and sliced fruit.

"Poor Giangi. He gets some champagne in him and goes crazy. But he's fun and knows everyone in fashion."

"Is he a good friend?" Simona asked.

"Sort of. We have friends in common. I had plans for this weekend, but they canceled. My . . . arrangements didn't work out. Giangi called this afternoon and said he was going to a fabulous party. It wasn't. I could have been in Sardinia this weekend, but . . . well, things don't always work out the way you want."

"You don't seem . . . his type," Simona said.

Boni chuckled and shook his head: "No, I'm not gay, most emphatically, but I do have gay friends. Giangi is well connected; he knows everyone in the fashion industry. I met him when we began designing the new Armani store in Dubai, which opens in a few days."

"Armani, wow, that must be exciting," Emanuela said.

"It is. In fact, my father is having a party for Giorgio in a couple of weeks at his apartment. Why don't you and Simona come as my guests?"

"A party with King Giorgio! I'd love to!" Emanuela squealed. "When is it?"

"Two weeks from tonight."

She put her hand to her mouth. "Oh, damn! I'll be in Paris for a bachelorette party that weekend. I've already bought the tickets. What a pity; I would have loved to have gone."

"How about you, Simona?" Alex asked.

She made a pensive face, appearing to take her time, not wanting to jump at the offer. "Two weeks from now . . . let's see. Next weekend I'm busy . . . I don't think I have anything the following weekend. But I don't know; that's not my crowd. I'm a private person. I don't know anyone in the fashion industry."

"Please come. You'd enjoy it." Boni reached into his wallet for a business card and dropped it on the bar next to her fingers. "Add me as a friend on Facebook and write a private message."

She slipped the card into her purse without looking at it. "I don't do much social media, sorry. Not even Facebook. My friends insist I join, but I don't have time."

"How about your e-mail or cell number?"

She reached into her purse and pulled out a phony business card with the law firm name and address, a front DIGOS used when an agent needed a phony contact. She scribbled her cell number and handed it over.

Boni glanced at it and slipped it into his shirt pocket. "I'll text you next week with the time and location."

"It sounds like fun. Oh, no, now I have to buy new clothes." She made a funny face like she was embarrassed. "What will I wear? You'll have to help me, Manu."

"Fun! I love to shop. Break the bank, Simona. Go in style. You only live once."

"My closet looks pathetic. I can't make it without a serious shopping session."

"You'll meet fashion people, designers, models, friends of Giorgio Armani, and my father," said Boni.

"What's your father's name?"

"Ghigo Boni. You might have heard of him."

She shook her head. "Sorry, it doesn't ring a bell."

"If you read gossip tabloids, you might have seen him and my step-mother. They go to parties, premieres, charity balls, that sort of thing."

"Are they celebrities?"

He grinned and rolled his eyes. "My stepmother thinks she is. My mother is American. She lives in New York. After they divorced, my father married an Italian woman. They have a daughter, Allegra, who wants to be a model. She's only seventeen but is starving herself, reading fashion magazines, watching the runway shows. She thinks she'll get hired if Giorgio sees her. Good luck, Allegra."

"A teenager around the house—that must be fun. Do you have any other brothers or sisters who walk the runway or are featured in fashion magazines?"

Alex's head snapped around to look into Simona's eyes. She knew about his brother having been killed in Iraq. She wondered if she was asking too many personal questions, but she was seeing how open he would be with her. He hadn't balked before. He seemed relaxed, a good sign that her curiosity had not come across as probing but as showing genuine interest in him.

Simona held her breath waiting for his answer. She knew agents had to be careful when they were undercover. Too much too fast could backfire.

"No. Not anymore. I had a brother. He died in 2003."

CHAPTER TWENTY-THREE

Two weeks later, a phalanx of agents stood in the hallway outside their offices when Simona came through the vaulted door into DIGOS. Their conversations were shifting between a popular reality show broadcast the previous night and a scandal about a PD left-wing politician taking bribes involving lucrative construction projects for Milan Expo 2015. But those conversations stopped abruptly when they saw Simona.

When she passed by them, one said, "Have fun last night, Simona?"

"Of course," she said, breezing past them.

Another said, "Isn't it early for celebrities to show up at work?"

"I had to drag myself out of bed so as not to keep my fan club waiting for me this morning." Chuckles from the hallway. None of these agents were on her team, and they were a bit envious of the attention she and Dario were getting with their investigation.

When Simona turned the corner, heading toward her office, another snide comment: "Hey, Simona, why didn't you take me to your posh fashion party? I heard there were gorgeous women there, outnumbering men two to one. Those are good odds."

An agent down the hall answered, "Nah, you wouldn't have fit in, Alfredo. You're a faithful married man with kids. The models are young, single, always dieting. They wouldn't be tempted to touch *polpettone* [hamburger meat] like you."

"Whoa! Hah!" the crowd in the hallway howled. "Good one, Stefano! Alfredo, you're an old, squashy *polpettone*!"

Stefano added, "Yeah, you can get sick and die from tainted *polpettone*."

Another howl, clapping, and cheering. "Alfredo, you're a *polpettone*—your new nickname!"

"Aw, shut up," Alfredo said, retreating into his office and slamming the door.

The hallway erupted in laughter, followed by more jeering and calls for Alfredo to come back for more teasing. A muffled string of words came from his office, possibly a curse, followed by more howls from the hallway.

Simona was grinning when she walked into her office. Dario looked up from his computer, chuckling at his colleagues' humorous bantering, a common practice in the corridors of DIGOS. "The gauntlet of wolves has been waiting for you. But you tamed them. How was your big night?"

Simona sat down and flipped up her computer screen. "Interesting, but it was a long evening. I saw firsthand how the rich and spoiled entertain themselves. They may have piles of money, but some don't have manners."

"I wonder what they would have thought if they had known that a DIGOS agent was an invited guest."

"Nobody knew, thank God." She looked up at the clock. "Is Amoruso in?"

"About five minutes ago."

"She texted that she wants to see me first thing. Come along, you should hear this, too."

They went back into the hallway. The wolves had been tamed, grumbling as she and Dario passed on their way to Amoruso's office. Simona fired one last salvo. "Ragazzi, isn't it time to get to work? I promise tantalizing gossip at lunch today. You'll hear about the celebrities I met. Lots of juicy details!"

Antonella's door was open. She was on her cell phone. She motioned for them to come in, ended her call, and punched in Giorgio's number. "Simona's here. Want to stop by?"

"Give me a few minutes."

"Good morning, Simona!" Antonella said in a hearty tone. "I can't wait to hear about your evening."

"I saw a slice of Milanese life that most people only read about. But more important, I learned something from Alex Boni that could be what we've been missing. But no more scraps for the wolves in the hallway, not until I've told you about it."

Antonella chuckled. "You returned their fire; they won't tease you anymore. So, how was it?"

"I haven't had time to finish my report but will in a couple of hours. As I was telling Dario, it was a very productive assignment. Alex Boni was with me a few times, and I observed how he interacts with guests and his family. Most important, I recorded a revealing conversation with him on my necklace microphone."

"I look forward to hearing it once Lucchini gets here. But who was at the party? Not that I'm curious like the wolves in the hallway, but maybe a bit," Antonella said, laughing at herself. "I look forward to reading your report, and so will Lucchini. But please start talking. How was the party venue?"

"As you know, it was at Alex Boni's father's two-story penthouse on Corso Venezia. Without a doubt, it's the most luxurious apartment I've been to. A bit too much glitz for a girl from Bergamo who likes to mountain bike and do yoga."

"Don't put yourself down. Look at what you've done in a few months, working a good case and getting invited to the family home of someone who might be involved in the Hussain group. I don't know anyone else who could have pulled that off."

"Thank you."

"Start with the background—who was there, and what did you see? Give us a little tour."

"Sure. The party was to celebrate the Armani flagship store in Dubai, designed by Ghigo Boni, which opened three days ago. He's also designing a new conference center in Milan CityLife, scheduled to begin construction next year."

"I read about it. I remember Boni got the contract. Pretty lucrative, a big city project. He's getting richer by the day. Continue, please."

"I got there a few minutes early. There was already a crowd at the ground-floor elevator, standing around as if they were waiting to get into San Siro. Giangi Marinoni, the fashion blogger I told you about, was already there, excited like a child with a new toy at Christmas, claiming it was the biggest party that week. Alex had the duty of greeting guests when they came off the elevator into the reception area.

"Ghigo Boni and his wife, Lucrezia, were host and hostess, along with their teenage daughter, Allegra, who wants to be a model. In the receiving line were Giorgio Armani; his beautiful nieces, Silvana and Roberta; and three male American models. I didn't get their names. Their Italian was juvenile, they could say *buonasera*, their names, pleased to meet you, the basic tourist words. Handsome men, obviously, but playing above their skill level, in my opinion. They just stood around, speaking in English to each other, eyes bulging at all the guys in the ballroom, including the security guards and waiters."

"They were props, I'm sure," Antonella said. "Not expected to say anything intelligent, just look elegant and flirt with the older women and the handsome single men, maybe invite them to a gay nightclub after the party."

"Yeah, I bet you could have found half the guests at the same nightclub for the post-party afterward."

"Celebrating their privileged social status, I'm sure," Antonella said. "So, tell us more."

"After I went through the receiving line, Alex walked Giangi and me into the ballroom. It was only about a third full; more people were still waiting downstairs to ride up in the elevator. The line was long, with black SUVs and taxis pulling up every couple of minutes with more guests who looked like they were going to a Hollywood premiere."

"And upset, of course, at missing out on the early champagne."

"How did you know? I heard comments later, including one woman saying too loudly, 'Why couldn't they find a better way to get us up here! I waited ten minutes in the dreadful heat! I went to Aldo Coppola today and spent five hundred euros to have my hair styled. And now look at me! I'm like a shaggy dog after a rainstorm!'"

They roared, Dario slapping his thigh, Antonella throwing back her head. "Rich and spoiled," Antonella said. "Narcissists expecting everyone to pamper them, treat them like royalty."

Simona continued: "In the ballroom, waiters in tuxedos were handing out Ruinart Blanc de Blancs champagne and tasty appetizers: trays of sushi, prawn canapes, oysters, Beluga caviar blinis, and lobster velouté served in shell-shaped Japanese cocottes."

"I love sushi," Dario said. "Oh, I wish I could have been there to sample them all."

"I'm drooling," Antonella added. "I would have had at least one of everything."

"And that was as the party was starting. Later in the evening, they brought around coconut milk gelato and minced peanuts for dessert."

"Did you try the gelato?" Antonella asked.

Simona held up two fingers. "Two scoops, my favorite of the whole evening. My sweet tooth was very happy."

"Those kinds of parties always have the most chic food, with the host and hostess trying to impress their guests," Antonella said. "Speaking of the Bonis, how did Alessandro treat you?"

"Quite well. A gentleman, in fact. Alex watched me in the ballroom as I was admiring the incredible elegance—a polished mahogany floor, an antique fireplace, eighteenth-century antiques, and contemporary furniture. He took me by the hand and pointed to three enormous glass chandeliers in the middle of the ballroom—a gift from one of his father's clients in Saudi Arabia. I said nice things about them, of course, but all I could think about was that if one of those crashed, it could kill someone. They were too gaudy for my style, and I didn't walk under them. Alex took me over to the grand piano, where a musician was playing Gershwin, Duke Ellington, Beatles, even Elton John tunes. Alex knew the piano player. He had a few words with him and introduced me. Then we walked over to see the modern art in a little room by the piano and fireplace."

"His own art gallery," Antonella commented. "How nice. What did you see?"

"A Picasso . . . two Matisses . . . a Boccioni . . . two Lucio Fontanas. A sculpture by Giò Pomodoro on a balcony that looked over Corso Venezia, where Alex made some startling revelations later in the evening about his father."

"Let's wait for that until Lucchini arrives," said Antonella. "I want him to hear it. Continue with the party."

"All right. Alex had to go back to the reception area. Giangi stuck with me through his first two glasses of champagne. We took a circular glass staircase up to a second-story terrace with a flower garden, trees, and a swimming pool illuminated by candles and torches. Not many people were on the terrace, but as the evening went on, more went to the pool and drank champagne. That's when their manners seemed to slip. I was quietly sipping champagne, nibbling caviar and prawns, and watching high-society elites lunging at the appetizers like they hadn't eaten in a week! Grabbing here and there, gobbling the food, hunting for a waiter with a fresh tray, pouncing on him, and emptying the tray in seconds. It was quite funny; even rich people can't get enough free food. I even saw a couple of men wrap prawns in napkins and stuff them in their pockets to take home. Probably to feed their cats."

Antonella and Dario both laughed. "I'm enjoying this," Antonella said. "You're like an actress on stage. You know how to engage your audience."

"After a few minutes on the terrace, Giangi and I went back down to the ballroom in time to see Ghigo Boni make a little speech, saying how honored he was to design Armani's new flagship store and how their friendship goes back years and will last forever. Everyone politely applauded and then went back to eating and drinking. Alex found me and walked me around to meet guests. A few I remember: *Assessore ai Lavori pubblici per il Comune de Milano* [Commissioner of Public Works] Luca Castelnuovo; his wife, Eleonora; the American consul general, Winston Bishop; and his wife. I don't remember her name, sorry."

"I met her at a Fourth of July party at the consulate," Antonella said. "A very nice lady."

Simona continued: "A little later, we met the superintendent of Teatro alla Scala, Jean-Christoph Fournier; his wife, Benedicte; and conductor Maestro Armando Bongiovanni, who is conducting the premiere of *Turandot* on December 7. He stood out from the crowd with a sweep of blond hair that touched his shoulders. I can imagine how his hair looks when he's on the podium directing the orchestra."

What Simona didn't mention was that she and Armando Bongiovanni had talked at length after the introduction, finding common ground about music, books, theater, and art. At one point, he took her hand, led her upstairs to the terrace, and said, "You're a very beautiful and charming young lady. I would be happy to meet you sometime later. Is that possible?"

"Ah, ah . . ." Simona said, at a loss for words. His soothing voice, warm smile, and the twinkle in his blue eyes had mesmerized her.

"Please don't think I'm being forward," he interrupted. "I've been traveling around Europe all year, a week in Prague, two in Amsterdam, another two in Moscow, a month in London. I haven't had time for a social life. I want to slow down a bit while I'm in Milan, see your famous city, and meet interesting people—like you." His roguish grin lit up his tanned face like he was under a theater spotlight.

"Well . . . you'll be impressed with Milan. Everyone is," she said, caught off guard at his hint. "What do you . . . have in mind?"

A modest smile spread into another warm grin. "I like you, Simona . . . your shyness . . . like a young girl . . . it's very touching."

"Me, shy? Why do you say that?"

"Because you don't know how to respond. Should I start over? Slow down a bit? I shocked you by being so direct. I don't meet many women who I'm attracted to so quickly."

"No, it's fine. I just never expected . . . here . . . my first time at a party like this . . . and I didn't think I'd find someone . . . so pleasant . . . and . . . interesting to talk to."

He bowed. "I confess, Simona, I feel the same way about you."

Her heart skipped a beat. Armando was polite, not like men who were eager to brag about themselves or be meddlesome, pumping her with questions not appropriate for a first conversation.

"Let's not lose this opportunity. Give me your number." He reached into his pocket, took out a smartphone, and started tapping on the screen as she gave him her cell number.

"I'll give you a call one of these days when I'm free. Coffee. Lunch. I'm in Milan for rehearsals the next couple of months. Maybe you can show me around, take me to a gallery, have a nice dinner."

"That would be lovely."

"Siiimoooooo, where have you been?" Her heart sank.

"Oh, no, it's Giangi."

"Giangi?" Armando said with a puzzled expression. "That sounds like a dog's name."

"No, Giangi's a gay fellow I know, a bit of a pest sometimes."

Giangi swept to her side, wrapping an arm around her waist, stretching to kiss her cheek. "Simo, I just met the most charming boy—man. He's wonderful! He adores me! I'm thrilled! A new man in my life!"

"Giangi, I'm pleased you're enjoying the champagne. Maestro, may I introduce you to Giangi Marinoni. He's a fashion guru and journalist."

Giangi glanced at him, smiled painfully, uttered, "Hello, how are you," and then turned back to Simona. "Come meet Rocco! He's soooo intelligent and dresses like a prince! I love a man who wears high fashion. You *must* meet him!"

"Sorry, Giangi, not now. I'll meet your new friend, but later. I'd like to finish my conversation here. Do you mind?"

Armando took her almost empty glass and said, "No, that's fine, you two can talk. I'll come back with more champagne."

"So, is this your new date for tonight, Simo?" Giangi asked when Armando walked away to find a waiter. "He looks . . . nice . . . great hair, by the way, but . . . unfortunately, straight. So sad. I'll leave him all for you. By the way, you were so busy with that *biondo* that you haven't heard all the ladies in the ballroom squealing like geese, 'George! George!' That was not for Armani. Guess who just arrived? George Clooney and Matt Damon!"

"So, you enjoyed talking to Armando, a very promising conductor," Antonella said.

"Yes, a real gentleman. I'd love to see him conducting some time."

"Maybe you will," Antonella said with a smile.

Simona blushed and looked down for a moment. "Let me continue; this is a fun story. Later in the evening, Armando and I were up on the terrace having a nice conversation when there was a commotion downstairs in the ballroom, with women squealing, 'George! George!' There was applause and laughter. We didn't know what was happening. Guess who had just arrived at the party?"

"Who?!" Antonella said.

"George Clooney and Matt Damon."

"Really? What were they doing there? Clooney has a villa on Lago di Como."

"As we later found out, Clooney and Damon are making a movie about recovering stolen Nazi art at the end of the war. They're shooting film in Europe this summer."

"Yes, I've read about it. The movie is *The Monuments Men*. It's been in the papers."

"Clooney and Damon are friends, and Clooney had invited him to Lago di Como. Armani has been wanting Clooney to appear in his ads, and knew he was going to be in Milan, so he invited him to his party."

"Did you meet them?" Antonella asked, her eyes widening.

Simona took her time, building suspense for an anecdote she knew they would enjoy. She cleared her throat. "Well . . . Clooney and Damon were making the rounds of the ballroom, shaking hands and hugging women who looked like they were going to faint. After that Hollywood entrance, they came up the stairs to the terrace."

Another pause. Antonella and Dario leaned closer to catch her every word. Simona cleared her throat again.

"So . . . I was talking to Maestro Bongiovanni again, and Clooney and Damon were being followed up onto the terrace. Then, out of the corner of my eye, I saw Clooney step away from Damon, leaving the women behind. He came up to the maestro and said, 'Armando! What a surprise. Wonderful to see you again!' They hugged and shook hands. Later the maestro told me they had met in Paris. Anyway, the next thing I know, the maestro introduces me to Clooney. He shook my hand and kissed me on the cheeks."

"George Clooney kissed you!" Dario said, gasping. He and Antonella laughed, shaking their heads.

"Exciting!" Antonella said. "I'll bet your heart was throbbing."

"It was. It was. He's even more handsome than his photos. His eyes are deep, dark . . . inviting. And his smile is so gentle and warm. No wonder millions of women have fallen in love with him after seeing his movies."

"Ah, were you falling in love with him?" Dario asked.

"Please, please, Dario. I was on duty, not one of the fawning tribe of jealous women staring at us."

"Then what happened?" Dario wanted to know.

"The maestro and Clooney chatted. The crowd was creeping closer to eavesdrop. Matt Damon came over, and Clooney introduced both of us to him. Damon shook my hand but didn't kiss my cheeks. He looked more shy. Handsome, but shy."

"You met two Hollywood stars in one night!" Dario said in disbelief. "You'll never forget it. Then what happened?"

"Sadly, it was soon over. Clooney told the maestro he and Damon had to leave, another party or something. Maybe to get away from the fans so they could have a quiet dinner by themselves. I imagine it gets tedious to have fans swarming around all the time. The last thing Clooney said to the maestro was, 'Come up to Como sometime. I'm going to be around for a while. Matt will be there, too. Bring your lovely girlfriend; it would be nice to see her again.'

"The maestro said, 'George, she's not my girlfriend. We just met tonight.' George gave him a sly smile and winked and said, "Maybe she will be. You can both be my guests. It was great to see you again.'"

Antonella said, "You might go to Clooney's villa?"

Simona held up her hand. "I don't think so. I will see Maestro Bongiovanni again only if I'm on duty at La Scala for the premiere. He's very busy, probably has girlfriends all over Europe."

Antonella smiled. "Marvelous anecdote, Simona. You probably won't put it in your report, but I want Lucchini to hear it."

As she said this, he appeared in the doorway. "What is it you want me to hear?"

"Come in! We were just mentioning you. Simona's been telling us fascinating tales of the Armani party at the Boni penthouse. You won't believe this, but she met George Clooney and he invited her to his villa on Lago di Como!"

"Really? Tell me! I want to hear about it."

Simona repeated the story, to everyone's amusement.

When they had all had a few laughs, Giorgio asked, "Was the Questore there? He mentioned it in passing."

"Yes, he was," Simona replied. "I saw him in the ballroom with his wife and Sindaco Giuliano Pisapia and his wife. Questore Taddei looked at me, made a puzzled face, and started walking toward me. I put a finger to my lips and turned to Alex. Questore Taddei turned away. Good thing. If he had come up to me, I would have had to introduce him to Alex, and my cover would have been blown."

"He's a cautious fellow, just curious," said Giorgio. "He asked me this morning what one of my agents was doing at an Armani party. Did you learn anything useful for us?"

"I did. Boni junior was busy during the party but sought me out a few times to introduce me around. Later in the evening, we had a revealing exchange on the terrace. He had been patient, a good host, but could barely hide his anger toward his father. He said, 'These are his people, not mine. Most of them are phonies, pretenders, sycophants, ass kissers.'"

"That's pretty harsh," Giorgio said. "Not unusual for a son to hate his father as a rebellious teenager, but not at his age. And he gets a paycheck from his father. Why would he be resentful?"

"I'm not sure how hard Alex works. He goes away almost every weekend, sailing on the family yacht in Sardinia, flying off to Paris, Rome, London for long weekends. He seems to be an errand boy, not someone his father trusts with serious work."

"And the resentment toward his father builds," said Giorgio. "That creates a lot of psychological pressure—working for him, getting paid well, but deep down he probably knows he doesn't deserve it. So he resents how his life has turned out."

Simona reached into her purse and took out a small tape recorder. "I want you to hear this, a crucial conversation I had with Alex." She pressed the "Play" button.

Alex's was the first voice: "Are you enjoying the party, Simona?"

"Of course. Your guests are very impressive and elegant. I like your sister. She said nice things about my clothes and asked how we met. She was polite, intelligent, a normal teenage girl who's seriously into clothes, fashion, and boys. Allegra knows what she wants, a career in fashion."

"She'll probably be successful if my father has anything to do with it. Her grades in school are good. She likes to read and talk about art and music. Fashion is her latest craze. Maybe it lasts, maybe not."

"Your father is charming, Alex. He introduced me to Armani, who didn't know me from Adam's house cat, but they both complimented me."

"I told Father about you before the party. He said you probably had more brains than the other girls I bring around. He usually doesn't like them and says they're only after our money."

A pause of four or five seconds with the sounds of glasses clinking and laughter in the background. Someone greeted Alex. They shared a few words, then he said, "My father . . . you see . . . look around . . . he's surrounded by VIPs, the filthy rich, powerful, many corrupt and nasty. But he's come a long way. He was a poor immigrant when he went to America. Struggled, had no money. He worked two or three jobs and got into university. He was obsessed with doing better than his father and escaping the poverty he had known growing up in Calabria."

"And look what he's done, Alex. He has a nice family, this beautiful apartment. He's successful in his business and knows important people. You should be proud of him."

More laughter and boisterous party noise in the background. Alex didn't say anything for another few seconds.

"I don't know how much I should say," he said, his voice lower, tense. "I can't forgive him for divorcing my mother."

A long pause, party noises in the distance. "Unfortunately, Alex, that happens too often. But children learn to adapt, love both parents, and not carry resentments about one or the other. That's not good for anyone."

"How do you know?" A sharp answer. "Were your parents divorced?"

"No."

Another pause, more laughter, and loud conversations far away. "It's not just my mother. I told you I had a brother."

"You said he died."

"Killed in Iraq in 2003. He was an army captain, awarded decorations and medals, a West Point graduate, the pride of my mother and father, the smart one. He could do no wrong. My parents worshipped him, bragged that he would go to law school after the army, get into politics, go to Washington, and become a powerful politician, not like the corrupt hacks here in Italy."

Another pause, the laughter subsiding. Boni's voice was clear, as if he were inches from Simona's microphone. "But me, I was just the younger brother. They didn't brag about me. They didn't say I was stupid, but they encouraged me to go to a school that wasn't prestigious like West Point. I didn't want to go to a military school. I just wanted to leave home. I graduated, worked a few years, traveled in America. My parents knew I wasn't going to set the world on fire like my brother. Father brought me to Milano when I was bored in New York and hired me so he could control my life more. He keeps me busy, but not with important work. He sends me to meetings with people he trusts but rarely asks me my opinion. Sometimes . . . I think my father is embarrassed about me, wishes it was me who had been killed in Iraq—"

"Don't say that, Alex. That isn't true. No parent ever wishes that. You're too hard on yourself. Give yourself credit. You have much to be grateful for. Be proud of what you have."

Another pause. Alex cleared his throat and greeted people passing. It was another fifteen seconds before he spoke to Simona.

"You are different from other women I know."

"What do you mean?"

"You listen to me. You shut up and listen. You don't brag about yourself or say ridiculous things to keep a conversation going. You don't seem like someone trying to marry into big money. You ask questions and are interested in what I have to say."

"I am."

"Then . . . I'll tell you something I don't share with other people."
He waited a few seconds before continuing. "I hated the Iraq war. It
was wrong, tragically wrong. Bush, Cheney, and Rumsfeld sent thousands of Americans to their death, including my brother. Thousands
of Americans returned with serious wounds . . . mental and physical. I
hate the American politicians for what they did. They're war criminals.
But they walk free, just like corrupt politicians in Italy."

Another pause.

"One day . . . one day in the future . . . they will regret what they have
done to Italy—the economy ruined, the rage against failed politicians,
people left with despair, no hope. They'll have something else to regret."

"I don't know what you mean."

A sigh from Alex. He cleared his throat, coughed, spoke in a whisper.
"I can't say. . . . It's just that . . . well . . . I know things . . . and . . . it
could be bad for these people here, the rich, the politically connected.
They have a perfect world now . . . but maybe not later."

Another pause before Simona responded. "Nobody knows what
is going to happen in the future. Politicians now in power could lose
their credibility, even their immunity, when they aren't reelected. Few
of them back in the nineties even went to prison. Is that what you're
talking about?"

"Not exactly. I've already told you too much."

She clicked off the recorder and set it on Antonella's desk. It was
quiet in the office. Antonella and Giorgio looked at each other, digesting
what Boni had said and its possible consequences.

"That was the end of the conversation," Simona said after a few
moments. "You can listen to the rest, but we were interrupted. People
came over to thank Boni for inviting them. Guests were leaving. We
moved through crowds, and he didn't say anything else important."

Giorgio said, "Fascinating. You caught him off guard. He'd probably had a bit to drink and felt comfortable opening up to you. He also
didn't think you'd say anything about what he told you. Do you think
you'll see him again?"

She shook her head. "I don't know."

Giorgio reached for the tape recorder. "I want the Questore to hear this right away. Boni is secretive. He said just enough to convince me he's involved in something we need to know about."

CHAPTER TWENTY-FOUR

On a Saturday afternoon in late November, Kareem was parked in an unmarked van with Esman, Kalil, and Tito on Via Daniele Manin across from Giardini Pubblici, the largest public park in central Milan. The wooded park was a popular weekend place for Milanesi to take leisurely walks, relax on benches around fountains, visit the Planetarium and the Natural History museum, or watch children on the playground. It was a sunny but chilly day, an opportunity to enjoy Milan's brisk autumn weather before the long winter months of snow blizzards, bleak overcast skies, and freezing temperatures sweeping south from the Alps.

Earlier that morning, Kareem had driven to his office in his Carefull van, parked it in the garage, and retrieved the keys to a small van without the company logo. He had driven near Esman's and Kalil's apartments, picking them up in alleys to avoid CCTV cameras on the street, and then on to Via Padova to pick up Tito behind the kebab café.

Driving to Via Manin, Kareem told the others, "I learned this technique at the training camp. Surveillance cameras focus on streets and building entrances, rarely on alleys, except behind government offices or buildings where criminals might break in. I checked a couple of weeks ago, and there are no cameras in your alleys."

"You don't think we're being followed, Kareem?" Tito asked.

"No, I'm positive. But I'm taking precautions. We're just two weeks away from the celebration. We'll follow the same procedure then . . . today is practice to show you the route and how we will work as a team."

Esman was sitting next to Kareem in the front; Tito and Kalil were in the backseat. Kareem reached between the two front seats and took out a clipboard with a calendar spreadsheet. Each day was divided into twenty-four hours and then into fifteen-minute segments. Scribbled on the calendar were Kareem's notes from the morning timetable.

"I picked up the van at 9:50 at Carefull . . . drove to Esman's apartment, picked him up at 10:45 . . . then to Kalil's apartment at 11:20 . . . and picked up Tito at 11:58."

He checked his watch: 12:20. "Two hours and thirty minutes from Carefull to here."

"Precise, Kareem. Just what you'd expect from an engineer," Tito said with a smile.

"Remember what they teach at uni: Measure twice, cut once."

Kareem flipped calendar pages to a date circled in red ink. "We follow the same schedule in two weeks." He lifted the page to a map of the city center. "Our target is five minutes from here." He circled a location on a map of the city center and then pointed to the end of Via Manin, where eight streets converged at Piazza Cavour, a busy commercial area with a pharmacy, cafes, shops, the Hotel Cavour, the Banca Monte dei Paschi di Siena, and a traffic island for commuters taking tram number one. "Traffic will be heavy that day, with people Christmas shopping. There will be police barricades at some intersections."

"Everyone knows where it is," Tito said. "One of the most famous landmarks in Milan. But I've never been inside. Have you, Kalil?"

"Never," he said with a scowl. "What would I do there?"

"Wear a designer suit with a silk tie and expensive loafers to make the infidels jealous of your elegant taste in clothes," Tito said with a chuckle.

"I wouldn't be seen with those filthy dogs! Or dress like them, even if I had a ton of money. They look like pimps with those fancy clothes!"

Kareem said, "Enough. We're here to plan our attack, not talk about clothes. We have critical details to discuss. Tito, give me the shirt in the backseat." Tito handed it over the seat to him.

"This is a Carefull employee shirt. I'll have one for each of you. I'll take a letter on Carefull stationery to the target's security office with fake names to get badges for you to drive through the security." He reached into his shirt pocket and took out his personal security badge with his photo.

"When we reach the building, Esman, Tito, and I will take an elevator to the upper floor. Kalil will leave in the van, drive six blocks to an underground garage, and wait there an hour, maybe longer. Don't wander; we'll be back. Be in the van when we return."

"I will," Kalil said.

"Will we have weapons?" Esman asked.

"Kalil bought two automatic pistols on the black market with Alessandro's money. You will have one, Kalil keeps the other, and Tito is the driver."

Tito said, "Kalil knows how to use them, don't you?"

"I have known guns since I was a child!" Kalil said, slapping a hand on Esman's headrest. "Guns are good. . . . They give you power. . . . No one messes with a man who has a gun unless he wants to die. All men should carry guns!"

Kareem held up his hand to stop Kalil. "Fine. We all would have had weapons and ammunition if the shipment from La Spezia hadn't been inspected and intercepted by the police. Two will be enough. Only use them in an emergency, which I doubt we'll have." He lifted the calendar spreadsheet and unfolded maps of the venue: several floors, elevators, bridges, the main hall, technical facilities, doors, stairways, and the loading dock.

He pointed to one of the upper floors.

"Here is where Esman and I will deliver our equipment three days before. Only the technical crew is allowed on the upper floors, not the public. The building has old wooden floors, cement steps, narrow hallways, and metal racks for electrical and ventilation gear. The control room is on this floor, but the upper floor is where the ventilation ducts are. I will go to the control room and inform the engineers that I'll be working on the upper floor for my final inspection. I'll return to the upper floor and unlock the door to the ventilation ducts. Esman will go to work, mixing the chemicals to create sarin. When he is finished, he'll connect to the ventilation ducts."

Kareem lifted a page to the diagram of the venue showing a large open area with doors, aisles, lobbies, hallways, and bathrooms.

"Directly below is the audience area. On Saturday, only staff are allowed inside before five o'clock. That afternoon, Italy's most powerful people will be drinking and socializing at a banquet at City Hall. Television cameras will be at the banquet, with everyone expecting a spectacular evening that they'll talk about for days. We'll make sure they have plenty to talk about for the rest of their lives . . . if they survive."

"Yes!" Kalil said, slapping Esman's headrest again. "We'll be heroes for our brothers and Islam!"

Esman winced as he leaned forward to avoid Kalil's slapping. "Don't hit that. You're irritating me. Stop it!"

Kalil mumbled, leaned back, and looked out the window. "I get excited. It will be a wonderful night. All the world will know what we have done—a great victory for Islam."

They all nodded. Esman turned to face Kareem and Tito and said, "It will take forty-five minutes to unload the canisters, attach metal tubes, secure safety valves, and check pressures. The chemicals are volatile. They have to be mixed carefully so there are no accidents—a fire or premature release."

"We did two tests at a Bovisa lab," Kareem said. "Esman works fast, no mistakes. As soon as he has completed his work, he'll set a timer to release the gas. I lock the door, we take the elevator to the ground floor, exit at the loading dock, and walk away. Twenty minutes after we leave, the timer opens the valves, the gases are mixed, and sarin enters the ventilation ducts and is distributed throughout the entire building, from the basement to the top floors. No one can escape."

Tito leaned forward and gripped Kareem's shoulder. "Excellent plan, Kareem! It will work. You're a genius!"

"Nothing is perfect," Kareem said. "I look for flaws, go over the timeline countless times, double-check everything, and then do it again until I know every detail is covered. Everything."

"Your engineer education paid off," said Tito. "I understand why you waited to tell us."

"One last detail. This Friday," said Kareem, circling a date with a black marker on his December calendar, "will be your last day of work in Milan. Don't act suspicious with your supervisors and colleagues.

Wish them a nice weekend. Leave your uniforms and belongings in your lockers. I know you'll want to celebrate, but don't do anything to attract attention. We will celebrate after we fulfill our plan."

"Praise Allah," Esman said. "I can't work another day on that filthy garbage truck. I feel like the garbage I'm picking up. I have a university science degree, but now I pick up soiled diapers, beer bottles, disgusting foods, bacon, ham, filthy clothes. Italians live like animals. Why should I have to handle their filth?"

"You could have stayed in Syria," Kalil said.

"No! I had to leave. If I hadn't escaped, I would have ended up in one of Assad's torture prisons. Never!"

"How do we leave Milan without being stopped?" Tito asked.

Kareem turned to a page with a timeline, destinations, and a crude map. "We finish around 4:00 PM . . . go down in the elevator, exit at the loading dock, and walk to the underground garage where Kalil will park the van. We drive to a brother's garage near Cinisello Balsamo, where I stored the van that Alessandro paid for. We drive six hours to a farm near Trieste, where we will spend the night with brothers who will give us new identities and passports. The next morning, we cross the border into Slovenia and split up. We will have different itineraries with money and documents to travel to safe locations with Muslim brothers. They won't know what you've done, just that a hero is coming. If any one of us is captured, he won't know where the others are. It's all been organized by brothers who smuggled out brothers with forged papers."

"A new country, new identities. Start new lives—better than here," said Kalil.

"Our Muslim brothers will help you get jobs, find apartments, get you sex slaves. If you're lucky, you can take a wife. She'll be honored to marry a hero of Islam."

"Sex slaves!" Kalil squealed. "I want blondes with breasts like melons! I won't marry them, just want to—"

The shrill scream of police sirens pierced the air. Their heads jerked to look out the front window. Kareem rolled down his window. The sirens grew louder, coming in their direction.

He pointed toward Piazza Cavour; three blue Polizia di Stato cars sped around the corner from Via Fatebenefratelli into Piazza Cavour, with red lights flashing and sirens wailing. Commuters at the tram station stopped and watched. Trams, cars, and motorbikes braked as the police cars swerved through traffic, turning onto Via Manin and speeding up.

"WHEEOO . . . WHEEOO . . . WHEEOO . . . WHEEOO!" the sirens shrieked, a wavering, high-pitched wail that punished eardrums. People stopped and turned to look at the source of the unnerving sound.

"*Cazzo!*" yelled Tito.

Drivers on Via Manin steered toward cars parked at curbs, letting the police cars cross the center line as they sped toward Kareem's parked van. A family was coming out of the park. The father was wearing a winter coat and holding two Saint Bernards on leashes. The dogs howled and tried to bolt back into the park, jerking the man backward. He nearly fell but managed to catch his balance. His wife, gripping the hands of the two children, pulled them to her side and away from the street as the cars raced toward them.

WHEEOOO . . . WHEEOOO . . . WHEEOOO . . . WHEEOOO. People on the streets covered their ears to mute the piercing sounds.

Esman braced his hands on the dashboard, knuckles white, veins bulging as if the cars were about to crash into the van in a fiery collision.

They all gasped. Tito swore again: "*Porca puttana!*"

The cars raced toward them, headlights bright, engines roaring, red lights flashing, sirens screaming, sunlight reflecting off shiny blue hoods like an approaching storm. Time seemed to stop. All eyes were on the cars that raced toward them, the red flashing lights blinding them momentarily.

A whoosh gently rocked the van as the first two cars raced by, the second so close their bumpers almost touched. There were four uniformed officers in each car, a blur that lasted milliseconds. The third car, meters behind, sped past, another whoosh vibrating the van.

WHEEOO . . . WHEEOO . . . WHEEOO . . . WHEEOO!

"*Va remengo ti e to senare!*" [Go to hell with all your dead ancestors!] Kareem cursed in a Veneto dialect.

They craned their necks to follow the speeding police cars behind them. Brake lights flashed red. Tires screeched. The cars made a sharp turn on Bastioni di Porta Venezia and disappeared, one, two, three, the sirens fading but still shrill.

The seconds of terror had immobilized Kareem, Tito, Esman, and Kalil. Their hearts were pounding, and adrenaline pulsing through their bodies, the hormone of fear.

The cars on Via Manin started moving, resuming normal traffic flow. The mother, bracing her two children, led them back into the park to a bench, where her husband held the dogs' collars as they continued to howl and bark.

"I . . . I thought they were after us!" Kalil yelled. "I was having a heart attack. I thought we were going to die here."

Kareem said, "The police don't know about us! Impossible!" He pointed toward Piazza Cavour. "They came from the Questura . . . around the corner. An accident . . . maybe a robbery. They're not looking for us."

Another siren wailed, an ambulance racing down Bastioni di Porta Venezia, following the police cars. "Probably a car accident—a bad one."

Esman and Tito squirmed in their seats, eyes wide, blinking rapidly, hearts still pounding, looking back where the police cars had disappeared.

"Oh, man, I thought—" Tito said, his voice quivering. ". . . No . . . they wouldn't know about us. Allah is on our side. Kareem is right."

"I hate police!" Kalil said, his hands still trembling. "In Egypt, police snatch dissidents off the street, throw them in the backseat, and beat them. They do it in daylight to scare people, to let them know what will happen if they speak against the government."

They sat in the van, the memory of the speeding police cars still terrifying, moments that would be relived in nightmares in nights to come.

"What . . . if the police come after us, Kareem? Aren't you scared?" asked Esman.

Kareem shook his head, eyes aflame with anger. "Not possible! God is with us and will protect us on the day of celebration. Have faith in Him!"

On Monday morning, Simona was on her computer, reviewing surveillance logs of the previous weekend. She read them twice, puzzled by the notation that none of the men had left their apartments on Saturday until late afternoon.

Kareem had been followed from his apartment as he drove to his office in his company van. He remained five hours and returned home at 3:45 PM.

Simona scrolled through previous weekend surveillance reports. All suspects had left their apartments in the morning on Saturday to do errands, go grocery shopping, or meet Muslim men at cafés for tea. They had spent the afternoons in their own neighborhoods, returning to their apartments by early evening.

She turned to Dario, who was reading *La Gazzetta dello Sport*. "Have you looked at the weekend surveillance reports?" she asked.

"Not yet. Why?"

"I don't know . . . something unusual . . . maybe just a coincidence. None of them left their apartments until late afternoon on Saturday, except Kareem, who spent a few hours at his office."

"What's unusual about that?"

"I checked previous weekend reports, because something didn't look right. On previous weekends, cameras got Esman and Kalil leaving their apartments in the morning. We followed them through the day until they returned in the evening. But last Saturday all of them—except Kareem— didn't leave their apartments until late afternoon. That's puzzling."

Dario put down the newspaper. "Could they have left their apartments secretly and met someplace? Maybe Kareem's office?"

She shook her head. "No. We would have followed them or seen them on cameras. They stayed in their apartments. That's what's strange."

"I guess so."

Later that afternoon, Simona mentioned this to Amoruso, who checked the logs on her computer. She scanned previous weekend surveillance reports. "I see what you mean. A coincidence? Strange. What do you make of it?"

"I don't know," Simona said with a shrug. "They've always followed routines during the workweek and on weekends—except for last Saturday. Why?"

"I know what you mean. Small inconsistencies could mean something major. Ask the agents who had weekend duty. See what they say. I'll mention this to Lucchini and see what he thinks."

That week, DIGOS in Napoli recorded a local cell phone call to an unknown cell phone in Milan. DIGOS in Napoli informed DIGOS in Milan that the originating caller was a known Muslim radical involved in selling forged passports and visas to Muslim men and women who had subsequently been arrested with the fraudulent documents before boarding flights to Iraq, Syria, Turkey, and Egypt.

DIGOS in Milan said the cell phone was registered to an old lady from Perugia, a retired primary school teacher who had died in January 2012 in a nursing home. The phone had been used three times after the old lady was reported deceased.

The recording went as follows:

"Are you ready?"

"Yes. Ready. We have a good plan. It will be a glorious party. Many will be there."

"We know. Will you be safe?"

"Yes. Our brother has arranged everything. He is very smart and has planned well."

"We are prepared if the party is not a glorious one. Unfortunate things may happen even with Allah by our side. We want to protect you if the party is canceled."

"Canceled?"

"Yes." There was a several-second pause. "Canceled . . . or postponed . . . or someone interrupts the party. We don't want this to happen, but be ready."

Another pause before the Milan caller answered. "I think I understand. . . . Yes, I do."

"We will protect you if it is canceled, postponed, or does not happen. We are prepared for the worst."

"What do you want me to do?"

"Leave the party. Get away. Come south immediately. Do you know what I mean?"

"Yes, I do."

"We will wait for you. We will know if the party is a glorious one . . . or canceled. We will be watching closely."

"I will come south like you request."

"You know where. From the last time."

"Yes, I remember your home. I will come. *Allahu Akbar!*"

CHAPTER TWENTY-FIVE

M orning sun was casting shadows across the Questura courtyard, where marked and unmarked Polizia di Stato cars were parked. Officers were coming up from the underground garage and finishing cigarettes as they walked into the building to take elevators to their respective departments. Four uniformed guards wearing traditional white caps, belts, and holsters and cradling automatic weapons stood at the arched entrance of the Questura, monitoring traffic along Via Fatebenefratelli. Stone barriers at the curb prevented unauthorized vehicles from entering.

Giorgio Lucchini was in Questore Taddei's office on the fourth floor for their morning meeting. The Questore's office had typical furnishings for his position as the head of the Milan police department: a mahogany conference table with antique chairs under a crystal chandelier; an eighteenth-century oil painting of naval combat; a photo of the president of the republic, Giorgio Napolitano; Taddei's family photos with his wife, children, and grandchildren; the flags of Italy, the EU, and Milan; a comfortable sofa and chairs. His desk was covered with files, a telephone console, and computers.

Before becoming the Questore di Milano, Taddei had started his career in the Questura di Cagliari, Sardinia, during the 1980s and 1990s, the "season of the kidnappings," when wealthy businessmen were taken hostage for months, if not years, in remote locations of central Sardinia by *Anonima Sequestri* gangs. Taddei's career had advanced rapidly; in 2002, he was appointed head of the Squadra Mobile in Rome, and in 2005, he became head of DIGOS in Palermo. In 2010, he was promoted to Questore in Milan, one of the most powerful positions in the Italian police bureaucracies.

Taddei was sipping his second cappuccino of the morning, brow furrowed. His appearance was dignified, like a judge: thinning gray hair brushed over a nearly bald pate, a prominent nose, watery dark eyes, thin lips, and sunken cheeks.

"We need a break in your case, Lucchini," he said to Giorgio, who was seated in a soft leather chair. "We have little new evidence since Boni confided to Ispettore De Monti about his anger at politicians and the American wars in Iraq and Afghanistan."

"It's been a month," Giorgio said. "We thought he might contact her, but he hasn't. She texted him a couple of times, but his responses were evasive; he was busy or out of town. I told De Monti to be cautious with him. We don't want her to be more aggressive, as he would ignore her, possibly thinking she was like other women, just after his money. We're tapping his phone, of course, but he never uses it with the Muslim group. We've had a team surveilling him, but we haven't detected any suspicious activity. He hasn't returned to the kebab shop on Via Padova or to the Islamic center in Viale Jenner."

"How about his money? Any unusual activity in his bank account?"

"Nothing so far. No suspicious bank transfers in or out of his accounts. We've noticed he has made almost daily withdrawals from ATM machines, all for 250 euros in cash, since mid-July. He could be funding the group with some of that cash out of sympathy and a passive-aggressive attitude toward his father."

"Dottor Lucchini, we need more. What are they planning? When? Who is involved? What did they receive in earlier shipments, and where is it stored?" Taddei's frustration showed on his face: pursed lips, stress wrinkles at the corners of his mouth.

"I know your concern, signor Questore. I'm frustrated as well. We're working long hours on surveillance, following the suspects every day, tapping their cell phones. They're a stealth group, disciplined. They probably know we're listening, but they're behaving normally. We talked with informants at the mosques, parks, and cafés that Muslim men frequent. Our informants have discreetly asked about them but haven't learned anything. Video surveillance cameras at mosques and near Muslim cafés haven't spotted them. It's puzzling."

Taddei sighed. "How much longer until you break this open? The Ministry of Interior calls every day. They want results, not just phone taps and surveillance reports that don't tell us much. Remember all the celebrations we're going to have in Milan around the holidays. You still believe Christmas is when they're planning their attack?"

"Yes. Our evidence comes from Mohammad, the terrorist I interrogated in Amsterdam. He met a Muslim from Milano at the Afghan training camp who told him about his plan to do something at Christmas. The dates Mohammad was in Afghanistan in 2012 are the same as when Kareem Hussain traveled to Pakistan. Pakistani intelligence confirms that Hussain was in Mansehra, where his father was born, but he did nothing to attract interest from local police. He had been to Mansehra as a child, again as a teenager, and again after he graduated from the Politecnico. And again last year. He speaks Urdu, Pashto, and presumably local dialects. He probably developed contacts in Pakistan, maybe al Qaeda or the Taliban. But neither Americans nor Pakistanis have anything to link him to either group."

Taddei frowned. "He's clever, covers his tracks, and is very intelligent. He's gotten this far, and we know little about him other than his travels, family ties, and profession. You believe the potential targets are the airports and underground stations?"

"Not only. We've gone through Carefull Services's important clients and identified the most prominent: Malpensa Terminal 2 . . . Linate . . . the Borsa [Italian stock exchange], possibly La Rinascente. Hussain supervises Carefull engineers responsible for the ventilation, lighting, security, and computers at these and other facilities. All of them are vulnerable infrastructure, ideal locations if you want to carry out a terrorist act with maximum damage and personal injuries. We're working with the security teams at these locations, monitoring gates where trucks and delivery vans enter. We track Hussain, and when he shows up, we inspect his equipment. He doesn't mind, never acts nervous or suspicious. He's a cold-blooded lizard. You can see it in his eyes."

Taddei grimaced. "Evil to the core. Heartless, no concern for the damage his group will do and the suffering they'll cause. I lose sleep worrying about your case. The symbolism of attacking airports . . . the stock exchange. . . . The Rinascente shopping center could be a target, the icon of Italian fashion and prestige packed with Christmas shoppers."

"We've started monitoring La Rinascente, too. You know what that's like, shoppers lining up at 10 AM, before they open, and then the place is packed until the 10 PM closing. We'll have agents at the entrances, on each floor, and at the loading dock."

"Dottor Lucchini, I think a prime target would be the international economic convention sponsored by IlSole24Ore at Palazzo Mezzanotte on December 11. That's a major event with European economic ministers, entrepreneurs, journalists, and corporate presidents."

"Yes, signor Questore, we've started surveillance around the Palazzo Mezzanotte, collaborating with the ROS squad [antiterrorism group] of the Carabinieri from now to the event. Unfortunately, Carefull Services has maintenance contracts there at the stock exchange, and we'll be following Hussain every step if he goes there. That event would seem to be a prime target for terrorists, with all the international finance officials attending. Luckily, the location is easier to monitor, without the large crowds of shopping centers or airports. A few hundred people, not thousands coming and going."

"Apart from Hussain, do you have any leads from the other suspects?"

Giorgio shook his head. "None. They're minor players, as far as I'm concerned. Bilal and Khan have manual labor jobs at Amsa and Rho. No problems with supervisors or others, no radical behavior. They keep regular schedules and are easy to follow. They're not the brains of the operation, but the muscle—drivers, guards, support. Cameras outside their apartments show when they leave for work. They return around 7 PM, occasionally go out for a meal or buy groceries, but are back by 9 PM. Wahd Gajani leaves Desio at 7 AM, arrives at his café at 9 AM, closes at 10 PM, and drives home. He takes Tuesdays and Wednesdays off. His son, Tariq, opens and closes on those days; his free day is Monday. No suspicious behavior from either of them.

"Hussain varies little from his daily routine. A team of agents is at his apartment at 7 AM. He leaves an hour later for work, drives to his office, and departs late morning to go to one of the airports or the stock exchange, where he spends the rest of the workday. After he returns home, another team monitors him until eleven o'clock, when he usually turns out his lights. Occasionally, he'll leave his apartment to pick up vegan sandwiches, salads, soft drinks, chips, and candy bars at a corner kebab shop."

"You're watching him every day?"

"Yes. It makes surveillance tedious. Our agents report identical entries daily, grumbling about how boring he is."

Taddei shrugged. "Police work is tedious; they know that. You never know when something critical is going to happen."

"We picked up personal information about Hussain from bugs we planted in his apartment. Most of his calls are about his job. Occasionally from his father in London or his mother in Verona, but they're not on friendly terms. He watches Al Jazeera, news from Pakistani TV, and Muslim chat rooms where they rant about terrorism, jihad, and infidels in the West."

"That's terrifying stuff. I've seen it translated."

"Yes, it is. Hussain is on there almost every night. He doesn't say much, except about American drone attacks killing civilians, innocent women, and children. He calls them massacres and says someone should pay for their war crimes. But he's never hinted that he's involved in anything."

Simona and Dario sat in an unmarked car across the street from Kareem Hussain's apartment at Piazza Ferravilla in the Città Studi area. They had arrived at 7 PM, replacing two DIGOS agents assigned to follow Hussain during the day. They were parked near a tram stop that provided an unobstructed view through branches of leafless trees of Hussain's apartment, his bedroom window, and another window off the balcony where his bicycle was covered with a tarp.

DIGOS agents had planted a bug on his computer and a camera in his apartment. They had snapped photos of his kitchen, his two bedrooms, and a hallway into a living area with a dining table, sofa, TV, and a desk with his laptop computer. His bookshelf held a random collection of university textbooks, novels by Italian and Muslim authors, copies of the Quran, and histories and photo books of Pakistan.

Simona flexed her fingers to warm up her hands. Evening temperatures were in the midteens, chilling the car until she or Dario turned on the heater, which blasted hot air and turned the car into a sauna until the heater was turned off.

Simona checked her watch. "Eight forty-five. He's probably not going to the kebab shop tonight."

Dario stifled a yawn and scanned a dashboard iPad linked to DIGOS. "The daily report said he stopped in Carrefour at six forty-five and picked up a salad, a large bag of fries, ice cream, two bottles of peach-flavored iced tea, a pound of coffee, and toothpaste. He stopped at the pharmacy for aspirin."

"Aspirin? He must have headaches."

"I'd have headaches, too, if I lived his boring life: a monotonous routine every day. He eats alone, watches TV, spends a couple hours on his computer. He needs a hot woman in his life to show him some fun and get him excited. Someone to come home to at night."

"He's not appealing at all. Creepy . . . too skinny, wears gray clothes every day. And his beard makes him look weird."

"Yup."

They sat in silence as winter winds blew through the trees, swirling fallen leaves in the deserted park. A local bus waited at an intersection for the light to change and then crossed in front of Hussain's apartment. A corner pharmacy was the only store open on the block; a barber shop, shoe store, and TIM outlet were all dark.

The street was almost vacant. A few people carried shopping bags, purses, or briefcases as they returned from work. Cafés and restaurants were largely empty. Waiters stood staring out windows as people passed by on their way home to have dinner with families, not at restaurants.

"Give me a cigarette," Simona said abruptly.

His head swiveled to look at her. "What?"

"Give me a cigarette."

"Why? You don't smoke."

"I'm starting tonight. Give me a cigarette."

"Really?"

"Yes."

"You could at least ask politely," he sputtered, reaching into his jacket for his Marlboros and tapping out one for her.

"*Please, Dario,* would you be so kind as to give me a cigarette?"

"Better. Need a light?"

"What do you think I'm going to do, eat it?"

"Hey, calm down." He flicked his lighter and lit her cigarette. She took a puff and coughed. "Have you ever smoked?"

"Of course."

"When?"

"Long time ago."

"How long?"

"Do you have to interrogate me just because I asked for a cigarette?" she said, her voice rising in irritation.

"Touchy, touchy," he said, lighting one for himself. "Just trying to be nice. Need anything else? Maybe one of my kidneys?"

"Don't make fun of me. I'm not in the mood."

Simona smoked aggressively, taking frequent puffs, coughing, and exhaling quickly like a novice smoker, holding the cigarette in the middle rather than toward the filtered tip.

"You don't seem the type to smoke."

"How would you know? We only work together. Even 'nice girls' smoke sometimes."

Dario took a drag and exhaled out the side window. "Yeah, a harmless act of rebellion. But you're not the rebellious type."

She scoffed and took another drag off her cigarette.

The tension in her voice was not new. She had been terse with him on their first duty assignments. Rookie jitters, he had thought, defensive pushback, nothing that irritated him. Part of the job, having a new partner, feeling each other out. But something was bothering her tonight. Dario knew the wrong tactic was to probe Simona when she was being defensive.

They smoked in silence, keeping the side windows open a crack. Simona surprised him when she said, "You don't know me very well, Dario."

Hmmm, why was she keeping that conversation going? He paused before answering.

"That's true, Simo, I don't know much about you." His tone was cautionary, a polite gesture to continue talking. "You mentioned a few things when we started as a team. . . . You're from Bergamo, worked for the police a few years. . . . Off duty, you go to yoga, the gym, and shop for antiques. You're friends with Manu, live in Isola, and have a rich boyfriend—Alfie?"

Her response was brittle. "Wrong. Alby. Formal name Alberico. He's my ex-boyfriend. I haven't talked to him in months."

The door had slammed again. They finished their cigarettes and flicked them out the window. Dario tried to restart the conversation, in a voice like a child asking for a cookie. "So when did you start to smoke?"

"A long time ago," she snapped. "None of your business."

Slammed and locked. It was going to be a long, cold night, inside and outside the car. Dario picked up the binoculars and focused on Hussain's balcony window. A shadow behind the drapes passed from right to left, meaning Hussain had come from the hallway into the living room, headed for the kitchen. The details were too trivial to mention. Plus, given Simona's mood, he wasn't interested in pretending to restart a dead conversation.

He lowered the binoculars to the entrance of the apartment building. A man wearing a cap and a winter jacket came out, pulled up the collar on his coat, turned right, and walked briskly, donning gloves. He went out of view at the corner on his way to a trattoria or a Chinese restaurant down the street. Dario looked back at the entrance. A woman and a child entered the building; the girl was around ten, the woman's age undetermined. They walked through a foyer and disappeared down a hall to the elevators. One of the diversions of surveillance that Dario enjoyed was the license to watch people without them knowing. The target was always a priority, except when that target was not in a location where escape was possible. Surveilling Hussain on a cold winter night was simple: watching lights in his apartment, the building entrance, and the garage exit if he left.

Dario's mind was wandering as he focused again on Hussain's lighted windows, curious about his reclusive behavior. Simona's voice startled him.

"I was under stress. A friend . . . a girlfriend . . . died from a drug overdose. Some creep in a bar slipped it in her drink so he could have sex with her."

Dario kept the binoculars raised and didn't respond. If she wanted to talk, he wasn't going to interrupt.

"She collapsed in my arms right in the bar. I . . . didn't know what to do. It was . . . horrible. . . . I'll never forget it."

She finished her first cigarette and flicked it out the partially open window.

"She died in a hospital that night. I didn't find out until the next morning. I was the last friend she was with. I started smoking because I was depressed. She was my best friend. Our families were close. My mother had known her father since they were children in Liguria. I blamed myself that she died. I quit smoking after a year, because I hated coughing in the morning and how my mouth tasted like soot."

A personal story, something she'd never shared before. "Sorry about your friend, Simo. I wasn't prying." Dario paused, contemplating whether he should share any personal information. "Four of my friends died from drug overdoses, but they had made bad choices in their lives."

"Oh."

"A common tragedy for too many youth . . . unfortunately."

They were both quiet for a minute or two. Dario checked the dashboard digital clock. A shadow moved past the balcony window. "He's watching TV," he said, picking up the binoculars again, observing for a few seconds, and then putting them back on the dashboard.

"What does he watch? Soccer? Certainly not silly reality shows."

"Mostly news, according to our camera."

"Yeah, a car crash on the *autostrada* . . . a corrupt politician getting arrested . . . another grisly murder in Puglia. TV is a waste of time. I don't see why anyone watches that trash."

"I like to watch soccer."

Simona looked out the window. The sidewalks were almost deserted. Families were home, enjoying dinner and watching TV. The children were playing. Parents were planning the weekend. It was a cold, dark, early winter night in Milan, with weather reports of a snowstorm over the Alps moving south.

"Is he still watching TV?"

"Yes. He'll probably be doing that until we leave." Simona picked up the binoculars and studied the shadow behind the curtain. "What does he do when he's on his computer?"

"Same as everyone else. Checks e-mail, plays video games, does social media. He also browses the web for radical Muslim sites, Al Jazeera, news from Pakistan, some porn."

She put down the binoculars, leaned back against the headrest, and closed her eyes. A minute later she opened them and stretched. "I'm going for a walk. I need fresh air."

"Don't go far."

Simona got out of the car and crossed the tram tracks, littered with crumpled newspapers, water bottles, and cigarette butts. She entered a small park and sat on a bench, gazing down the tracks toward the Milan skyline through low, dark clouds. Frigid temperatures crept through the scarf around her neck, through her leggings, and between her gloves and wrists. She lowered her woolen cap down over her forehead and wrapped her arms around her down jacket. She sat alone, felt alone, and shivered, feeling a sadness she had not experienced in a long time.

Being with Dario on night surveillance was causing her agitation that she couldn't disguise. She was fulfilling a professional duty while her mind drifted to another place with a man she'd rather be with, enjoying an evening she dreamed about, a once-in-a-lifetime experience she'd probably never have again.

She bit her lip, clenched her fingers in her gloves, and shivered. Her distress was so powerful that she felt like crying. But she couldn't, not on duty with Dario. Better to be by herself on a cold bench in a vacant park, with streetlights shining pale yellow cones of light on empty streets and sidewalks.

Tears came to her eyes and trickled down her cheeks. She brushed them away with a gloved hand and blinked away more tears.

She glanced up at Hussain's lighted windows. How long had it been since she had looked? Thirty seconds? A minute?

The damp, frigid air smelled of dried leaves, dead grass, and moist soil. Simona exhaled mists of warm vapor and looked down the tracks at the Milan skyline: spears of white light, flashing red beacons, a foggy haze of lights from skyscraper hotels, offices, and apartments.

She stood up, returned to the car, and turned on the ignition. A blast of hot air flooded the car, clouding the windows.

"It's freezing outside," Dario observed.

"Give me another cigarette."

Dario stifled a laugh. "Whatever you say. I exist to serve your every desire." He repeated his ritual, lighting her cigarette and waiting for her response.

She ignored his remark and smoked in silence, exhaling out the window, staring at Hussain's apartment. When she finished her cigarette, she flicked the butt onto the tram tracks.

"Will this evening ever end?" she said, puzzling Dario by her rambling. "I can't imagine a more exciting Friday evening, waiting for Prince Charming to invite us up to his apartment and spill his guts about his dastardly deed. We arrest him, take him to the Questura, and go home to bed. But no, he hides in his cave while we freeze our asses off. Friday night," she repeated, shaking her head. "Everyone else is . . ." she stopped.

Dario let her words stand without replying. Simona fidgeted with the keys, picked up the binoculars, pointed them at the windows, and then put them back. She let out a sigh.

"What's going on with you? You're acting weird."

"Didn't your mother teach you to mind your own business?"

"She did. Didn't your mother teach you to be polite?"

"Okay, okay, yes, she did." She sighed again. "I don't mean to be rude. . . . I'm just . . ." Her voice faded.

Stalemate. For the next hour, they took turns looking through the binoculars at Hussain's windows, stepping outside the car to stretch, walking around, and returning when the freezing temperature drove them back into the heated car. Neither spoke, the tension a silent vise against conversation.

At 10:59 PM, she started the car and put it in gear. "Let's get the fuck out of here. We're done."

Dario called the DIGOS duty officer to tell him that their shift was over Hussain had not left his apartment, had his lights on, and was watching TV. When he closed his phone, Simona snapped, "Give me another cigarette."

He took out his pack, lit one for her, and handed it across without saying a word. She smoked with one hand on the wheel, the other holding her cigarette at the cracked window.

"Can I trust you?"

What was this? "Sure."

"I mean it. You mention a word, and I'll never talk to you again."

"You can trust me. What's going on?"

She took a deep breath, eyes straight ahead. "Guess where I could be tonight?"

"Not a clue."

"Lago di Como. At George Clooney's villa."

"Really?"

"Yes, God damn it. Armando called me yesterday." Her voice was rising in agitation. "George Clooney invited him to his villa and mentioned bringing me. He remembered me from the Armani party. I could be with Armando at Clooney's Lake Como villa this weekend. It would be so romantic. I haven't had a fun weekend since . . . since . . . oh . . . forever it seems." Her normally calm voice was high-pitched and strained, revealing her suffering.

"Instead you're with me on a boring surveillance that turned up nothing. You're pissed. I don't blame you. Maybe Armando will invite you to another party."

"Forget it! He's conducting *Turandot* at La Scala for the premiere next month. He has rehearsals, meetings, and events with VIPs and musicians all week. Tonight was his only free time until after the premiere."

"Sorry. I didn't know that. I understand why you're upset."

"This fucking job messed up a perfect weekend with a very nice man. He's thoughtful . . . intelligent . . . kind. I don't meet men like that," she said, frustration in her voice. She ran a gloved hand over the steering wheel, tapping with the other hand. "Instead, I'm driving to the Questura after night duty spying on a terrorist who never goes anywhere at night, stays in his apartment alone, watching porn and listening to weird Arabic music on his iPod!"

"Did you try to get a replacement?"

"How? It was too late. Our shift was on the books. I couldn't ask Amoruso for a replacement. She would have thought I was sacrificing work for a frivolous weekend on Lake Como. I couldn't do that. Imagine if that got around the office?"

They were approaching Piazza Cavour, a minute from the Questura. "Simona . . . you did the right thing. You kept your assignment and didn't try to find a replacement at the last minute. I'm sorry things didn't work out, but there'll be another time. Armando seems like a gentleman. He'll understand."

"I told him I had to visit my ill mother in Bergamo this weekend. Isn't that the lamest excuse? He probably thinks I'm a mamma's girl, tied to her apron strings. Ooooohhh," she groaned.

She felt tears forming and brushed her eyes with her glove.

"Our shift is over," said Dario. "Go home and have a good cry. You made the right decision. You're a detective. We make sacrifices for our job, sacrifices that affect our families, friends, health, even love. We're working a critical investigation. What is more important, a night on Lago di Como with glamour boys or being on duty, where you belong?"

They pulled into the Questura. Two uniformed guards waved them into the courtyard. Simona parked in the back of the courtyard, took out the keys, and dropped them on the dashboard. She reached for her purse and set it on her lap but didn't open her door. The courtyard lights shined on the car's hood, reflecting on her blank eyes staring ahead.

Dario glanced over, sensing her thoughts were far away, not just imagining being on Lake Como with Armando, but having regrets about the personal sacrifices she was making to be a police officer.

He reached over and put his gloved hand over hers, which were gripping the straps of her purse. "Want a ride home?"

She blinked, back in the present. "No. I need to walk."

"See you in the morning. Call me if you need to talk."

At eleven thirty that evening, Hussain was trolling the Internet for news, finally clicking on a web chat line with a link to his contacts in Afghanistan.

Earlier in the evening, he had called his father, who had invited him to London over the Christmas holidays, saying it had been almost two years since they had been together. Hussain had been tentative, saying the Christmas holidays were busy at work, and told his father that coming in January was a better time. It was a short call, five or six minutes, like a business call rather than a family conversation. Hussain got one call from his supervisor about a schedule change. All of the calls were intercepted by DIGOS phone taps.

DIGOS had also tapped Hussain's computer, tracing e-mails, web searches, blogs, and forums that he browsed. But this night, he clicked on a web chat room that had complicated passwords and security firewalls to minimize unauthorized access. DIGOS, however, had access, using sophisticated cyber tools used by police forces.

The chat room was a known terrorist site in Afghanistan. The short digital conversation triggered alerts at DIGOS, and they reported the chat immediately to Lucchini, Taddei, and the Ministry of Interior.

"Are you ready for the party?"

"Yes. All the guests are prepared. It will be a big party."

"The biggest. All of us will be watching, celebrating your success. We wish we could be there."

"You will see it all. Everyone will see it. They will praise God."

"God will rejoice that brothers have brought Him so much joy. Your reward will be great in heaven. Your name will live forever. Praise to Allah."

CHAPTER TWENTY-SIX

Nico Brebbi squinted at the digital clock on his nightstand. It was 6:13 AM Too early to get up. He needed to doze for a few more minutes. He closed his eyes and rolled over in bed, bizarre dreams still sloshing around in his subconscious. As the dreams vaporized, Nico's brain emerged from slumber, prompting him to the day ahead.

It was one of the most important days of Nico's year: December 4, the dress-rehearsal performance of Giacomo Puccini's *Turandot* at Teatro alla Scala, where Nico, at forty-five, was the youngest technical director in the theater's history. The rehearsal performance was for families and guests of La Scala staff in preparation for the premiere on December 7, followed by a banquet for Italian VIPs, politicians, foreign diplomats, and elite Milanese families in Milan's city hall, across the piazza.

A thousand dignitaries would attend the premiere, and millions of Italians would watch the performance live on TV or on big-screen monitors around Milan. The audience in the theater, on the streets, and in homes would be thrilled by the dazzling arias, choruses, elegant costumes, stirring drama, and staging of one of the most beloved operas in the history of music.

Nico lay still. His digital clock ticked another minute. He kept his eyes closed, breathing slowly, to snatch another moment before surrendering to the reality that his day had already begun.

His right arm was stretched across the pillow next to him, which was cool and empty since his former girlfriend, Carlotta, had broken up with him in June. She soon had been replaced on the second pillow by a gray Chartreux female cat called Pamina, a gift from Nico's former lover and colleague and now best friend, Lidia, La Scala's set designer.

One of the reasons for his breakup with Carlotta was that she couldn't tolerate Lidia's constant presence in Nico's life. Lidia had refurbished Nico's "total white" loft apartment on Piazza Caneva, which had been featured in *Elle Decor* and *Casabella* interior design magazines. More requests from other magazines were pending in Nico's e-mail.

Summer had started lonely for Nico, who remained in Milan to supervise the annual maintenance before the season-opening premiere. But in August, Nico's social life blossomed when he met Aurora, twenty-six, during his vacation in Ischia. Aurora was a part-time law student, part-time belly dancer, and full-time joy. Talkative as a jabbering jaybird, Aurora made Nico laugh like no woman had before. She was uninhibited and carefree with a wicked sense of humor.

After Nico had returned to Milan in September, a friend had introduced him to Iwona, thirty-three, a Polish bombshell who worked in Paris for a well-known brand as a jewelry designer. Nico and Iwona had dated sporadically, since she was getting over a boyfriend and not sure if she wanted a relationship so soon. She traveled to Paris, Milan, and New York with her job and was making very good money. Iwona was a gentle soul, content to drink wine at a café and talk about art, literature, and movies. She was good company, intellectually stimulating, and a passionate lover.

Excited to have two new women in his life, Nico was surprised when a third showed up, Valentina, twenty-three. A performing arts student in the drama, art, and music program at the University of Bologna. Valentina's drama class had come to La Scala in October for a backstage tour and lectures. She was the prettiest girl in the class, and she listened attentively to Nico's lecture, thanking him profusely and kissing him on both cheeks. Moments later, Nico found Valentina's cell phone number scribbled on a tram ticket inside his pocket. They arranged a quick dinner, and she spent the night at his apartment. They had slept together only three—or was it four?—times, each a memorable experience.

Three women had changed Nico's life, recharged his passion to fall in love, make love, and enjoy life again. And he was. But how would he manage three girlfriends during the December holidays? He did have a plan . . . sort of.

On December 10, after the premiere of the ballet, he planned to drive to Bologna for a weekend with Valentina.

On December 15, he would fly to Naples to see Aurora.

On December 19, he would return to Milan to see Iwona before she flew to Poland for a holiday visit with her family.

Nico expected that all three women would want to be with him during the party-filled week between Christmas and New Year's. How could he juggle his calendar to see all three of them without letting them know about each other? Oh, the challenge of being a handsome and available single man in Milan with so many beautiful and alluring females.

How did he get so lucky? How long would his good fortune last? He certainly didn't want to end up unhappily married like he had been in his thirties. He still winced when he thought of that first disastrous attempt at commitment. Thank God, he and his wife had had no children. They had been married only two years.

Nico pondered his dilemma, running his fingers over Pamina's soft fur, floating in delicious thoughts of seeing Valentina, Aurora, and Iwona soon.

He squinted again at his digital clock: 6:28 AM Reality time. Out of bed. Shower. Dress. Leave cat food and water in the bowls. Get on his BMW motorbike, put on his helmet, and start his important day!

Peeking out from the entrance of his apartment, Nico decided against taking his motorbike. He checked his iPhone weather app; a snowstorm was sweeping south from the Alps, forecasted to blanket Milan by midnight. Nico opted to take tram 14 to Piazza Cordusio. He put on his new Belstaff coat, wrapped a cashmere scarf around his neck, put on fur-lined gloves, and walked to the tram stop. Fifteen minutes later, he stepped off the tram, seeing ahead the familiar facade of La Scala through a white blur of falling snow.

Nico walked one block to Piazza della Scala and turned down Via Filodrammatici, a wind tunnel of freezing air and falling snow. La Scala employees were entering the double glass door, tracking snowy footprints across the polished tile floor.

Nico reached inside his coat for his badge and swiped it across the security turnstile. Once through the gate, employees split up, some moving toward first-floor offices and the stage, others queueing at a bank of elevators in the hallway. The mood was festive as employees took off gloves, blew on cold hands, and greeted each other, patting backs and talking excitedly about the rehearsal performance.

"*Ehi, Nico, come stai?*" A young stagehand from Rome greeted him.

"*Ciao, Vinicio, tutto bene, e tu?*"

"*Mannaggia a' Giuda, che cazzo de freddo!* Every winter I miss the capital so much. You Milanese live at the North Pole. I can't get used to that. Yesterday my sister was strolling on the Ostia beach, wearing only a sweatshirt!"

Nico laughed. "But you have the honor of taking part in La Scala's premiere, the most exciting opera event of the year! Aren't you thrilled?"

Vinicio made a sweeping gesture with his arms and said, "*Me' cojoni!*" [You bet my balls!] Then he went for the stage door, followed by colleagues.

Nico greeted others as they jammed into the elevator, doffing wool caps, hats, and gloves and sharing the excitement of working at La Scala's rehearsal performance.

The elevator was almost empty by the time Nico reached the fifth floor. He turned down a hallway, passing Rudolf Nureyev ballet rehearsal studios, offices for technical directors, and storage rooms for sound and camera equipment.

He opened the door to his cluttered office of tables with tools, electrical parts, and technical manuals; chairs; and his desk, with two computers and an internal telephone console. He took off his coat, shook off snow, and went to a vending machine for his first coffee of the morning. He sipped it standing by his desk and watching snow swirling over the back roof, a stucco dome that rose eight stories above the street.

A red blinking light on his phone console indicated he had voicemail messages. Before he responded to any of them, he turned on the computers. One was connected to the Internet and another to La Scala's internal cameras showing real-time activity throughout the theater: backstage, side stages, front lobby, balconies, box seats, main floor, rehearsal rooms, and the formal lobby on the fourth floor.

Nico's eyes moved from screen to screen. A crew was arranging the set for Act I, which took place in a Chinese palace. Another crew was placing props onstage for the opening scene of Act I. A lighting crew was checking bulbs on the proscenium and the front stage lights. Electrical technicians were checking connections for the smoke and haze machines. Experienced and specialist *macchinisti* were testing twenty-by-twenty-meter mechanical bridges and stage compensators that moved sets between scenes and raised and lowered the wooden panels forming the center stage.

Two forklifts were moving lumber and wooden boxes from the stage into temporary storage bins in the sidewalls. A hoist was lowering mechanical panels of lights to the stage for final inspection. Audiovisual technicians were testing monitors, recorders, amplifiers, generators, and microphones at a console board on a lateral stage. Ushers proceeded through theater rows, dusting each seat and checking for possible malfunctions.

Nico's close friend, Ivan, the stage manager, was in his booth on stage right talking on his headset to crews in charge of the curtain, lights, sound, and orchestra pit.

Nico listened to his voice mails and punched the first button to talk to an assistant stage manager in the orchestra pit.

"*Buongiorno*, Nico. Leandro here. Ivan is busy. I have a problem with faulty lights on three music stands in the pit. Can you call someone to fix them?"

Nico punched a button to a lighting crew and asked them to take tools and lightbulbs to the orchestra pit.

For the next half hour, Nico took calls, listened to messages, and scribbled on a notepad routine tasks for his morning. No crisis yet; assistants were taking care of minor problems. It was hours before the curtain would be raised, plenty of time for the crises he'd have to address.

At nine fifteen, Nico took the elevator to the basement cafeteria for a quick breakfast. He stood in a long, slow-moving line that reached into the hallway. The cafeteria was crowded, with each table occupied. Used plates, cups, and utensils were stacking up, as workers behind the counter were busy serving coffee and plates of *cookies* and *brioches* to hungry staff. Nico greeted everyone by name—wardrobe fitters, production assistants, electricians, mechanical bridge crews, and a fireman. After gobbling down a *brioche* at the counter and drinking a cappuccino, Nico walked up two flights to the stage for his first inspection.

A small army of technicians was working on the twenty-by-eighteen-meter stage from the raised curtain to the rear wall. The eighty-meter-high ceiling reverberated noises of crews shouting directions, tools clanging, forklifts rumbling across the stage, and the screech of metal scraping across metal of twenty-meter-long bridges positioning sets and panel stages for the first act.

Nico walked toward the center of the stage as crews called out to him. He answered each person by name. "Buongiorno, Tony! Manfredo! Gigi! Beppe! Ornella! Ready for the dress rehearsal?"

"*Certo, Nico! Come sempre!*" one of them replied.

Nico walked around the stage, greeting technicians, shaking hands, patting people on the back, thanking them for their diligence, and sharing the pre-performance exhilaration, knowing that each person would endure stress, anger, and frustration over the next twelve hours before they could go home for a well-deserved rest—and return in three days for the premiere.

Nico's chest swelled with pride as he walked around the stage where many famous opera premieres of Donizetti, Rossini, Verdi, and Puccini had been performed. He spent the next hour going from crew to crew, observing their work, talking to assistants, and asking if they needed his help.

Stage crews were the unsung heroes of La Scala, specialized teams responsible for complex tasks that dazzled audiences when world-famous singers, actors, and dancers performed in front of glamorous sets and artistic props created by craftsmen in the theater's workshops.

What audiences couldn't see between acts behind La Scala's red curtain were crews flipping switches, pressing buttons, and pulling levers that guided mechanical bridges to transport sets, props, and stage panels. When the curtain rose for Acts II and III, audiences were dazzled by stunning new sets positioned precisely in minutes by experienced stagehands.

When he finished his morning rounds, Nico walked over to the stage manager's cubicle, where Ivan was talking on his headset. Nico made the "okay" gesture with his thumb and forefinger. Ivan returned the gesture, indicating that everything was perfect, at least for the moment.

At 11:15 AM, Nico returned to his office. His phone was flashing six new voice-mail messages. He had muted his mobile while making his first stage inspection. He listened to his messages in reverse chronological order. They were all routine, and each would take a minute or two to resolve. The newest message was the most urgent; it was from Didier Aubry, the experienced but excitable French costume designer.

"Nico . . . I need you now! Emergency!" Didier screeched, his voice high and shrill, his words flowing like water cascading over a falls. *"Ce n'est pas possible!* My costumes are falling apart in front of my eyes! I'm going to have a heart attack! My career is ruined! A disaster! The silk veils of Liù's costume look like a garbage bag! And the color is *totalement faux!* Wrong! Horrible! Orsola is ignoring me! Help me! Please! Where are you? Come see me now!"

Nico had expected a panicked plea from Didier. It was the dress rehearsal performance, and everyone was anxious, none more so than Didier. He and Nico had worked together for fifteen productions during his career. Before every dress rehearsal, Didier was on the verge of jumping off a cliff. A thread exposed on a costume would send him screaming at the staff, one of whom could repair it in seconds without the drama. Didier was brilliant and his sketches had touches of genius, which was why everyone tolerated his eccentricities.

Nico took the elevator to the third-floor wardrobe suite. He greeted the seamstresses by name. He considered them the artistic geniuses, modestly paid but proud of their work and highly respected in the theater world. The singers were celebrities, but these wardrobe workers labored just as long, under different pressures, and produced costumes considered the finest in the world.

Designers and seamstresses were putting final touches on costumes and hats laid out on tables with pins, checking every inch of fabric, securing buttons, hooks, zippers, and seams. Sewers at machines stitched sleeves and cuffs on blouses, while seamstresses at mannequins hand-stitched collars to coats and dresses, inspected costumes, and verified that meticulous detail work had been done and that the costumes were ready to be delivered on racks to dressing rooms.

The mood in wardrobe was boisterous, with seamstresses and designers joking and teasing each other. Conversations carried across the room while Italian hip-hop's most famous band, Articolo 31, played from speakers.

The head seamstress, Orsola, spotted Nico. "Nico! Come over. I want to give you a hug!" she said over the chatter and music. When Nico reached her, she opened her arms. "I knew you'd show up soon, darling, even if you're busy. So are we. It's going to be a wonderful rehearsal. My family is coming tonight, including three grandchildren. I have five now, two babies. Maybe they'll come next year."

"Congratulations, Orsola! My sister and her husband are coming tonight. But they'll leave the children with the babysitter."

"Maybe a girlfriend is coming?" Orsola said, a twinkle in her eye.

"Not tonight. They're—they're," he stammered, "she's in Venice for the week."

"They? You have more than one girlfriend?" She wagged a finger. "Nico, Nico, you need to settle down. Find a nice Milanese girl. Start a family, little children to come home to at night who call you *papà*. They would make you happy. You don't want to grow old and still be single."

Nico blushed. "I don't think I will, Orsola. Next year I'll invite a special guest."

She pressed her hand against his chest. "Promise? Next year! I won't forget." She looked over her shoulder toward Didier's office. "I know why you're here; it's Didier, isn't it? He's mortified about Liù's costume."

"He said it looks like a garbage bag."

She rolled her eyes. "If I had that material, I'd never use it for garbage. Nothing to worry about; I've taken care of it. I called Veronica at the Ansaldo and asked her to send five silk samples in nuances of the same color so he can choose. Shipping hasn't delivered from the loading dock; probably they'll be here any minute. He'll find the color he likes. We'll take care of it."

"Like always."

She put her hands on his biceps and squeezed. "Nico, he's like you with your girlfriends: If you're with a blonde, you want a brunette. If she's got brown hair, you want a raven beauty."

"Orsola! I'm not that kind of guy!"

She winked like a teasing mother. "Nico, Nico, you're a gentleman, a kind man, a real Don Giovanni!"

"I don't know about that, Orsola," he said, embarrassed by her flattery. "I just behave myself and try to be kind."

"That's why they fall for you like flies, Nico! But you're not here to talk about your love life. You came because Didier called."

"Yes," he said, eager to move out of Orsola's spotlight. "He left a message and was very upset, as you know."

"We all know Didier's tantrums at rehearsal performances. He doesn't listen to us. He needs you to calm him down so he doesn't have a heart attack. Please go see him," she said, nodding her head toward Didier's office.

Nico could see Didier in his corner office with the glass door closed. He was bending over a dressing table, examining sleeves and lace cuffs on a woman's dark blue costume.

Nico knocked and entered. "*Bonjour*, Didier. I got your message. How can I help?"

Didier looked up, peering over his bifocals. "Nico! Liù's costume for the first act is a total disaster! Orsola is ignoring me. My career is ruined. I can't send Liù onstage looking like a garbage bag!"

Nico walked over and raised his hands in a gesture of confidence. "Don't worry, Didier. I talked to Orsola. She's waiting for new silk samples from Ansaldo. They could be at the loading dock already."

"Oh, *merci bien*, Nico. I couldn't live without you!" He came around the table, almost tripping as he bumped the corner, and reached to hug Nico. Nico patted him on the back, feeling Didier's heart thumping through his sweat-damp shirt. He really was going to have a heart attack one of these nights.

"Orsola would never let you down. You know how she cares about your needs. She's the best in the world!"

Didier grabbed Nico's hands and squeezed them with his sweaty fingers. *"Merci, mon cher! Merci encore!"* Didier gushed. He dropped his hands and pivoted to return to his work, again bumping the corner of the table. He was humming a tune and bending over to get back to work.

Nico left Didier's office and walked through the aisles where Orsola was working. She whispered, "I heard everything. We've been telling him that all morning, but he never listens. He's wild on days like this. Thinks the world is ending. We just avoid him and do our work."

"Good luck. Let me know how it goes."

She patted his cheek. "Nice to see you again. Nico, always to the rescue."

"First crisis of the day. . . . I'll have another dozen before the curtain rises."

Leaving the wardrobe studio, Nico took the elevator to the sixth-floor offices for technical staff in charge of La Scala's electronic infrastructure, lighting, heating and air conditioning, audiovisual, backup generators, Internet, internal video, and electronic security. When he got off the elevator, he recognized a familiar face in the crowded hallway, Kareem. There was a man behind him, and both of them were wearing blue Carefull shirts. Kareem was pushing a dolly with a metal container with leather handles.

Nico raised a hand in greeting. *"Ciao*, Kareem. Everything okay?"

Kareem looked up. *"Ciao*, Nico. How're things on stage? Hysterical as usual?"

Nico stepped to the side to let crew pass in the hallway. "Everything's under control—for the moment, at least." He checked his watch. "I just left wardrobe, a minor fire to put out. Next is a meeting with DIGOS for the security procedures scheduled for Saturday. What do you have?" he asked, looking at Kareem's dolly.

"Just delivering a piece of equipment."

"New equipment for rehearsal? Couldn't you have done it earlier, not today?"

"It was scheduled for yesterday, but our engineers added a couple of new features. We installed the original equipment this summer." He looked at the box on the dolly. "This is upgraded software and new switches for the digital monitor we use at airports and the stock exchange. It lets us make precise adjustments at Carefull without being here. My technician and I will hook it up and run a couple of quick tests. I'm sure I called you last week to tell you about the installation."

Nico frowned. "Hmmm, I don't remember. Did you try my mobile?"

"I'm afraid not. I used your office extension. I thought I left a voice mail." Kareem was getting anxious; he wanted to get away. He turned the dolly away from the wall.

"I didn't get a message. Next time, try my mobile if I don't pick up your call when I'm in my office."

"Will do, Nico. Better run. I'll install this, escort my technician to the exit, and go back upstairs. You know where I'll be in case you need me."

"See you later, Kareem. And please wait until tomorrow before testing your new equipment. I don't want any technical problems during the dress rehearsal."

They departed, and Nico resumed thinking of his schedule before his meeting with DIGOS. But for a moment, he reflected . . . Kareem delivering equipment on rehearsal day. Shouldn't he have known about this before? But Kareem was reliable, efficient, and well-respected by La Scala engineers. He knew what he was doing.

Nico returned to his office, answered phone calls, and followed crews onstage. A few minutes before 1 PM, a security guard at the entrance called to say that dottor Lucchini and his team were in the lobby for their appointment.

"Please escort them to the fifth floor. I'll be at the elevator."

Nico moved chairs in front of his desk. Did he need two? Three? He put four in a semicircle. He straightened up his desk, moved coffee cups and trays to a sink, and put magazines and manuals on a corner table away from his desk.

He went to the hallway and waited at the elevator. A minute later it arrived, and out stepped Giorgio Lucchini, a young woman Nico didn't recognize, and a man who looked familiar.

"*Buongiorno,* dottor Lucchini," Nico said, reaching out to shake hands.

"*Buongiorno,* Nico. You remember Vice Ispettore Maurizio Baraldi from last year." They shook hands.

"I have a new officer this year, Ispettore De Monti. She's new to DIGOS. This will be her first La Scala assignment." Nico smiled and shook her hand.

"Welcome to La Scala. Come to my office, please."

He led them to his office and motioned to the chairs he'd arranged around his desk. His male radar made a quick analysis of Ispettore De Monti: attractive, modest makeup, pretty eyes, and a perfect complexion. No wedding ring, reddish-blonde curly hair, black slacks, Dr. Martens boots, a padded jacket, and a scarf around her neck.

"I'm sure you're very busy today, Nico," Giorgio said. "We'll just need a few minutes to brief you on the inspection. Our agents and dogs will be here on Saturday afternoon at one o'clock."

"Yes, dottore, the staff has been notified. We feel secure when DIGOS is protecting the theater's guests, especially for the premiere, with all of the VIPs, politicians, and diplomats in the house. How many will you have on duty?"

Giorgio opened a folder and handed him a three-page memorandum about police surveillance. Nico put on his reading glasses and scanned the roster of names, titles, police branches, phone numbers, and locations where agents were assigned.

"Let me run through it quickly," Giorgio said. "For the premiere, we'll have thirty agents in the theater, men dressed formally in tuxedos, female agents in evening wear, on all floors, in box seats, backstage, and in the balconies. You can recognize them by this medallion on their clothing."

Giorgio took a medallion from his pocket and handed it to Nico. It was euro-sized and hexagonally shaped, with a turquoise border, a white crescent at the top, and a scarlet center.

"The Carabinieri will wear the same," Giorgio continued. "They will have twenty in the theater, working in pairs in the background."

"Discreet and official. You keep us all safe."

"That's our job. On the day of the premiere, we will have about four hundred police on duty inside and outside the theater—Polizia,

DIGOS, Carabinieri, Vigili Urbani, and Guardia di Finanza, with mobile radios to the COT—the Centrale Operativa Territoriale at the Questura command center."

"Reassuring, dottore. We can't have any unfortunate incidents. Our VIPs, the audience, and millions watching on TV count on us to provide entertainment without disruption."

"On Saturday," said Giorgio, "we'll sweep the theater at one o'clock. No one will be allowed to remain inside. After the doors are sealed, agents with dogs from the Polizia di Stato's Unità Cinofila will sweep the entire theater for explosives or suspicious material to be removed."

"I've already sent everyone a notice," said Nico, "but they know your procedure. It's standard. Our stage manager will order everyone to leave by five minutes before one I'll be the last to exit. When we return, we will have at least four hours before the curtain goes up. Will you attend the dress rehearsal, dottore?"

Giorgio shook his head. "No, sorry. I have a meeting with the Prefetto and the Questore about the premiere. Baraldi and De Monti are your contacts. They will be in charge of the DIGOS team for the performance. You can reach me through them."

"I will be on the third floor, left side of the stage, along with De Monti," said Baraldi. Simona smiled, and Nico returned the smile, lingering a moment to admire hers.

"I will attend the premiere with my wife," Giorgio said.

"You'll enjoy the evening, dottore, a superb production of *Turandot*."

Giorgio looked at his watch. "Good. It's all organized. Baraldi will take De Monti around the theater to show her where our agents will be assigned."

"I've reviewed reports from past premieres," Simona said. "I've memorized the theater floor plans, backstage, offices, and storage."

"Have you attended La Scala before?" Nico asked.

She lit up. "Of course! My parents brought me to Rossini's *Cenerentola* when I was ten years old. I've seen *Tosca*, *La Traviata*, and Strehler's great stage direction of *Le Nozze di Figaro* and *Lucia di Lammermoor*. My favorite is Franco Zeffirelli's *La Bohème*."

"Mine, too," Nico said, smiling. He liked Simona, a DIGOS agent with a pleasant manner, a soft voice, and beautiful eyes. "Puccini's my favorite composer. You'll enjoy *Turandot*—all the costumes, gorgeous singing, and the exotic characters. I've loved Ping, Pang, and Pong since I was a little boy."

Giorgio stood, followed by De Monti and Baraldi. They shook hands across Nico's desk, and Nico moved toward the door. "Thank you for coming, dottore. A pleasure to see you and your colleagues." He shook hands with Baraldi and De Monti, bowing slightly when he touched her hand.

CHAPTER TWENTY-SEVEN

Simona De Monti stepped down from the DIGOS trailer parked behind La Scala on Via Giuseppe Verdi and started walking toward Piazza della Scala. It was a drizzling, cold day, 2°C, with brisk winds sweeping down the corridors of Milan's streets. It was December 7, dedicated to Milan's patron saint, Sant'Ambrogio, and the date of La Scala's annual premiere performance. Amoruso had just called and said that she was leaving the Questura and coming to the trailer to supervise DIGOS agents in the piazza and in La Scala.

Chain barricades had been placed on streets and sidewalks on Via Manzoni and Via Santa Margherita, leading to Teatro alla Scala. The festive premiere always drew rowdy demonstrators who tried to block streets, hold protest rallies, and shout political slogans at TV cameras and VIPs attending the premiere. Milan's historic center was also packed with shoppers on Christmas buying sprees in Galleria Vittorio Emanuele, on Via Manzoni, and in the city's world-famous fashion district, *quadrilatero della moda*.

When De Monti reached Piazza della Scala, she searched for familiar faces among the sea of DIGOS, Polizia di Stato, Carabinieri, Guardia di Finanza, and Vigili Urbani officers monitoring protestors around the perimeter. Uniformed police wore visored helmets and bulky bulletproof vests and carried riot shields. DIGOS agents were more discreet, wearing plain clothes, boots, caps, holstered Beretta automatic pistols, and bulletproof vests under leather coats and padded jackets.

Protest permits required demonstrators to organize separately, not mingle, not cross barricades, not throw smoke bombs, and not start fights. Police were on guard for the inevitable ugly disruptions: angry demonstrators tossing smoke bombs, lighting firecrackers, throwing eggs or rocks, and shouting profanities. Disruptions were usually brief, as beefy police officers would arrest a few, handcuff them, and escort them to police vans.

No TAV protestors carried banners demanding the closing of the train tunnel being bored under the Alps between Italy and France. A "No More Immigrants" group waved signs and shouted demands that Italy ban refugees from Africa and the Middle East:

"Send immigrants back to Africa!"

"Italy for Italians!"

"Stop polluting our country!"

The protestors represented a cross-section of Italians: teenagers, college students, and adults; some with children on their shoulders, others with craggy beards, boots, jeans, black rucksacks, kaffiyeh scarves, and ski masks.

De Monti spent an hour walking around the Leonardo da Vinci statue in the piazza and mingling with colleagues, all of them eyeing slogan-shouting protestors waving banners and signs. A few minor disruptions had quickly been shut down by vigilant police.

De Monti made a thorough, one-person patrol of the perimeter, starting at one corner of the piazza and then reversing her path so she could gauge the possible flash points. When she'd finished her patrol, her mobile radio beeped. It was Amoruso. "Ciao, Simona. I'm in the trailer. Where are you?"

"Good afternoon, dottoressa. Reporting from Piazza della Scala. Minor problems so far; three or four troublemakers rushed the barricades, knocked one down. The Carabinieri grabbed them and hauled them off. That quieted things down."

"I've been watching," Amoruso said, referring to the Carabinieri van parked at the perimeter with CCTV cameras on its roof. "It's early. I expect things to get out of hand later. Police vans are standing by on Via Verdi and Via Filodrammatici. The real agitators show up when TV cameras are there for VIPs arriving in government cars and police escorts."

"I saw the vans on Via Verdi. Haven't been to Via Filodrammatici yet."

"How long will you remain at the piazza?"

"Another hour or so. I'll go with the others at three o'clock to change into formal wear in the theater and make a final sweep before the doors open at five."

"Check in when you need to. I'll stay in the trailer until five thirty and then go to the theater to meet Lucchini and his wife."

"Would you like me to report to the trailer before we go into the theater?"

"No reason. Call me after the four o'clock briefing before they send you to your assigned area in the theater. Will you see the maestro today?"

Simona sighed but didn't pause, not wanting Amoruso to detect her anxiety about him. "Unfortunately, no. He's busy. He texted me yesterday. I wished him good luck with the premiere. To be honest, I'd be embarrassed if he saw me tonight wearing the DIGOS medallion. I told him I work for a law firm."

"I'm sure he doesn't mind where you work."

Simona bit her lip. She had not handled the maestro situation well. She had turned down his invitation to Lago di Como when she had surveillance duty at Hussain's apartment. The maestro had invited her to lunch in Brera a week later, and she had accepted. She had been touched by how warm he was that day. He had said he hoped to see her again before he left Milan. He had offered her a ticket for the rehearsal performance, but she had turned him down, not wanting to admit that she would be a police officer on duty that night.

Simona's emotions were in turmoil at the irony. She was excited about her assignment for the La Scala premiere but frustrated because duty interfered with her personal life. She was a police officer with serious responsibilities. But she was also falling in love with the maestro, the most exciting man in her life.

Duty. Female desires. Why should one negate the other? She hoped she would be assigned in the theater during the performance and not backstage, where she might bump into him. She didn't want to risk the maestro seeing her with her police medallion, as she would have to confess that she had not told him the truth when they had met at the Armani party and again at lunch in Brera. Twice she had lied, regretting her decision, delaying the inevitable when she would tell him she really was a DIGOS agent.

At 3 PM, De Monti joined her on-duty DIGOS colleagues. They left the piazza for the employee entrance to La Scala on Via Filodrammatici and took the elevator to the basement dressing rooms used by extras.

Two rooms had been reserved for the police to change into formal wear. The women's dressing room was small but enough to accommodate eight female officers. De Monti's formal evening wear had been delivered in the morning. She stepped into a private dressing area and changed into an above-the-knee, black, sleeveless cocktail dress, a pink silk scarf, diamond earrings and a pearl necklace her mother had given her, black ankle-strap pumps, and a black Gucci purse. She pinned the police medallion to her dress and returned to the main dressing area, carrying her purse, which contained her cell phone, Beretta pistol, silencer, and DIGOS identification card.

In the main dressing room, hair stylists and beauticians were styling hair and applying makeup on her female colleagues. Simona waited her turn and then sat in front of a mirror while a stylist teased and sprayed her hair, combing out curls that touched her shoulders. A beautician applied fresh lipstick, rouge, eye shadow, and mascara. When she finished, she looked at Simona in the mirror. Simona was smiling, pleased to have such exclusive treatment by theater artists.

"Che bella! Sei una delizia, cosi! Semplice e chic!" [You're beautiful! You're stunning like this! Simple and chic!] the beautician said, beaming at her.

Simona thanked her, stood up, and looked in a full-length mirror, turning to see her profiles. Yes, she did look glamorous! If only Maestro Bongiovanni could see her: formally dressed, hair styled, with fresh makeup applied by an artist. She looked like a fashion model, but in reality, she was a cop on duty.

De Monti waited for Baraldi and Volpara outside the men's dressing room with its open door. Carabinieri from the ROS squad, DIGOS agents, and Guardia di Finanza officers were teasing each other as they preened before mirrors, wearing designer tuxedos, formal dress shoes, cummerbunds, black ties—and police medallions.

"Simona, you look ravishing," Baraldi said when he saw her waiting at the door.

"Thank you, Maurizio. You look great, too. Unfortunately, we're cops on duty—*not* members of high society. We're carrying guns, badges, looking for bad guys. We could be wearing combat boots, jeans, and caps tonight; no one would pay attention to us. They'll be jealously fawning over their friends—who is the prettiest, who is wearing the most expensive dress—and admiring each other's jewelry."

"Oh, come on. I haven't seen you look so elegant since you joined DIGOS."

"Are you flattering me, Maurizio?" she teased, raising an eyebrow.

He opened his arms in a gesture of invitation. "Just a little, maybe. Would you come to dinner with me tonight?"

"I'd love to. Where are we going, Cracco's?"

He grinned. "Not tonight, sorry. But you could be my guest when we have those delicious sandwiches and snacks they've prepared for us before the doors open at 5 PM"

"Oh, Maurizio," she said, pouting. "I thought you were a real gentleman. All you offer me is sandwiches?"

"Sorry. I wish I could offer you Cracco's legendary *insalata russa caramellata*. But we have to eat something. We're on duty until 2 AM and won't even have a break for some beer or wine."

"Such a pity, and you know it will be torture watching the VIPs at the banquet without touching anything. I read in *Corriere della Sera* what they're serving, and it's mouthwatering."

Volpara came out of the dressing room, patting his black hair, which had been trimmed and gelled by stylists. "Well, well, look at this. They made you into a movie star—almost," Simona teased.

He blushed. "You think so? I don't know about that. I'm cheap. I pay 20 euros for haircuts at the barber shop around the corner. But here they gave me a 200-euro styling."

"Did you tip your stylist?"

"Actually," he said with a chuckle, "I was going to, but then my stylist—a fifty-year-old man dressed like a twenty-five-year-old—made a pass at me. He said I looked like a cop in a TV series and asked for my phone number!"

"Did you give it to him?" she asked, giving him a wink.

"Of course not. I said it was top secret!" They laughed, enjoying a rare moment of bantering as colleagues and friends.

Stylists were finishing their last DIGOS customers, trimming hair, beards, eyebrows. Simona took out her cell phone and snapped a few photos. "Look at them, primping like peacocks. I'll show some photos to their buddies at our briefing tomorrow. Imagine the jeers and howls."

"Peacocks!" Volpara said. "We'll never live it down. Lucchini and Amoruso will fire us."

"They'll love it," she said checking her watch. "Time to get to work. It's almost four. We've got a last briefing in the theater. Doors open at five; we have to be at our stations."

They took the elevator to the ground floor and walked down a carpeted hallway into the theater. Rows of La Scala's plush red seats were all empty, but soon they would be occupied by the elite of Milan, national politicians, and foreign dignitaries. De Monti and Volpara joined their formally dressed colleagues, taking seats near the orchestra pit for the final briefing before the doors opened.

It was a new experience for many of them. They had attended performances at La Scala before, but never when the theater was empty and quiet. They looked around the splendor of the eighteenth-century design, including lush folds in the blood-red curtain with gold braid and the logo of La Scala. Four floors of boxed seats and two upper galleries swept around the oval theater, divided by the *palco reale,* the royal box used by the former king of Italy and the royal family, where the president of the republic, the mayor of Milan, and other high government officials would be seated that night. Globe lights on each level and the chandelier hanging high above lit the theater as bright as a summer afternoon.

The ranking officer from each police agency passed out diagrams of the theater and assigned positions on the four levels of boxed seats, the two upper galleries, the staircases, the elevators, the lobbies, and backstage. Each officer had a mobile radio tuned to a frequency connecting with the COT (*Centrale Operativa Territoriale*) command center.

There were no questions. The officers knew their assignments and were familiar with the layout of the theater. "To your stations," a Carabinieri captain announced to end the briefing. The officers stood and walked up the aisles and out of the theater to take elevators to their assigned security posts. DIGOS agents were assigned throughout the theater, backstage, and in the audience. Baraldi, De Monti, and Volpara were assigned to the floors to the left side of the stage.

Agents took the elevator to various floors with dressing rooms and rehearsal studios occupied by actors, dancers, performers in costume, and musicians in tuxedos. In empty wardrobe studios, mannequins posed naked beside tables strewn with bolts of cloth, sewing materials, wigs, sleeves, and bodices. A DIGOS agent was left on each floor.

After the backstage agents were in position, they returned to the first-floor hall of soloist dressing rooms, walking single file in a stream of backstage crew and wardrobe specialists, overhearing the buzz of exuberant conversations about last-minute emergencies, a constant in any theater.

De Monti, Baraldi, and Volpara passed an open elevator as two people entered. De Monti glanced in.

She froze. Kareem Hussain was at the back of the elevator wearing a blue shirt with a Carefull logo. For the first time, she was almost face to face with Hussain after months of studying his surveillance photos. He looked vaguely sinister: beard, gaunt face, sunken cheeks, a blank stare. She noticed two men wearing blue Carefull shirts on each side of Hussain. One was Esman Bilal. Somebody was standing in front of the third man; all she could see was that he looked dark-skinned, possibly Middle Eastern, like Kareem and Esman.

The elevator closed with a soft whir.

De Monti gasped and turned to Volpara and Baraldi. "Hussain! I just saw him with two others. Bilal and someone else."

"Hussain is supposed to be here today," Baraldi said. "It was in the Carefull log. You saw Bilal?"

"Yes—and he's *not* a Carefull employee!" she protested. She glanced at the digital display of the elevator passing the second and third floors and stopping on the fourth floor. She grabbed her radio and called Amoruso, her voice tense. "Dottoressa, Hussain and Bilal are here. I just saw them in the elevator. And another man, all wearing Carefull shirts. Bilal doesn't work for Carefull. Why is he here? Dottor Lucchini has to know."

"Just a minute. Let me get to a computer," Amoruso said from the DIGOS trailer. Over the radio, the three agents could hear chairs skidding across the floor, conversations in the background, and Amoruso asking colleagues for a computer. A door opened and slammed, and someone said, "Demonstrators getting out of hand. Let's go. There's a fight, throwing rocks." There was commotion in the trailer, feet moving across the floor, the door opening, agitated voices. The door slammed shut. Then quiet in the trailer except for the tapping of keys on a computer.

A moment later, Amoruso said, "Here it is. . . . Hussain was scheduled for La Scala Wednesday and today. Bilal and Khan are at their apartments. Gajani is at the kebab shop. Are you sure you saw Bilal?"

"Yes! No doubt. He was only a few feet from me. I recognized him immediately."

"So he's NOT at his apartment," Amoruso said. "How did he get there?"

"Dottoressa . . . remember a couple of weekends ago, everyone except Hussain didn't leave their apartments until the evening? I think they found a way to escape surveillance cameras."

"Yes, I was suspicious, too."

"The third man *could* be Khan," De Monti said emphatically.

"*Mio Dio*, three of them in the theater! I've got to call Lucchini."

Amoruso pressed the button on her radio to link her and De Monti with Lucchini on a DIGOS channel. "Dottore, we have an emergency. I have De Monti on the line. She says Hussain and Bilal are in the theater with a third man, maybe Khan."

"All three in the theater?" he exclaimed. "They can't be. Are you sure?"

"Yes, sir," De Monti confirmed. "I saw them on a backstage elevator. The third man looked dark-skinned, but I didn't see his face."

"You're positive?"

"I was in front of the elevator. They were so close I could almost have touched them. I've seen hundreds of photos of them. I'm positive they're Hussain and Bilal."

"Signor Prefetto!" Lucchini said, raising his voice to get the attention of everyone in the command center, which included the

Prefetto, Questore Taddei, the colonel of the Carabinieri, the head of NOCS, the chief of Vigili Urbani, and the General of Guardia di Finanza, all watching CCTV cameras of unruly demonstrators in Piazza della Scala.

Lucchini rose from his chair. "We have an emergency! A cell of terrorists is in La Scala."

A ripple of panic went through the command center. "Terrorists?" the Carabinieri colonel said in disbelief. "How could they get inside La Scala? I thought they were planning an attack at the IlSole24Ore conference at the Borsa next week."

"Maybe . . . maybe," Lucchini said, choosing his words carefully, ". . . we were wrong. I'm sorry. We'll deal with the Borsa later. The threat might be La Scala. Tonight."

"How could they? You've been following them—for months!" said the commander of the NOCS.

"Yes, yes, I know. We've been surveilling them. They've been very secretive, no intelligence from phone taps, no tip-off from the Muslim community. But one of my agents saw them minutes ago. They could have chemicals to make sarin gas. It would be *disastrous* if they released them in the theater."

"Are these the chemicals that came from La Spezia? The Muslim terrorists?" the commander of Guardia di Finanza asked.

"Yes."

"What shall we do?" the Prefetto asked, his hands trembling as he took off his glasses to wipe his forehead. "We'll have to cancel the premiere to guarantee the safety of the guests and the artists."

The Prefetto looked around the conference table, looking for nods that they supported his decision. No one nodded. They all looked at Taddei and then Lucchini.

"Wait!" said Taddei, raising his hand and turning to Lucchini, next to him.

Lucchini said, "We can't cancel the premiere. The whole world is watching us."

Taddei supported his decision. "It would be a major victory for terrorists—and a total defeat for the Italian police forces."

The tension in the room was eerie. There was silence for a few seconds as they considered the gravity of the situation and the consequences of making the wrong decision. But there was no time for debate.

"No!" the Prefetto protested. "I'm not risking lives just because we have an opera premiere. The Ministry of the Interior will have my head on a silver platter if we let the performance go on and something happens. We're canceling it."

Questore Taddei was quick to respond. "With all due respect, could we take a moment to consider another option? Instead of canceling immediately, we could delay the premiere, which would give us time to apprehend the suspects. La Scala can say there's some minor temporary technical problem—electrical, elevators, the sound system. We've had heavy snow the last few days; water leaked through the roof."

Nods around the room. Eyes moved to Lucchini.

"I agree with the Questore," he said. "Give us time to arrest the terrorists and remove them from the theater. Let the La Scala director handle the postponement, tell the staff, the artists, the media. Emphasize it's temporary until the minor problem is fixed. We can't have the press think we're ordering it; it has to come from La Scala."

A flash on three of the CCTV monitors caught everyone's attention. Another flash, a cloud of smoke, another flash, another cloud of smoke. Protestors rushed the helmeted police, who were holding bulletproof shields, as smoke obscured the entrance into the galleria. The Carabinieri ROS team and Polizia di Stato's DIGOS reinforcements rushed to the melee, pushed back protestors, knocked down signs, grabbed protestors, and pulled them away. Smoke rose in the air, sweeping over the Piazza della Scala. Within seconds, the protestors pulled back, and a wall of shielded and helmeted officers cornered them, grabbing arms and pushing protestors against walls.

One by one, the commanders looked away from the monitors, knowing there would be more outbursts that evening. They had all experienced chaos at public events in recent years, even been a part of violence earlier in their careers.

Lucchini cleared his throat. "I'm confident my agents will find the terrorists before they do any harm. Signor Prefetto, my team is pursuing them. Let me call my deputy. They'll find them before the first guest enters the theater."

Taddei looked around the conference table and interpreted that the decision had the support of everyone in the command center. "Signori, I completely trust Dottor Lucchini and his team," he said. "Signor Prefetto, we'll take full responsibility for this decision. We'll have the terrorists in our hands within minutes. No one will be harmed."

The colleagues around the table nodded in support of Lucchini's proposal.

"You all agree?" the Prefetto asked.

One by one, they all answered, "Yes . . . yes . . . yes . . . yes . . . yes." The Prefetto looked at Lucchini, raised his palms as an expression of agreement and said, "Dottor Lucchini, I want the terrorists captured within fifteen minutes. If they're not, we'll cancel the premiere." He looked at the large clock above the conference room fireplace. "It's 4:35. Alert your team they have a deadline: fifteen minutes."

Lucchini picked up his mobile radio. "Dottoressa Amoruso. Ispettore De Monti . . . the command center has made a decision. . . . You have fifteen minutes to find the terrorists and arrest them. Don't create a disturbance in the theater. We don't want the media to find out."

"Yes, dottore!" Amoruso said. "I'm on my way to the theater now. De Monti, what's your status and location?"

"We're on the second floor, going to the upper floors, where we suspect they are."

"I'll be there in minutes with backup."

De Monti turned to Volpara and Baraldi. "To the fourth floor! Take the stairs. The elevator's coming down; we can't wait for it to come back."

She grabbed Baraldi's arm and pushed him and Volpara into the stairway, letting them lead, they leaped two steps at a time. De Monti unstrapped her shoes and ran up the steps, one at a time, her bare feet slapping the tiles like paddles. The stairway ascended twelve steps and turned back to twelve more steps to the next door. They passed the third floor, arrived at the fourth, and ran to the ballet and musicians' rehearsal rooms. Baraldi threw open the door, Volpara behind him, both puffing from racing up two flights of stairs. They held the door for De Monti.

The hallway was crowded, with performers and crew moving in both directions. The three agents waited by the elevator, catching their breath and peering over heads in the crowd.

"See any blue shirts?" De Monti gasped.

Volpara stood on his tiptoes, looked one way and then the other, and scanned the crowded hallway. "None," he said.

"Elevator's on the sixth," De Monti said, pointing to the display.

"Here's Cella and Morucci," Baraldi said, pointing at their colleagues weaving through the crowded hallway. When they reached the elevator, Baraldi ordered them: "We're looking for Hussain and Bilal. Search this floor. We're going to five and six."

Volpara pushed open the door to the stairs and dashed up the steps in the lead, with Baraldi following and De Monti several steps behind. Volpara reached the fifth floor, pushed open the door, and held it for them. The three exited into the hallway. Fewer people than other floors. No blue shirts.

De Monti was wheezing, out of breath. She paused a couple of seconds before she pressed the button on her radio. "Dottore, we're on the fifth floor. We'll check here, then sixth."

"Amoruso is on her way to the theater," responded Lucchini. "I'm sending backup to all exits. Everyone on this frequency, keep it open for the DIGOS team in the theater."

De Monti, Baraldi, and Volpara made their way down the hallway, pushing open doors to empty offices and rehearsal studios with musicians practicing on flutes and stringed instruments. No blue shirts.

De Monti reached the women's restroom and pushed open the door. Three women in Chinese costumes, possibly from the chorus, were at sinks, combing their hair in front of mirrors.

"Did men in blue shirts come in here?" De Monti asked, her voice cracking.

They stared at her. "What? Men? This is the women's."

She let the door close and took her Beretta from her purse. She held it at her side, her heart thumping. Of course, men wouldn't go into the women's restroom; they'd be in the men's restroom next door. She heard water running in a sink, and then it stopped. A towel torn from a dispenser. She waited outside the door, her Beretta by her side.

The door swung open. De Monti gasped. Maestro Armando Bongiovanni was coming out, wiping his hands on a paper towel.

"Simona! You have a gun!" Armando was stunned. "What are you doing here? You're wearing a police medallion! What—"

"Armando!" Adrenalin was pumping through Simona, her heart pounding from the shock of seeing Hussain and Bilal in the elevator, running up the steps—and surprising Armando at the men's room.

"I'm . . . DIGOS . . . working . . . the theater." She gasped, her voice brittle between gasps, regretting that she was sounding like she was talking to a criminal.

"DIGOS? You said you worked for a law firm."

"No. Sorry. We need you to go downstairs. We're doing a last-minute inspection." She spoke rapidly, her words running together.

"But—but I can't," he stammered. "I'm rehearsing musicians in the studio."

"Please . . . escort them downstairs. No alarm, we just need to inspect the floor."

He shrugged. "I thought they did that earlier today."

She shook her head. "But now we're doing a final inspection. Don't worry, just routine."

"Very well," he said, a puzzled look on his face. "I'll do as you say . . . but still . . ." He moved toward the rehearsal studio and pushed open the door. "Everybody . . . we have to leave."

"What's wrong? Leave? We're rehearsing," one of the startled musicians answered.

"We need to go downstairs. Bring your instruments. We'll finish rehearsal in the orchestra pit." Armando held open the door, motioning for them to hurry. They rose from their chairs, reached for music on the stands, and scrambled to file out of the studio, carrying sheets of music, flutes, clarinets, and an oboe, muttering about the strange situation.

Armando guided his musicians down the hall like a teacher ushering schoolchildren to class. When they reached the elevator, Armando turned to look back at Simona, still confused about encountering her, learning she was DIGOS, and seeing her carrying a deadly weapon. He raised a hand, a pleading gesture, "Are you okay, Simona? I don't understand—"

She was firm. "I'm fine, Maestro. No reason for alarm. We're making a final inspection." She managed a smile, brief assurance that she was just following orders, all routine. She surprised herself when she said, "I'll see you later."

He nodded, "Okay . . . okay . . . yes . . . let's . . . okay." Then the elevator door closed behind him.

Simona stood in the hall, trembling from the surprise encounter with Armando and his reaction to her telling him she worked for DIGOS. In a few seconds, an important part of their relationship had been altered; she had told him a lie. Even casual relationships depend upon trust. Would she ever see Armando again, despite his last words?

She was still trembling when Volpara said, "So that's the maestro. . . . "Nice-looking fellow. You surprised him. Did he know you were DIGOS?"

"Forget it," she snapped. "We've got work to do and—"

"No one else on this floor," Baraldi interrupted. "Let's get to the next floor."

They hurried to the stairwell, pushed open the door, and ran up the steps, De Monti trailing. Volpara opened the sixth-floor door.

The sixth floor was almost empty compared to lower floors: one technician carrying filters for floodlights, two men behind him carrying a box of floodlight bulbs. "Any men in blue shirts on this floor?" Baraldi demanded.

"What? Blue shirts?"

"Men in blue shirts," Baraldi repeated, louder and more forcefully. "The Carefull team. You know Kareem Hussain?"

The technician with the filters looked up. "Yeah, I do. He's on the upper floor. I was there a minute ago."

"What's up there?" De Monti asked.

"Technical. Lighting, heating, audio, video. Sometimes Carefull goes there."

"We're DIGOS," Baraldi said. "Take us up. We'll follow."

"Are you really DIGOS?" He set down the box. "What's going on?"

Volpara pointed to his medallion. "See this?"

"Okay, I'll take you up." They went into the stairwell and hurried to the seventh floor.

An empty hall. A different layout from the lower floors. No tiled floors, painted walls, or domed light fixtures. Wooden and cardboard boxes, carts, tools, three dollies resting against a wall. Dust shavings on a wooden floor blotched with stains and scarred with scratches and gouges.

"They went that way," the man said, pointing down the hallway to three closed doors.

"What's there?" Baraldi asked.

"Technical controls . . . thermostats, heating and air conditioning . . . mechanical bridges . . . lights for everything—stage . . . footlights . . . floodlights . . . theater . . . lobbies . . . balconies. Ventilation . . . audio . . . video . . . TV cameras . . . all here."

"You know Nico Brebbi?" De Monti asked.

"Sure, he's the technical director, my boss."

"Call him. Get him here. Now!"

She called Amoruso. "Dottoressa, we're on the seventh floor, all technical. One of the crew saw Hussain here a few minutes ago. I've told the technician to get Brebbi here. Are you on your way?"

A flurry of shouting, cursing, and harsh banging came over the radio when Amoruso clicked to talk. "I'm still on the street!" she shouted. "Demonstrators are blocking Via Filodrammatici!"

De Monti could hear the *oomph* of bodies pushing against bodies, shouting, cursing, sirens, yelling. "We're pushing them back, but it will take me a couple of minutes! I have backup with me."

Lucchini interrupted: "Ispettore De Monti, this is Lucchini. Don't engage until Amoruso gets there."

"Yes, sir."

CHAPTER TWENTY-EIGHT

"Dottoressa," De Monti said into her radio, "we're on the seventh floor. Take the elevator. Nico Brebbi, the technical director, is coming. We think Hussain, Bilal, and the third man are on this floor."

"Via Santa Margherita still blocked," Amoruso responded. "Protestors on the ground. Carabinieri pulling them away. It's pretty rough. Wait for me. A couple of agents are escorting me through the crowd. I'll get there as soon as I can." The sounds of shouting, crowds yelling, and sirens came over her radio.

Lucchini spoke again on the police frequency. "Theater exits secured. DIGOS and ROS are taking care of the demonstrators blocking Via Santa Margherita. Everyone on this frequency, keep channel 22 open for DIGOS team in the theater backstage. Volpara, Baraldi, and De Monti, go to channel 22 and update your location and situation."

The three agents switched channels from the COT command center to channel 22. Volpara answered, "Dottore, we're on the seventh floor backstage. We're searching this floor. There are several doors leading to technical equipment. We're waiting for Nico Brebbi to help us."

Volpara, Baraldi, and De Monti lowered their radios and started toward the closed doors, Berettas drawn, backs to the wall. The narrow hall was open, with a metal railing that looked over the stage, six floors below. They could glimpse crews putting final touches on props, sweeping floors, and moving boxes and tools. Above the stage, a network of girders, mechanical bridges, cables, and ropes dangled from the ceiling like metal intestines.

De Monti glanced at the chasm a meter in front of her. She felt dizzy with the flash of a childhood memory when she had fallen off a wall onto a stone path, had lost consciousness, and had awoken to the pain of cracked ribs.

One misstep would plunge her over the railing, falling to the stage. She turned her face, looking at the back of Volpara's head as they both moved silently along the wall. They reached the first door: a metal plaque with the numeral 17 on the wall. They stopped to listen. No sound behind the door.

They moved to the second door, identified by a plaque with the numeral 18. A faint hum behind the door, barely audible beeps. No human voices.

The third door, 19. At first, no sound. Then a muffled murmur. Silence. Another murmur. Voices? A sound like a metal pinging on metal. A hammer? A whoosh. Air being released from a tank? More murmurs.

Volpara pointed at the door and mouthed, "*In there.*"

De Monti nodded and looked down the narrow hall that led to a semidark enclosure. She pointed it out to Baraldi and Volpara and shrugged her shoulders in a gesture that indicated *What's that?* They shook their heads and retreated down the hallway away from the doors.

Back by the stairwell, De Monti again pointed toward the open area beyond the third door. "Where's that go?"

Baraldi shook his head. Volpara whispered, "Don't know."

"Let's check it out. It might be an escape route. Maurizio, stay by door 19. Dario and I will see what's there."

The two of them returned down the hall, Baraldi moving over to door 19. De Monti and Volpara moved to the opening, letting their eyes adjust to the dim light. A single bulb illuminated the open space: a floor of wooden planks and exposed wooden beams packed with wires, cables, and insulation padding.

They looked around. Metal racks around the perimeter held wiring and color-coded plastic and metal cables that converged in a center console of blinking lights, gauges, and meters. Wires and cables were strung like spaghetti from the console to the stage below. Through an open beam, De Monti and Volpara could see the stage proscenium, La Scala's red curtain, and the orchestra pit. Above was the ceiling of La Scala's domed roof.

De Monti pointed to a narrow rectangular gap in the wall ahead. They walked on the planks and peered out. Below was the interior of the theater, two long, carpeted aisles from the rear to the orchestra pit, rows of red seats, three floors of box seating, two upper balconies, and the rear VIP gallery. Police agents in formal dress stood by each door that led into the theater.

Directly in front of them was La Scala's massive chandelier, which hung from the ceiling by gold cables. The agents had sat under that chandelier minutes before. Above the chandelier, two men in a control booth were testing floodlights focused on the stage and red curtain.

De Monti and Volpara stepped back and walked on wooden planks to the hallway, where Baraldi was listening at door 19. Murmurs . . . quiet for a few moments . . . more murmurs. Impossible to distinguish words. One murmur was a low voice. The second murmur was a stronger tone, accented, as if asking questions.

The agents moved silently to the stairwell. "They can't go that way," De Monti whispered, pointing to the space they had inspected. "No doors. They have to come this way. We'll guard these doors."

A moment later, the elevator arrived. The door opened and Nico Brebbi came out, followed by Amoruso and two plainclothes DIGOS agents, Berettas by their sides. De Monti put her fingers to her lips.

"A mess on the streets. We got an escort," Amoruso whispered with a snarl. De Monti pointed down the hall. "Is that where they are?" Amoruso whispered, squinting to inspect the narrow hall and open space over the stage.

De Monti said in a low voice, "They're in the last room. Nico, what's in room 19?"

Brebbi was visibly nervous, with a sweaty forehead and eyes darting to look at the officers standing alongside him with drawn weapons. "Ventilation ducts," he whispered in a shaky voice. "All areas of the theater." His hands were shaking. He made fists and pressed them to his side, still shaking.

"Where terrorists could introduce toxic gases into the ventilation system?" Amoruso asked.

He shuddered. "Oh, my God, yes. But how did they get there?"

"Do you know Kareem Hussain and Esman Bilal?" De Monti asked.

Brebbi's head bobbed. "I know Kareem. He works for Carefull Services. Bilal? No, I've never heard of him. Who is he?"

"Brebbi, we need to get in there immediately," Amoruso said, her eyes continuing to look down the hall and over the railing, squinting at the open space that De Monti and Volpara had inspected. "Do you have a key?"

Brebbi fumbled in his pocket and took out a ring of keys. "Yes, this one." He handed it to Amoruso, who pointed down the hall to the semidark room. "What's down there?"

"Just the area above the proscenium, orchestra pit, and control mechanisms."

"Any place to escape that way?"

"No."

"Let's go." Amoruso led everyone down the hall. When they reached room 19, she motioned to all of them to form a semicircle in front of the door.

Amoruso motioned at Brebbi to knock on the door. He knocked and said in a shaky voice, "Hello? Is anyone inside? This is Nico Brebbi . . . making final rounds. Who's in there, please?"

Silence. Amoruso put her hand on the doorknob and turned. It was locked.

"No! Don't come in!" a shout from the room.

"Kareem, is that you?" Brebbi said, his voice quivering.

"Nico, yes, it's me," said the voice behind the door. "We're running a final test. Wait."

Amoruso motioned for everyone to have their silencers in place. When she saw they were ready, she raised her weapon, holding it near her shoulder. All the agents copied her stance.

Amoruso stood between Brebbi and the door, inserted the key, turned it, and pushed open the door. It was slammed closed immediately.

Back-and-forth murmurs from the room. Agitated, different voices. Then a burst of anxious dialogue:

"Muoviti con quell'affare!" [Quick with that device!]

"Cazzo, non posso fare troppo in fretta!" [Fuck, I can't rush things!]

"Non hai ancora finito?" [Haven't you finished yet?]

Amoruso turned the key again and pushed the door open a few inches, revealing an overhead electrical light and metal racks from floor to ceiling packed with wires and cables. The door was forced shut again.

"Police! Open the door!" Amoruso ordered.

No answer. Loud murmurs, rising in tone, arguing in Arabic.

Amoruso signaled the two plainclothes DIGOS agents wearing bulletproof vests to break through the door. They stepped back and slammed their shoulders against the door, forcing it open, but only halfway, as the door bumped into something.

"Aaah!" a grunt from inside. Something hit the floor. A shrill voice from inside. *"Porca troia!"*

The agents pushed again, forcing the door open almost all the way. They squeezed into the narrow room. "Police! Raise your hands."

"No!" a voice screamed from behind the door.

Two gunshots from the room: a *pfft* from a silenced DIGOS weapon and a loud *BLAM!* The second gunshot inside the room was muffled by the thick walls.

Brebbi shouted, "Aiieeh!"

The first DIGOS agent inside the room screamed and fell back against his partner. Baraldi forced the door open farther, but it was pushed back again. Then it flew wide open. Two men in blue shirts bolted out, swinging arms, shoulders, and fists, pushing Amoruso and Volpara against the metal railing over the stage. A pistol butt slammed Baraldi in the cheek and eye, knocking him to the floor. A shoulder slammed De Monti against the wall. She fell to the floor, hitting her head.

Brebbi was the only one not hit in the brief melee. He stared in disbelief, too shocked to move, his mouth gaping at the violence in his theater.

The men in blue shirts jumped over De Monti and ran down the hall, Bilal trailing. He half turned and aimed his pistol. *BLAM!*

Volpara grunted and fell to his knees, clutching his waist. Drops of blood spread across his white formal shirt. He collapsed, falling on De Monti, who was still sprawled on the floor.

Amoruso had recovered from hitting the railing. She knelt on the floor, raised her pistol, and fired twice. Bilal was pushing open the stairwell door. Hussain was behind him, half turned, both men's left sides exposed.

Pfft! Pfft!

They slammed back against the door jamb and fell to the floor, red holes in the left side of the chest of their blue shirts.

The plainclothes agent in room 19 ran out and yelled, "Morucci down! I shot one in the head! He's on the floor!"

De Monti struggled to her knees and was almost pushed down again as Amoruso ran past her, using one arm on the wall to keep her balance as she raced down the hallway, her weapon pointing at Hussain and Bilal thrashing on the floor. She stood over them, pointing her pistol at Bilal's head, then Hussain's. Their eyes were glazed, unfocused, with dilated pupils. Both were moaning.

Amoruso stepped on Bilal's hand, which was holding his gun, and kicked the weapon to the wall and down the hall. She knelt and pointed the barrel of her weapon at Bilal's head and then at Hussain's. Neither moved.

She was breathing heavily, not taking her eyes off the two downed terrorists. One of Bilal's hands was twitching; the other was under his chest. Hussain was faceup on the floor, with one leg flopped over, arm extended, a long knife in his open palm. A trickle of blood streamed from his open mouth.

De Monti and the plainclothes DIGOS agent ran up behind Amoruso. The agent put his weapon to Hussain's head. The hall reeked with the smell of cordite. "Got 'em," Amoruso said, not taking her eyes off Hussain and Bilal.

The stairwell door swung open. Six uniformed and plainclothes police stopped in the doorway when they saw Amoruso and the DIGOS agent on their knees, pointing weapons at the heads of the downed men.

Amoruso looked up and said in a voice that was surprisingly calm, "Two down here . . . one in a back room. Tell Lucchini we have all three. Three DIGOS injured. . . . Get doctors here immediately."

It was 4:49 PM.

CHAPTER TWENTY-NINE

ico Brebbi remained on the seventh floor as Amoruso supervised the DIGOS agents securing the area. Forensic technicians snapped photos and collected evidence. An emergency medical team lifted Baraldi, Volpara, and Morucci onto gurneys to roll into the elevator. De Monti followed them into the elevator to be examined at the hospital.

Lucchini had arrived and taken charge of the scene. Nico watched him brief the superintendent of La Scala, Jean-Christophe Fournier, who had been escorted up in the elevator by two DIGOS agents. Fournier was one of the most recognized celebrities in Milan, the subject of TV interviews as well as newspaper and magazine articles, and a featured guest at elegant balls, parties, and receptions.

He was just as well-known for his striking appearance: nearly six feet six inches, skeleton-lean, with a bale of white hair, a hawk's beak nose, a prominent chin, and teeth that gleamed like bleached coral. He resembled a statue of a Medici pope.

"Terrible! Terrible! Never in my life!" Fournier blustered, his face red as a lobster, his hands trembling, "How could this happen . . . tonight? I can't believe it!"

Lucchini put a calming hand on his shoulder. "Monsieur Fournier, let us finish our work here. I promise everything will be ready in time for the premiere."

"When? It's 5:05!" he said, stabbing a bony finger at his watch. "The police and Carabinieri won't let me open the doors. We'll have the first guests arriving within minutes. And what do I tell the president of the republic . . . the French president . . . the ministry of culture . . . the mayor of Milan? They're arriving in a half hour!"

"I will take care of that with our police teams. Please calm down, monsieur. We will have the area secured soon, but you have to postpone a few minutes."

"How long?" he fumed, spit exploding from his mouth in rage. "I can't believe this! Delay the premiere? Never! Performers will be onstage in minutes! What do I tell them?"

Lucchini looked straight into his eyes, even when Fournier looked away. "Just that there was a minor technical problem," Lucchini said calmly. "Something with electricity . . . a problem with the stage. . . . You decide," he said, his voice calm, as if he was complimenting a waiter on a pasta dish.

Lucchini's manner soothed the superintendent. "Very well . . . *très bien* . . . you say so . . . I will tell them. How long? Five minutes . . . ten minutes?"

"No longer than ten minutes."

"Ten minutes!" he exhaled, closed his eyes, then opened them, with a look of determination. He glanced down the hall at Nico and motioned for him to come close. "Very well. Nico, we have to delay the premiere—by ten minutes. First time in our theater's glorious history! Nico, inform the artistic and technical staff. Immediately!"

He harrumphed and lifted his head so his Adam's apple protruded from his wrinkled neck. "Very well. I'm off!" he said to Lucchini, his dignity restored.

Lucchini put a hand on his elbow for his last words. "We will handle this delay with the utmost care, Monsieur Fournier. Signor Brebbi will inform the personnel we have a technical issue that is going to be solved. But, as superintendent, you have to inform the TV reporters and RAI that you're postponing the premiere for a few minutes. Blame the snowstorms of the past days. Invent an extra security measure. Coordinate with your press manager and Signor Brebbi, but no one else has to be involved. Don't tell *anyone* what happened here. You two are the only ones who know the truth."

"Of course, dottor Lucchini! I'll prepare a statement with my press manager at once."

Thirty minutes before the curtain rose, Nico was outside Ivan's cubicle, explaining that the delay was an unfortunate electrical malfunction between the seventh floor and lights in the orchestra and front stage.

"I heard noises up there, banging, shouting. What the hell was that?" Ivan said angrily.

"Nothing, nothing. I was there," Nico said with a shrug. "I shouted at a technician who dropped a box of floodlights. They exploded in the box; otherwise, glass would have landed on the stage. We were lucky."

Ivan looked at Nico like he was telling a bad joke. "You're kidding me, Nico! Don't joke about the premiere. Everyone will think we're clowns!"

"Don't worry, Ivan. Just let me have the microphone. I'll inform everyone about the delay. The performance starts at six-ten due to a small accident, a minor technical problem that we're about to fix. Fournier will take care of the press, the VIPs."

"But this is La Scala! People expect us to get everything right. All the world is watching us! We're not a kindergarten class doing a Christmas pageant. I don't believe a word about this minor problem. What's this all about? Tell me."

"Bad things happen, Ivan, even with premieres," Nico said.

Ivan sighed. "Whatever you say," he said, handing him his headset. "Nico . . . we've known each other for, what, twenty years? This story you're telling me is crazy. And I don't believe you. But no time to argue. You owe me a drink. No, make that a dinner, an expensive one. Lots of wine. Then you'll tell me what happened, every single detail of it."

Nico shrugged and raised his hands in a "What can you do?" gesture. "One day, Ivan . . . I promise . . . one day." Nico put on the headset, made a brief announcement about the delay, and then walked away, telling technicians that even La Scala could have technical problems.

Nico went to the dressing rooms to speak with the lead singers and then into the rehearsal studio to brief Maestro Bongiovanni and the orchestra. While he was in the studio, a TV monitor showed the superintendent announcing before RAI TV cameras that ". . . the theater apologizes . . . for the first time in La Scala's long and glorious history . . . I have to announce a brief delay of ten minutes for the premiere . . . due to a completely unforeseen, minor . . . very minor . . . technical malfunction. My paramount concern . . . as always . . . is to guarantee the safety of all our guests . . . our artistic and technical staff. I humbly ask that our audience will forgive us and let us offer to the world . . . the best *Turandot* ever produced by this theater!"

An RAI journalist thrust a microphone at Fournier and demanded, "Tell us what happened! What was the problem? Was there any danger for La Scala staff? Who caused the problem? Will they be fired?"

Fournier ignored him, stepped away, and left the room, followed by his press secretary and two assistants.

Nico imagined the superintendent, as soon as he was behind closed doors, hoisting a glass of champagne with trembling fingers, gulping it, and walking out to greet the VIPs. The monitor showed guests streaming into the theater, taking off coats, greeting friends, and making their way to the bar for a drink before taking their seats.

At 5:45, Nico was backstage as performers took their marks on the stage and musicians entered the orchestra pit to tune their instruments.

Nico loved the pageantry and drama of *Turandot*, which was adapted from a seventeenth-century tale, *One Thousand and One Nights,* about a Persian emperor who will give his eighteen-year-old daughter, Princess Turandot, to any suitor who can answer three riddles. If the suitors fail, they will be executed. Prince Calaf takes the challenge and answers all three riddles, but Princess Turandot still doesn't want to marry him, until the end.

Nico looked over the stage at the assembled cast, admiring their costumes and majestic presence: the beautiful Italian soprano who played Princess Turandot, the British bass Emperor Altoum, and the star tenor, Volker Bachmeier, as Prince Calaf, impressively handsome with wavy blond hair, bejeweled rings on his fingers, and silver bracelets on his wrists. Prince Calaf stood by himself, dressed in a floor-length, black leather coat with large sleeves. The toes of his black slippers peeked from under his coat like mice.

Nico's favorite *Turandot* costumes were those worn by the members of the Emperor's court—Ping, Pang, and Pong. They wore full-body, satin, oriental costumes in geometric patterns of bold green and blue against a scarlet background. Each wore a pointed cap in scarlet with a bell-like ornament and a chin strap.

After wardrobe made final touches to the lead singers' costumes, wigs, and caps, the performers made a small circle, hummed scales to loosen their vocal cords, and sang measures of their opening arias.

In the wings stood rows of dancers dressed in white tunics, sleek pants, theatrical masks, and oriental bonnets. The dancers stretched their arms, did knee bends to limber their leg muscles, and pressed palms together in resistance exercises.

Nico looked up at the digital clock. It flashed 5:49. The backstage hum stilled. At 6:00, the stage manager instructed the lighting crew to dim the front lights twice, indicating to the audience that it was ten minutes before the curtain would rise. Chattering in the theater hushed, and the audience settled into their seats. The huge room became quiet, except for gentle coughs and the rustle of programs.

The *primo violino* in the orchestra pit stood and played the note to tune all instruments. A cacophony from the instruments followed and lasted a couple of minutes, then stilled. Maestro Bongiovanni, in a tunnel below the orchestra floor, checked his cuffs, twirled the baton in his fingers, and hummed the first measures of the overture.

At 6:10 PM, Maestro Bongiovanni boldly climbed four steps into the orchestra pit, strode under a spotlight at the podium, and bowed at the audience. Thunderous applause erupted, grew louder, and then stilled as the audience settled back into their seats. Bongiovanni smiled and bowed left, center, and right. Then he turned and raised his baton.

The stage manager cued the lighting crew above the chandelier. They flicked switches, and three bright floodlights shined on La Scala's distinctive blood-red curtain. A few gasps came from the audience. The spectacle was about to begin.

Maestro Bongiovanni pointed his baton at the brass section and flicked his wrist. Trombones, bass, trumpets, and percussion thundered the overture's opening crescendo. An electric current raced through the audience. Ushers stood rigidly, waiting for the curtain to rise. When it did, floodlights shined on Chinese singers and dancers about to perform. A cymbal from the orchestra pit crashed. Tenors and sopranos raised their voices in a thundering chorus.

The mandarin announced that any prince seeking to marry Princess Turandot must answer three riddles. If he fails, he will be executed. The chorus screamed for blood!

"Popolo di Pekino!
La legge è questa:
Turandot, la pura, sposa sarà
di chi, di sangue regio,
spieghi i tre enigmi
ch'ella proporrà."
[People of Pekino!
The law is this:
Turandot, the pure one, spouse will be
of who, of regal blood,
explains the three enigmas
she will propose.]

Turandot was live!

EPILOGUE

Giorgio Lucchini waited in the conference room as DIGOS agents filed in. He was on the podium, leaning against a table, exhaustion evident in the way his body sagged. His tired eyes followed each agent as they made their way into the room. The lines at the corners of his mouth seemed more pronounced, and his cheeks had a gray sheen. Muscles tensed on his neck.

It had been three days since the La Scala premiere. Since that night, Lucchini had been swept up in the frenzy, at the center of the post-shooting investigation, the one police official everyone wanted to reach. He'd received countless phone calls and texts and had attended meetings with Milan political officials, the Carabinieri commander, the head of ROS, Questore Taddei, and Lucchini's supervisor at the Ministry of Interior in Rome, who had flown to Milan with intelligence officials.

Lucchini had slept little, traveling in a caravan of DIGOS vehicles to the Questura, the Carabinieri headquarters, the mayor's office, and the San Paolo hospital to check on the condition of Baraldi, Volpara, De Monti, and Morucci, who'd been injured in the attempted escape by the terrorists. Lucchini had kept in touch with Amoruso, who was in charge of questioning coworkers and supervisors at Carefull, AMSA, and the Rho sanitation department, along with searching the apartments of Hussain, Bilal, and Khan, as well as Gajani's home in Desio.

On the morning of the third day, Lucchini had asked Amoruso to schedule a debriefing with DIGOS staff to update them and assign follow-up investigations.

At 6 PM, DIGOS agents filled three rows of chairs in the conference room and stood silently along the walls waiting for Lucchini to speak.

His weariness was obvious; no one was going to indulge in even casual chatter in his presence. He had their complete attention.

Amoruso sat in the front row beside De Monti. It was Simona's first day back at work. She had spent a night in the hospital and two days at her Bergamo home nursing a slight concussion. A fading, purplish bruise on her cheek reached one eye, from when she had been slammed against a wall when the terrorists had exploded out of the room. Her left eye was partially closed, and she wore a narrow bandage over a cut on her eyebrow where her face had hit the wooden floor.

Lucchini waited for the last of the agents to enter. When the door was closed, he cleared his throat, pushed away from the table, and stood erect.

"Thank you all for showing up. We're all busy, so let's not waste time," he said, his voice weak from all the reporting he had done with officials. "I want to debrief you about the confrontation at La Scala and the shooting of terrorists Hussain, Gajani, and Bilal. The newspapers and TV have reported an incident, but we have kept critical details secret from the media.

"The three terrorists were rigging four canisters with chemicals to introduce sarin gas into La Scala's ventilation when Amoruso, De Monti, and Volpara's team stopped them. In ten more minutes, poisonous gas would have filtered throughout the theater, seriously injuring and possibly killing guests. Only you—and the highest level of police and intelligence branches—know this. It will remain classified with no dissemination to anyone outside this room."

Everyone nodded. DIGOS had a reputation for having no leaks of critical intelligence of their operations.

Lucchini gestured to the front row, where Amoruso and De Monti were seated. "Our team—led by Amoruso, De Monti, Volpara, and Baraldi—prevented that from happening. They performed to the highest standards DIGOS is known for."

Murmurs of praise went around the room. Agents started to stand and applaud until Lucchini gestured for them to remain seated.

"Unfortunately—as we expect in such dangerous situations—we had injuries. De Monti suffered a slight concussion, a black eye, and a bruised cheek." He gestured to De Monti, who nodded but didn't stand.

"Maurizio Baraldi, Febo Morucci, and Dario Volpara are in the hospital. A bullet struck Morucci's bulletproof vest and punctured his spleen. He lost a lot of blood and had several transfusions during surgery. Baraldi suffered a fractured cheekbone and eye socket when one of the terrorists struck him with a pistol butt. He's on pain medication and antibiotics and will return to work soon. A bullet pierced Volpara's side and punctured his colon. He also had several transfusions during surgery and is recuperating. We expect Volpara and Morucci to be released in a few days and return to work when they've fully recovered.

"Our agents survived." He paused for a moment, smiled briefly, and then continued. "None of the terrorists did. Tariq Gajani was shot by Baraldi at close range in the enclosed room and died at the hospital. Hussain and Bilal died in ambulances."

The shoot-out had been the main topic in the DIGOS office since the premiere. The agents' colleagues were injured and hospitalized; the terrorists were in the morgue. Hearing it officially from their commander was significant for morale and solidarity. Lucchini understood this. He was following a protocol that the most critical information about an investigation was best delivered by the commander.

"We were surveilling *four* terrorists, Hussain, Bilal, and Gajani—the son, not the father—and Kalil Khan."

Lucchini paused, looking around the room, making eye contact with his top agents. "Khan was not apprehended after the incident. We haven't been able to find him."

He paused for a moment and gestured toward Amoruso. "Dottoressa Amoruso and her team have searched Khan's apartment. They removed his clothes, cell phones, documents, a few letters, pornographic magazines, and an old computer. We have learned little from his roommates, who say they don't know where he is. He hasn't reported to work since the premiere.

"Agents have questioned people in cafés, markets, and stores in Khan's neighborhood, as well as at the mosques and the Islamic Center. Khan was a shadowy figure, not well known, with few, if any, friends. We assume he escaped, driving the getaway vehicle. We are studying CCTV footage from parking garages near La Scala for license plates that departed that night. We have search bulletins and Khan's photo at security checkpoints at airports, train stations, highways, border crossings, and ports. DIGOS in Naples has notified us that they intercepted a call the evening of the premiere from a suspected terrorist link. An unknown man called and sounded frightened."

Lucchini nodded at Gerardo Annichiarico of the IT center, who was standing by. "Here is a recording of the phone tap that Naples sent," Lucchini said. "We believe this is Khan's voice." A crackle was audible as the agent opened the conference room's audio channel.

> *"Pronto."*
> *"Pronto, I'm listening."*
> *"Where are you?"*
> *"Going south. The party has been stopped."*
> *"Your friends didn't make it?"*
> *"No."*
> *"Have they been eliminated from the guest list?"*
> *"Yes."*
> *"When will you be here?"*
> *"Couple days."*
> *"We'll be waiting. Allahu Akbar."*

Lucchini waited a few moments to let everyone contemplate the significance of Khan's escape. Then he continued. "Let me wrap up by telling you what we have learned from the American Alessandro Boni. He has been interrogated with a team of expensive attorneys present, hired by his father. He denies prior knowledge of the event, but we're continuing to question him. He admits he gave Hussain thirty-thousand euros for what he was told was a cyber-hacking operation of people Boni considered his enemies. Our psychiatrists have read the transcripts and consider Boni a borderline paranoid with vague delusions about revenge.

"Boni's brother was a U.S. Army captain killed in Iraq. The psychiatrists believe his death triggered something in Boni's fantasies about avenging his brother's death. Associating with the terrorists was part of this, but we don't know what else he might have been up to. We've searched Boni's apartment, office, and cell phone records, and we've questioned people at his work and apartment, as well as his social contacts. Our investigation of Boni will continue until we exhaust every possibility that he might have been involved."

Lucchini paused, looked out over the room, and asked if there were any questions. When no one raised a hand, he began discussing follow-up investigations, the search for Khan, and agents assigned to replace Baraldi, Morucci, and Volpara.

When Lucchini dismissed the meeting, the agents filed out the door. Simona stood up and found her phone vibrating in her coat pocket. She took it out, sat down again, and saw a text from Maestro Bongiovanni: *Ciao, Simona. How are you feeling? I've been worried about you and hope I can see you soon. Can we have dinner tonight?*

She grinned, thrilled to hear from Armando again. When he had texted her after the premiere, she had texted back that she had minor injuries from a scuffle with street demonstrators after the performance. He had texted her the next day, asking if he could come by for a visit. She had responded that she was recuperating in Bergamo and would be returning to Milan soon.

She tapped on her phone: *I'm fine. At work for a meeting. I have a black eye and a bruised cheek. Why would you want to see me when I look like I was mauled by a dog?*

She waited for his answer, which took only seconds: *I don't care what you look like! I miss you. Dinner tonight? 9 PM?*

She paused and texted: *Well . . . maybe.* Before she sent it, she chuckled and added a comment: *Maybe I'll wear an eye patch.*

He responded quickly: *No eyepatch! You're too beautiful to hide even a black eye.*

I won't scare you?

Never! I reserved a table at Aimo & Nadia for 9 PM I miss you!

She answered: *Me too. I'll leave the eyepatch home. Love, Simo.*

THE END

ACKNOWLEDGMENTS

N o book is the sole work of one writer. I was fortunate to have many who helped me along the journey that became *No One Sleeps*. Elena Ciampella is my talented Milan researcher who offered invaluable commentary developing the plot, characters, and insights into contemporary Italian life, for both this book as well as *Thirteen Days in Milan*. Another Milanese, translator Benedetta Calzavara, also provided critical suggestions on Italian history, language, settings, and customs. I'm indebted to sources in the Milan Questura and other Italian institutions who prefer to remain anonymous.

My editor, Pamela McManus, was a steady hand ironing out the kinks in the narrative. Pamela and I have been working together for more than twenty-five years on this book and others in my earlier career as author and publisher. We enjoy each other's company while working on a project and socially when we share our good fortune to be Californians after growing up in the Midwest.

I also appreciate the contributions and encouragement of Eric Sylvers, Bojana Murisic, Marco Ottaviano, Aaron Maines, Caterina Cutrupi, Bryan Lee, Doug Kennedy, Catherine Dunning, Vanessa Jackson, and Wendy Sizer.

I continue to read widely on Italian history and culture. I'm fortunate to live in Monterey, California, and have access to the extensive library in studies of international terrorism at the Middlebury Institute of International Studies at Monterey (MIIS) and other libraries.

BIBLIOGRAPHY

The Shadow of the Crescent Moon, Fatima Bhutto, Penguin Press, 2015.

The Making of a Terrorist: Recruitment, Training, and Root Causes, Volumes 1–3, Edited by James J. F. Forest, Praeger Security International, 2006.

A Kidnapping in Milan: The CIA on Trial, Steve Hendricks, W. W. Norton, 2010.

Farewell Kabul, Christina Lamb, William Collins, 2015.

Terrorism: A History, Randall D. Law, Polity Press, 2009.

Counterterrorism, Dr. Marie-Helen Maras, Jones & Bartlett Learning, 2013.

Way of the Knife: The CIA, A Secret Army, and a War at the Ends of the Earth, Mark Mazzetti, Penguin Books, 2013.

Islamic Extremism: Causes, Diversity, and Challenges, Monte Palmer and Princess Palmar, Rowman & Littlefield Publishers, 2008.

Terrorism and Global Disorder: Political Violence in the Contemporary World, Adrian Guelke, I. B Tauris, 2006

Inside Al Qaeda: Global Network of Terror, Rohan Gunaratna, Columbia University Press, 2002.

Al Qaeda in Europe: The New Battleground of International Jihad, Lorenzo Vidino, Prometheus Books, 2006.

The Mind of the Terrorist, Jerrold M. Post, Palgrave MacMillan, 2007.

The Reluctant Fundamentalist," Mohsin Hamid, Houghton Mifflin Harcourt, 2007.

Notes

1. *A Kidnapping in Milan: The CIA on Trial*, Steve Hendricks, W. W. Norton, 2010, p. 32

2. Ibid., pp. 122–123

3. Lorenzo Vidino, *Al Qaeda in Europe: The New Battleground of International Jihad* (Amherst, New York: Prometheus Books, 2006), pp. 216–219

4. Vidino, p. 226

5. Hendricks, pp.167–169

6. Hendricks, p. 220

7. Hendricks, p. 147

8. Hendricks, p. 273

ABOUT JACK ERICKSON

Jack Erickson writes in multiple genres: international thrillers, mysteries, true crime, short mysteries, and romantic suspense.

He is currently writing a series of international thrillers based in Milan featuring the antiterrorism police, DIGOS, at Milan's Questura (police headquarters). Book I in the series is *Thirteen Days in Milan*. Book III, *Cadorna Station*, will be published in 2017.

The models for Erickson's thrillers are three Italian mystery series: Donna Leon's Commissario Brunetti in Venice, Andrea Camilleri's Inspector Salvo Montalbano in Sicily, and Michael Dibdin's Aurelio Zen in Rome. All three series have been produced on television at BBC, PBS, RAI, or Deutsche Welle.

Erickson travels throughout Italy for research and sampling Italian contemporary life and culture. In earlier careers, he was a U.S. Senate speechwriter, a Washington-based editor, and RedBrick Press publisher. He wrote and published several books on the emerging craft brewing industry, including the award-winning *Star Spangled Beer: A Guide to America's New Microbreweries and Brewpubs*.

Before he began writing fiction, Erickson was a wealth manager for a national brokerage firm in Palo Alto, California.

Erickson's Milan DIGOS thriller series and his other books are available on your e-reader, smartphone, or tablet.

Sign up for his newsletter at *JackErickson.com*

Made in the USA
Columbia, SC
08 November 2017